WINTER STUDY

"Chilling…Barr's visceral descriptions of the winter cold nicely complement the paranoia."   *—Publishers Weekly*

"Strong, evocative writing…frigid winds blow through *Winter Study* as the suspense heats up."
—South Florida Sun-Sentinel

"Barr skillfully uses archetypal images of the wolf to deepen the suspense."   *—The Washington Post Book World*

"Fast-paced, intricately plotted, and filled with foreboding."
—St. Paul Pioneer Press

"Riveting."   *—Minneapolis Star Tribune*

RESOUNDING PRAISE FOR
NEVADA BARR, ANNA PIGEON, AND

ENDANGERED SPECIES

"Barr is a splendid storyteller."
—Los Angeles Times Book Review

"In Anna Pigeon, author Barr may have created the most appealing mystery series heroine to come along since Sue Grafton's Kinsey Millhone."   *—The Cleveland Plain Dealer*

"Vivid…skillful…Barr, a park ranger herself, has the tools to make the island seem real, from the wicked insect life to the glow of the moon on the Atlantic."   *—Detroit Free Press*

continued…

NEVADA BARR

BLIND DESCENT

AN ANNA PIGEON NOVEL

BERKLEY BOOKS, NEW YORK

THE BERKLEY PUBLISHING GROUP
Published by the Penguin Group
Penguin Group (USA) Inc.
375 Hudson Street, New York, New York 10014, USA
Penguin Group (Canada), 90 Eglinton Avenue East, Suite 700, Toronto, Ontario M4P 2Y3, Canada
(a division of Pearson Penguin Canada Inc.)
Penguin Books Ltd., 80 Strand, London WC2R 0RL, England
Penguin Group Ireland, 25 St. Stephen's Green, Dublin 2, Ireland (a division of Penguin Books Ltd.)
Penguin Group (Australia), 250 Camberwell Road, Camberwell, Victoria 3124, Australia
(a division of Pearson Australia Group Pty. Ltd.)
Penguin Books India Pvt. Ltd., 11 Community Centre, Panchsheel Park, New Delhi—110 017, India
Penguin Group (NZ), 67 Apollo Drive, Rosedale, North Shore 0632, New Zealand
(a division of Pearson New Zealand Ltd.)
Penguin Books (South Africa) (Pty.) Ltd., 24 Sturdee Avenue, Rosebank, Johannesburg 2196,
South Africa

Penguin Books Ltd., Registered Offices: 80 Strand, London WC2R 0RL, England

This is a work of fiction. Names, characters, places, and incidents either are the product of the author's imagination or are used fictitiously, and any resemblance to actual persons, living or dead, business establishments, events, or locales is entirely coincidental. The publisher does not have any control over and does not assume any responsibility for author or third-party websites or their content.

BLIND DESCENT

A Berkley Book / published by arrangement with the author

PRINTING HISTORY
G. P. Putnam's Sons hardcover edition / March 1998
Avon Twilight edition / April 1999
Avon mass-market edition / August 2001
Berkley mass-market edition / October 2009

Copyright © 1998 by Nevada Barr.
Interior map copyright © 1998 by Jackie Aher.
Cover photographs: Shutterstock. Cover design by Rod Hernandez.
Interior text design by Laura K. Corless.

ISBN: 978-0-425-23063-3

BERKLEY®
Berkley Books are published by The Berkley Publishing Group, a division of Penguin Group (USA) Inc.,
375 Hudson Street, New York, New York 10014.
BERKLEY® is a registered trademark of Penguin Group (USA) Inc.
The "B" design is a trademark of Penguin Group (USA) Inc.

PRINTED IN THE UNITED STATES OF AMERICA

10 9 8 7 6 5 4 3 2 1

For Andrea, Jim, and Andrew Goodbar.
Without their expertise and generosity
not only could this book not have been written
but I would never have been lured
into the beauty of the underground.

With deep appreciation of the staff of Carlsbad Caverns National Park, particularly Dale Pate, Paula Bauer, Harry Burgess, and Frank Deckert. Among them, they educated, enlightened, amused, advised, and kept me safe on what turned out to be some of the most amazing journeys of my career. People like those at Carlsbad Caverns make me remember that the hackneyed phrase "our National Parks are our greatest heritage" is the simple truth.

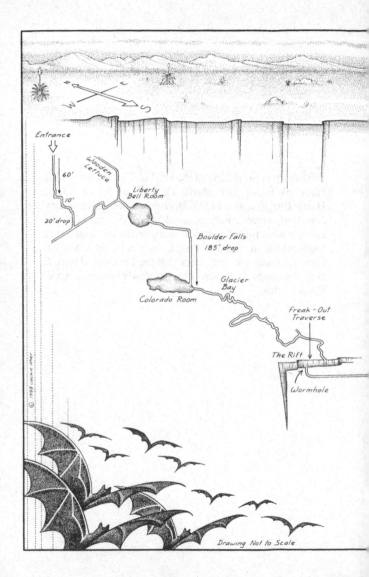

Entrance

Wooden Lettuce

60'

10'

20' drop

Liberty Bell Room

Boulder Falls
185' drop

Glacier Bay

Colorado Room

Freak-Out Traverse

The Rift

Wormhole

© 1998 Jacqui Oakley

Drawing Not to Scale

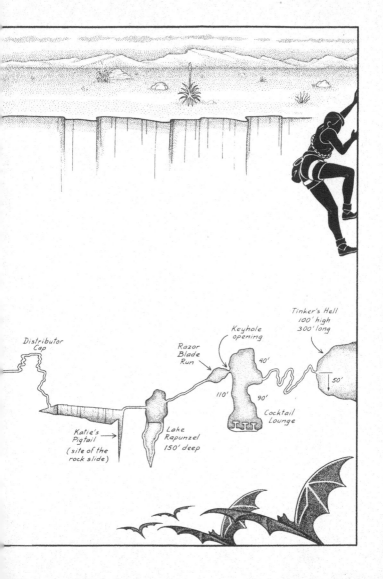

Distributor
Cap

Katie's
Pigtail
(site of the
rock slide)

Lake
Rapunzel
150' deep

Razor
Blade
Run

Keyhole
opening

110'   40'

90'

Cocktail
Lounge

Tinker's Hell
100' high
300' long

50'

ANNA HADN'T SEEN so much dashing about and popping in and out of doors since the French farce went out of fashion. Given the pomp and posturing surrounding her, she felt like a walk-on in *Noises Off.*

Anna Pigeon was on the overhead team, the second wave to hit CACA—the official if unfortunate National Park Service abbreviation for New Mexico's Carlsbad Caverns, home to two of the most famous caves in the world, the original cave, known and exploited since the late 1800s, and Lechuguilla, discovered in the 1980s and yet to be fully explored.

Though Carlsbad was less than an hour's drive from the Guadalupe Mountains, where Anna had worked some years back, she'd been down in the cave only once. The parts of Carlsbad open to the public were highly developed: paved paths, theatrical lighting, named formations, benches to sit on while changing film. At the bottom, some seven hundred fifty feet underground, there was a snack bar and souvenir shop. When hot dogs and rubber stalactites had been brought into this pristine heart of the earth, their ubiquitous companions came as well: rats, cockroaches, and raccoons.

It could be argued that the open areas of the caverns felt as much like a Disney creation as Space Mountain. There were no dangerous mazes, no precipitous heights, no tight squeezes. Still, it was a cave, and so Anna had passed on repeat trips. Given the inevitable nature of things, she would spend much of eternity underground; no sense rushing on down before the grim reaper called for her. Her love of bats might have overcome her fear of enclosed spaces, but if one waited, the splendid little creatures were good enough to come out and be enjoyed in less stygian realms.

This December she had been sent to CACA from her home park in Mesa Verde, Colorado. Trained teams consisting of park rangers from all over the region responded to catastrophes that ranged from hurricanes to presidential visits. This time it was the injury of a caver.

Had the caver been hurt in Carlsbad Cavern, extrication would have been simple: pop her in a wheelchair, roll her down to the snack bar and onto the elevator. She'd have been home before her mother knew she was missing.

But this caver had been injured in Lechuguilla. The cave was on NPS lands near CACA's headquarters. Lechuguilla was closed to the general public for the protection of both the cave and the visitors. Nearly ninety miles of the cave had been explored but it would be many years before it was fully mapped. Lech was a monster man-eating cave, dangerous to get into and harder to get out of.

Two days into Lechuguilla, a member of the survey team had been hurt in an accident. Not surprisingly there'd been a contingent of experienced cavers at Carlsbad at the time, a small but dedicated group given to squeezing themselves into dark holes and living to write home about it.

Before Anna and her teammates had descended on the park, the cavers had begun doing what they did best: getting one of their own back. Procedures in place from the last, well-publicized rescue from Lechuguilla, in 1991, the NPS had mobilized in record time. Within four hours of the report, Anna had been on a plane to El Paso. By the time she reached Carlsbad more than two dozen others from the southwestern region had arrived.

With the overhead team came the inevitable Porta-Johns, food trucks, and power struggles.

On duty less than three hours, Anna was happy to sit out the political squabbles in Oscar Iverson's snug little office. There, far from the madding crowd, she manned the phones in her official capacity as information officer, doling out approved statements to a press already panting for another media glut like that generated by the Baby Jessica case in Texas. When she was eight hundred feet below the surface of the earth and two days' travel from the light of day, a grown woman in a limestone cave was almost as good as a baby in a well shaft.

For the past half hour reporters had been getting short shrift. Anna was reading. By chance she'd picked *Trapped!*, the story of caver Floyd Collins, off Iverson's shelves. It detailed the gruesome death and media circus surrounding the entrapment of a caver in the 1920s. Collins had become wedged in a tight passage; his attempts to wriggle free had brought down loose dirt and rock, entombing him from neck to heels, his arms pinned at his sides. For thirteen days, friends had made the dangerous descent to feed him, while up above concessionaires sold food and souvenirs to an ever-growing crowd of vultures gathered in curiosity, sympathy, and morbidity. On the fourteenth day rains so softened the earth that the access tunnel collapsed. Collins was left to die alone.

Scrawled in the margin of the book were the words "fact: wedge victims die."

Transfixed by the same dread a woman in a stranded VW might feel watching a logging truck bearing down on her, Anna was glued to the book. Iverson, Carlsbad's cave specialist, gusted into her sanctuary, and she dropped *Trapped!*, glad to be rescued from its bleak pages. He waved her back into his ergonomically correct office chair and folded himself haphazardly over the corner of the desk.

Housed in an old stone building built in the 1920s, the office was small, crowded by two desks, the walls lined with metal shelving and stuffed with books. Sprawled over the cluttered desktop, Oscar looked as homey and leggy as a spider in his web. Long limbs poked out the fabric of his trousers at knee and hip. His arms, seeming to bend in several places along their bony length, were stacked like sticks on his thighs. Come Halloween it would take only a little white paint to pass him off as a respectable skeleton. A mummy of the sere and unwrapped variety would be even easier. The man looked made of leather, hide tanned by the desert, hair coarse and straw-colored from the sun. Anna guessed he was close to her age, maybe forty-five or -six.

"Got some bizarre news," he said, banging his heel softly against the metal of the desk.

For whom the bell tolls, Anna's mind translated the hollow ringing.

"Now that the relatives have been notified we can release the name of the injured woman. Frieda Dierkz. And she's asking for one Anna Pigeon."

Shit, Anna thought. It tolls for me.

"Frieda?" she echoed stupidly.

Iverson shot her a startled look. "Don't you know her? From the intensity of the summons, I got the idea you two were best buds."

"Buds." Anna's mind was paralyzed, not so much by shock as by incongruity. Hearing Frieda's name in reference to the victim of the rescue was akin to running into one's old grammar school teacher in an opium den.

"She's the dispatcher at Mesa Verde," Anna managed. "We're . . . friends." They were friends, fairly close friends, and Anna wondered why she'd sounded so half-hearted.

"Dierkz was on the survey team," Oscar said patiently, his washed-out hazel eyes trying to read Anna's face.

It wasn't an earth-shattering revelation. Most cavers led

other lives. They were geologists and physicists, beekeepers and bums; regular folks who had been bitten by an irregular bug that compelled them to creep beneath the skin of the world every chance they got. Anna had seen the photos of a helmeted and mud-bedaubed Frieda grinning out from nasty little crevices Anna wouldn't go into for love or money, and she'd listened with half an ear about her upcoming "vacation." She'd just not put two and two together.

"What does she want me for?" Without much caring, Anna noted the disapproval sharpening Iverson's gaze. She could guess where it came from: cavers helped cavers. It was an unwritten law of survival. Who else was going to fish them out of the god-awful places they insisted on pushing their way into? Iverson stared, and Anna stared back, refusing to apologize or explain. A moment passed, and his look softened. Perhaps he reminded himself she was not a caver but a mere mortal.

"The injury is worse than first thought." He spoke slowly as if Anna had a learning disability. His voice was low, gentling. She would have been irritated at the condescension had she not known Iverson always talked that way. "The caver who hiked out said a broken leg. Painful but not life-threatening. Apparently the rock that smashed her kneecap struck a glancing blow to her left temple as it fell. She was knocked unconscious but only briefly. We just got a second report. It was brought out by a member of another team surveying in the Great Beyond. He met up with one of Dierkz's team in Windy City and brought out a message. She's been slipping in and out of consciousness and has suffered some disorientation."

"Head injury," Anna said. "Bad news."

"Bad news," Iverson agreed. "Peter McCarty, a member of Dierkz's team, is an M.D. in real life. That's the good news. She's got a doctor with her. McCarty recommended we get Ms. Dierkz what she wants. She's agitated, and it is not helping her medical condition any. He feels it would soothe her if she could have a friend there."

"A lady-in-waiting?"

"Exactly."

A chilling image filled Anna's mind: herself crouched and whimpering, fear pouring like poison through her limbs, shutting down her brain as the cave closed in around her. Adrenaline spurted into her bloodstream, and she could feel the numbness in her fingertips and a tingling as of ice water drizzling on her scalp. To hide her thoughts she rubbed her face.

"Will you go?" Iverson asked.

Anna scrubbed the crawling sensation from her hair with her knuckles. "Just deciding what to wear."

Oscar looked at her shrewdly, the long, narrow eyes turning the color of bleached lichen. "Let me rephrase that: *can* you?"

"I don't know," Anna answered truthfully. "Can I?"

"Caving?"

"None."

"Climbing?"

"Some."

"Rappels sixty to a hundred fifty feet. Ascents ditto, naturally. Rope climbs with ascenders."

"I can do that."

"Crawl on your belly like a reptile?"

Jesus. "How much?"

Oscar laughed, a huffing noise concentrated in the back of his throat and his nostrils. "Not much where we're going. Lechuguilla is a big place. Huge. It's where the NPS stores Monument Valley during the off-season."

It was Anna's turn to laugh, but she didn't. "The crawls," she said. "How much is 'not much'?"

"Three or four good crawls."

"An oxymoron."

Iverson sat, letting her absorb the information. His heel rang its dull music from the side of the desk. Anna quashed an urge to grab his ankle, stop the pendulum. She tried to think of Frieda, alone and confused, hurt and afraid. She tried to think of friendship and honor and courage and duty. Cowardly thoughts of a way out pushed these higher musings aside: claims of a bad heart, a dying mother's call, or, if all else failed, "accidentally" shooting herself in the foot.

"Can you?" Iverson asked finally. Her time had run out.

Over the cringing claustrophobia, her mind had begun to chant the Little Engine That Could's mantra. She gave the cave specialist the edited version. "Sure."

OSCAR IVERSON HAD vanished into what in any other law enforcement organization might have been gloriously termed a council of war. Under the civilizing influence of the NPS it was called a "team briefing." In an attempt to feel unity and coherence during cuts and downsizings, the Park Service had begun to overuse comforting words: team, group, symposium, cluster. Words to keep from feeling alone and, if necessary, to diffuse the blame.

Anna had been handed over to two cavers from Palo Alto, California. Timmy, a man who when aboveground was actually employed as a bona fide rocket scientist, though he preferred a less incendiary title, and his wife, Lisa, a New Zealander who had caved all over the world, enjoying photographic junkets in places with such alluring names as the Grim Crawl of Death.

Had Anna been able to focus on anything other than not getting the shakes, she might have enjoyed the transformation process. Like an ugly duckling in an old movie, she was made over from head to toe. She was fitted with a brimless helmet and a battery-powered lamp strapped on with elastic. The batteries, three C-cells, resided in a black plastic case at the back of the helmet. The pack Timmy and Lisa put together for her was unlike anything she had used before. An elongated sack with a drawstring top, it was worn on the hip, with the strap over the opposite shoulder, like a woman's purse. A second strap secured it loosely around the waist.

"It's a sidepack," Lisa explained as Anna fussed with the unfamiliar equipment, unable to get comfortable. "In tight squeezes you can slip it off easily and shove it ahead. Or tie it to your foot and drag it behind."

Dumbly, Anna nodded. The image gave her the willies.

"You could probably take a regular pack where you're going. Tons of room," Timmy said, and Anna wondered what had given her away, the bloodless lips or the slight trembling in her knees. She doubted Timmy's words were meant kindly. There was a coldness in him that she suspected was born of contempt. In the narrow world of a specialty—diving, climbing, caving—cliques formed, egos became wrapped in layer after layer of shared hype, of the glamour of overcoming real and imagined dangers, of feeling the exquisite pleasure of keeping secrets denied the uninitiated. Devotees ran the risk of becoming intoxicated by their own differences. Finally they came to resemble the stereotypical Parisian; if one couldn't speak his language, and flawlessly, the conversation was over.

Screw him, Anna thought uncharitably.

"How about Razor Blade Run?" Lisa asked her husband. Lisa was in her forties and wore her hair in two long plaits that reached to the back of her knees. Her face was round and gave the impression of being lumpy, but her eyes were fine, and Anna'd seen a smile transform her into an exotic kind of beauty.

"Okay, you'll need a sidepack at Razor Blade," Timmy conceded. He was a spare man, shorter than his wife and leaner, with pale wisps of hair defining upper lip and chin. His eyes, colorless behind tinted glasses, took on a faraway look as his hands continued buckling the web gear girdling Anna. "And the Wormhole," he said finally.

"And coming out of Tinker's," his wife added.

"I get the picture," Anna snapped.

Chastened, the two cavers stopped talking. It was clear they were sensitive individuals, aware they'd offended. Equally clear was the fact that they hadn't a clue as to why. The few cavers with whom Anna had ever conversed insisted that they, better than anyone, understood claustrophobia because, when wedged in some tight Floyd Collinsian crack with the very real possibility of never getting out, they felt fear.

They understood nothing. That was not claustrophobia. That was logic, survival instinct, an IQ test. Anna sniffed, an exclamation remarkably close to "harumph."

Lisa looked up with limpid gray eyes, the tails of her braids brushing Anna's boot tops. "Too tight?" she asked, and reached to adjust the buckle that cinched the webbing around Anna's upper thigh and under her buttock.

"No," Anna said, and, with an effort, "Sorry."

Again the acceptance. Again the total lack of understanding. Apparently idiosyncratic behaviors were not cause for comment in the caving community.

"You'll want it tight," Timmy said. "Once you get your weight on it things loosen up considerably."

Anna knew that. But for the pack, the gear was familiar. Climbing equipment: seat and chest harness, locking carabiners, rappel rack, Gibbs ascenders, D-ring, JUMAR safety. All the chunks of metal and rope intended to keep a caver in one piece on the way down and on the way back up. From a lifetime's habit of safety, Anna watched as each link was forged in the chain of devices designed to defy gravity.

Letting Timmy and Lisa tell her things she knew, dress her as if she were a baby, she contributed little. Much of her brain was given over to a jumble of dangerous thoughts, dangerous because a preoccupied climber can very easily become a dead climber. A moment's inattention, an unclosed D-ring, an improperly threaded rack, an unlocked carabiner, and suddenly the whole house of cards—and the climber—comes tumbling down.

Anna longed to call her sister, Molly, to talk about friendship and irrational fears, duty and human frailty. Since there was no time for a chat with her personal shrink, she went through her mental files and pulled out everything she could remember her sister having said about coping with phobic reactions. Desensitization, the slow increasing of exposure to the feared situation; no time. Relaxation exercises. Anna snorted, and Lisa and Timmy stopped what they were doing to look at her expectantly.

"It's good," Anna said. "Perfect. Thanks." Lisa beamed her transforming smile. The gear was hers, lent to Anna for the duration. Anna smiled back, appreciating the woman's generosity. By rights Lisa should be the one going in. She was a strong and experienced caver. She hadn't been to Tinker's Hell, the part of Lechuguilla where Frieda had been injured, but she'd been on three survey expeditions into the cave, trips of five days each. Anna knew that at times of high drama, along with concern for the injured and the desire to be of help, there was an overpowering need to be a part of the adventure. In a way she'd cheated Lisa out of that.

"Climbing I'm comfortable with," Anna said. "Let's go over the rest of it."

The three of them were in a largish room outside the chief of resource management's office in a building down the hill from Oscar's office. It was of the same soft-hued native stone as the other buildings. The inside was clean and open with a beautiful old fireplace filling one wall. The grate was cold, seldom, if ever, used. The air was warmed to a uniform seventy degrees by modern methods. Anna would have welcomed the comfort of living fire. Through the window, opening onto stairs leading up the hill to the other buildings, Anna could see that a thin drizzle had started. Cold, gray, winter rain, falling on concrete. Soft, lifeless rain. Ray Bradbury rain.

Drama queen, Anna cursed herself, and turned abruptly to the pile of debris on the chief's blond wood conference table, the guts of her sidepack waiting to be inventoried.

"How much do you know?" Timmy asked.

"Pretend I don't know anything and you'll be pretty close," Anna said.

His manner might have warmed a degree or two. Her admission of total ignorance took him off guard. "Okay," he said. "We'll start from the beginning." His thin voice took on a pedantic drone, and Anna felt a vague stab of pity for all the Stanford undergrads sitting through whatever classes fledgling rocket scientists were required to sit through.

"Three sources of light," he intoned. "Light is more important than food or water. Your headlamp." He pointed with a long pale digit that looked well suited to a creature living deep underground. He waited. Apparently he wouldn't continue the lecture without classroom participation, so Anna nodded obediently.

"With spare batteries and bulbs. A flashlight." He pointed to a neat blue Maglite, brand-new and jewel-toned. "And what's your third source?" The tinted lenses winked at Anna, and she wondered if she should raise her hand before speaking.

"A candle?" she ventured, thinking of Tom Sawyer and Becky Thatcher.

That was the wrong answer Timmy had been fishing for. "Anachronism," he said triumphantly. "A candle in Lechuguilla is akin to a firefly in a whale's gullet, charming but not illuminating."

"We carried candles for years," Lisa volunteered. "When we switched out we noticed neither one of us had thought to bring matches." She laughed, a high whiffling sound. Her husband was not amused.

"Third source: another flashlight. More batteries." He stowed the lot away in the bottom of the pack.

Anna picked up a wide-mouthed plastic bottle from the pile. The top was a white screw-on cap with the letter "P" written on it with a Sharpie permanent marker. "What's this?"

"Just what it says," Timmy replied. "You pack it in, you pack it out."

"There's one urine dump near the permanent camp on the way out," Lisa added helpfully. "If you need to you can dump it there."

"Don't use it," Timmy said. "Pack it out."

From her brief exposure to caving literature, Anna half remembered discussions on how the salts and sugars of human wastewater could, over time, alter the cave environment significantly. A filtering system to remove these components from the waste so only pure water would be left behind was in the works but was yet to be realized.

"Number two," Lisa said.

Anna's mind snapped back to the lesson at hand. Evidently she had missed number one.

"Feces," Timmy said succinctly. Anna had not missed number one. He held up a pile of zipper plastic bags. "In the bag. Zip it. Double bag. Zip it." Fleetingly Anna thought this would make a heck of a commercial for Glad-lock green-seal bags. "Wrap it all in tinfoil. Pack it out."

"Burrito bags," Lisa said, and Anna detected a hint of mischief in the guileless eyes.

Caving, deep, serious caving, was beginning to take on the trappings of an expedition into outer space.

THINGS MOVED QUICKLY, and for that Anna was grateful. This was not a time she would welcome interludes for deep introspection. Shortly before four P.M. Oscar Iverson and a man he introduced as Holden Tillman picked her and her gear up at the resource management office. She was unceremoniously stuffed into the back of a covered pickup truck along with packs, ropes, helmets, and other assorted paraphernalia. She would have preferred the distraction of conversation to being left alone with her thoughts. That option denied, she stared resolutely out through the scratched Plexiglas over the tailgate.

The ceiling of clouds had fractured. An ever-widening strip of blue pried open by the last rays of the sun shone on the western horizon. Rain and the season had leached the desert of color, leaving a palette of gray to be painted by the sunset. Drops of water clinging to the catclaw and sotol soaked up the light and refracted it in glittering facets of gold. The stones and black-fingered brush dripped with molten finery. Faint rainbows bent over the desert, where rain still fell through veils of light.

Anna mocked herself for feeling like a woman in a tum-

brel, jouncing through her last glorious moments toward
the guillotine and the vast unknown. Still, she rather wished
the day had closed without this final hurrah of heavenly
fireworks. A sunless world would have been that much
easier to leave behind.

After too short a ride, the pickup pulled off the rutted dirt
road into a wilderness parking lot incongruously marked off
with concrete curbs. Anna'd been too engrossed in morbid
imaginings to recollect the twists and turns they'd made
through the wrinkled landscape, but she guessed they were
only three or four miles from the headquarters buildings.
The discovery of Lechuguilla in the backyard had put Carlsbad Caverns National Park in the odd position of having
doubled in size overnight. Oscar had likened the experience
to "finding Yellowstone in your basement."

Holden Tillman opened the tailgate, and the three of
them divided up the gear. As they started the hike to the
mouth of Lechuguilla, Oscar filled Anna in on the team
briefing. Holden Tillman was officially titled Underground
Rescue Coordinator. He was in charge of all activities subterranean. The NPS had borrowed him from the local Bureau of Land Management office because of his expertise in
caves and cave rescues. Oscar assured Anna he was, in caving circles, known as *the* Holden Tillman.

A quiet person with an aw-shucks drawl, Tillman seemed
half embarrassed and half amused by Oscar's effusions.
"Oscar's going to write my eulogy," he told Anna, a slow
smile blooming beneath a brown brush of mustache. "He
just wants to get some practicing in before I'm dead."

Anna liked Holden right off. She hoped nothing happened to change that. Experience taught her her first impression of people was dead wrong as often as not. This
time she had a gut feeling it wasn't. Tillman was of an age
with Iverson—in his forties—but there the resemblance
ended. He was a small man, maybe five-foot-eight and a
hundred thirty pounds with skin that looked shrunk to fit
a wiry, muscled frame. Crow's-feet radiated from the corners of his eyes to curve down in unbroken lines along the

sides of his face. His forehead, wide and slightly sloping, was cut by horizontal lines as sharp as old scars. The effect of this network of time was a wizened soul, blessed with wisdom and, possibly, "the sight." At least that was the fanciful image that floated up from an old fairy-tale illustration buried in Anna's memory.

Despite narrow shoulders and small frame, Holden carried a prodigious amount of equipment. Though half a foot shorter than Oscar, arms and shoulders were corded with muscle where Iverson's were mapped in bone. Anna guessed his pack was seventy or eighty pounds but it didn't bow his back or take the spring from his step. As he walked ahead of her along the trail Anna heard sotto-voce snatches of song. She laughed. Holden sang the digging song Snow White's Seven Dwarfs sang on their way down into the mine.

Anna saw the cavern sparkling with a million lights and peopled with benevolent spirits. Despite herself she felt better than she had since Iverson had brought her the news of Frieda's head injury.

Holden and Oscar, along with CACA's superintendent and the chief of resource management for the caverns, had organized a four-person team that would follow the two men Anna was with. The second team would carry a stretcher for the evacuation, medical supplies Dr. McCarty had requested, and a Korean War-vintage field phone with spools of wire so Holden would have telephone communications with the surface during the carry-out. The logistics were staggering, and Anna was duly impressed that the details had been hammered out in such a short time. There were people for every aspect of the rescue: cavers who would do nothing but rig the drops for hauling Frieda up the long vertical and near-vertical ascents; cavers to schlep water, packs, garbage, batteries, and food.

Anna listened to the plans being rehashed by Holden and Oscar as they walked single file along a ridge above a dry creek bed, and she began to wonder what would undo her first: her fear of enclosed spaces or her fear of crowds. The sheer absurdity freed her mind, and for a time she was able to shut out the human murmurings and enjoy the hike.

They were on a plateau to the north of the gypsum plains that spread down into Texas. What vegetation managed to eke out a livelihood from the parched soil kept a low profile. Little had grown to greater than knee height, and there were barren spaces between plants. With the lifting of the clouds and the dazzling clarity of the rain-washed air, Anna could see to the edge of the world, or so it seemed, and the world was all high, clean desert, burnished with gold.

Even knowing she walked over limestone honey-combed with passages, she couldn't imagine a less likely place to find the entrance to a world-class cave. She pictured the plateau cut into thin sections and placed between sheets of glass like the ant farms she'd seen as a child. Beneath her feet, creeping through those twisting tunnels, were human beings.

"There it is." Oscar interrupted her musings. They'd walked down a slope and crossed the stone bottom of a wash to climb again. Ahead of them was more of the same: low hills dotted with desert shrubs and cactus. "See that green spot?" Iverson pointed to a cluster of stunted trees poking from a fold in the hills. "That's it."

Anna took his word for it.

Within a few minutes they'd reached the trees, and still she was none the wiser. Not until they climbed down four or five feet to where the oak trees had found soil to root could she see the entrance. Back in the rocks an opening maybe twenty feet wide, thirty long, and ringed by heavy overhanging brows of rock, showed darkly.

Over the years Anna had made any number of rappels from ten to two hundred ten feet. After the first step, she'd thoroughly enjoyed the trip. Suspended like a cliff swallow over lakes in the Absaroka Beartooth, dangling above a sea of dusty live oaks in northern California. There was an above and a below. Here, she noted with an unpleasant tingle, there was neither. In the theatrical light of coming evening, the entrance to Lechuguilla looked like a portal, one lacking the standard three dimensions agreed upon by the real world.

She'd read of holes described as yawning, gaping, hungry—words that suggested an orifice, an appetite. The sixty-foot drop leading into Lech didn't fit any of those adjectives. Rather than sentience, it suggested a departure from life. The last rays of the sun skimmed its surface, lighting the stone for fifteen feet or so. Below that, nothing. Night took all.

"Hi ho," Holden said happily.

Iverson began checking ropes secured to bolts near a tree that showed scarring from when it had been used as an anchor in previous descents. "The climbs are all rigged. We leave them that way along the main trade routes—established routes through the cave. We've found it does a lot less damage to the resource to leave the rigging in place than having every expedition rerig each time."

"Me first, you last?" he said to Holden as he threaded the rope through his rappel rack.

Holden nodded. Oscar leaned back and walked, spider-like, from sight. The sun slid below the horizon, and Anna felt suddenly cold. "It's getting dark," she said, and hoped Tillman hadn't heard the faint whine beneath her words.

"So?"

"Off-rope," drifted up from the black hole.

"Good point," Anna said, threaded the rope through her rack, pulled on her leather gloves, and unhooked the safety. "On-rope," she shouted down, and stepped back into the darkness.

2

AS SHE RAPPELLED down, Anna closed her mind to all but the task at hand. Peripherally she was aware of the change in temperature, of the quick coming of night as she fell from the last vestiges of the sun. Mostly she concentrated on the play of the rope through her gloved hands, the pressure of the web gear holding her up. Below, in an inkwell of stone, she could see Oscar Iverson's lonely light winking as he moved his head. Peter Pan's whimsical directions came to mind: first star to the right and straight on till morning.

Having touched down, she freed herself and called "Off-rope" to let Holden know he was clear to descend. Moments later, sixty feet above, she saw his silhouette in the small triangle of gray that was all that remained of the world.

Switching on her headlamp, she studied the bottom of the shaft, absorbing each detail in hopes of crowding out unnecessary thoughts. The area was small and everything she expected from a cave: irregular, colorless, and dirty.

The air smelled of things long buried, of damp and basements, of rotting cardboard and stale bat guano. The floor was uneven, and there were signs of the guano mining that had taken place around 1914. Piles of loose dirt attested to more recent digs.

This entry to Lechuguilla, originally called Old Misery Pit, had been known for years. Like many other caves in the area it was merely a deep hole melted into the limestone, valuable only as a source of fertilizer for the California citrus crops. But there had been tantalizing drifts of air coming from the rubble. The cave was "blowing." Following these ephemeral leads, cavers dug repeatedly in attempts to search out the bigger cavern promised by the passage of air. In 1986 they finally broke through to what was arguably one of the most important discoveries ever made by the caving community. They'd pushed into a system that not only promised to break records for length and depth but housed an unusual number of stunning decorations and cave formations.

Her knowledge of Lechuguilla's history exhausted, Anna turned her headlamp on Oscar, looking for distraction from that quarter.

"Over there," he said, indicating a darker slit in the floor. "You can hear the cave breathe."

Anna didn't tell him the last thing she needed was to hear the damn thing breathing.

In a tangle of beams from three headlamps, Holden disengaged from the rope. The entire descent had taken so little time, neither Anna nor Oscar had bothered to take off their packs.

"Onward and downward," Oscar said, and walking to an unpromising looking hole dug into the bottom of the shaft, picked up a nylon rope Anna'd not noticed before and wove it deftly through the metal ladder of his rack. "A nuisance drop—maybe ten feet. On-rope." And he was gone. "Off-rope" floated up seconds later.

The hole was hand-dug and dirt-walled. To Anna it looked as unstable as the caves the children used to dig in the sand pit behind the local airport in the neighborhood where she grew up; caves the airport operator was always dynamiting for fear some hapless little gene would get itself culled from the pool before its time.

Anna went second. The bottom of this drop was more rank and evil than the first. From a landing barely long enough to lay a coffin down, a ragged hole cut through to another chamber. Beyond this uninviting aperture, Anna could see a spill of light from Iverson's lamp. Then that was snuffed, and she felt terribly alone.

A blinding eye winked over the lip above. "You off-rope?" Holden asked.

"I guess." Anna couldn't move. A creeping numbness was flowing in from her fingertips. As it passed through her insides she felt her bowels loosen and bile rise in her throat. "I don't think I can do this," she said.

Holden landed beside her as lightly as a feather and flipped open the rack to free the rope. "Were you talking to me?"

"No." Anna didn't trust herself to elaborate.

Holden dropped to his knees and skittered out of sight through the crevice. "We having fun yet?" she heard him say.

Mechanically, she got on hands and knees and followed. From the look of the tiny room she entered, things were going to get worse before they got better. Hacked from native soil, the space was too low to stand upright in. The far side was higher but partially blocked by a slide of dirt and rock. Nowhere could she see anything that even obliquely promised the wonders she'd heard spoken of in connection with Lechuguilla. Oscar and Holden crouched with their backs to her, their helmet lights pointed toward the floor, where they groveled before some god hidden from the eyes of unbelievers.

Light swung in a dizzying arc and struck her in the face. "Ta da," she heard Holden say.

"Down the rabbit hole," said Iverson.

Vision cleared, and Anna saw the altar at which the men

worshipped. Sunk into the floor was a heavy metal manhole cover with a T-shaped handle welded to its center.

"Cover your eyes," Iverson said, but Anna couldn't. She was transfixed. Grasping the handle he pulled the hinged trapdoor open, swinging it on a counterweight. Corrugated metal drainpipe set vertically in the ground was exposed. A ladder welded to one side led down. Wind gusted from below, blowing dirt into Anna's eyes.

"It blows. Hoo-ee, does it blow," Holden said. "By the air coming out of here it's been estimated Lechuguilla might go three hundred miles or more."

"From where?" Anna asked, and was embarrassed when the words came out in a wail.

"Air pressure," Iverson said. "When it gets low outside, the cave exhales; high outside, it inhales. Pressure equalization is all it is. You last, me first?" he said to Holden. The other man nodded, and Anna wondered if they consistently put her in the middle so she couldn't escape. Iverson slid easily into the pipe and pulled the trapdoor closed behind him. The sudden stillness was a boon for Anna's nerves.

"How long is that?" She pointed to the culvert.

"Twenty feet maybe. It was installed to stabilize the entrance. You can see the soil up here shifts when we get rain."

"Clear," reverberated through the metal conduit. Holden laughed. "Oscar goes down in record time. The pipe's so small he can't use the steps. He's too long from hip to knee. Coming out is what really gets to him." He pulled open the trapdoor, releasing an angry blast of warm, wet air, warmer than the air aboveground. Lechuguilla maintained a temperature of about sixty-eight degrees with close to a hundred percent humidity year-round. In this case it was a blessing. In a colder cave Frieda would be at risk from hypothermia in addition to her other ills.

"M'dam." Tillman gestured toward the culvert with the pride of a maître d' indicating a coveted window seat.

Down the drain.

In that instant Anna knew she had to confess her short-comings, admit her fears, and get out of the hole with as much speed and grace as she could muster. Most people would be understanding. Even cavers would see that it was better to bow out than to fall apart once inside and, at best, provide the rescuers with a second casualty to evacuate or, at worst, endanger other members of the team. Not going would, in a way, be the more courageous choice. Facing up to one's failure. All this went through her mind in a calm and orderly fashion as she watched her body, possessed by demons, crab-walk over to the open culvert and begin the climb down.

Holden dropped the trapdoor. Anna felt the tremors through the palms of her hands, but she didn't hear the clang of finality. Her mind had shut down. She had no thought but of her next step, her booted toe reaching for the rung beneath, the catch of her pack on the pipe above, the circle of light inches in front of her eyes.

The culvert emptied out into a crawl space much the same as the one she'd just left. Anna chose not to think about it. Having hollered back up the culvert to let Holden know she was clear, she turned her back on the escape hatch and crawled after the faint glow of Iverson's lamp. The air in her lungs compressed until she breathed in short gasping sips. Perspiration, born cold and feeling like ice water, drenched her armpits. She wanted to weep for herself.

Then the passage opened up. Not gradually but with a suddenness that must have shattered the composure of the first men digging into the cave. Jules Verne time, Anna thought, breathing a bit easier, and pushed herself to her feet.

A tunnel big enough for a locomotive led away to the southwest. "Tunnel," with its connotations of smooth walls and unhampered passage, was not the right word. The space Anna stared down was more a fantastical corridor, walls and floor and ceiling merging, growing together in rock outcrops and smooth pale beards of liquid stone, separating again, leaving behind delicate towers to reemerge into recesses maybe six feet deep, maybe going into the shadowed heart of the world for a thousand miles.

A path had been worn down through this cluttered basement of the desert. Orange plastic surveyor's tape marked both sides, the dirt between pounded and tracked. This surprising touch of humanity gave Anna back a morsel of control, and she felt the grip of muscles on the scruff of her neck loosen somewhat.

The trail wound through enormous blocks of limestone studded with rough grayish-white formations called popcorn, then vanished in darkness beneath a low arch in the rock. Though impressive, and the size a relief to her fear-tightened mind, the cave had no life and no color. In a land devoid of sunlight, color was superfluous. Everywhere the puny beam of her headlamp touched was gray or white or brown. The paucity of light circumscribed the area, making it no larger than the small circle illuminated, creating a sense of fragmentation that was disorienting.

In the world above, the memory of which was already fading, there were signs and portents, clues that let one know one was alive: breezes, birdsong and crickets, the sound of distant thunder, the smell of sage. Here, the silence was absolute, the only sounds those of their own making. With the manhole closed, the air moved, but much more slowly, and the only smell was the dank odor of ancient rock. In this place unmarked by the rise and fall of the sun, the tides, the seasons, time ceased to have meaning.

With a thud and a scrabble, Holden Tillman joined her at the commencement of the passage. "Pretty neat, huh?"

"Neat."

"This is nothing. Wait till we get in the cave."

Iverson ducked into sight from beneath the arch. Something in the cast of his features, the set of his shoulders, had changed subtly. The unhitched movement of his joints had tightened up, become smoother. Responsibility wrapped around him, tying up all the loose ends. He radiated competence.

"Frieda and her team are on what is usually a two-day trek—maybe a day and a half. It'll be at least that hauling her out. Traveling fast, I figure we can get there in seven hours. Maybe a bit less. We've been over this before, but we're going to go over it again. I can make it. Holden can make it. If you don't feel up to it, Anna, now's the time. No loss of face. We leave all testosterone topside. Heroes are a pain in the butt down here."

"I'm okay with it," Anna said, wondering at the ease with which she kissed off her last chance.

"If you get too tired, start getting stupid or scaring yourself, let me or Holden know. We'll take a break, eat a bite, swap some stories. Can't leave anybody by 'emselves down here. Hodags'll carry 'em off."

"Cave spirits," Holden said solemnly. "Mischievous little beggars."

"Got it," Anna said, relieved she'd never be left alone in the vast gullet of New Mexico with only her own brain for a playmate.

After a couple hundred yards the passageway came to an abrupt end, the floor dropping unceremoniously away into a pit so deep that light was lost. Water dripping from the ceiling laid a slippery layer over gold-colored stone that poured over the lip into the void. Two stalagmites, just more than knee high, protruded like eyeteeth on either side of the trail. A climbing rope was anchored to one of them, its hefty weave of nylon looking as insubstantial as a spider's web in the formidable throat of limestone.

"Boulder Falls," Iverson told Anna. "More a pit than anything, but 'Boulder Pit' lacked poetry. The descent is one hundred eighty-five feet. Half of it free fall. Me first—"

"Me last," Holden finished.

Iverson hooked up his descent gear and, bracing a foot to either side of the line, walked backward, his weight on the rope, his body angled out over the shaft.

The descent didn't frighten Anna. She trusted her gear and her ability. It was the thought of going yet deeper into the ground, farther from the light of day, that made her queasy. She turned her back on the falls and looked at the already familiar face of Holden Tillman. He reached up and switched off his headlamp. "You might want to do the same," he said. "Save batteries every chance you get."

Anna clicked her light off and was instantly lost in a universe of such utter blackness that she had a sense of vertigo. Afraid to move so much as a centimeter in any direction, she sat down cross-legged where she was. An unwelcome wetness seeped through the seat of her trousers. Should anyone notice, she hoped they wouldn't think the moisture had originated from within. Given the shock of total light deprivation, it was not impossible.

As she sat in the seep puddle, the darkness began to harden around her. It was not a mere absence of light, it was a substance, an element, a suffocating miasma that filled her ears, clogged her nostrils, bore down on her shoulders and chest. When the pressure on her eyelids became such that she could feel the black leaking like raw concrete into her brain, she reached up and switched on her lamp.

Probably thirty seconds had passed since she'd turned it off.

The light pushed the cave back to its former size, and she breathed deeply, embarrassed that her sigh of relief was so audible.

"Lookie," Holden said, politely ignoring her personal crisis. "Cave pearls."

To the left of the trail, in a shallow basin on the lip of Boulder Falls, was a formation cavers called pearls. They formed much the same way pearls formed in oysters. As water dripped from above, rolling around grains of sand, the limestone in the liquid began to coat them. Because of the movement the pearls stayed free rather than being captured in a static formation.

"There used to be one in Liberty Bell. A big one we called the Jupiter Pearl," Holden said. "It had a red dot on it. Every time you came through, the dot was in a different place, orbiting around its tiny solar system."

"What happened to it?" Anna asked just to keep the conversation going. She didn't care, and that shamed her. People caught up in themselves, trapped in their own web of fear and greed, were the worst possible custodians of the wilderness.

"Some SOB stole it."

Anna nodded, trying to communicate a concern she knew she should feel. To her the pearls lacked beauty. They were misshapen and dirt-colored; their wet convex surfaces looked like things not quite alive: stumps oozing, eyeballs set aside for unimaginable Frankensteinian monsters.

"Want a piece of candy?" Holden held out a red Jolly Rancher, and Anna accepted it gratefully.

"I'm sorry about the Jupiter Pearl," she said to pay for the treat.

"So it goes," Holden said. "And then it's gone."

The sadness in his voice cut through her cloak of self-pity. In more ways than one, the underground was the only true wilderness remaining. The lead where Frieda had been injured had been discovered Tuesday. Thursday of the same week Anna found herself sitting, staring at Holden's beloved cave pearls. She would be the twelfth or thirteenth person ever to walk where they were going, ever to see whatever it was they were going to see. No animal—human or otherwise—had made its home here. No planes flew overhead in any real sense. Helicopters couldn't airlift the lost and injured to safety. The cave was within easy walking distance in miles to restaurants and VCRs, yet the far rooms of Lechuguilla were among the most remote places on the globe. Intellectually, Anna could see the attraction. Viscerally, she still wanted to go home.

"Off-rope," boiled up from the pit at her back. An echo accompanied it, hinting at cavernous spaces and irregular walls.

"I know," Anna said irritably. "Me next, you last." Having gone meticulously through the drill: clipped in safety, called "on-rope" to clear the fall zone, threaded the rack and replaced the JUMAR safety on a harness 'biner, she eased over the edge of the falls. The terrain revealed by her lamp provided footing as she gently touched the cliff face on the descent. Then the cliff undercut, and her feet dangled free. She held herself from the wall with her left arm, the right paying out rope from below the rock. In an instant the wall was a memory. She hung suspended in the middle of nowhere, of nothing.

She paid out twenty or more feet of line, then stopped. Perhaps she swung gently, held safe by a few links of metal and nylon, seventy feet above a floor she couldn't see— probably would never see but in the niggardly scraps afforded by a headlamp. With no up and no down, no walls, no horizon, all sense of motion was lost. Her light pried into darkness but reached no destination. All that existed was the bright yellow-and-blue weave of the line that held her, and the rough russet of her battered leather gloves. An ideal rappel for an acrophobe. Without any shred of visual evidence, the mind refused to grasp the situation fully.

Anna had stopped for a couple of reasons. The first was habit. Whenever possible on a descent she liked to stop partway down and take in the view. It was a time of absolute freedom: freedom from one's fellows, from one's job, even, in a way from the law of gravity. With this absolute freedom came absolute peace. In this instance, since the rope and her own gloved hands failed to fascinate, there was no view to speak of. But even given the peculiarities of the place, a remnant of peace remained.

For the first time in a long while, she was alone. The men, one a hundred feet above, the other nearly as far below, could have been on the face of the moon, such was her momentary isolation.

Time, snatched away by the urgency of Frieda's head wound, was by some alchemy of darkness and suspension, returned for the nonce, and Anna felt able to steal a minute or two to collect what had become a stampede of thought and emotion. Buffeted by personal terrors, hands numb and mind driven inward till it was as choked as the place she had crawled into, she was of no value to anyone. Worse, she was a danger to herself, to others, and to the fragile life of the cave. One of the tales of degradation she'd been told by Lisa as they readied her gear was of an aragonite bush deep in the cave. A delicate structure of pure white growing from the cave floor in intricate crystallized branches with minute "leaves" that glittered like diamonds. On this surreal object of beauty someone had dumped his human waste, shattering the minuscule spires with ordure. This monument to human coarseness could never be washed away by rains, dried and whisked off by the wind. The cave had no way of cleansing and renewing itself. Each misstep left a track for all eternity.

Hearing the story, Anna was repulsed as she was meant to be. But, though she would not have admitted it to Lisa or Timmy, she could empathize with the transgressor. When fear and fatigue reached critical mass, the higher instincts were lost. In their place came a rough anger, a grasping for immediate needs regardless of the consequences, whether that need manifested itself in snatching the last mouthful of water or relieving oneself without taking the time and energy to assure no damage was done in the process.

It was toward this shameful and dangerous mind-set that Anna knew she was headed. While she still had a modicum of control, she had to make one of two choices: go back or get over it. She sincerely hoped that in the extremity of her need, should she call for someone they would come. Frieda had called.

Going back was out of the question.

She took a deep breath and let the claustrophobia build in a vacant center of her skull. Terror gushed from her pores in a sweat that stank of fear. A metallic taste flooded her mouth, and her hands grew so cold and stiff she wondered if the rope would slip though the fingers of her right hand and leave her to plummet to the rocks below. Though she remained upright, she had the overpowering sensation of falling in all directions at once.

When terror had filled every cell of her being, she gripped the rope tightly and pressed her cheek against it.

Screwing her eyes shut she braced herself against the detritus in her head and willed it to move. Not gone, she told herself, knowing that was too much to hope for. Just stored away in a vault. Later, when she was out of the cave and Frieda was safe, she would give herself permission to go completely insane if that was what was required.

Sharp pain cut between her eyes, and she could almost hear the creaking and snapping as she mentally bulldozed the mountain of neurosis to the back of her mind.

For half a minute more, she dangled with her eyes closed. Her head hurt, but feeling was returning to her hands. The fear was not vanquished. It hung over her, a huge and precariously balanced boulder ready to come crashing down and crush her at the first loud noise or brush of air. Being wired with a panic button on a hair trigger was not reassuring, but, with luck, it would never be pressed. If it was . . .

I'll burn that bridge when I come to it, she told herself. Until then she could think again; there was room to care for others. She could go on.

Rapidly she began paying out rope, descending to the bottom of Boulder Falls, where Iverson welcomed her with the light from a small battery-powered star.

3

THE HELLISH PACE set by Iverson was a godsend. Traversing the rugged subterranean landscape took all of Anna's concentration and all of her skills. The interior of the planet did not seem governed by the same laws of physics as its exterior. Or perhaps it was just that the route was nonnegotiable. One couldn't pick and choose passes or climbs; one went where there was no dirt in the way.

Such were the demands of travel that majesty and grandeur were lost. Anna wasn't sorry. Hard physical work was a balm for her soul. Vast slopes of scree were painstakingly descended. Boxcars of stone, upended and angled in a hundred ways, stacked against each other until they formed smaller passages of their own. Hands were used like an extra pair of feet for balance. Chunks of stone slid underfoot, and ankle-breaking traps opened between rocks the size and stability of bowling balls.

Names went by with the black velvet-clad scenery: Colorado Room, seen as a series of slides framed by the limiting scope of headlamps; Glacier Bay, great pale glaciers calving in a sea of night. Windy City, Rim City.

Anna used her body in a way she seldom had since childhood. Though occasionally alarmed at being called out of an early and long retirement, her muscles gloried in the exercise. As she bent and stretched, hopped from boulder to boulder in faltering and moveable light, slid down talus slopes on butt and heels, hauled herself up rocks, scrabbling with fingers and toes for purchase, it came home to her how stultifying the dignified world of grown-ups had allowed itself to become. How limiting and unsatisfying to deny our simian ancestry by walking always upright and sitting in chairs, throwing away natural powers for some inherited code of decorum.

Wriggling through a narrow chimney, knees and elbows thrust against the rock, she remembered a story she'd been told by a friend who led canoe trips for Outward Bound in the Boundary Waters of northern Minnesota. He'd taken a group of physically disabled people on a two-week trip. It wasn't a luxury vacation. Everybody did what they could, filling in the gaps for one another.

The story that stuck in Anna's mind was of a man who suffered from a crippling case of muscular dystrophy. In his late twenties, he'd been wheelchair bound over half his life. His greatest fear was that his house would catch fire. If he couldn't get to his wheelchair, he would burn to death.

During the trip this man was unable to carry canoes or gear on the many rough portages. But he chose not to be a burden to the others. He discovered an untapped talent. Clad in protective clothes, he crawled and inched and slithered, dragging his legs over fallen logs, across rocky beaches, and through weed-choked ravines.

By the end of his sojourn in the wilderness, his fear of burning to death in his own home was gone. "I can crawl out," he said. "I never thought of it. Shoot, I could crawl the six miles to the fire station if I had to." He'd regained some of his lost mobility.

The guy would have made a heck of a caver.

They'd been traveling ninety minutes, had gone less than three-quarters of a mile, and had ventured into the earth four hundred feet, when they came to the North Rift.

The rift was a great crack running northwest to southeast, splitting the known world of the cave as a cleaver might halve a melon. Pointing with his light, Oscar picked out a hand line, threaded his rack, and descended. At the T-shaped junction where passage met rift, the cut was only fifteen feet deep. Moments later he was climbing up the far side. A cringing, spine-scraping crawl later they emerged next to a huge fissure. The Rift gone mad.

"Jesus," Anna breathed as she cleared the last tumble of rock. Iverson was seated on a square block of breakdown the size of a refrigerator. The stone was sheared as neatly as if a gargantuan mason had done it with a chisel. Pieces, varying in size, clung to the edge of the precipice. She scratched her way up to sit gingerly beside Oscar, her hands hooked on the back of their limestone couch lest the pull of the deeps should suck her down. "Shouldn't there be a sign here that reads 'Beyond This Point Be Monsters'?"

"Left goes up to the North Rift," Iverson said. "Right is the main route to the rest of the cave. We go right."

The word "impassable" came to mind. Above, stone vanished into the gloom. Blocks the size of rooms jutted from the walls. Where she and Iverson sat, it was about thirty feet wide, the far side smooth, vertical, offering nothing in the way of an inducement to cross.

"Right?" Anna said.

"Right."

"How?"

Iverson smiled. "There." He painted a curved surface of rock above her with his light. The wall of the rift bulged slightly and bent around in a southwesterly direction. On closer examination, Anna could see where a rope had been strung. The trail—using the term loosely—was suspended along the wall eight or ten feet above where they sat. Pitons, bolts were frowned upon in wild caves. Driving these man-made anchors into living stone left scars. The rope above them made use of a motley assortment of natural anchors: BFRs, Big Fucking Rocks; jug handles, natural holes in the rock; and stalagmites.

Below, the rift fell away in a rugged canyon. Light served only to beckon forth the shadows and veil secrets. It struck her as odd that all of it—this tremendous gorge, the seeps and falls and spires—could continue to exist in the total absence of light and life. Like the philosophical tree falling in the theoretical forest, with no one to hear, not so much as a gnat or a dung beetle to take note, did it really exist? Apparently it did. "How deep?" she asked.

"Here? Maybe one hundred twenty-five feet or so. It varies, of course. Nobody's ever really done much exploring down there."

As far as Anna was concerned, that left it wide open as a habitat for impossible creatures from the underworld. It was no mystery why the ancients peopled caves with evil spirits and placed their hells deep within the earth.

"Definitely a No Falling Zone," Iverson said mildly.

Anna turned her light on his face. He was smiling with what looked to her like genuine delight. "You really are a creepy person, you know that, don't you?"

Holden Tillman eased up beside them and swung his legs over the edge. Anna kept all her appendages on solid ground, her legs folded neatly under her, tailor-fashion.

"So," Holden said, uncapping his water bottle and pausing for a long pull. Anna followed suit, checking first to reassure herself there wasn't a "P" scrawled on the cap.

"Freak-Out Traverse," Holden said, and waved toward the roped cliff face with his water bottle.

"Gee, why do you think they call it that?" Anna asked.

Holden didn't seem to notice the sarcasm. "Interesting story," he said. "See below the rope there? That great, big, old, solid-looking pokeoutance, just exactly the right size to wrap your arms around and hang on to for dear life?"

He traced the rock outcrop he described with a golden finger of lamplight. It was the obvious place to make the traverse. Anna had wondered about the trail being set so high above the starting point.

"We got here. Me and a caver named Ron. I, being the gentleman that I am, insisted Ron have the first crack at it. 'Oh, no,' he said. 'After you, my dear Holden.' 'I wouldn't dream of it. After you,' says me. So he goes first. Ron gets to that big, old, friendly rock and spread-eagles himself across it like a love-struck starfish. And that sucker starts to move. The thing is on ball bearings. Hence 'Freak-Out Traverse.' I let Ron name it. I'm just naturally generous that way."

Even in the wandering half-light, Anna noted the twinkle in his eyes.

"Everybody rested and rejuvenated?" Iverson asked.

A sheer curtain of panic, like heat rising from the desert, quivered behind Anna's breastbone; panic not at the traverse but at going on instead of turning back. Gideon, the horse she'd ridden on backcountry patrol when she was a ranger at Guadalupe, and she had this discussion at every fork in the trail, Anna insisting they go on, Gideon determined to take every opportunity to go back to the barn.

Rest stops were going to be bad news.

"Ready," she said, and was the first to get to her feet. Movement was good, work even better. She felt herself almost looking forward to Freak-Out. That should take up every shred of her thought processes for a few minutes.

After Freak-Out the going got somewhat easier. Though a good deal of effort went into climbing on, around, and under the blocks, little of it was heart-in-mouth stuff.

Shoving her hands in cracks, her face in the dirt, reaching into darkness, squeezing through the narrow ways, Anna came to appreciate the sterility of the cave environment: no spiders, grubs, scorpions, rattlesnakes, wasps, tarantulas, ants, or centipedes. She burrowed and barged her way through with more or less complete confidence that, as predators went, she was pretty much alone. Given the forced intimacy with blind crevices and dank hidey-holes, this was definitely a plus. This far in there wasn't even any evidence of that benign resident, the cave cricket. For the first three or four hundred yards she had seen a few of the harmless, spectral insects, but cave crickets found their food on the surface or in the twilight zone where the outer world reached within. They seldom wandered more than an easy cricket commute from the terrestrial world.

Partway down the North Rift, half an hour's travel and not quite a hundred yards as the crow flies—should a crow choose such a batlike endeavor—Iverson stopped again, perched this time on a narrow ledge, his lamp extinguished. Lest he startle Anna and make her lose her footing, he announced himself shortly before her light strayed across his aerie. "I'm here," he said softly.

Anna squawked, her heart leaping so forcefully it felt as if it pounded against the rock she embraced. "Don't do that," she said when breath returned and she'd found a stable roosting place.

"Sorry," Iverson said politely. "I guess 'I'm here' are the two scariest words in the English language."

"Nope."

"Uh-oh?" Iverson guessed.

"Floyd Collins," Anna said, and he laughed.

Holden joined them and switched off his lamp. Having no taste for the darkness, Anna let hers burn. "Better be careful," Holden warned. "Oscar's a light leach. He'll drain your batteries faster than a disgruntled Hodag."

Hodags, Anna knew from earlier banter, were known for sucking the energies from cavers' batteries, tying shoelaces together, and swapping the caps on water and pee bottles when annoyed in some fashion. "Leach away," she said. She wasn't turning her light out.

Just beyond the cranny where Oscar had curled his bony frame was a tilted tyrolean traverse. A line was anchored around a boulder on the side of the rift where the three of them sat. It ran over the chasm and up to another anchor, a jug handle on the cliff face five yards above them on the opposite side. Anna had used a tyrolean once on a recreational climb in the Rockies. For some reason they gave her the willies where a good vertical ascent failed to. Maybe it was that one had to lie horizontal. Gravity seemed more virulent when one's back was turned to it.

"Who rigged the traverse?" she asked. Her insecurities were showing.

"Me and Holden," Iverson said.

"I sure hope we were sober," Holden added.

"From here on we're in new country," Oscar said, and Anna could hear the quiver of anticipation in his voice.

"You've never been to Tinker's Hell?"

"Nope. Neither of us. Just got to pore over the surveys. Might never have gotten to go either. The chief"—Iverson referred to his boss, George Laymon, Chief of Resource Management for Carlsbad Caverns—"has been keeping a tight lid on who goes in here. After the big push in the 1980s they closed the cave to all but scientific research and restoration—"

"And anybody who knew somebody they could lean on," Holden put in, and Anna was reminded of the usually friendly but still existing rivalry between federal land management agencies, in this case the NPS and the Bureau of Land Management. Ostensibly the Park Service was dedicated to total conservation. The BLM espoused a more commercial view, leasing and exploiting some of the resources of public lands.

"Hey, it's who you know," Oscar said equitably.

The closing of Lechuguilla was an old bone of contention. "How do we know where we're going?" Anna asked, bringing the conversation back to a subject nearer her heart.

"If you don't know where you're going, you're liable to end up someplace else," Holden said philosophically. Anna heard telltale crackling as he unwrapped a Jolly Rancher.

"House rules," Iverson told Anna. "You survey as you go: maps, sketches, measurements, the whole enchilada. No scooping booty."

"It happens," Holden said. "Somebody gets excited and boldly goes where no man has gone before. But it's severely frowned upon."

"Do they lay orange tape like we've been following?" Anna asked.

"Them's the rules," Holden said, and she found herself immeasurably relieved, though she knew the tape was laid more for the cave's protection than that of the cavers. If each expedition followed precisely the same trail, never veered from between the lines, a majority of the cave would remain untrammeled. Oscar looked at his watch. "Seven P.M.," He said. "We've been on the go just over two hours. With luck we'll be there by midnight. Everybody holding up okay?"

"Okay," Anna echoed.

"The Wormhole," Iverson said. Clicking on his headlamp, he ran the beam along the traverse to where it was anchored on the far side. Below the jug handle securing the line was an irregularity in the stone about the size and shape of an inverted Chianti bottle. The opening was flush with the wall: no ledge, lip, or handholds; no nooks or crannies to brace boots in.

"You're kidding," Anna said hopefully.

"I'll admit it looks tricky," Iverson said. "You want to go first, Holden?"

"And rob you of the glory? No indeed."

Iverson peeled off his pack and began strapping on ascenders.

The one time Anna had been on a tyrolean traverse it had been a simple horizontal move over a river valley under kind blue skies with the music of frogs to keep her company. They'd not used ascenders, just strung the traverse line through a trolley on the web gear and scuttled across with much the same movements used when shinnying along a rope. Because of the steep tilt of this traverse—close to forty-five degrees—ascenders were needed.

Mechanical ascenders were a relatively simple invention that had revolutionized climbing. A one-way locking cam device about the size of a pack of cigarettes and shaped like a tetrahedron was strapped to the right boot above the instep. An identical device was attached to the left foot but on a tether that, when pulled out to full length, reached the climber's knee. This ascender was tied to a thin bungee cord and hooked over the shoulder. Once this awkward arrangement was complete, the rope to be climbed was hooked through both ascenders and a roller on the climber's chest harness. Thus married to the rope, it was a not-so-simple matter of walking, as up an invisible ladder. Raise the right foot; up comes the Gibbs ascender. Put weight on the right foot; cam locks down on the line. The foot is firm in its stirrup, and the body is propelled upward. This movement tightens the bungee, which in turn pulls the second ascender up along the rope. When the left foot steps down, the cam locks and another "stair" is provided.

Anna had used Gibbs ascenders enough that she was proficient, but she always enjoyed watching a master. The ascenders, so arranged, were called a rope-walker system. On the right climber that appeared literally true. Anna had seen men walk as efficiently up two hundred feet of rope as if they walked up carpeted stairs in their living room.

"Croll," Iverson said as he rigged a third ascender into his seat harness. "Ever used one?"

Anna shook her head.

"Like falling off a log," he assured her.

Rotten analogy, Anna thought, but she didn't say anything.

"Get the packs ready," Iverson said to Holden. "Once I get settled, I'll bring them across with a haul line."

"We'll use the haul line, too," Holden told Anna. "Ever so much more civilized."

As Iverson rigged himself to the traverse, Anna watched with a keen interest. One lesson, then the test. It crossed her mind how much better a student she would have been if in school the options had been learn or die.

Crouching on a thumb of rock as big around as a plate, eighteen inches of it thrust over the chasm, Oscar attached his safety, clipped his Croll into the rope, wrestled his two foot ascenders onto the line, then pushed till his torso and buttocks hung like a side of beef a hundred twenty feet above God knew what.

Anna kept her headlamp trained where he would find it useful, kept the light steady and out of his eyes. It was all she could do. There was no room for a second pair of hands to help him.

Holden was occupied with the business of tying the packs into trouble-free bundles that could easily be hauled across. Along with personal gear were medical supplies requested by Dr. McCarty, among them oxygen. In the case of a head wound it might be the only thing that could keep Frieda's brain tissue from permanent damage.

Iverson finished and snaked an elbow over the line so he could hold his head up. "Check my gear?" he said to Holden.

"Right-o."

Having been checked out by a fresh pair of eyes, Oscar began rope-walking over the rift. Suspended at four points along the line, his body was nearly horizontal, spine toward the center of the earth. As always in a traverse, there was an element of sag. It made the operation of the ascenders inefficient, and progress was measured in inches. As the line began to angle, rising steeply toward the Wormhole, the slack was taken up. After a few strangled kicks to get the cams to lock down, Oscar climbed like a pro, covering the last thirty feet in as many seconds. The rig was a work of art; not so much slack that he was head-down at the bottom, but enough so that he was standing upright when he reached the hole.

In the scattering light, Anna could see his skinny arms weaving some sort of magic near the top of the traverse, where his shoulders blocked her view.

"That's the tricky part alluded to earlier," Holden said. Anna was startled at the nearness of his voice. She could feel his breath against her cheek. In their absorption, they'd knelt shoulder to shoulder on the edge of their limestone block like a couple of White Rock fairies in a troglodyte nightmare.

"What's he doing?" The words gusted out, and Anna realized she'd been holding her breath.

"There's no place to be, and the Wormhole's so tight it's sort of pay-as-you-go. He's changing ropes. Hooking onto the rebelay. He'll let himself loose a little bit at a time as he gets that part of himself into the hole. The hard bit is feeling for the Gibbs down at your feet. Sort of like tying your shoelaces when you're halfway down a python's throat."

Iverson squirmed a moment more, Anna and Holden so entranced they forgot to talk. Then it was as if the rock swallowed his head. It was gone, and only the body remained, twitching with remembered life. The shoulders were next, melting seamlessly into the cliff, the pathetic stick legs kicking in short convulsive movements. Hips vanished, and Anna and Holden's lights played over a pair of size-thirteen boots flipping feebly. The image was ludicrous, but Anna didn't feel like laughing. Hands reappeared, only the hands, gloved and bulky. With no assistance from a corporeal body, they fussed and fluttered and danced like a cartoon drawn by an artist on acid.

"Removing the foot ascenders," Holden said. "Last link."

Abruptly, the hands were sucked back into the limestone. The boots followed. All that remained to indicate that any life-form had ever existed was the gentle swaying of the rope.

"He's good," Holden said admiringly. "The man is good. He could thread himself through all four stomachs of a cow and never even give her the hiccups."

Anna eased back from the edge of the rock and rearranged legs grown stiff from too long without movement. "Me next," she said, and was pleased at how normal her voice sounded.

"Not yet. Oscar will holler when he's ready. There's no room to turn around in the Wormhole. He's got to crawl on up a little ways. There's a chimney. He'll go up, spin himself about, then come back down so he can get the gear and pull you in. One of you guys will do the same for me.

"The creepy-crawly part of the hole's fifty feet or so." Holden answered Anna's unasked question. "Then it opens right up. Big stuff like we've been doing."

Anna nodded. She'd not wanted to ask, but the Wormhole was eating away at her hard-won control. Fifty feet; she measured it out in her mind. Frieda's backyard in Mesa Verde was fenced to keep her dog, Taco, from wandering. The posts were eight feet apart. Anna had helped replace four of them at the beginning of the summer. Fifty feet: six postholes. She could swim that far underwater. Sprint that far in high heels and panty hose. Fifty feet. Nothing to it.

"All set." The words reverberated across the chasm, and Anna and Tillman trained their lights on the orifice that had swallowed Oscar. A disembodied hand waved to them from the solid fortress that was their destination.

"Now you next," Holden said. "Have fun." He smiled and she smiled back, glad to know him, glad to have him with her. Holden Tillman's smile was better than a bottle of Xanax.

Anna was always careful with climbing gear. This time her attention to detail was obsessive. The contortionist movements required to hook ascenders with half her body bobbing over a crevice she couldn't see the bottom of required that each movement be thought through before it was attempted. She was glad the ranger from Rocky Mountains who had taught her to climb had insisted she practice everything one-handed, and by touch, not sight. Tillman trained his lamp on her hands and watched.

"Looks good," he said when she had finished. "See you on the other side."

Anna nodded and pulled herself hand-over-hand along the rope till she could begin to kick in with her rope-walkers. For a brief eternity she floundered like a fish in a net. Because the Gibbs wouldn't lock regardless of how she angled her feet in an attempt to get the cams to catch, she was muscling her way along, using the strength of her arms and shoulders. Bad form, and something she couldn't maintain for any length of time. Exertion made the line sway. Coupled with the wild dancing of shadows every time she moved her head, it was dizzying. Adrenaline, already high, rose to poisonous levels.

Closing her eyes, she forced herself to relax, let the rope and metal take the weight. After a steadying breath, she began again her crippled walk, this time with more success. The rope inclined, tension increased, the cams locked and unlocked fluidly. Much to her amazement, she found she was enjoying herself. Deep in the bedrock of the Southwest, and she was probably as high as she'd ever climbed. She laughed aloud and hoped Holden wouldn't mistake it for hysteria.

The ascent was over too soon. Head against the wall, feet over the rift, she dead-ended. By craning her neck she could look back far enough to see the opening she was supposed to get into. It was nothing short of miraculous that Iverson had managed it without aid. She felt utterly helpless.

"Oscar?"

"Right here." An ungloved hand, looking sublimely human, came out several inches above her face and the fingers waggled cheerfully. "Put your arms over your head like you're diving."

It took a minor act of will, but Anna got both hands off the traverse line and did as she was instructed. Fingers locked around her wrists, and she was drawn into the Wormhole. Stone brushed against her left shoulder and her face was no more than two inches from the rock above. The dragging pulled her helmet over her eyes. Newly blind, her first sense that the environment had changed was the warm sweet smell of sweat mixed liberally with cotton and dust. An unseen hand tipped her hat back so she could see. Rock had been replaced by a maroon tee-shirt with pink lettering so close to her face she couldn't read it. She was less than an inch below Iverson's chest. The space was closing in. Her lungs squeezed and her throat constricted. An image of fighting like a maddened cat, clawing back out to fall into the abyss, ripped through her mind.

Now's not a good time, she warned herself. "What next?" she asked, needing to move.

"Is your rear end in?"

"Feels like it."

"Okay. There's space to your right. You're going to have to stretch over, reach down, and let loose your foot ascenders."

Anna bent to the right at her waist. She tried to bring her knee up but cracked it painfully against the rock. Second try and she could feel the ascender on her boot. After a moment of fumbling she pulled the quick-release pin securing the cam and plucked the line out. "Got it," she said.

"Left is harder, but you're short and flexible," Iverson said encouragingly.

Anna grunted and pretzeled farther over in the slot that sandwiched her in. The left proved easier. Small blessings. She'd take what she could get. "I'm loose."

"Get your body as straight as you can," Iverson told her. She squirmed her bones into a line. Every movement was dogged by difficulty. Clothing and gear caught and dragged. Her hard hat pulled, choking then blinding her. Fear built. She began to count in her head to drown out the distant buzz of panic, a sound like a swarm of angry bees.

"Okay. Good. Grab my knees and pull yourself the rest of the way in."

Anna worked her arms back over her head and felt the warmth of Oscar's thighs. Hooking her fingers behind his knees, she dragged herself toward them.

"Watch your light!"

She stopped just before she rammed his groin with the apparatus. "Caving is not conducive to human dignity," she grumbled.

"Nope. Just to long and meaningful relationships," Oscar said, and Anna laughed to let him know she appreciated the effort. "You're home free. Take off your helmet and push it ahead. Keep going till you come out in a place that looks like it's made of cheese. Wait for us there."

Inching along like a worm, Anna oozed between Oscar's legs. The passage opened enough so she could roll over onto her stomach, then closed down again so tight she had to turn her head sideways to make any progress. The bees whined, the noise threatening sanity.

She scratched ahead with her toes. Tugged forward with fingertips and stomach muscles. Humped along like a caterpillar, ignoring the rake of stone knives down her shoulder blades. Each foot achieved was a goal to be celebrated. When she thought she couldn't take any more she was granted a reprieve. The Wormhole bored out of the wall into a large room, and she spewed gratefully to the floor.

Oscar Iverson's choice of metaphor had been apt. As if she had entered a mouse's dream of paradise, Anna had arrived into what looked like a giant piece of Swiss cheese. Uniformly pale round passages twisted away in all directions. Without moving she could count twelve openings, some as small as the Wormhole, some big enough to walk through upright. The place was a three-dimensional maze, confusing and disorienting. But it was bigger than a bread box, and Anna contented herself with that.

In less than twenty minutes the men joined her. "Eight thirty," Iverson said, looking at his watch. "We're way slow. Everybody okay to pick up the pace?" Too tired to speak, Anna nodded. Packs were redistributed, and they resumed travel. Again Oscar set a brutal pace. Anna worked until there was no room for thought, for observation, no room even for fear. Holden's promise held true; there were no more creepy-crawly bits and only a handful of places they had to chimney- or stoop-walk. The earth's interior was so riddled with airspace it was a wonder great tracts of the Trans-Pecos didn't collapse periodically.

Wonders flashed past in a sweating stream, caught in light fragments like views from a rain-streaked train window. Falls of liquid stone the color of old brass emptied into a lake so clear that the bottom, thirty feet down, looked no farther away than Anna's toes. There was no way around it, and the three of them stripped naked lest their filthy clothes sully water kept pure for millennia. Clothing was put in zipper-lock plastic bags to keep it dry. For the climb back out of the water-filled room, they donned rubber beach shoes so they would not scar the perfect surface of the flow-stone, tumbling in a waterless fall frozen in place for all time.

After the lake, they dressed and laced on their boots for Razor Blade Run. Aragonite bushes, white and as freeform as coral, bloomed in the utter stillness. The slightest touch by a passing caver was enough to snap the delicate crystals. Tunnels of these fragile, razor-sharp feathers were eased through with aching slowness and a constant mantra of "be careful. Look out. Big one. Take it slow . . ." from Iverson.

"Watch those big feet. Laymon says Oscar walks like an elephant on a pogo stick . . ." from Holden.

Anna's legs carried her. Hands grasped rope. She poured water down her throat. Miracles passed by.

By the time they arrived in Tinker's Hell, where Frieda lay, it was after two in the morning. Anna hadn't slowed the cavers down. She hadn't gotten hurt. And she hadn't gone nuts. All in all, a successful day.

Tinker's, where the survey team was camped, was an immense chamber; Shea Stadium could have been tucked inside with room left over for a taxi stand. Anna, Holden, and Iverson entered through a jumbled corridor devoid of decorations and uniformly dirt-colored. The passage emerged halfway between the floor and the ceiling of Tin-ker's, spilling onto a high balcony guarded by a natural parapet of stone. Oscar was astraddle this wall drinking water when Anna came into Tinker's Hell.

Every muscle in her body melted with fatigue. Aches and pains would come with rest. For the moment she felt only warm and liquid, her mind as pliant as her limbs. With a poorly concealed grunt of exhaustion, she dumped her pack and dragged herself up beside him.

Sixty feet below, in the immense room, was a scene of rampant destruction. Breakdown littered the floor; blocks of limestone, some the size of houses, lay one on top of the other like the building blocks of a spoiled giant flung across his nursery. Amid this majestic rubble were cones and pillars of gold and burnt umber, stalactites and stalagmites that had been growing for countless ages and now lay broken and scattered.

"Jesus," Anna said. "Earthquake?"

"Who knows? I've never seen anything like it. But the breaks are old, old, old. Whatever happened, happened a long time ago."

Holden joined them, his light weaving in with theirs as they looked at the magnificent ruin.

"Yup," Holden said after a few minutes' study. "It looks like a bomb hit a tinker's cart. Have you spotted the camp yet?"

From his pack Iverson dug a secondary light source, a powerful six-cell flashlight, and played the beam over the jagged floor. Near the end of the great room, on a flat place tucked up near the left-hand wall, his light picked out the litter of humanity. Looking pathetically small and fragile in the confusion of elemental stone, six people lay in sleeping bags. The wrinkled forms were soft and shapeless, like larvae on a deserted patch of beach. The necessities of human existence—packs, stoves, water, and food—were piled neatly at one end of the clearing. The group had been there four days, one since Frieda was hurt. The camp appeared clean and well organized.

"Another twenty minutes and vacation's over," Iverson said.

They donned packs and started the tedious climb down to the cavern floor. This time Holden Tillman led.

Underground operations had officially commenced.

BY THE TIME they neared the camp, Anna was so tired she was stumbling. It was as if her brain, recognizing that the end was in sight, had quit holding her muscles together. The only workable mode of travel across Tinker's Hell was boulder-hopping. At each leap, she found herself keeping her center of gravity closer to the ground. When Dr. Peter McCarty came from the camp to meet them, she was traveling on all fours, the wolfman reverting to type.

McCarty and Tillman exchanged greetings, and introductions were muttered. Anna dredged up a nod. A handshake was beyond her. She was even too far gone to protest when McCarty took her pack to carry it the last ten yards. At that point she doubted she'd have put up much of a fight if he'd offered to carry her.

Even with the stamp of the cave on him and five days from a showerhead, Peter McCarty was a handsome man. Not a matinée-idol pretty—Anna would have found that off-putting—but with enough flaws to keep his face interesting. His lips were chiseled but a little too thin, his jaw strong but with a crude boxiness at the angle of the bones. His voice was light but pleasant, with an adenoidal quality to it as if he suffered from a slight head cold. His curling brown hair was thinning at the hairline. Anna guessed his age to be forty, or near enough—it didn't matter.

He and Holden fell into a close, whispered conversation, needing to share information but not wanting to disturb the sleepers. They'd forgotten to douse their helmet lights, and feeling mildly righteous, Anna switched hers off and leached from them as she staggered in last and folded onto the floor. She was too tired even to sleep without being told to and sat lumpishly staring at them as they conversed in tones too low for her to make sense of.

At length, Holden broke away and came over to where she waited, beyond patience and nearly in a state of catatonia.

"Frieda?" she asked.

"No better, no worse."

"Good news," Anna said. With a wound to the head, it was. Deterioration of levels of consciousness or motor control augured evil, usually swelling or bleeding in the skull that, unchecked, would create deadly pressure.

Holden nodded. "Peter is putting her on a hundred percent oxygen with a non-rebreather. He's got things well in hand. He separated Frieda from the others to give her a little quiet and privacy. He wants you to bed down over near her. Don't talk to her, he said. Let her sleep. Just be there in case she wakes up."

"Got it."

Holden pointed out the recumbent form that was Frieda Dierkz. In his shielded light, Anna could see the leg, an air-splint from foot to mid-thigh. Dr. McCarty was fitting the non-rebreather oxygen mask over the woman's face. Frieda was fighting his attempts to help her, moving her head from side to side and moaning in such a way that Anna was overcome with an irrational fury toward her tormentor.

Biting back words she was bound to regret, she knelt in the dirt near her friend's head and laid her hand on her brow. "It's me, Anna," she said softly. "I got here as fast as I could. You couldn't have hurt yourself in the Bahamas or Paris, could you? It had to be here. You are such a pain in the butt, Frieda."

"Interesting bedside manner," McCarty said dryly.

Frieda stopped fighting. The tension went out of her muscles, and her breathing evened out.

"Ooh. Hey," the doctor said. "Maybe I'll have to give it a try."

Anna laughed. "Where are you from?" she asked on impulse.

"St. Paul, Minnesota." She couldn't have said why, but it didn't surprise her. "I'm glad you showed up," McCarty said wearily. "Let's go with the nasal cannula at six liters. I don't want her getting agitated again."

Anna handed him the appropriate tubing and, when he had it in place, turned the flow to six liters per minute. He watched her carefully. She didn't bother telling him she was an EMT. Doctors seemed to make a point of being aggressively unimpressed by that tidbit of information.

McCarty took his patient's pulse one last time, then turned his light on Anna's face. She didn't like being diagnosed, and busied herself with her pack. "Sleep," he prescribed. "Do you need something to help you?"

Too tired to laugh at him, she managed a "No thanks," and was rewarded by his departure.

She didn't pull out her space blanket or take off her boots. Laying her head on the unkind lumps in her side-pack, she was instantly asleep.

So deep was her unconsciousness that when she was awakened she didn't know if minutes or days had passed. For a horrifying moment she didn't know where she was; then, with no decrease in the horror, she did. Such was the suffocating blackness, Anna was blind, deaf, and dumb with it. Black filled her lungs, and she couldn't get enough air. Fighting the drawstrings of her pack, she felt for and found the little blue Maglite. Clicking it on, she carved a space big enough that she could breathe. The pounding of her heart racketed in her ears, and she had to go to the john desperately; a mere Baggie seemed inadequate to the task.

Breathing evenly, she quieted her heartbeat to a dull thunder. Through it she heard the noise that had pulled her from sleep: her name, a sound so insubstantial it could have been the whisper of a ghost. "Anna . . ." and an exhalation.

On elbows and knees, she crawled over to Frieda. "I'm here," she said.

"Anna . . ." again, and something about a lake with marble clouds, and Taco throwing up on her good shoes.

Shading the light, Anna studied her friend's face. The skin was flushed on forehead and cheeks but white and drawn around the lips. Automatically she checked Frieda's pupils. Equal and reactive. No battle signs showed behind the ears. No fluids leaked from ears or nostrils, and the flesh around her eyes was not discolored. McCarty would have looked at all this, Anna reminded herself; still, she checked.

Frieda's gaze skimmed across her face and wandered to the impossible darkness above. "Thirsty," she said. Anna fed her sips of water, scared to lift her head lest there was a neck injury, scared of choking her to death if she didn't.

"Stay with me, Frieda. I came all this way. Don't leave me now," Anna pleaded. "I'm not leaving you."

Frieda's hand closed convulsively on Anna's tee-shirt, bunching the fabric tight around her ribs. "It wasn't an accident," she said clearly.

"What? What wasn't an accident?" Anna demanded.

"Lily pads ruined," she whispered, and Anna could see that reason had fled.

"Frieda," she begged, but the woman's eyes closed. Anna resisted a cruel urge to shake her.

Not an accident.

Marble clouds, dog vomit, and lily pads: Frieda was delirious. It didn't take Freud to figure that out. But there'd been a moment's clarity. And a reason Frieda had asked for a friend, a noncaver friend from outside.

Anna sat back, traced her finger of light over the feet of her companions. "God, but this sucks," she muttered. Curling herself around Frieda like a Viking's dog on his master's funeral ship, Anna laid her head down once more. If anyone wanted to get to Dierkz, they would have to tread on some part of Anna's anatomy to do it. It was all she could do till morning.

Morning was two days away.

4

THE NEXT TIME Anna was dragged from sleep, the effect was not so jarring. People were on the move. A lantern pushed back the dark walls until the camp seemed almost spacious. Voices softened the sepulchral stillness, and there was the smell of coffee. The odor was weak, the brew undoubtedly instant, but it was enough to stir Anna's sluggish mind.

Lying motionless, she watched the wakening camp. This far from the sun, all was shrouded. Shadows claimed more than light, and light cloaked as often as it revealed. Focus flickered, changeable as candle flames, as a lamp caught one plane, then another, lopping off a nose with moving shadow, sparking an eye bright as opal. Colors were fired and quenched, leaving comet trails on the retina as they passed. Beams sought out sudden horizons at varying distances, and the cavern appeared to be expanding and contracting; an uncertain and secretive world, more hidden than would ever be told.

Anna fantasized about bringing great mercury-vapor

lamps in and cranking up the wattage. The movie *Interview with the Vampire* had given her a similar feeling, though to a much lesser degree. She needed to see the sun rise.

Rolling onto her side, she realized that while she slept someone had spread a space blanket over her to keep off the chill. Fear had laid down with her, and at this sign of interference, she instinctively reached for a weapon. The reflex was a mere flick of her hand, aborted before her hand had moved even a finger's width. Here she was not a law enforcement ranger. Her assignment had been quite specific. Ladies-in-waiting didn't customarily go heavily armed. Anna was without so much as a hat pin.

Remembering her nocturnal exchange with Frieda, she wondered how much danger there was. What was delirium and what was the truth? That, too, was wrapped in shadow. She looked over at her friend. Frieda's eyes were closed. If she slept, Anna didn't want to disturb her. She lay a bit longer, taking advantage of the extended night to see what fellows she had fallen in amongst.

Holden, Oscar, and Peter McCarty were huddled around a single lamp, heads low and close, fannies in the air. Anna guessed they were going over surveys of the cave, discussing the care of Frieda as she was subjected to the rigors of her rescue.

A big man, his face lost in darkness, stood a few feet behind them, listening but contributing nothing. Light from the floor caught the bottom of the cup he held, the edges of two large, soft-looking hands, and the underside of a jaw bearded in short red-brown whiskers as thick and shiny as a cat's fur. His bulk took Anna by surprise. He was more than six feet tall and easily weighed two hundred pounds. She'd thought all cavers would be lean and lithe, eel-like. She wasn't sure whether the man's size suited her or not. Should she follow this large subterranean specimen, she would be assured of never getting wedged in a tight spot. Anywhere he could get through would be a breeze for a person Anna's size. Then again, should he become stuck fast when she was behind him, a considerable wall of human flesh would stand between her and freedom. It would take weeks to eat the man; he had that much meat on him.

Behind him, closer to the cavern wall, was a woman cast in a more classic cave formation. Working by the light of two helmet lamps, facing into her camp like lanterned turtles, a lanky woman, so thin that anorexia came to mind, banged gear into packs. Her movements were abrupt, each cached item cracking in protest as she smashed it against the rest. Long straight hair, not caught back in a braid or bandana, swung around her bony shoulders with the angry switch of a mare's tail. Every few seconds she flung it irritably back from her face. As the curtain of hair was raised and the lamps painted her face, Anna noted sharp, clear features. Each was exaggerated just enough that the woman would never be considered truly pretty. Her nose was well shaped and large, her jaw thin, jutting slightly and ending in a squared-off chin with a hint of a dimple. The widely spaced eyes were long, exotic, and slightly unnatural looking. Her mouth was her best feature. The upper lip was well cut with a cupid's-bow fullness, the lower pouted but so girlishly it charmed rather than irked. Anna guessed she was in her late twenties.

"How is Frieda doing?"

Anna rolled over to see a woman hunkered down on her heels not three feet behind her. Anna had neither heard her coming nor sensed her presence. For protection, Frieda would have been better off with a Lhasa apso, she thought sourly.

"She's going to be fine," she said firmly, hoping Frieda could hear and take comfort.

The uninvited guest nodded slowly. She had a round bland face and dark hair pulled back under a bandana that had once been green. The kerchief was tied across her forehead in the fashion of pirates, artists, and outdoorswomen. "Frieda is one tough lady," she said after giving the matter some thought.

Bovine, Anna thought, but it wasn't an insult. The woman brought to mind not the cow-like traits of stupidity or of being easily led, but of solidity and being slow to anger. The image was helped along by dark brown eyes, black and liquid in the dimness, and her size. She was nearly a match for the bearded man. Unfolded, she was probably close to five-ten with broad hips and heavy thighs. She wore shorts and a white tee-shirt, the sleeves rolled above her shoulders. A soft layer of fat hid the muscle, but Anna was willing to bet she was terrifically strong.

"Zeddie Dillard," she said, and stuck out her hand. Damp hair curled from her armpits, and Anna was impressed. Zeddie wasn't more than twenty-four, yet she was as comfortable as an old hippie.

"Anna Pigeon."

Clanking cut into their exchange of pleasantries, and both looked to where the skinny woman knocked a cookstove into its component parts.

"Tantrums on the River Styx?" Anna asked.

"That's the doctor's wife," Zeddie replied with a careful lack of inflection. "And that's what's got her so pissed off."

"That she's Peter McCarty's wife?"

"That she's *the doctor's* wife."

"Ah."

"Zeddie Dillard, amateur psychiatrist and oracle to the stars," the woman said, and laughed. "Coffee?"

Anna was warming right up to Ms. Dillard. "Cream?" she asked hopefully.

"Better. Magic white powder that turns into cream if you stir it with a little plastic stick. It might not work down here," she added as she rose to her feet. "All there is to stir with is the community spoon."

"I'll be with you as soon as I've visited the ladies' room," Anna said.

Zeddie took a flashlight and used it to point out a black gateway between two sizable blocks of stones. "Unisex johns. Easier on the cave," she said. "Put that pointy rock in the path. Privacy guaranteed."

Destination confirmed, Anna worked her way up from the ground. Everything hurt. The aggressively three-dimensional nature of caves ensured that she had been battered equally from all directions. She felt as if she'd been beaten up by experts. Muscles unused for decades cried their lament as she hobbled toward the powder room. Bruises made themselves felt in places that never came into contact with anything more abusive than a down comforter or silk underpants.

Nothing was easy.

Anna was accustomed to the practice of cat-holing, digging tidy holes for waste and covering them. She'd burned enough toilet paper in the wilderness to raise the stock of Scott Tissue a point or two. And she knew why it wouldn't suffice. None of the normal elements of the terrestrial world were at work here, no self-cleaning features built in. Pack it in; pack it out. With stoicism if not good cheer, she completed her toilette as she'd been told: a neat rectangle of aluminum foil, Lisa's "burrito bag." Anna laughed in spite of herself.

Zeddie was waiting with fresh-brewed water. Anna added brown powder and white powder and told herself it was coffee with cream. The group had gathered around an upended flashlight that took the place of a campfire. The people she'd observed earlier were there, as well as another man who had not been in camp before. In his forties, he looked in good physical condition. His hair was blond and cut short, reminiscent of the Nazis in World War II movies, but his face wasn't hard. If anything, he looked slightly timid, slightly aggrieved. He was clad in a muscle shirt and cutoffs so short Anna made a mental note not to get behind him on a steep climb unless she wanted to get to know him a whole lot better.

Zeddie saw where she was looking and muttered, "Brent Roxbury. Fortunately for Brent, there are no fashion police in a cave."

"Is Frieda any better?" Roxbury asked, interrupting their less-than-kind gossip. The question sounded genuinely concerned, and Anna felt mildly guilty. To make it up to him, she forgave him the short-shorts.

"The same," she replied, sorry she didn't have better news. As Anna looked at the ring of concerned faces, Frieda's words of the night before seemed absurd. It was possible she had been thinking clearly and yet had been mistaken. If a blow to the head could erase the trauma, surely it could scramble the facts. Frieda might have been recalling an event from the delirium, a dream so real that in a confused state it would be remembered as gospel. Memories could and were implanted, often so deeply that even faced with proof that an event never actually occurred, a person couldn't shake the feeling from muscle and bone that it had happened.

If the words were true, just as Frieda had said, no psychological voodoo involved, then one of these individuals radiating sympathy and love had pushed a rock on her. Unfortunately, in a place as rigidly controlled and inaccessible as the bowels of Lechuguilla, the last-minute solution of the wandering hobo with homicidal tendencies was unworkable.

"We haven't met," Anna said to half the group, wanting to hear their voices, feel the clasp of their hands, in hopes a sense of their trustworthiness would be communicated.

"Sondra McCarty," Zeddie said, adopting the hostess role. McCarty's wife was braiding her hair with both hands, a thick cloth-covered band held ready in her teeth. Anna got neither a voice nor a handshake but merely a grunt and a nod.

Zeddie went around the circle. "Dr. Curtis Schatz." The big man with the furry chin looked up from where he sat. His eyes were obscured by glasses framed in mock tortoiseshell. The lenses caught the light and reflected back blank space.

"Hello," he said in a flat voice that gave absolutely nothing away and left Anna feeling snubbed.

"Two doctors," she said just to say something. "That's lucky."

"Not really," Schatz drawled, but without Holden's Texas warmth. A "Tennis, anyone?" effeteness lent his words a snobbish air. "I'm a doctor of leisure and recreation."

Anna laughed, realized it was not a joke, and laughed again. "Sorry," she said.

"No problem." Schatz returned to his coffee. Again no handshake. Near the center of the earth, life tended toward the informal.

"Curt's a professor of leisure and recreational studies— park planning stuff—with a state university in New York." Zeddie came to Anna's rescue with the biographical details. "He's sketching this trip."

Anna remembered Oscar discussing survey team responsibilities. Always, when mapping, besides measuring distances and surveying angles, someone sketched the rooms, the landmarks, the passageways, formations, fossils, and anything else of interest they could squeeze in. Depending on the sketch artist, the drawings varied from stick-like cartoon pictures that documented where an object was and its rough shape, to things of beauty in and of themselves.

"This is Brent Roxbury." Zeddie introduced the last of the strangers as if they'd not already raked him over the coals for his sartorial inelegance.

Brent did shake hands. His grip was firm and dry, as apparently sincere as his asking after Frieda's health.

"Brent's a geologist," Frieda said. "He teaches and does a lot of work for the Park Service and the BLM."

Sondra had finished her hair. She pushed forward and stuck out her hand. "I'm a freelance writer," she said. The gesture, belated, and the announcement were out of place. Anna wasn't put off by it. Though she couldn't remember exactly when or why, she knew there'd been a time when she was younger that she'd felt as she imagined Sondra was feeling: ignored, undervalued, outclassed. Her husband was a doctor. He was probably fifteen years her senior. It had to be a hard act to follow. Anna took the proffered hand. The woman's grip was hard, competitive. Anna resisted an impulse to shriek and sink to her knees in exaggerated pain.

"I write travel and adventure articles for the *St. Paul Pioneer Press Dispatch* and travel magazines in America and Great Britain." Her credentials and résumé complete, she dropped Anna's hand.

At a loss for an appropriate response, Anna mumbled, "How do you do?" and left it at that.

Holden was pinching his wrist, pressing the minuscule button on the side of his watch. In the ubiquitous gloom even the green glow of a Timex night-light shone vividly. It was 6:23—A.M., Anna assumed. There was no way of knowing, but her body suggested she'd gotten four hours' sleep, not sixteen. In an hour or less, the team that followed, bringing gear and rigging, should arrive. This would be one of the last times this group would be alone together. As soon as the others came, the machinery of the rescue effort would fall in place and they would be swept up in the momentum.

It was on the tip of Anna's tongue to ask what had happened, how Frieda had come to be hurt, when Holden said, "Okay, before the world starts happening to us, let's go over what we're going to need. Just us chickens. Everybody else is extra."

Anna was just as glad her question had been preempted. It was too late to catch the perpetrator—if there was a perpetrator—off guard. Everyone had ample time to perfect a story. But, had she asked, an official version would have been created by the simple expedient of publicly relating it. Hearing five unofficial versions might prove more enlightening.

Holden spoke just loud enough that one could hear if silence and attention were maintained. When Anna'd been in high school it had been one of Sister Mary Corrine's favorite techniques. Thirty years later and seven hundred feet underground, it still worked. They hung on Holden's every word. Three things were paramount: speed, care of the patient, and care of the cave. The rescuers would keep to the trails even when it made things more difficult. On Tillman's watch not a single aragonite crystal was to be sacrificed. Looking at each in turn, he told them their duties.

Anna and Sondra were ladies-in-waiting. Their task was

to see to Frieda, make sure she was comfortable and secure, calm her if she became agitated, let Holden know if she needed to rest. Peter was to focus on Frieda's health, commission any help he needed with drugs, dressings, and services, monitor her vital signs, and keep Holden apprised.

Curt was given the task of carrying heavy objects. "Born to sherp," he said with a resignation that made Anna laugh. Zeddie was to carry packs and water. There would be others to help her, Holden promised, but it was her job to see that the core group—the eight of them—had what they needed during the carry-out and at the next camp. Holden estimated they could evacuate Frieda in approximately forty-eight hours; two twenty-hour days broken by an eight-hour sleep. Cavers from outside—and by this he meant anyone not in what he had chosen to call the core group—would bring in food, rigging, water, and medical supplies. There were people to lay phone line, prerig major obstacles at the Rift, the Boulder, and the entrance, and do liaison work and requisitioning. Cavers would be assigned to carry the Stokes when needed, and would cart out garbage and derig the hauls behind the evacuation party.

At rests and in camp they would segregate themselves. Those outsiders who could or wished to would rotate to the surface to be replaced by fresher, rested people. Holden wanted Frieda to be surrounded by people she knew. He wanted to keep her trauma and stimulation to a minimum.

For Frieda's peace of mind, Anna would be rigged with her on all the hauls, traveling up with the Stokes. When hands-on carrying of the litter was not required, only Anna, Dr. McCarty, and Sondra would be allowed near her. Holden didn't want Frieda swamped with good intentions.

Anna listened with a growing sense of confidence. She could feel it spreading through the group. When she could get a moment alone with Holden or Oscar, she would tell them of Frieda's assertion that her injury was not accidental. Till then, the arrangement that kept her near Frieda and most others away was tailor-made for her needs.

Lights flashed from the far end of Tinker's Hell. The cavalry had arrived, and the meeting broke up. Sondra McCarty waylaid Anna as she walked back to where Frieda lay.

"Ladies-in-waiting," she said, her voice dripping with conspiratorial scorn. "That man's a dinosaur from the pregnant-and-barefoot school. Doesn't he think we're fit for men's work?"

Anna was dumbstruck. For ten years she'd made a living doing what was traditionally considered men's work. Being a lady-in-waiting required more courage and stamina than she'd ever bargained for. "Hey," she said when her silence had grown too long to be considered polite. "It's a job."

"Yeah. Well. For you, maybe," Sondra said, and Anna knew she'd been written off as hopelessly bourgeois.

A team of twelve cavers rattled into camp, bringing a raucous confusion of light and sound. Packs were dumped and fallen upon, their innards jerked forth for inspection. Peter McCarty was handed a bundle earmarked for patient care. He tucked it under his arm and made a beeline for his patient. Until Anna knew for sure what had harmed Frieda, she didn't intend to let anyone mess with her unobserved, not even her private physician.

"And good morning to you," McCarty said as Anna joined him. With his good looks and instant attentiveness, she could guess part of his wife's problem. The man was a natural flirt. Or a habitual one. She doubted he meant anything by it; the response had just become ingrained into his patterns. Squatting on Frieda's other side, she trained her headlamp not on the doctor's face but on his hands.

"Frieda," he said, "Anna and I are going to fit you up with a catheter so you don't have to go traipsing off to the loo. It will be a wee bit uncomfortable for just a minute." His voice was reassuringly conversational. Anna would have liked to have absolute faith in the man, but it was a luxury Frieda couldn't afford.

Together they cut away the injured woman's trousers. They were lined with soiled toilet tissue, a homemade diaper the doctor had taken care to provide till his equipment arrived. At each step in the procedure, Peter explained what he was doing, dividing his remarks between Anna and the unconscious Frieda. His hands were ungraceful-looking, the nails chewed down to the quick, but his movements were sure and gentle.

When the catheter was in place, McCarty pulled an over-sized handkerchief from his hip pocket and shook out the square of cotton. A baseball was printed in the middle, the words "I do believe in the Twins, I *do*!" stenciled in a semicircle around it. "Not exactly sterile," he said, "but clean and unbesnotted." Draping it carefully over Frieda's lap, he secured it with safety pins to preserve her dignity.

Their patient was settled, as comfortable as they could make her. McCarty began gathering up his supplies, and Anna asked him how the accident had happened. Her light was on his face now to see if muscles might betray something voice had been schooled not to. Watching for lies was a professional habit and, though Anna was a fairly decent practitioner of the art, she had learned not to count on it overmuch. Some liars were just too good, some honest people just naturally twitchy. Still, it was a place to begin.

McCarty glanced over his shoulder. The move was not precisely furtive; maybe he was only judging the time left till they moved Frieda out. Anna had noted that quick, unfocused glance before. It was the one crack in his armor of charm. Though seemingly attentive, one sensed he checked to see if anyone more interesting was in the room before committing his time.

Either Anna won, or she'd imagined the game; McCarty turned back to her.

"Nobody knows for sure," he said. "Possibly not even Frieda. The brain has a way of protecting us from memories that are too painful to be relived."

"Did anyone see it happen?"

"Nope. We'd split up to explore possible leads out of Tinker's. Most of us were fairly close to camp. Brent thought he had a going lead in the upper quadrant. There." McCarty picked up his hard hat, switched on the lamp and used it to point out a crack seventy or eighty feet up the back wall. "He and Curt climbed to that ledge. Brent went inside. Curt waited on the ledge, sketching. Sondra was photographing a broken formation. Zeddie and I had been pushing a lead behind that mountain of breakdown." Again he used the light to point. The vastness of the chamber swallowed the beam before it reached its objective.

"So you were with Zeddie. Who found Frieda?"

"No. It got kind of squirrelly. Our lead petered out. Zeddie was headed back to camp and I was going to collect Sondra when I heard a yell—high, like a bird or a stepped-on cat. There was no way to tell where it came from, but it sounded enough like a cry for help that I think everybody pretty much started trying to get to wherever they thought it was. We ran around like the proverbial headless chickens. Then we all started shouting at each other, so if Frieda called a second time there was no way to sort it out from the general hubbub.

"Zeddie was the one who found her. She'd known where Frieda was going. Neither of them thought the lead had much promise, it wasn't blowing to speak of, but if you don't check them all out, you know the one you skipped leads to the bottom of the world and the next guy is going to find it.

"Frieda was in a crawl space, vertical, mostly breakdown—unstable stuff. Zeddie had gone down twenty feet and could just see Frieda's head. A rock the size of a basketball but pointy on one end had lodged between Frieda and the side of the passage. The weight rested on her shoulder, wedging her in.

"Zeddie got down as far as she could, squatted over Frieda, and lifted the rock straight up. Talk about clean and jerk! Zeddie's no slouch in the weight-lifting department. She pushed it up over her head. Curt and I got hold of it and brought it the rest of the way. It was a good forty pounds. Frieda's lucky it didn't crush her skull or break her collarbone."

"Curt was there when you got there?"

"No. Wait. Yes. He was trying to get Zeddie to let him go after the rock."

"So Zeddie pulled Frieda out?"

"No. That was a group effort. I doubt even the amazing Zeddie could lift a hundred and forty pounds of dead weight straight up. She got out, and I went down and got a cervical collar on Frieda. We tried to be careful, but you know how it is. For all the protection we could give her spinal column we might as well have hooked a tow chain under her armpits and yanked her out with a backhoe.

"It was lucky she was unconscious. We didn't know her leg was broken till we had her out where I could get a look. The pain would have been horrific."

"Frieda never said what happened? Wasn't she conscious at first?"

"Her level of consciousness wasn't stable. She knew who we were but not where she was or what had happened. As near as we could guess, she was climbing down and loosened some rocks as she went by. When she was below them, they broke loose. The first one hit her right leg at the knee and sheared off the top of the tibia. That must have been when she called for help. Then the second rock hit her in the head.

"Guesswork, but informed guesswork," he said with a laugh. "That's a doctor's bread and butter."

Having finished with the story and clearing up the medical paraphernalia, he stood, unfolding with the ease of a dancer. "When we get you tucked up snug in the Stokes," he said to Frieda, "I'll get you on an IV to keep your fluids up."

Anna didn't know whether Frieda had gotten Peter's message, but she had: keep talking. There was no way of telling what got through to Frieda, but all possible lines must be used to tether her to this world when temptation urged her to wander into the next.

Since Anna hadn't bothered unpacking so much as a change of socks the night before, she had nothing to do for the moment. Sitting near Frieda's head, she took her friend's hand between her own. "I know, I know, I'd never dare take such a liberty if you were awake," she said as she pressed her friend's fingers. "But, hey, there's not much you can do about it, is there? And I don't know if it comforts you, but it sure soothes the hell out of me. This cave stuff is for the birds. Bats." For a moment she sat quietly, playing Frieda's inert fingers against her palm. "Think about this," she said after a time, talking as much to herself as to her friend. "According to the good doctor, everybody was by themselves, near you, all shrouded in darkness when the rocks fell. Except maybe Brent and Curt. They were together, but I'm not clear exactly how together. This of course narrows things down not one whit. Cogitate upon it and then wake up and tell me all."

Frieda moved and made a noise in her throat. Anna held her breath and waited, but Frieda never opened her eyes.

5

THINGS HAPPENED FAST and so smoothly that Anna's estimate of Holden Tillman—already high—went up a notch or two. His quiet authority overlaid strict self-discipline. In another man it might have been abrasive, but Tillman created the illusion that he had time for everyone, an ear for every concern. In addition to a gentle, self-effacing humor, his manner provided the lubricant that allowed a disparate collection of people to operate with singleness of purpose.

Anna and Peter packaged Frieda Dierkz. She was strapped snugly in the Stokes, her hands crossed on her chest and lashed in place with soft bandages. A helmet with a Plexiglas face shield was fitted over her head and a stirrup beneath her left foot so, should she become able at some point, she could keep the weight off her injured leg when the litter was tilted. The oxygen bottle was secured between her knees.

Because of the radical ups and downs of the rubble-strewn path to Tinker's exit, the standard method of carrying a litter would have subjected Frieda to a bumpy ride. So Holden strung the sixteen people out along the path, and the stretcher was passed between two lines of cavers, eight on a side, moving Frieda from hand to hand in the fashion of a bucket brigade. As the stretcher left a caver's hands, he or she scrambled ahead, keeping the line always unbroken, always moving forward. In an effort to make her journey as uneventful as possible, the stretcher bearers would stand between stones and pass the Stokes overhead rather than lower Frieda and pull her up again, squat on their haunches on the high ground and keep the Stokes moving levelly a foot or so above the rock.

The men were as motley a group as one could hope to assemble behind any one cause. One had a gray-shot beard and hair that tangled like Charley Manson's in his heyday. Another resembled an undergraduate from a conservative midwestern seminary. Various points masculine in between were represented. Most worked shirtless. In the cave's humidity, exertion brought body heat up. Sweat glistened on bare backs between streaks of dirt. Bound by convention even this far below Emily Post's basement, the women sweated beside them in tee-shirts and running bras. Lisa was there, her Rapunzel braids looped up under her hard hat, along with two other women Anna had not seen before.

Like a column of ants passing a grasshopper up the line, they moved the injured woman across the ruptured floor of the cavern. Running, climbing, waiting, lifting, and running again, Anna worked all the kinks and aches of the previous day out of her muscles. Later there would be hell to pay, but for the present it was good to be moving.

She'd thought more bodies in the limited space would exacerbate her claustrophobia. In the tighter crawls she believed it still would, but in the vast dark of Tinker's Hell, the crowd made things feel less alien, less likely to close down in an inky tidal wave and blot out the fact that humans had ever dared venture there.

A sense of purpose brought with it a rush of high spirits that those who had been stranded with Frieda sorely needed.

Though the injured woman was seldom far from the minds of her rescuers, there wasn't an aura of grim determination but laughter and hard work and sharing. As Anna took a long pull on a water bottle offered by a stubby caver from Kentucky, she thought how good it was for people to be heroes, how much joy and confidence had been lost when the American public turned the care of themselves and their neighbors over to the impersonal rescuers of government agencies: police, fire fighters, paramedics, park rangers.

Heroism had become almost taboo. Citizens were discouraged from mixing in "official" business. When the occasional soldier came forward and stopped a robbery or captured a would-be rapist, the next day's papers would be full of bureaucrats decrying the hotheaded interference and painting a somber picture of what-ifs in an attempt to dissuade any further outbreaks of vigilante kindness.

A time or two Anna had been guilty of it herself. There were reasons: civil suits, idiots doing more harm than good, well-meaning people hurting themselves in their enthusiasm. But much of the time the help was turned away simply because it was too much fun playing hero. Nobody wanted to share the glory.

Buoyed up on this beneficent rapture, Anna was of two minds. The good and kind Anna, who had learned to open doors for nuns, wanted to spread this wellspring of self-worth among the peoples of the earth. The real Anna figured the general public would just bollix it up, and let her good intentions wash down her throat with the tepid canteen water.

The carry to the end of Tinker's took just over an hour. In the terrestrial world the sun would be rising. The rescuers were fresh, morale high, and no significant obstacles stood in the way. At the base of the climb to the balcony from which Anna had first seen the cavern, Holden called a stop. It was a near-vertical ascent scabbed by breakdown that created a more difficult haul to rig than a clean cliff face would have presented. There were nine hauls of varying difficulty to be rigged between Tinker's and the Rift.

Holden and Oscar would rig those they came to. Teams from the surface would be doing the same. Working like the builders of the first transcontinental railroad, the teams would meet somewhere in the middle.

The Stokes with its precious cargo was set well away from the fall zone, where stray feet and stones might compromise the patient's safety. Sondra made a halfhearted offer to stay with Frieda, but it was clear she itched to be in the center of things. Anna was glad to excuse her. Tucked back on a slab of breakdown, sheltered beneath a protective overhang of limestone, she looked after her patient and left the next round of heroics to those on better terms with the underworld. She adjusted the Stokes to make sure the head wasn't lower than the foot and the whole contraption was in no danger of moving of its own volition. She took Frieda's pulse, checked her IV and catheter. Her skin was cooler to the touch than it had been the previous night, and she seemed to be resting easier, sleeping rather than comatose.

The climb to Tinker's entrance was alive with light and color. Under the dreary dun of the planet's skin, yellow helmets, aqua tee-shirts, and red and orange ropes shone with startling clarity. Line and personnel were snaking up the slope with a grace that, sequestered from the chatter and grunts, was balletic in its grace.

Professor Schatz's vee-necked undershirt, more brown than white from dirt, was plastered to his body with sweat. He climbed stolidly up what looked, from Anna's viewpoint, to be an impossible incline. Around his waist, pulleys, trolleys, ascenders, carabiners, and webbing in gaudy hues hung like the tool belt of a carpenter from another galaxy. Crossed over his chest were two coils of rope, sixty pounds of gear at a conservative estimate. He moved with the supercilious good humor of a bear everybody thinks is tame.

Zeddie Dillard's thick frame flitted from place to place with astonishing speed. She carried nothing, and Anna surmised she was checking the rigging, though she'd thought that was Oscar's job.

Halfway down Tinker's, McCarty could be seen, a mere scrap of color bobbing on a rough sea of stone. Freed from stretcher-bearing duties, he made his way back to the old camp to gather packs that had been left behind.

Anna's eyes slid back through the kaleidoscopic darkness in time to catch Sondra looking after her husband with an expression of disgust. Mrs. McCarty wrinkled her long nose and curled her lovely lips as if she'd just sucked up a mouthful of sour milk.

On Sondra the expression didn't seem out of place, and Anna realized that the young woman spoiled her looks with a mask of discontent. Chances were she'd been asked to fetch packs, had turned the request down, and now felt she'd somehow been cheated out of the good assignment. A saying of Anna's long-deceased father floated to the surface of her mind and made her smile: "That woman would complain if you hung her with a brand-new rope."

Oscar was lost in the throng. Helmeted, dirty, flitting between light beams, the cavers were nearly indistinguishable. Anna spotted Holden only because of his bright pink shirt and silver helmet. He'd already reached the balcony. There he directed a symphony of ropes. The Stokes would be hand-carried, but it had to be rigged.

Anna's home park, Mesa Verde, was reached by a winding road cut into steep hillsides. She had worked her share of low-angle rescues, dragging the victims of automobile accidents up through the oak brush to the road. There was no way to avoid the back-breaking work. On a near-vertical, the Stokes would be rigged, a line fore and aft, so, should the carriers slip, the patient wouldn't be dropped unceremoniously back down the way she'd come, but the weight of the litter would be borne by human arms and backs. The only thing that could be depended on was that wherever one ended up standing there was never room to lift the way the safety films advised. Hands clutched where they could, held where they had to, and moved the litter on. Doan's Pills and Ben-Gay took care of the details after the party was over.

Anna caught sight of Brent Roxbury climbing stairsteps of stone three and four feet high. Below, a man laughed, and Lisa, her braids swinging in loops beneath her helmet, averted her eyes. Evidently Brent's attire was exposing his shortcomings.

"Anna?"

"Yeah?" Anna said, trying to catch a glimpse of Brent's retreating form for the same reason people stare at car wrecks.

"Anna?"

"What?" she demanded, mildly irritated. As the word fell from her lips she realized who was doing the talking. Crabbiness vanished, replaced by a relief so powerful it bordered on euphoria. She scooted over to Frieda, wrapped mummylike in the coffin-shaped Stokes. "Welcome back," she said. Frieda struggled feebly. Picking at the knots in the bandages, Anna explained, "Sorry. We tied your arms in so they wouldn't fall against anything and get hurt. The main rescue team is here. You're in a Stokes at the end of Tinker's Hell. They're rigging the lines to haul you up. See?" She leaned back so Frieda could see the activity on the rock wall and know that she was safe and cared for.

Frieda tried to lift her head and moaned. The helmet and cervical collar kept her from moving much, but the effort had caused her head to hurt.

Anna cursed herself for her exuberance. She'd all but told Frieda to sit up and have a look around.

"What's wrong with me?" Worry colored her words, but Frieda sounded calm, in control. Anna was so proud she felt her heart swell until it became a lump in her throat. Trussed up helpless, deep underground, she doubted she would behave as admirably. To banish the lump, she reminded herself that Frieda liked burrowing in the dirt.

Fussing with bandages and buckles, she told Frieda all she knew of her injuries. She was careful to relate nothing of the speculation surrounding the accident. Frieda's mind would still be vulnerable, open to suggestion. When she finished, she forced herself to stop fiddling with Frieda's packaging. The woman was stable. Anna was only reassuring herself.

Frieda blinked up through the clear Plexiglas safety screen on the helmet they'd fitted her with. Seeing her friend's discomfort, Anna eased it off, careful not to change the alignment of Frieda's cervical spine.

"Thanks," Frieda said. "Let me sit up."

"Better not."

"Shit. I feel like such an idiot. I'm fine. If my leg wasn't broken, I could walk out of here. I'm tempted to call the whole circus off and crawl out. It's been done."

Anna knew that. Years before, after the last big publicized rescue, a caver had broken an ankle a long way in, near the Leaning Tower of Lechuguilla. Rather than subject himself to the Sturm und Drang of a grand rescue, he crawled the two days out. He wore through his own kneepads and the kneepads of every member of his team, but he self-rescued.

"It's not your ankle," Anna reminded Frieda. "It's your knee. Not to mention your brains are scrambled. Besides"— she gestured to the cascading humanity on the wall, each caver busy and intent—"everybody is having such a good time."

Frieda snorted, but there was a thread of laughter in the rude sound. A good sign.

Anna questioned her about her hurts, asked all the things she'd been taught to ask to test for disorientation or brain injury. Frieda had a vicious headache that hurt down into her left shoulder, and her leg throbbed, but she knew who she was, where she was, and who was president of the United States. The only question she'd missed was "What day is it?" and since Anna wasn't all that sure either, she'd let it pass.

Anna backed off, let the patient rest. Frieda lay staring at an invisible sky. Her jaw-length red hair was stuck to her cheeks. In a sudden spill of light from above, the freckles across her face stood out black against her unnatural pallor.

McCarty had cleaned and bandaged the wound on her temple, but an ugly bruise spread from beneath the dressing, blacking the corner of Frieda's eye and suffusing her cheekbone with angry purple.

"Last night you woke up and talked to me," Anna said. "Do you remember?"

Frieda thought for so long that Anna worried this was not an end of the crazies but only another moment of clarity in ongoing delirium.

"No," Frieda said finally. Her voice was strained as if the effort of remembering had exacerbated the pain in her head. "I had zillions of dreams. All bad. Not nightmare quality, just the can't-find-your-keys-show-up-at-work-naked variety. On and on. Every time I'd think I was awake and could stop, something bizarre would happen and I'd realize I was back in the dreams." She reached for the water bottle and Anna pressed it into her palm. When she drank, water spilled down her cheeks. Anna wanted to wipe it away but didn't. Frieda wouldn't appreciate being mothered, and it was an art Anna was not sufficiently skilled at to risk rebuff.

"You said 'It wasn't an accident.' Was that part of a dream?" Anna kept her voice intentionally casual. What she knew about head wounds would fit in chapter twelve of an EMT manual. A chapter she hadn't read in a while. It just made sense not to fever an already traumatized brain with unnecessary fears.

"Did I?" Frieda asked. Anna waited, letting her work things through at her own speed. "Shit," Frieda said after a time. "Everything is like those stupid dreams. Piecemeal. Broken film."

"It's okay," Anna said.

"I remember all of us splitting up to follow a handful of leads. I remember going down a crack in the breakdown on the cavern floor. Maybe I heard something?"

Anna kept quiet. Anything she suggested would only add to Frieda's confusion.

"I must have been looking up." Frieda fingered the bruise

on her temple. "Shit," she said again. "Maybe I saw some-thing. I think I saw something. Somebody's hand. That might have been what I meant. I remember I saw a hand above me on a big fucking rock. Get thee behind me, Hodags."

Anna thought Frieda had slipped back into her dream world, then remembered Hodags, like their German cous-ins, the Kobold, were spirits that didn't take kindly to foul language. Frieda was metaphorically throwing salt over her shoulder, knocking on wood.

"Did you see the hand before the rock hit you in the head or after?" Anna asked. The hand could have belonged to Zeddie, lifting the stone from Frieda's shoulder.

"I don't know."

Anna could hear the weariness in her voice. She didn't want to overtire her. One more question, she promised her-self, then she'd stop, "Was it a man's hand or a woman's?"

"Gloved," Frieda replied with certainty. "Damn."

"Don't push," Anna said. "It'll come back."

"You won't go away, will you?" Frieda asked. Both women heard the fear in her voice. Frieda didn't approve of it. "No big deal," she said. "It's probably all bullshit. Scram-bled brains."

"Probably," Anna said, helping her save face. "But I've got to stick close anyway."

"Why?" Frieda sounded stubborn.

"So nobody will put me to work."

Frieda tried to laugh, but it came out as a moan.

"Hey, is that Frieda talking?" Sondra McCarty was five yards off, pulling her lean frame up onto a rock. "Oscar said to come back and see if you needed relieving or anything."

If someone wanted Frieda dead, then comatose was surely the next best thing. Till Anna knew more, Frieda would be safer with the status quo. "No, just muttering. She's still delirious." Anna found Frieda's hand in the dark-ness and squeezed it. "Delirious," she repeated, and felt an answering pressure. Anna knew the ruse would not be foolproof. They could lie to Sondra and the others, but she was going to have to take Peter McCarty into her confidence. Frieda needed something for the pain. This far from the hospital, shock could kill her as surely as the most determined assassin.

Anna wanted Frieda to pretend she remembered nothing, but quoting "in for a penny in for a pound" as her rationale, Frieda opted to tell Peter everything. Anna didn't put up an argument. For her own peace of mind, Frieda needed to trust her doctor. McCarty agreed to go along with the lie that she was still delirious—not because he deemed it necessary but because Frieda became upset when it looked as if he wouldn't. He seemed more annoyed than alarmed by the disembodied glove on the rock. Anna couldn't remember hearing a theory so thoroughly pooh-poohed since she'd told her sister, Molly, Jimmy Newton's idea that Dad and Santa were one and the same.

McCarty laughed, shrugged, did everything short of actually saying "pshaw." The fact that he did it with humor and a thick gob of charm didn't let him off the hook. He put Anna's hackles up. If she'd had a tail, by the end of the performance it would have been lashing. She kept her misgivings to herself. There were two possibilities: the doctor had a reason for wanting Frieda to think it was all a dream, or it actually was all a dream and, knowing a whole hell of a lot more about head injuries than Anna ever would, he had chosen this method of allaying his patient's fears.

However unsatisfying to the ego, Anna hoped it was the latter. Still, she watched him closely as he gave Frieda a shot for pain. Hovering, a suspicious and sweating guardian angel, Anna realized if McCarty wanted Frieda dead he could easily have killed her in the hours before Oscar, Holden, and she had arrived.

Unless he didn't think she'd wake up.

Unless he didn't think she'd remember if she did wake up.

Remember what? An attempt on her life? Surely there would have been a reason for attempted murder. Hope she would have forgotten that reason? Not likely, not unless that reason had occurred moments before the rock fell, and even then traumatic amnesia wasn't something anyone would count on, especially not a doctor of medicine. In a heretofore undiscovered crack in the earth there was no secret Frieda could stumble on, and it was unlikely, though not impossible, she'd overheard anything compromising. Peter McCarty's too hearty skepticism was making more and more sense.

The doctor left. Anna listened till the sound of his going was gone. "Frieda, are you awake?" she whispered.

"Hard to tell," came the reply.

"Do you have any idea why somebody would want to push a rock on you?"

"No reason. I'm a *secretary,* for Chrissake."

Anna wasn't sure being a secretary was as harmless as Frieda thought, but she understood the thrust of the comment. And it was unlikely any NPS secrets—as if a bureaucracy the size of the Park Service could actually keep a secret—from Mesa Verde, Colorado, would get her killed this deep in New Mexico. In anything but James Bond stuff, the power of secrets tended to have only local jurisdiction.

"How about personal animosities," Anna pushed. "Somebody on the survey team?"

"No way. I'm a frigging saint. Oops. Make my apologies."

Frieda was succumbing to the medication, and Anna had to quit badgering her. It was her opinion that "frigging" would be acceptable to even the most persnickety spirits; still, on Frieda's behalf, she said, "Sorry, little Hodags. She's not herself at the moment."

6

IF TWO PEOPLE know a secret, it is no longer a secret. On long car trips Anna and her sister used to amuse themselves by planning the perfect murder. The catch was always that you couldn't tell anyone, not a soul. And where's the fun in doing anything perfectly if no one else knows about it?

Oscar was the first to pay his respects. McCarty, he said, felt duty-bound to tell him and Holden of the change in the patient's condition. His tone left no doubt that he felt Anna had been remiss, as indeed she had. Extenuating circumstances, she told herself as she squirmed under his reproachful stare.

In the way of runaway secrets, the tale spread without any traceable source—each person told one other, someone overheard, someone deduced. Within an amazingly short period of time, Frieda's lucidity went from secret to news.

As the Stokes was moved up the incline, cavers greeted her, welcomed her back to the world of the living. Never comfortable with subterfuge, Dierkz dropped the pretense and answered as best the pain medication allowed until a squat clean-shaven caver from the outside, boasting EMT status, as if EMTs weren't a dime a dozen in this crew, got so officious Frieda became anxious. Then Holden asked the rescuers to dispense with their good cheer and let her get what rest she could, given she was being trundled up a steep slope.

For reasons of his own, which were possibly sinister but more likely intended to save Frieda from embarrassment, Peter McCarty had left the gloved hand and the possible murder attempt out of his report.

Anna had no idea if this boded good or ill. If someone wanted Frieda dead, perhaps not knowing she was aware of the attack would stay their hand. Then again, maybe if everyone knew, it would discourage a second attempt. The whole thing was too much for Anna's beleaguered mind; the ravings of a head injury patient and the paranoia of an admitted claustrophobe weren't much of a basis for a meaningful dialogue with reality.

Shelving these vague possibilities, she put her back into carrying Frieda home. With each step taken, each rock climbed, they were that much closer to getting out. Left to herself, she knew she would set an underland speed record from Tinker's to the surface, but even the creeping gait of their human caterpillar was heartening.

The passage out of Tinker's closed down so tightly a person couldn't walk upright. It narrowed until shoulders and hips brushed the sides. Well back on the balcony, between the Stokes and the cavers derigging the first haul, Anna felt fear rise in a freezing tide. To hold it at bay, she busied herself checking every knot, buckle, and hook on the Stokes. The stretcher couldn't be rigged and hauled through the passage. Given the horizontal as well as vertical twists and turns, it couldn't be passed from hand to hand. At every step of the way it would require lifting over rockfall, easing across crevices, working under projections of limestone. The stoop-walk in front of them would be impossible to rig; consequently Anna assumed Holden would be a while figuring out the logistics. She planned to use that time to compose herself for an interminable incarceration in a very small space.

"Everybody listen up," Holden said, and she felt an icy poke in her innards followed by an irrational anger. Tillman had already worked out the carry. Did the man never sleep?

The cavers, most of whom were crowded onto the balcony or perched like colorful crows on rocks nearby, fell quiet. Those who weren't actively engaged in derigging had their headlamps switched off. Holden moved the beam of his light from one face to the next, and they appeared like actors in the spotlight, each with his own bizarre tale to tell before the curtain came down.

Counting his sheep, Anna realized, and she was put in mind of a long ago and long forgotten Sunday school. Fleetingly, she wondered if Jesus of Wherever counted his apostles with the same half-loving, half-annoyed, totally concerned look, reading people for fatigue, injury, fear— any weakness that could harm them or the cause.

"This passage is one hundred sixty-two feet long. There are only two rooms big enough to stand up in, and there're not many flat enough to set the Stokes down. What we're going to do is turtle it." Judging by the intrigued looks that flickered from the darkness, "turtling" wasn't a classic maneuver culled from the most recent edition of the *Manual of U.S. Cave Rescue Techniques.*

Deferring often to Frieda to make sure she knew that she was part of her own rescue and not just one hundred forty pounds of packaged meat, Holden talked them through the next leg of the journey. Turtling was evidently a process he'd learned from his predecessor at the BLM. Like many things that worked, it wasn't in the pages of any how-to book. Though to give credit where credit was due, the few books on cave rescue Anna had looked at agreed that the most important piece of equipment in an underground rescue is the rescuer's brain.

One by one Holden sent them into the passage. Half a

body length apart, they were to get on hands and knees and pass the Stokes along their backs, a shoulder-wrenching premise, but workable. When Frieda reached the head of the line, the trailing cavers would close ranks like an inch-worm taking up its inch. The litter would be pushed to the last two backs, the leading fourteen would spread out far-ther up the passage, and Frieda would recommence travel over the soft shells of Holden's turtles.

Of necessity, Anna would be separated from her patient. She tried to work up a good case of anxiety over that, but at the moment, she really didn't care. She was the third turtle sent in. Dr. McCarty and his wife were in front of her, Curt Schatz directly behind. Due to the congestion and the knowledge that large chunks of flesh and bone walled her in fore and aft, the passage felt much tighter than it had when she'd come through eight hours before.

Eight hours. Anna marveled at the number. On a good night she could sleep that long. In Lechuguilla it seemed a lifetime.

To have something to think about other than the fact that the walls were going to close in, she wondered if her hair would have turned snow-white by the time she reached daylight, as was reported in old ghost stories. Not that it had that far to go. Since Cumberland Island, when she'd hacked it off short, the gray had become more evident, streaking both temples in the timeless fashion of the Bride of Frankenstein.

Lechuguilla had been formed in a rather peculiar man-ner. It hadn't been carved out by underground rivers as many eastern caves had been. Surface water percolating downward had not dissolved the limestone as Anna once thought. Deep in the petroleum-rich land beneath New Mexico, hydrogen sulphide waters welled up to mix with the fresh water and oxygen at the water table, creating sul-phuric acid. The acid ate away the stone. The result was a cave that was formed without the sobering influence of gravity. Corrosive acid burned along cracks and fissures, chewed away the softer places, and created intricate mazes, deep pits, shafts, and crevices that grew away from one another in a dizzying manner.

The passage Anna and her fellow turtles traversed exhibited this lack of respect for rhyme and reason. In the skittering glow of her headlamp it resembled a seascape rolled in on itself. Stones were pale gray and pitted all over with holes of varying sizes, from the merest pinprick to sockets she could have stored a bowling ball in had she been a bowling ball kind of girl. Nothing had been worn smooth. Edges retained the razor sharpness they'd been honed to in their geological youth, some hundreds of thousands of years before. Rocks as capricious as clouds lowered down from the ceiling. Sharp-edged scythes, rude fingers poked from all directions, forcing her to one side then the other, pushing out at waist level in a dragon's head daring her to climb over or squeeze beneath. The floor rolled and buckled, spewing up till Anna skittered over on belly and elbows, dropping away in cracks she chose not to consider the depth of. All melded seamlessly together. The effect was exhausting, disorienting. Space-time relations taken for granted aboveground ceased to exist. In the roiling rock-filled chaos, distance couldn't be measured in feet or miles. Minutes and hours tangled until she felt as stoned as she had a hundred fifty feet below the surface of Lake Superior, suffering from nitrogen narcosis.

"Nice butt."

Curt Schatz's flat drawl filtered through from behind her. His tone was devoid of lasciviousness, malice, or condescension. She'd never heard the words without one or all of these accouterments. Clearly she'd misheard. She stopped and turned, bending down to push her helmet under a curtain of limestone. "Pardon?" she murmured politely.

"Nice butt," Curt repeated. "I couldn't help but notice. Since I started caving I've become something of an expert. I've followed some of the finest butts in the business. Yours is up there. Better than Peter McCarty's. But don't tell him I said so. He prides himself on that sort of thing." He smiled showing small white teeth, perfectly even. In a fairy-tale princess, they might have been described as pearls. Peeking out from his thick beard they lent him the rakish charm of a wolf pup.

Anna laughed. "Better than Dr. McCarty's?"

"Yup," Schatz said. "And I know Pete's butt like the face of my own mother."

Anna returned to the business of wending her way through New Mexico's lower intestine, but she felt cheered. No more airspace presented itself. The tonnage between her and the sky remained unchanged. Yet the anxiety squeezing the blood from her veins was momentarily lessened. Where there was humor there was a fighting chance of remaining sane.

Such were the isolating influences of Lechuguilla's topography: a turn in a passage, a change in elevation, an upthrust of formations, and all light and sound was cut off. Smaller, more agile, Anna left Curt and was once again as alone as if the earth had buried each of them in their own personal grave.

Dr. McCarty and Sondra were on the far side of two pincers of rock coming together under a wall of calcite drapery that folded down like velvet curtains to within sixteen inches of the bottom of the passage. Anna recognized the formation as the place she was to stop. The crawl was too tight to pass through except one at a time, but the floor beneath was uncharacteristically flat. Here she was to wait for Frieda to be brought across the backs of her fellows. Anna and Curt would set the Stokes onto the floor and feed it through to the McCartys. They would move it far enough up the passage that the cavers could congregate on the far side of the crawl and the mechanism of the turtle ferry would be started up again.

Anna sat down, her fanny pleased with the smooth flooring, her body pleased with a rest. Sweat poured down the sides of her face, burned her eyes, and ran in a small river between her breasts. Mixing with the ubiquitous dirt, it formed a streaked layer of mud over skin and clothes. She pulled her helmet off and scratched at tickles creeping through her hair. No doubt this left her locks standing Medusa-like in snaky ire, but she could not have cared less. On some primitive level she was beginning to enjoy being dirty, to see each layer of crud as a testament to her undaunted perseverance. Maybe she'd turn into a caver yet. She switched off her headlamp to test out the idea.

With the dousing of the light she became aware of a faint play of gold from beyond the crawl space: the McCartys. It was a comfort, and she watched it come and go, wishing Professor Schatz would hurry up. Even discussing the nether parts of Peter's anatomy was better than sitting alone with only her thoughts for company. A minute more passed in this lonely internment before she flicked her lamp back on and shone it down the way she had come. No sign of life. Perhaps Curt had stopped to wait for the turtle in his wake. Zeddie Dillard, Anna remembered.

Lamp off again, she sat a few minutes more, drank water, and tried not to think about anything. Without action it proved an impossible task, and she decided to belly down and investigate the crawl so she could better prepare Frieda for the experience when the litter arrived. The space allowed for a lizard-like creep using elbows and knees but little else. Trusting to the McCarty's light, Anna left her hard hat and lamp behind. From the forced march in, she knew the crawl wasn't long—maybe eleven feet—then it opened into a small chamber, one of the few places in the tunnel large enough that two or three people could stand upright with some degree of comfort.

By the time she'd nearly wriggled through, her head a foot or less from the opening to the room, she was able to hear the doctor and his wife. Their voices had the unmistakable pitch of a marital squabble. Unable to resist the puerile temptation to eavesdrop, she lay still and listened.

"You wanted to be blackmailed," Sondra was saying heatedly. "And at the same time I thought I loved you."

"You don't now?" The doctor's voice had lost its bedside bonhomie and rang cold in the closed chamber.

A pretty darn good fight, Anna thought happily. Anybody else's troubles had to be a relief from her own.

"I'm beginning to wonder if I ever did," Sondra snapped. "I'm sick to death of watching you play doctor, knowing everybody is laughing themselves sick at my expense."

"Frieda's hurt," McCarty said mildly.

"You can always manage to make yourself necessary, can't you? Is there anything you won't do to make yourself indispensable to women?"

This was answered by silence, and Anna wished she could see their faces. She pictured anger and resentment on Sondra, maybe touched with that absolute disgust she'd noted earlier. Peter McCarty was harder. Would he look hurt? Reproachful? Arrogant or vain?

"And maybe I wasn't talking about Frieda," Sondra went on when the silence began to lose its power.

McCarty sighed, a theatrical gust that Anna could hear down in her rabbit hole. "You can always leave," he said.

"Right." Sondra laughed without joy. "You'd like that, wouldn't you? What? You expect me to go back to being a secretary? Fetching coffee for editors, old fat white men who have less talent in their whole bodies than I've got in my little toe?"

"If you ever got anybody coffee—which I doubt—I suspect they had the good sense not to drink it," Peter snapped. There was anger in his words this time; his pose of world-weary patience was slipping. Sondra must have scented weakness. When she spoke again, she redoubled her attack.

"I'll leave all right. When I'm ready. Maybe sooner than you think. All I need is one good story. When I go I'll take everything but your toothbrush and your little black book. If you lift a finger to stop me, I'll see your license is jerked, *doctor*."

"I wouldn't push your luck if I were you." The trite comeback was so laden with ice and threat that Sondra fell quiet.

Anna decided this was not a good time to pop out of a

hole in the floor and yell "surprise." Moving as quietly as possible, she squirmed backward, filling the cuffs of her trousers with dirt until, hind parts foremost, she regained her little patch of land on the inside of the crawl way.

"What's it like?" Curt had arrived. He sat in inky darkness, his long legs and heavily booted feet sprawled over their tiny room.

"Squishy," Anna said succinctly. "Could you not breathe for a bit? I think there's only enough air for me."

"No problem."

He was quiet while Anna clambered over his knees and settled herself on a rock bracketed by his boots.

"Let me go through first," she said. "The crawl space is way too small for you. You're going to get wedged. I don't want to be stuck behind you."

"Will you bring me sandwiches?" he asked. He seemed utterly imperturbable, his voice light and laconic for so bulky a man.

"Nope. Once I'm out of here I'm never going to let anything between me and the sun again. I'll buy a convertible, sleep out of doors."

"I won't get wedged," Curt said. "My father was a rodent. My mother says a rat, but after further research I'm inclined to believe he was a common field mouse. I inherited his bones, mouse bones. Mine can fold in on each other allowing me to pass through apertures too small for mortal men. Once, on a dare, I crawled through the pop-top hole in a Coors can."

"Hah."

Half a beat of silence followed, then he added this note of verisimilitude: "I did have to strip down to my shorts to do it."

Darkness reclaimed them, and that total absence of sound that is peculiar to caves. Not a whisper of air, not a sound of the movement of grasses, birdsong, running water, the stars spinning in their orbits. Anna took it as long as she could. To break the silence before it solidified, she asked, "What brought you to Lechuguilla?"

"You're not of the Minnesota connection? I'm surprised Frieda thinks so highly of you. Where are you from?"

"Originally, California."

A groan.

"Northern California."

"That's okay then. Not Minnesota, but you get snow, right? I used to teach at the University of Minnesota. I got my Ph.D. there. That's how I hooked up with Peter and Sondra. Met him at a grotto meeting. He married her. Caving is a small world. Especially in Minnesota, land of ten thousand lakes. If there are any caves there, we call 'em aquifers."

"Zeddie?" Anna asked.

"Doubly connected. Frieda and her sister were pals. And she was an undergraduate. She had me for Leisure 101."

"How did she do?" Anna asked for lack of anything better to say.

"She was a vacant-eyed little snipe," Curt said as if this fact were obvious. "All students are vacant-eyed little snipes."

Anna couldn't tell if he was joking or not. "Was Brent a student of yours? Adult ed," she added, realizing Roxbury was probably ten years Curt's senior.

"Are you suggesting Brent is a vacant-eyed little snipe?" Curt asked innocently.

Anna fumbled around for a minute, grateful for once for the darkness. Curt relented. "No. Brent's an outsider. Either Zeddie or Frieda asked him on. Or maybe he was tagged on by George Laymon. We needed another surveyor. I've worked with worse."

From Schatz, Anna gathered this was high praise indeed.

"Frieda's parents lived in Anoka," Anna remembered.

"She used to be a patient of McCarty's," Curt said. "Or maybe it was her mother. I can't remember. I met her on an expedition in Mexico."

"Peter is a GP?" Anna asked.

"Gynecologist."

"Jesus. Why is that funny?"

Curt said, "If you're going to talk about stirrups and things, I'm going to leave the room. I'm very shallow. It's one of the things I like most about myself."

"Turtling!" was shouted down the insulating passage behind them. They buckled on their hard hats, dragged Frieda over three more spines, set the Stokes on the floor, then pushed it through the crawl space to the waiting hands of the McCartys.

One more inching of their sixteen-bodied worm, and Frieda was delivered from the cramped passage.

The tunnel opened into a low-ceilinged room studded with formations and ending in a lip ten or twelve feet across and a couple of feet deep. A yard below was a second step of like dimensions, then a ninety-foot drop into a pit. The opening where they emerged marked the pit's halfway point. It continued upward, smooth as poured cement, for another forty feet. On the far side, going out of the top, was a black hole, shaped like a keyhole, about nine feet high, wide at the bottom then narrowing in to a wasp-waist of rock to open again in a slit no more than a foot and a half wide and half again that long.

The pit, Anna remembered, was dubbed the Cocktail Lounge. At one time it had been partially filled with water. Formations shaped like giant golf tees—or cocktail tables, if one hailed from New York City—had formed in the bottom. There were seven in all, made of stone coming out of solution as it dripped from above over the millennia. Beneath the water, it had built up in slender columns. When it reached the surface, the stone spread out in ever-widening circles, floating like petrified lily pads on the lake. At some point the water had drained away or dried up and left only the pit and the nine-foot-high tables looking as if they were made of alabaster and inlaid with gold. Every square inch of the formations was covered in decorations. Small puff excrescences called popcorn studded the columns. Tiny stalactites dripped by the thousands from the undersides of the tabletops. Layer after layer of stone had formed with such delicacy and infinite variety that the formations presented larger-than-life sculptures by a mad, genius god fascinated with rococo baroque.

They made Anna nervous. They were so beautiful, a testament to the sanctity of the deep caverns; she knew she was doomed to stumble over her bootlaces and take them all down like a row of priceless dominoes. Infamy would dog her to the grave and beyond as it would the man who had smashed Michelangelo's *Pietà*.

Schatz, Dillard, Tillman, and Roxbury were rigging the descent. The others rested and kept out of the way. Anna edged over to where Frieda lay in the Stokes.

"I've got to sit up," Frieda said. Anna understood. Too long on one's back was disorienting. She left Frieda and returned with McCarty's permission to let her sit as long as she had help, wasn't left alone, and the cervical collar remained in place.

"God, that feels good," Frieda said as she gently worked her arms and shoulders. "Have you ever had a tooth crowned? Lain in the dentist's chair till you felt you were going to La La Land or bite the next finger that came into your mouth?" Anna nodded. "Like that."

She drank from the water bottle secured in the Stokes near her hand. "Are we alone?" she asked.

Anna looked over her shoulder. They were on the end of the ledge. The others seemed occupied; no one listened. "As alone as we'll ever be down here," she said sourly.

"Good. I'm tired of being a good sport, a real trooper. This sucks. I hate it. I hate everybody and everything, and I especially hate this blasted cave and sincerely hope all caves the world over fill with bat shit. God," she said with a deep-seated sigh. "*God,* but I needed that. Now I can be cheerful and grateful and optimistic for another hour or so."

Anna and Frieda were in the midst of a repast consisting of Beanie-Wienies, granola bars, and cold Chef Boyardee ravioli; treats Anna packed in, unable to face a diet of MREs, government-issue meals ready to eat.

A caver Anna'd seen but not spoken to invaded their

picnic. Irritation, always close to the surface in an enclosed world, prickled under her skin. This was the guy who had badgered Frieda on the haul out of Tinker's. Despite the confined space, he managed a swagger. Munk, Kelly Munk. Anna fished his name out of the fog of conversational fragments she'd swum through during the past eight hours.

Munk was young but not young enough to be excused, early thirties. Muscles bulged from hours at the gym. Flat, tiny ears were stuck on a square head. Muscle ridged the points of his jaws. Anna recognized the type. The only description the Hodags would approve of was egomaniac. Every EMT class had one; the world was a TV show, and he was the star.

"Since we've got a minute, I thought I'd check your packaging," he said. "You're putting a lot of strain on this group. What do you weigh? One fifty? One sixty?"

Frieda's mouth crumpled at the corners. Confidence and courage leached away.

Munk reached to rearrange the patient's catheter tubing.

"Don't." Anna grabbed a meaty wrist.

Munk sat back on his heels, his eyes small, carplike. "She's not packaged properly. Holden may be an okay caver, but he's no EMT."

A number of arguments came to mind, but Anna knew she'd be wasting her breath. "Go away," she said.

"I think Frieda—"

"Away. Far, far away."

"Ahoy!" rang out from across the void.

A dozen lamps switched on, beams crisscrossing like searchlights at a mall opening, to center on two figures waving from a narrow aperture on the opposite side and near the top of the chamber that opened into Razor Blade Run. The response from the cavers in the lounge was exuberant. Everyone, including Anna, shouted and hullabalooed like castaways sighting a ship. The energy of the rescue, the quest, the cause, made them all brothers, tied them together in a way they would miss when the littles of the workday world pried them apart again.

"Landline!" came the shout.

"Good work," Holden called back. Energized by the sight of the others, the rigging team returned to work with redoubled vigor.

Holden came over to where Anna and Frieda rested. An uncompromising look from the mild blue eyes relieved them of Munk's presence. "How're ya doing?" Holden asked as he straddled a rock and made himself at home.

"I'm good," Frieda said firmly. "You guys are doing all the work. I get a free ride."

"You'd do it for any one of us," he reminded her. "And will probably have to this year or next."

Frieda didn't say anything, but it was clear she appreciated the thought.

"Are you up to being famous for a minute? Now that they've brought the phone line down you can bet there's going to be a newspaper guy on the other end wanting to talk to the heroine."

Frieda looked pained. "I hadn't thought of that," she admitted.

"You don't have to do it. You don't even have to make any excuses. If it bothers you, we'll just make like static and hang up. That equipment is left over from the Korean War. Who's to say it's not going to break down?" He smiled what he probably thought was a wicked smile, but on his worn and weathered face it was so sweetly mischievous, Anna could have kissed him.

Knowing she had an out gave Frieda courage. "I'll talk," she said. "My folks are probably glued to the television, sweating bullets. They're old. I was Mom's midlife crisis. If I don't call for three days they think I've been carried off by white slavers. I can imagine what they're going through with this mess. They'll feel better if they hear from me that I'm still alive."

"Don't worry," Holden said. "It won't be just you yakking. As soon as a phone shows up, all of a sudden everybody's got somebody they've just got to talk to. We'll probably take a half-hour break for the doggone gabfest."

He glanced at his watch. "Not so bad, I guess. By the time we get up that other side we'll have been truckin' for nearly seven hours, and Razor Blade Run is going to be a fun one to rig. Be good to have everybody fresh."

The three of them looked across the pit to the keyhole in black on the ceiling. Razor Blade was rimed with a miniature forest in glittering aragonite crystals, a winter wonderland in snow white that stretched for nearly twenty yards. Some of the flowers were of a size and intricacy seldom seen before and never in such abundance. Aragonite bloomed in wild snowflake patterns, crystals growing from white rootlike bulbs of the same substance. Lechuguilla's treasure was its formations and the wonder they created in the too-often jaded imagination of man.

Tears started in Frieda's eyes. The first Anna had seen. "No way," she said. "I won't do it. This litter will go through there like a bulldozer. What I don't ruin, you guys will, manhandling me. Get me out." She began to fight the straps that held the lower half of her body in the Stokes. "I'll walk it. Get me a stick."

She fell back, tears streaking the mud on her cheeks. "There's not a stick for a day's travel in any direction," she said.

"Lean on me," Anna offered lamely, at a loss how to comfort her.

"It can't be done," Frieda said.

Holden smiled. It was inoffensive. The smile of a child. *"Au contraire,"* he said. Anna could almost see the miles of rope and rigging stringing through his brain like the solution to a complex trigonometry problem.

He started to lay a hand on Frieda's arm but didn't, and Anna sensed for the first time what an essentially shy man he was. "I got it covered. Remember who you're talking to here: Mr. Leave Nothing. Not Even Footprints. Lookie." With his light he pointed to the narrow top of the keyhole. "We're gonna rig you through there. No decorations. Straight line, like thread through the eye of a needle. Bad climb, good haul. You've got to go by your lonesome. There's just room for the litter. Not even a place for your scrawny little lady." He winked at Anna.

"Good. Okay." Frieda was so relieved she would have agreed to be shot through the keyhole by a cannon. Holden stayed a minute longer to give her a chance for second thoughts. "Really," she said at last. "Alone is fine."

"I didn't doubt it," Holden said.

When he'd moved out of earshot, Anna asked, "Why didn't you tell him about the glove on the rock? Both he and Oscar should know." Anna's only reason for not reporting it was Frieda's return to consciousness. In regaining her mental powers, she had regained the right to make her own decisions. "Do you want me to call him back?"

"No. Don't," Frieda said. "Life is too embarrassing as it is. An attempt on my life. Who'd believe it? Even I don't believe it. I can't remember anything that makes sense. Let's leave well enough alone. Please."

It didn't feel "well enough" to Anna, and it went against the grain to leave it alone. She'd ever been one to give sleeping dogs a good poke just to see if they were faking it. But she would go along with Frieda because she didn't want to upset her. And she had no proof, not of malfeasance, or even of negligence. Thirty hours—give or take—and they would be out. Thirty hours in a crowd all looking after Frieda's well-being. She would probably be safe.

For the descent to the floor of the Lounge and the haul up the other side, Anna was rigged along with the Stokes. A spider, a confluence of lines attached to the litter, met several feet above Frieda's midsection. Anna was tied into this spider, the Stokes cutting across her at waist level. Thus secured, she was always with her patient, there to reassure, to push the litter out from the wall when necessary, to handle any problems that came up en route.

Frieda was in good spirits, and it was contagious. They made it through the magnificent tables without destroying a single formation. On the ascent Anna found herself actually having a good time.

As promised, phone service awaited them at the top.

Twelve or fifteen cavers were scattered around the low-ceilinged room that connected the Cocktail Lounge with Razor Blade. The space resembled the inside of a giant clam shell. Elliptically shaped, the floor and ceiling of bedrock, it came out in a concentric circle from the keyhole to a wide slot. At its highest point, the ceiling was five feet from the floor. There was little that human impact could destroy, making it the ideal place for the teams to congregate. All of the core group, including Oscar and Holden, had made the ascent. The other cavers were a mix of the rescuers from the first team and the three men responsible for providing the phone line.

Frieda was sequestered near the back of the clam shell, Holden's pack and helmet laid down like sentinals guarding her from all but Anna, Sondra, and the doctor. Peter McCarty was with her, taking advantage of the flat bit of earth to perform central nervous system tests he had been unable to when his patient was comatose.

Anna had done those tests she was familiar with. Frieda's limbs responded, she had feeling in her extremities, and there were no palpable deformations along her first eight vertebrae. Beyond these simple reassurances, Anna was out of her league and relieved to have someone with training double-check her work. Though it surprised her somewhat, she was also relieved to be given a respite from her duties as chief lady-in-waiting. Physically it was no more demanding than the jobs of any of the others. Often it proved less strenuous. When Frieda rested, Anna rested. It was the caring that sapped her strength. For Frieda she had to be strong, optimistic, unafraid. When she thirsted, she asked Frieda if she wanted a drink. When rope cut through her clothing to rub raw her flesh, she checked her patient to see if she suffered like discomforts. It was good simply to sit and be selfish.

The "phone booth" had been established up near the keyhole, where those using it would be afforded at least the illusion of privacy. Always needing to be near the spotlight, Sondra squatted close by, sitting on her helmet, a notebook on her lap. Playing at being a journalist, Anna thought uncharitably. Maybe Frieda's rescue was the one big story she thought would give her the financial freedom to abandon what was apparently a loveless marriage. Schatz sprawled nearby, looking for all intents and purposes dead to the world.

Oscar used the phone, then Brent Roxbury, and finally Holden. After he'd been on the line for maybe three minutes, Sondra slammed her notebook shut like an angry schoolgirl and huffed over to where Anna was sitting.

"*The New York Times.*" She spit out the words. "They're onto this story. Like they can know anything." She flopped down, glaring at Anna as if waiting for her to take up the cause and fume with her.

Anna was too tired. "You'll have the first-person I-was-there angle," she said consolingly.

"Who'll care? By the time we get out of this hellhole it'll be old news."

"I guess." Anna concentrated on unwrapping a Jolly Rancher Holden had given her at the last rest stop. She wished Sondra would go away. Petty concerns in the face of disaster irritated her. She remembered a self-important tour guide from one of the many buses that plagued Mesa Verde during the tourist season. An elderly man in her group had collapsed on the porch of the museum, dead of a massive coronary. They'd practically had to pry the guide's grasping fingers from the corpse's wrist so they could shock him in an attempt to restart his heart. The woman was livid, spouting New Age bullshit about how she needed to say good-bye to his spirit. Later, when Anna was tying up the loose ends, it turned out the guide didn't even know the man's name. She'd traveled with the group for three days and had never been interested enough to remember it.

That was about as close as Anna had ever come to taking her baton to a visitor who wasn't actually breaking any laws.

"I told Holden I'd talk to the *Times*," Sondra said. "He said they declined. Those sons of bitches have no interest if you're female. Screw the truth. White male only wants to talk to white male. Big surprise."

Holden Tillman's race would be pretty hard to discern over the phone, but Anna didn't say anything. Maybe the newspaper business was as sexist as Sondra believed. It wasn't a circle Anna had ever moved in, or ever wanted to.

"Anna," Dr. McCarty called, and she looked over to where he sat with Frieda. "Frieda's going to do her phone interview now. Want to come keep her company?"

Grasping at any excuse to leave, Anna pushed herself to her feet. As she stoop-walked toward the back of this cave-within-a-cave, she could hear Sondra grumbling, "Anna. Of course. Anna. Now I suppose there's only *one* lady-in-waiting . . ."

"It's Katie Couric," Peter called.

Sondra gasped. Or hissed. Anna couldn't tell with her back turned. In spite of herself, she laughed. She didn't much care if Sondra heard or not. The woman was beyond help.

Frieda did splendidly. Dr. McCarty's central nervous system exam had freed her from the cervical collar, and she was in excellent spirits. Whether she liked it or not, she was both a good sport and a trooper. She was charming and gracious and brave and funny, lots of good stuff to quote on the six o'clock news. Or the ten o'clock news. Anna no longer had any sense of time. The little numbers the hands of her watch pointed at, then passed, had ceased to have meaning.

Phone calls finally at an end, Holden delivered the good news. At least it was good to everyone but Anna and possibly the doctor's wife. For the past five minutes he had closeted himself in a cranny near the keyhole with Peter McCarty. When the two men emerged it was to tell the rescue party that their hellish pace could be relaxed. Frieda was stable and alert. The break in her tibia was in no way life-threatening. With this fortuitous development they could afford to move more slowly, take greater care not to harm any of the natural resources of the cave.

Like a good citizen, Anna joined in the cheer, but her heart was creating a bizarre sensation in her chest by racing and sinking simultaneously. Thirty hours had seemed an eternity. Forty-eight rang in her ears like a death sentence. Get a grip, she told herself coldly. Pretend you are in a movie theater, a mall. The strategy was transparent; movie theaters and malls had doors.

Holden went on to tell them anyone feeling the need to could rotate out. A cave rescue made special demands. Those unaccustomed to it, not in perfect health, or "off their feed" for any reason were to go and Godspeed. They'd already given several lifetimes' worth.

"That's me," Sondra said, and her husband pretended not to hear.

Anna wanted to go. Like a drowning woman wants air, she wanted space and sunlight. In an act of mind-bending courage, she put temptation from her and said nothing.

Holden's rigging through the high slit above the aragonite forest of Razor Blade was a work of artistry. He edged through, a line tied into a carabiner at the back of his belt. A rig and tag line were pulled through using that first line as a tow. Pulleys were anchored at either end by running webbing around a boulder on the Lounge side and a formidable stalagmite on the far end. As he had promised, Frieda went through as neatly as silken thread through a needle's eye.

It took considerably longer for the rescuers, now nineteen in number, to creep and contort through the lower, decorated passage. They went on the buddy system, two at a time, with orders to take it slow, warn each other of endangered formations, and never, under any circumstances, stray from the existing trail. In Holden, Lechuguilla had a staunch protector.

Razor Blade opened on Lake Rapunzel, so named, Oscar said, because the only way to the lake was across fifty-five feet of flowstone, a stunning formation created by eons of trickles leaking down the side of the basin to leave behind golden locks that cascaded as enticingly as the imaginary damsel's tresses.

Traveling in, they had passed through the chamber, but Anna had seen it only fleetingly via scraps of light that served more to irritate her exhausted retinae than to illuminate the room. Now, as it turned out, her lucent fantasy of earlier in the day had come true.

Along with the rigging team working from Rapunzel to the cave's entrance came two newspaper photographers, sent by the *Times* and allowed in by George Laymon and Carlsbad's superintendent, to record the rescue. They had brought powerful floodlights. When Anna corkscrewed out of the aragonite embrace of Razor Blade, the room and lake were bathed in light. She laughed and clapped her hands like a delighted child. For that instant she was no longer tired, no longer afraid.

The chamber was made of magic. From where she stood on the lip of the run, liquid gold poured down to a lake as crystalline and blue as a summer sky. Beneath the water's surface floated great clouds of white stone, appearing as ethereal as any she'd watched forming over the mountains of southern Colorado. This jewel was in a setting befitting its splendor. Flowing draperies ringed the water in a delicate golden tracery. It staggered the imagination to know this was all made of solid rock. That it had remained hidden from human eyes for the short eternity of its existence lent it a mystical aura. Anna was transfixed.

In short order, bustling humanity compromised the beauty. Zeddie hovered at the drop, checking anchors as the teams began rigging the descent to the water from Razor Blade Run and the shorter climb up a second golden fall to a bleak section of the cave dubbed Katie's Pigtail.

Sublime became surreal as a giant alligator flopped into the diamond waters.

"What in the heck . . ." Anna heard Oscar whispering beside her.

"It's Frieda's ride."

Anna turned to see Holden looking particularly delighted at the gray-green amphibian. "It's Andrew's favorite. The boy has a deeply generous heart."

Andrew, Anna recalled, was Tillman's four-year-old son.

Oscar shook his head. Fatigue robbed him of his sense of humor. "Somehow I think the Park Service could have come up with a few inner tubes that would have done the job."

"Oscar, Oscar, Oscar," Holden said sadly, a man lamenting the failure of a promising protégé. "Inner tubes are *unclean.* Andrew's 'gator is clean, lightweight, easily packed, and designed to float supine bathers."

Even in whimsy, Tillman had a plan. The alligator was ideal. Anna was sorry when he commanded a moratorium on photographs of the actual crossing. It would have made a picture worth having, but Holden wanted his people to keep their minds on their work and not on how their naked hind ends were going to look on the front page of the Sunday paper.

Every caver to cross Lake Rapunzel stripped down to helmets and rubber water socks, then sponged off with water brought up from the lake in plastic pitchers. Their clothes and packs would be ferried over on the alligator as soon as Frieda no longer needed it. Once they had climbed the opposite wall to the entrance of the Pigtail, they would dress and put their boots back on.

Frieda was the only one to remain clothed. The Stokes was wrapped in plastic and a second float put on top of Andrew's alligator to keep her out of the water.

Again Anna was hooked into the spider on the Stokes. This time she was joined by Oscar and Peter. Her job was to watch Frieda, theirs to keep the litter away from the flowstone so the formation would not be scarred. Naked people of all shapes and sizes dangling from ropes over a pint-sized paradise; the picture so tickled Anna she had to think dark thoughts to keep from giggling.

KATIE'S PIGTAIL WAS a miniature version of the North Rift. A jagged crack bordered by breakdown, it cut upward for close to thirty yards, ending in a choked crawl that led into the Distributor Cap—the Swiss cheese room where Anna had waited on the way in while Oscar and Holden negotiated the Wormhole.

The Pigtail wasn't as impressive as the Rift. At its deepest it was forty-two feet, and at no place was it more than ten or twelve feet across. As at the Rift, a litter could not be carried along the breakdown on either side of the drop.

A team from the outer world worked from the far end stringing a traverse so the litter could travel in a more or less straight line. Because of the emergency situation, a power drill and pitons had been okayed by the superintendent, saving the rescuers the time required to find natural anchors: jug handles, arches, stalagmites, knobs, boulders.

Near the end of the Pigtail a pile of breakdown created a wall that continued down to clog the end of the slot. It was this mountain of rock and scree they would climb to reach the exit. Forming the base of this sliding heap of earth was a wedge-shaped boulder fifteen feet across at the top and six feet at the foot. It was lassoed with webbing secured with locking carabiners. The traverse rope was attached to the webbing and so to the boulder.

Faces, arms, and legs burnished bronze by sweat and dirt, cavers crawled everywhere. Cracks were crammed with bodies wrapped in various colored ropes. Ledges held packs, water carriers, and those with no immediate task. Shadows scurried over surfaces to be swallowed by the canyon below and the crevice above. Instructions, questions, and remarks hollered by workers caromed off the walls till conversation was broken down into meaningless words.

In the cacophony of sight and sound, no one was easily recognizable. Like ants, they all looked the same. Sitting at the mouth of the Pigtail with Frieda, Anna had to close her ears and shut her mind to escape the suffocating congestion.

Within two hours the rigging was complete. All personnel not needed for the traverse went on ahead. Noise abated. Once the Pigtail was behind them, the team would break up, most of them leaving for the surface. The core group would remain to set up camp in the Distributor Cap.

Since escape was beyond the realm of possibility as far as Anna was concerned, she found herself looking forward to the departure of the others. As welcome as they had been hours earlier, they were coming to seem an absolute crush of humanity, a veritable horde of interlopers. And she wasn't dreading camp as much as she thought she would. Movement toward the surface was a balm to her soul that allowed her to go on with some show of equanimity, but fatigue was overriding paranoia. Every cell in her body cried out for rest. Regardless of personal demons, she had little doubt that she would sleep like a log.

When all was in readiness, Holden came back to the ledge where Anna and the Stokes roosted.

He'd had less sleep than she. No one had worked harder; no one had taken fewer rests, yet aside from a miner's tan of filth, he looked none the worse for wear.

"How do you do it?" Anna asked in admiration.

"Coffee breaks," Holden said simply.

Coffee. Anna would have given a year of her life for a good hot cup of coffee. "Where?" she almost wailed.

Holden tapped the pocket on the front of his tee-shirt. "Next to my heart." He pulled out a small foil envelope of Taster's Choice instant, ripped off a corner, and tapped the contents expertly into his bottom lip like a farmer taking chaw. "Good to the last crystal."

Frieda was as tired as any of them. Without the concealing mask of dirt, her face showed it. Her skin was drawn and pale and her eyes were staring, too much of the whites showing. For the hauls, Holden needed her awake and moderately alert so she could tell them if she was in any distress and needed to stop. There was a limit to the amount of pain medication Dr. McCarty could give her and still leave her with enough brain power to work on her own behalf. Though no one but Anna was permitted to hear a word of complaint from her lips, Frieda was not the best of patients. Anna suspected she hurt a good deal more than she would admit and took less pain medicine than she needed, as if by suffering she was somehow paying her way.

"Ready for a last push?" Tillman asked Frieda.

"Ready whenever you are. I'm the one's been napping all day."

"This is rigged like a dream," he promised. "You'll be in camp in no time. I got a special room in the Swiss cheese earmarked. You two can have it all to yourselves to do lady things."

When this was over Anna wanted to meet Holden's wife and his little boy. A man as fine as Tillman didn't just spring into being all of a piece like Venus on the half shell. Somewhere along the line he had been shaped. Anna had the feeling she would be right at home with those sculpting influences.

Anna and Frieda were tied into the web of ropes. Two pulleys, anodized in red, white, and blue, were set to roll down the main traverse, a thick lavender rope. The Stokes was tied into the system with webbing, two lines through each of the four carabiners locked onto the frame of the litter and running up to locking 'biners connected to the bottom of the rollers. A gray line attached at the same point. This would be used to pull the Stokes and Anna along the crevasse. A second, purple rope, lighter than the traverse line, was connected as well, but with its own carabiners, a tag line so the Stokes and its dependants could be retrieved in the event of a malfunction. Each system had a backup, and each connection had been checked by Holden, then rechecked by Oscar and, apparently on her own agenda, by Zeddie as well. Neither Anna nor Frieda had any compunction about trusting their lives to the cat's cradle of ropes.

Nothing in Lechuguilla was designed for the easy access of humans. Katie's Pigtail was no exception. The crack was irregular; the sides of jutting rock looked as if they had only recently been torn from the opposing wall. The stones were white overlaid with dirt that sifted from above. Below, all was darkness, a band of unrelenting night cutting raggedly away from the farthest reach of the lamps. The right side of the Pigtail was concave, gaping holes where chunks of rock had fallen away. On the left was a fractured ledge, a footpath for mountain goats. It was here the remaining rescuers would make their way. Three-quarters of the way to the exit, the crevasse was crossed by breakdown, immense slabs forming a natural bridge. Five yards beyond was the landing where they would start the climb to camp.

Katie's Pigtail couldn't be rigged in the neat in-line haul that Holden had managed above Razor Blade. For most of the way the rigging was tucked up close to the left-hand wall. The ledge was too fragmented to hand-carry the Stokes. It would be suspended over the drop and moved along by pulleys and haul lines.

Anna hooked into the spider, she and Frieda were lowered over the edge of the drop. Anna's feet were flat against the wall, her fanny over thin air. The Stokes was held several inches above her airborne lap. By using the strength of the muscles in her thighs, she would be able to "walk" the Stokes over the rough patches along the edge. The haul line did the work of moving the litter forward. Wherever on the goat track cavers could find perches, they waited to help her manipulate the litter around obstacles.

Knowing this was the last work of the day gave strength to Anna's flagging spirits as she began the long crab-walk to the exit with Frieda. Ropes slid, pulleys rolled. Muscles in her thighs and butt burned, but the Stokes slipped and bumped along without mishap. At Holden's order, no one talked. His voice, light and clear as he supervised from the false floor of stone bridging the canyon, issued commands and encouragement. Foot by foot they passed through the maw of the Pigtail. Anna could see her own exhaustion and elation mirrored in the faces of the others; a dance, a symphony, a poem of human effort and mind.

The first hint that something had gone wrong was the call "*Rock!*" carried down the black canyon on a gust of fear.

7

LIKE A FLICK of foam on the crest of a tidal wave, the shout was borne down on a thunderous roar. In the insulated chamber, sworn to long silence by the earth itself, the noise consumed everything in its path. The stone beneath Anna's boot soles quaked. The Stokes chattered against the limestone. Anna could feel the frame ratcheting in her hands. The feeble clacking of metal was lost in the greater chaos. Helmet lights slashed at the darkness, cutting across each other in the void, vainly seeking the source of the racket. In a second Anna saw those beams turn from gold to brown. In another instant they were smothered completely.

Silt-out, she thought inanely, her mind grasping at a diving incident years before. Dust: the earth was reclaiming the canyon they crept through. Curling down over Frieda, Anna grabbed both sides of the Stokes and hung on. Her hard hat was pressed against the Plexiglas protecting Frieda's face. Anna thought she heard Frieda screaming, but it might have been her own voice.

Ropes slipped, and there was a sickening skid downward. Then something broke loose, and they fell as one falls in a nightmare. Sudden weightlessness, a sense of utter helplessness, as all that was once real, once stable, is sucked away. Without sight, there were no walls streaking by, no floor rushing up. There were just the wind and the breathless drop.

Without warning the ropes caught, and Anna was jerked above the litter, the webbing slashing at the soft skin of her groin. Upended, she snapped back against the canyon wall, elbow cracking into an unforgiving surface. The litter was still between her hands, the weight of it threatening to drag her arms from their sockets. Maybe lines still held it, maybe they didn't. Anna wasn't going to let go and find out. As long as the spider held, she could hold, she told herself.

She lied. The leather of her gloves began to slip, a slow rotation that would pry her fingers from the metal. Squeezing with every muscle in her body, Anna willed her bones to weld to the aluminum. "I got you, Frieda," she said over and over, as if by repeating it it would continue to be the truth.

By the light of her lamp she could see Frieda's face below her. Through the gauze of swirling dust she looked no more than twelve years old. "Grab me, Frieda. Grab my wrists." In what appeared to be slow motion, Frieda reached up. Anna could see the articulation of her fingers, opening like petals of a flower in time-lapse photography.

Grinding as of enormous gears out of sync clogged her ears and squeezed the gray matter in her skull. Dust boiled down in an opaque swirl, burning her eyes and lungs. Frieda vanished in a noxious cloud. "Grab hold," Anna cried. Dust forced her eyes closed, stopped her breath. None of her senses would function. She felt a terror so primal she could no longer even speak. Fingers closed around her wrists. Good girl, Frieda, she thought, and clenched eyes and teeth and hands against the onslaught.

Gradually the noise abated. The invisible freight train

roaring down their canyon turned away, the rumble following it. Pressure lifted with the relative quiet. The sound of rocks skittering touched lightly on the ear like the burble of a mountain stream. Anna remembered to breathe and was rewarded by a hacking cough expelling dust-saturated air. She opened her eyes. In the brown glow of her headlamp she could see her left arm and Frieda's face. Through the Plexiglas Frieda looked up at her, and Anna saw her own fear mirrored.

Stillness reigned. Anna craned her neck, peering over her shoulder. The lines held. The traverse rope was at a drunken angle, but it was taut, and the spider looked solid, a testament to Oscar and Holden's rigging expertise.

"Whoa," she said. "They've still got us. We can let go. Easy." Frieda loosed her hold on Anna's wrists, leaving a burn where she'd gripped bare skin. "Me now. Sheesh. My hands are stuck in the 'on' position." Anna laughed shakily, and Frieda managed a smile. Before Anna could pry her fingers from the metal, another sound assaulted them, a screech like tires on pavement. "Jesus fucking Christ, what—"

Grinding began again, pulverizing Anna's words. Irrationally, she thought she'd brought it on by offending the Hodags. That and an unformed thought about the eye of the hurricane were raked from her mind as the momentary stability of the Stokes was lost. Ropes that held them in their tangled web dropped half a foot, caught. For a heartbeat they rested; then those same lines that had kept them from falling snatched them from safety. Anna and Frieda didn't so much fall as hurtle. The foot of the Stokes was dragged down, towed into the inky depths as if hitched to a leviathan that dived for the bottom.

Anna's neck whipped back with the suddenness of their descent. A rope burned across her cheek. She felt the drag on her flesh but not the pain. Heart and lungs were left behind. In the brief second afforded, she was disappointed her life didn't flash before her eyes. There had been times she would have liked to revisit, faces she wanted to see once more. On the heels of this spark of dream came a craven hope that if they had been buried alive, this fall would kill her.

Black on black, she struck with a violence that knocked thought aside, hammered her knee into her chest. She folded. Her helmet struck something with such force she could feel her brain skid in its pan. Her left shoulder slammed against the rocks. A faint pop reverberated up through tissues to her ear—a break or a dislocation. No pain, not yet. Air gusted from her chest, the wind knocked out of her. She'd not felt that paralyzing inability to inhale since she was a little girl and had fallen off the horizontal ladder on the playground of Johnstonville Elementary.

Through the panic of asphyxiation came a piercing realization: her earlier prayer for death was bogus. Regardless of where she'd landed, she wanted to stay alive. A line from *Rosencrantz and Guildenstern Are Dead,* a play her husband, Zach, had starred in Off-Broadway, reverberated in a voice she'd thought lost to her, something to the effect that life in a box was better than no life at all.

Air returned in a trickle, and Anna sipped greedily till her lungs expanded. With oxygen came pain. Her shoulder throbbed down to her fingertips. She'd not let go of the Stokes, and her left hand was pinned beneath the metal. During the fall, she had become wadded up. Knees under chin, arms down around her ankles, she knelt in a ball on an unstable surface. As she fell—or, more likely, as she landed—her headlamp had been lost. Darkness was absolute, viscous. Of the three sources of light she'd been cautioned to carry, two were in her sidepack, somewhere above her. If above still existed.

Frieda's lamp had been extinguished as well. Anna could not tell which direction was up and which down, whether they had landed on the bottom of the Pigtail or were caught partway down. She had no idea if she bled or was whole, if Frieda was with her or gone. Only sound remained to keep her company; a distant grumbling as if the people the earth had swallowed for her supper didn't agree with her.

For half a minute Anna was unable to move. Blindness, dizziness from the blow to her head, left her with a sense of disassociation. The pain in her shoulder, fingers, the cramping in her thighs, were distant echoes from a body she had once inhabited. The only true sensation was stark terror. Fear if she moved she would fall again, farther this time. And fear that she was alone and would die alone in the dark.

Anna was never to find out if this panic would have passed on its own, if she would have been able to function again without help. A light came through the dust storm of night and touched the wall several yards above her. "Down here," she managed. Her voice was so tiny she could scarcely hear it herself. Fear she would be passed over, the search plane would never again fly near her life raft, sent a spurt of adrenaline through her veins. "Down here," she yelled so loudly she wondered that she didn't set off another fall of rock.

Lamps began appearing, brown muted smudges that came and went in the haze like will-o'-the-wisps. Shouts and cries accompanied them, but none reached to where Anna crouched.

"Light," she shouted. "Get me some light down here."

"Hang on." Oscar Iverson's voice cut through the fog, and she was comforted. She could hear the scramble of feet and lines. A fine rain of dirt pattered down on her helmet.

"Frieda?" she ventured. There was no reply. Keeping her right hand clasped tightly on a projection of stone above her shoulder and moving carefully so as not to dislodge them should their perch be as precarious as she feared, Anna worked her left hand from between the rock and the Stokes. The pain was intense but not unwelcome. It clarified her thoughts, burned through the mind-numbing terror. When her hand was free, she pulled the glove off with her teeth and began a tactile exploration of the territory beneath her.

Between her knees was the cool Plexiglas of Frieda's

face shield. Anna wiggled her fingers under the edge and felt the warmth of her friend's throat. Without help from her eyes she sought the carotid artery the way she'd been taught years before at a trade school for emergency medical technicians, feeling first for the hard shell of cartilage that protected the esophagus. Nothing but too-pliant flesh met her touch. Risking the fall, she released the stony projection and brought her right hand down. Using her left to hold the shield up, she felt Frieda's face. There was no stickiness of blood or slippery ooze of mucus or cerebral spinal fluid leaking from nose or ears. With gentle strokes, she checked the exposed parts of Frieda's skull and forehead. She seemed to be all in one piece. Anna's fingers tapped gently down over feathery eyebrows to touch Frieda's eyelids. They were wet.

"Frieda?" Anna said softly. There wasn't a flicker of response. She moved a fingertip lightly down the lid to the bridge of the nose. Not blood but tears: Frieda's eyes were open. Anna's fingertips rested on the sclera.

"Frieda?" Anna said again, and heard a note of hysteria in her voice. "Get Dr. McCarty down here," she yelled.

"Almost there." Looking up she could see the boots and butts of two cavers descending in a halo of murky light. When she looked down again the illumination had spread. In diffused sepia tones, like those of an old photograph, she could make out the barest outline of where they had come to rest. Katie's Pigtail bottomed out a foot or two below the wide shelf where the litter had landed. The Stokes was at an angle, propped in the ell where wall met floor. Lines tangled around it, some vanishing into the dark like snakes fleeing the scene. Anna had landed on top of the litter, her knees on Frieda's chest.

In the swaying shadows she could see Frieda's face. The shield had become detached from her helmet on one side. Anna lifted it off. Eyes open, lips slightly parted as if she meant to speak, Frieda stared at the limestone wall. Where her esophagus should have been was a shallow depression the size of a saucer. That was why Anna had been unable to find it in the dark. It had been crushed, smashed flat when Anna's knee had driven through the soft flesh of her throat.

"I killed you," Anna said tonelessly.

"We're almost there," came Iverson's voice. "Take it easy."

"I killed her," Anna told them. "I killed Frieda."

8

WITH THE GIFT of light, Anna found the courage to move. Her left arm was useless. Even if it wasn't broken, the pain was so great her muscles lacked all strength, and she couldn't put any pressure on it. Keeping the weight off Frieda with her right arm, she got free of the Stokes and knelt by her friend's head. With her weak hand beneath Frieda's chin, Anna pinched her nose closed and tried to blow air into her lungs. The trachea was too damaged. No air could flow through. Twice more she tried, then Oscar and Peter McCarty arrived.

"Crushed esophagus," Anna said, and, "Emergency tracheotomy?" She'd seen Jane Fonda do it once in a movie about a doll maker. It was not sanctioned for EMTs by any state board in the continental U.S. Pocket-knife and Bic-pen procedures were frowned upon by a litigious society not given to trusting the kindness of strangers.

In this instance McCarty echoed Anna's thoughts verbatim. "We've got nothing to lose."

She moved back, making room for him. Lines weaving

through gear and metal tied Anna and Frieda together, and Anna knew it would always be so. She no more blamed herself for ending Frieda's life than she would have blamed a rock that had effected the same end, but together they had traversed the Pigtail. Together they had shared the terror of the ropes giving way. Together they had fallen. Anna had not only been there at the moment Frieda's life had winked out but, however unwillingly, had been the instrument of her death. That connected them.

"She's gone," Dr. McCarty said. "There was too much trauma. The spine may have been snapped."

An involuntary shudder rattled Anna's frame. Graphic images, the mechanics of her kneecap cracking Frieda's bones were too much. To her embarrassment, she started to cry, not a quiet flow of seemly tears but salt water and snot and great gulping sobs. Her heart and mind felt as if they had burst, swollen tender blisters full of poison. She could no more stop her weeping than she could have stopped the litter from falling.

Arms went around her. Hands removed her helmet. Fingers stroked her hair. A voice murmured in her ear. Still, she could not stem the tide of emotion. Grief she could have borne with silence if not dignity; she'd done it before. Pain she could carry without undue complaint. Even the shock and the fear might have been tenable. It was the helplessness that unmanned her. An overwhelming sense of being utterly lost.

"I'm going to give her a sedative," she heard Peter say. From the movement against the top of her head she realized it was he who held her.

"Not till we're out of here and have camp set up," Oscar returned. "She needs all her wits about her for the climb out."

They spoke as if she wasn't there. With her tears she had abdicated. At least in the minds of men. They didn't understand tears; the difference between giving up and stepping down for a moment, collapsing and crying "I can't go on," then, refreshed, lifting one's burdens and pressing onward.

Anna fought free of Peter's protective embrace and mopped at the mess on her face with the tail of her tee-shirt. The coarseness of the gesture went unnoticed by the three of them. There wasn't a clean hanky for a long ways.

"I'm okay," she growled. An untimely case of the hiccups robbed her statement of its force. "Just a bad patch there. Frieda—" Tears yet unspent rose in her throat and eyes. Anna stopped trying to talk and breathed in slowly till they receded. "Frieda's dead?"

"Dead," Peter repeated.

"Can we get out of here?" Anna asked. "Out of the cave?" She kept her voice dead-level. She expected the answer to be "no" and did not want them to know how desperately she needed it to be otherwise.

"I don't know," Oscar said. Peter turned his head to listen. His light fell on Iverson and Anna saw his face. Age had settled on him with the layers of dust. She wouldn't have thought his seamed, mummylike skin would have the elasticity to tell any more tales of use, but it was there. Exhaustion pulled at the rims of his eyes, responsibility pinched his thin lips, shock sucked the blood from his tanned hide, leaving it more gray than brown.

Seeing him this way could have further demoralized her. Oddly it had the opposite effect. Had he been a paragon of strength, she might have been tempted to fall apart and let him pick up the pieces. Recognizing his humanity brought to the fore a playground sense of justice. It wouldn't be *fair* to fall apart. It wouldn't be kosher to make him carry her load.

"Okay," she said. Given the context, the word was meaningless. She intended only to buy herself a little time, to indicate she heard and understood, that she could be relied on. Whether the last was true or not, she didn't know.

With meticulous attention to detail, proving to someone—herself, probably—that she was still a viable member of the team, Anna began unhooking herself from the Stokes. Her fingers now opened and closed, the wrist and elbow moved without too much pain. Apparently her shoulder had only been badly bruised. She didn't mention that or the blow to her head to Peter McCarty.

Distracted, he didn't press her. He asked questions about her and Frieda's fall but was easily satisfied. They had yet to hear what had occurred up near the rockfall. The doctor might have his work cut out for him. Anna could see the lack of confidence in the uncomfortable shift of his blue eyes and the uncertain, almost childish, crimp of his mouth. McCarty wasn't an ER doctor or a television hero. He was a gynecologist on holiday. Chances were good he had less experience with emergency medicine than Anna, Oscar, or Holden. But he had the M.D. after his name, and in the eyes of the world, that made him responsible.

He and Oscar had rappelled down using two short lines Oscar had been carrying to rig the ascent at the end of the Pigtail. They anchored to a formation that grew out of the wall above like a petrified rhinoceros horn. Anna watched as they strapped on their ascenders for the climb back up. Her gear resided with her other two light sources under Zeddie's care. If Zeddie still lived.

Peter worked in grim silence. Understanding Anna's need for information, an imposition of order—or maybe just needing to talk—Oscar told her everything he'd seen, heard, or surmised.

"Peter and I were right above you and Frieda," he said. "We heard that . . . that noise . . . and looked up. Something let loose in the pile of rock up by the Distributor Cap. I heard it more than saw it. Kind of a weird shift in the shadows, but I could tell it was coming down. I think it started off small. Then a ton of rock hit the boulder we'd anchored you guys into. It must have shifted."

That would have been the first short drop.

"I thought that was it, but something big got torn out," Oscar went on.

The second grinding.

"The anchor boulder hopped. I mean *hopped*," he said. "Like it had come to life. It staggered, rocked backward, then hopped, hit the bridge, and went down."

Anna's leviathan.

"After that the dust got so bad I had to turn away, put my arm over my face. Didn't see much for a while."

"Holden?" Anna asked. He'd been on the stone bridge directing the operation.

"Don't know," Oscar said, his voice suddenly hard. "He's fast. He may have got clear."

"Anybody else hurt?" Anna pressed.

"Like I said, I don't know," he snapped. Strain came across as irritation. After a moment he went on, his unspoken apology accepted. "Most of the others went ahead. They must have gotten clear. The Distributor Cap is solid. I'm betting this was a local slide."

Peter McCarty was locking his ascenders onto the rope. He had said scarcely a word since he'd pronounced Frieda dead.

"Will you be okay with . . . You know, here?" Oscar asked almost as an afterthought. "As soon as I'm up I can send down my climbing gear."

"Thanks," Anna said. "I'll be here."

They left her a flashlight, and for that she was grateful. Watching them walk back up the wall of the chasm, she hugged it to her chest as if it were a magic wand.

Alone again, she crawled over to where Frieda lay. There was nothing with which to cover her face. By the light of the flashlight, Anna closed her friend's eyes and folded her hands on her chest. They wouldn't stay put, and she had to hook the elbows against the frame of the Stokes to keep them in place. Why it was important, she wasn't sure, but it was. Death required ritual, even ritual that wasn't completely understood. Anna found herself wishing she knew the words of the last rites. All that came to mind from a distant and spotty religious training were the first lines of the Twenty-third Psalm. "Yea, though I walk through the valley of the shadow of death I will fear no evil." The sentiment was apt, so she spoke the words aloud. They were all she could remember. The rest of the psalm was inextricably tangled up with the *Charge of the Light Brigade.*

"Sorry," Anna whispered. "It's the best I can do." Clicking off the light she sat cross-legged near the Stokes, one hand resting on Frieda's shoulder, and listened to what was going on above.

Remembering the drop, then watching the men climb, she estimated they'd fallen close to thirty feet. Dust was thick in the air but had ceased to boil and twist like a live thing. In increments almost too small to note, the lamps were growing brighter. Sound, human notes, were discernible, but just barely. They seemed far off and impossibly lonely.

"I'm scared, Frieda," Anna admitted. "I wish you were here." Tears came again but quietly this time, a steady stream of sorrow cutting channels through the dirt on her face.

One of the lines used to descend began to snake up the wall. The slithering frightened Anna till she shined her light on it and knew it for what it was. Half a minute later came the call "Heads up." She used her light to follow a burgundy sidepack, streaked with mud, down the rock face. It came to rest a few feet from the foot of the Stokes. She made no move to retrieve it.

"Got it?" came a call.

"Got it," she shouted, and continued to sit and stare as if it were an alien object for which she could not fathom any practical use.

Now that the time had come to reenter the fray, take up those burdens she had righteously eschewed abandoning, she wondered if she had the wherewithal to do so. There was an undeniable appeal to sitting in the bottom of the ditch with Frieda, unmoved and unmoving, letting emergencies be dealt with by others. For a bit she indulged this desire, finding deep wells of self-pity to justify inaction.

"Shit," she said finally, that being as close to a personal philosophy as she could muster. "I guess I'm not dead yet, Frieda." She pried herself up from the rock and retrieved the pack.

Oscar's gear was a rotten fit, but it was a short climb and

it would suffice. Once she was rigged she turned back to Frieda. It was time to say good-bye. She doubted they'd be alone together again. And, soon, Frieda's soul, if such a thing actually existed, would take flight, rise effortlessly through the layers of bedrock. It crossed Anna's mind to kiss her friend, but it wasn't something she would have done had Frieda been alive. It seemed impertinent to do it now that she was dead. Anna racked her brain for a gift to leave her with, but the dead are hell to buy for. The answer came in a flash of insight a superstitious woman might have taken as a message from the Other Side.

"Taco," Anna said, naming Frieda's middle-aged golden retriever. "I'll take care of Taco," she promised. "As if he were a cat." She waited a few seconds more, but there was nothing left but a hollow mountain and the smell of dirt.

9

FOLLOWING THE LIGHTS, Anna left the standing rope to Frieda in place and edged along the chasm. While she picked her way over the precarious goat track, a shouted dialogue echoed from one end of the Pigtail to the other. Besides registering that probably more people had survived than not, she paid little heed. Her attention was taken up by the placement of each foot. Ambient anxiety had settled on one thought: that she would fall again. And, though she'd gone beyond where the Stokes lay, there came with anxiety the horror that she would again land on Frieda. Knowing the fear was irrational did nothing to dispel it, and Anna crept and clung like a lifelong acrophobe.

At the end of the rift where the lights pooled, she joined Holden, Oscar, Peter, and Brent. When he saw the anchor shift, Holden had leapt from the bridge. Protected by the stone, he survived the landslide. In his Texas drawl he admitted, "The first step was a doozy." Rubble flowed into the end of Katie's Pigtail, burying the exit through to the Distributor Cap. By the time the slide was over, a mountain of dirt was between them and the way out. The fall created a stairway of rock down into the rift. Holden had been able to crawl up to the lip of the Pigtail.

Unhurt, Brent Roxbury had already started the demoralizing process of fussing over Holden. Though necessary to a degree, Anna knew it increased the sense of helplessness. She was too tired and helpless herself to interfere.

As near as Peter could tell, Holden's right ankle had been broken by the fall. As they shared their news with him, something else broke as well. Cracks appeared in his composure when he asked after Curt and Zeddie. They had been stationed along the Pigtail between Oscar and Holden. No one had seen them since the rockslide. The cracks widened, weakening the bones of Holden's face when Oscar told him Frieda was dead. Maybe it was Anna's knee that had crushed the life from her, but it was Holden's anchor that had given way. Nothing that had happened to Holden himself seemed to interest him. He ignored what had to be the painful examination of his ankle, sucked dust into his lungs as if it were the purest of air while he hefted both the boulder and Frieda's corpse onto his bony shoulders. An unsettling reflection of the feelings of those around him, despair marked his face like passing years. Anna recognized the temptation that had grabbed at her in the way he scrubbed imaginary cobwebs from his cheeks, the way his eyes lost focus as if he saw something beyond the rock walls. Holden was in shock. He wanted to give up, to lie down, pull disaster over his head like a dark blanket, and grieve. A broken ankle was a ticket to this lonely escape. Had Anna had an injury worth speaking of she might have used it to hide behind.

She thought she was too tired and shaken to care about anything, but she watched him grappling with his devil as if she'd bet the farm on the outcome. Oscar Iverson was there and he was functioning, but Holden Tillman was of the cave itself. In some unfathomable way, she felt should he give up, the cave would take him—take them all. Even should they be freed, when they returned to the world their souls would be left behind under tons of limestone.

"Goddamn, but I'm tired," Anna said too loudly, blowing away the morbid fantasy.

A minute shift occurred in Holden's dull stare. He was looking at Anna, his light on her face.

"Oscar," he said in a reasonable facsimile of his old voice, "we've got to teach Anna the fine art of cowboy cursing."

"Dad blast it," Oscar said, and Anna heard the relief behind the words. He'd sensed Holden's return as well.

"Gol *dang* it," Holden said. "The power is in the diphthongs."

Remembering her last great blasphemy before all hell broke loose, she gave it a try. "Shucks," she said tentatively.

Everyone laughed. Brent's laugh was shrill, an alarming whinny. There was an edge of desperation to it. Still, it was good.

"Darn tootin'," Holden approved.

"We're going to have to rig a litter for you." McCarty jerked them abruptly back from the oasis of forgetfulness they'd forged.

The only litter they had was in the bottom of the rift, housing the remains of Frieda Dierkz. A clutch of icy fingers tweaked Anna's insides, and she waited for Holden's retreat back into the quietude of victimhood.

"My ankle's not broken," Holden declared. Wordlessly, Anna cheered his obstinacy. "Fix me up so I can get by."

Anna and Oscar understood perfectly. McCarty was nudged aside. The two of them ransacked packs and first aid kits and built Holden a walking cast that kept his knee and ankle rigid. With duct tape and three of the lightweight, ladderlike aluminum rappelling devices they tied his foot and lower leg into a brace he could put his weight on. Dealing with the pain and awkwardness was up to him.

"Everybody okay?" It was Zeddie Dillard coming crablike over breakdown from the direction of the goat track. Hailing her as Lazarus woman, they all but fell on her neck and wept. At least that was how Anna interpreted the calls of: "Where have you been?" Brent. "Now there's a good-looking woman." Oscar. And, "Is Curt with you?" Holden.

Of the six of them, she appeared to have weathered the incident the best. She'd suffered no physical injury. She'd not seen the litter fall, Frieda dead. Unlike Oscar, Holden, and Peter, she carried no burdens of responsibility for a crushing past or an unpromising future. Added to these was the blessing of youth and its attendant sense of immortality. Anna doubted it had occurred to this strong, determined young woman that something as paltry as the elemental forces of nature could snuff out her life.

Zeddie had tested the phone line, she told them. It was dead, probably sheared during the avalanche. Curt was unhurt, she reported. After the fall, she had seen Brent attending to Holden, and she and Schatz had passed the lines where Peter and Oscar descended to the Stokes. Since matters were being handled on the fall end, they had gone back to the beginning of the Pigtail to check on the others. Curt stayed back with four of the rescuers from outside who had been trapped.

"I thought it best we not all come thundering up here till we knew how things stood." That said, Zeddie waited expectantly.

Truth was, nobody knew how things stood. Holden rose to the occasion, drawing the invisible albatross of leadership back around his neck. "You did just right," he assured her.

"Did anybody . . ." Zeddie's question petered out as she nodded at the pile of earth beneath and behind them.

That they squatted on the burial ground of the perhaps undead had not occurred to Anna, and she shivered uncontrollably. To have her one hundred fifteen pounds instrumental in the death of another of her fellows was insupportable.

"No," Holden said firmly. "The others made it to the Distributor Cap before this happened. If anybody went up there after that, they had to sneak by. Everybody was out."

Anna released breath she'd not known she was holding and laughed—a rush of air without sound—at the image that had held her in thrall; grasping hands thrust through the soil from a movie. Probably Stephen King.

"Frieda?" Zeddie said.

"Didn't make it."

Anna watched the woman's face as the simple words sank in and thought she saw genuine sadness through the grime. In a spill of light, she caught sight of Roxbury at the same instant. He had already heard the news, yet sorrow and something else—a gestalt of expressions suggesting a painful and very personal loss—crumpled his face a second time.

"What happened?" Zeddie asked, and Anna drew breath to confess.

"She was killed in the fall." Holden forestalled her. "After the anchor gave way and brought down the mountain there was nothing anyone could do. Anna was lucky not to be killed too."

The statement was more than an exoneration of Anna. It was an acceptance of the blame. He'd chosen the anchor that had carried Frieda and Anna to the bottom of the rift.

"I'm betting the anchor held, that the slide started above the boulder and knocked it loose," Oscar said in an attempt to ease his friend. "The anchor was sound. Rocks from above must have dislodged it. There couldn't have been any way to foresee that."

Brent Roxbury interrupted with a strangled noise.

"If you're having a heart attack, I'm not up for CPR," Anna said unsympathetically.

For a second he searched for words or breath, then he said, "Listen." They froze in a sudden tableau, expecting a reprise of the horrible grinding. Instead came a musical cadence of taps, clear and sharp and obviously man-made.

Again Brent whinnied.

More taps.

Anna laughed, and Oscar with her. They were saved.

"Well," Holden said, a ghost of the twinkle flickering through. "Somebody answer the doggone door."

Zeddie was the quickest to respond. She scuttled up the

newly fallen scree to where the taps emanated from. In her haste she started another rock slide, a tiny one this time, but enough to remind them how inherently unstable the slope was. Deep in timeless and unweathered earth, jagged corners unsoftened by the influence of wind or water, breakdown was cemented in place with a dry mortar of silt that had filtered down fine as dust over the centuries. Without external forces to act upon it, this bedding went untested through soundless, lightless years. Once the delicate fabric was disturbed, it flowed like sand through an hourglass, trickling from beneath, shifting rocks that had been held unmoving for eons.

Having unclipped a carabiner from a belt loop on her trousers, Zeddie rapped it smartly against a stone. No reply.

"I think it's too light," she said, meaning the aluminum alloy of the 'biner.

McCarty dug a hammer from his pack, possibly the kind used to tap on patients' knees. "Try this," he said, and tossed it. Fortunately Zeddie's hand was sure even in the faint and shifting light, and she caught it. This deep within the earth nothing could afford to be casual. Greater threats than Hodags were ready to make mischief at every turn. Shadows waiting to swallow tools, holes to snap bones, passages like mazes to capture lost souls.

Hostile work environment, Anna thought, and no one to sue.

Using the hammer, Zeddie banged three times in quick succession. Three raps came back and the cavers sent up a ragged cheer that ended as spontaneously as it had begun.

"Does anybody know Morse code?" Oscar asked hopefully.

"SOS," Zeddie offered. They all knew SOS.

"I think that's been established," Iverson said dryly.

Another flurry of taps were exchanged for the reassurance of both parties. Nothing of moment could be transmitted, but the message that they were not alone, not forgotten, that help was on the way was enough.

"How long do you think it will take them to get through?" Brent said, and Anna was grateful he'd saved her from being the first to ask.

Holden and Oscar looked at each other in mute conference. Holden shrugged. "I'd only be guessing," Oscar said.

"Guess," Anna demanded, unable to help herself.

"A day. Maybe two."

Anna's heart shriveled up till it felt the size of a wizened lemon. "Twenty-four-hour days or eight-hour days?"

"Could go either way," he replied unhelpfully.

Holden took over. "We got nothing to dig with and the best we can do to help is get out of the way. They're going to be pushing out on this slope, and it'll slide again before they're done. We've all put in close to a nineteen-hour day. Everybody's shot. Till we've rested we're just accidents waiting to happen. We'll set up a base of operations back at the other end of this hole. We've got beaucoup water. Rapunzel goes down forever. This cave's got enough air to be considered a wind tunnel in some parts of the world, and we've got food. Lechuguilla's warm and dry. All we've got to do is get comfy and wait for the cavalry to arrive. My guess is old Oscar here is being conservative. We only need wiggle room, not the Holland Tunnel. We'll be out of here in eight or ten hours. Let's go spread the good word."

Though he'd chosen to be brave, macho, noble, and all the things that Anna and, she was sure, the others had hoped he would be, Tillman remained a cautious man. Because of his ankle he tied himself between Oscar and Brent, the strongest of those in their truncated group. It could have been argued that McCarty was sturdier than Iverson, but he hadn't recovered from the trauma of the avalanche or Frieda's death—whatever demons stopped his voice and drained the blood from his lips.

Consumed by an all-encompassing fatigue, Anna was unable to take much interest in McCarty's well-being. Body, mind, and spirit were exhausted. The ache in her arm and her fear of falling kept her awake. The lure of the lamp kept her moving forward. She'd come to believe there were no flat level places in all of the inner space of Lechuguilla. The "trail" they'd been calling the goat track was like the dotted line on a cartographer's drawing; it existed only in their minds. Reality was a stretch of rock that could be navigated only by borrowing from the traveling techniques of spiders, monkeys, starfish, and weasels.

On the careful trek back, McCarty was in line behind Anna, taking up the last position. "Sondra?" he said with the startled intonation of a man remembering a package left behind in a taxicab. He had to say it a second time before the import penetrated Anna's haze of self-absorption.

"Sondra?" she echoed stupidly, and ceased all movement to summon the energy required to process the idea. "Zeddie!" she hollered when the thought had percolated through the layers of dulled emotion.

"Yeah?" Zeddie called back. Anna could just see her, down on all fours like a muddy St. Bernard, fifteen or twenty feet ahead.

"Is Sondra back with Curt?"

A moment's silence followed, then the almost inevitable response: "Wasn't she with you?"

Anna swiveled her head to see if the message had reached the doctor. It was the only part of her anatomy she felt she could disturb without danger of dislodging her corpus from the rock face. With the poor light and the distance, she could scarcely read his reaction, but it looked as if as much guilt as worry. Maybe he realized how late in coming was this concern for his missing spouse. Anna studied him an instant longer, trying to see if relief mixed with concern on his face. If it did, she missed it.

"She told me she was going to rotate out," Anna remembered.

Now the doctor did look relieved, and Anna mirrored the sentiment. Intrigue in addition to all else that had happened might have proved to be the proverbial straw.

Camp was luxurious by caving standards: there was a fairly flat spot for everyone to lie down on. At Holden's insistence, food was eaten. Most were so tired they would have forgone the meal to avoid the effort of lifting the spoon from container to mouth. Understanding the need to fuel the body, Anna ate mechanically. The disappearance of Sondra was hashed and rehashed. The four cavers who had taken up the rear position on the Pigtail had spoken to her early on during the rigging but hadn't seen her since the actual haul began. Anna dutifully repeated her hopeful tale of Sondra's opting to rotate out. No one had seen her going ahead with the others, but such was the crush of cavers and the business of the traverse they might easily have missed her. She'd not told her husband of her plans. None but the four newcomers seemed to think that unusual. Anna wasn't the only one who'd noted the relationship between Peter and Sondra was strained.

Consensus was that Sondra had gone out. Either that or she lay under the rock and dirt of the slide. Despite the slimness of this possibility, Anna knew Holden would have spent the night digging but for the fact that by the time Peter McCarty had mentioned she was missing it was too late, she'd have been long dead. Holden wasn't one to risk the living for the dead no matter how good it might look on paper.

Chewing, swallowing, drinking warm water, it occurred to Anna that Peter might have waited on purpose. A rock slide would be a convenient end to an inconvenient marriage. Anna had no idea what power Sondra thought she had to jerk her husband's medical license, but if it was true and half an hour's malicious silence could remove the threat for all time . . .

Anna's punch-drunk brain fumbled at the thought for a while, then let it go. Odds were against it. At any rate it would be unprovable.

Oscar and Holden did a commendable job with their pep talks. Oscar's was filtered through fatigue and Holden's a near-crippling sense of guilt, but they served their purpose. The team was given hope and cohesion. Lisa, the long-braided caver who had been trapped with the core group, was a practicing Buddhist. She said a prayer for Frieda that Anna was too tired to follow, but she appreciated the gesture.

One by one they made the creeping journey from their bivouac to the mouth of the Pigtail where there was a good "squatting rock" and they could perform their evening ablutions. Limited space precluded both a ladies' room and a men's, so an empty water bottle was set in the trail. If the bottle was upright, the loo was available, if on its side, *ocupado.*

Throughout the bustling and munching, the coming and going, Holden and Oscar sat huddled in conversation. If asked a direct question or detecting a need of a team member, they would break from their tête-à-tête, only to return to it the moment they were no longer wanted. They spoke so quietly Anna couldn't discern individual words. She didn't have to. She knew as surely as if she sat with them that they were rigging and rerigging the traverse, mentally stalking around the anchor boulder, asking each other if they could have seen something that signaled instability, if they'd missed a tell-tale sign that might have saved Frieda's life. Unless cause and effect were established, this was a conversation Holden Tillman was going to have with himself for many years to come.

Finally, tucked in close as sardines in a can, the cavers bedded down. Anna was sandwiched between Curt Schatz and Lisa. Where she would have expected a deepening of claustrophobia, she found comfort. Lamps were extinguished. Before the heavy night of the underground could oppress, Zeddie began to sing. Her rich alto reverberated from the stone and filled all the cracks and crevices with humanity, pushing back the unforgiving dark. A truth Anna had long suspected was ratified: we are one another's angels. No unearthly sound could have been so glorious.

"Life is like a mountain railroad with an engineer that's brave. We must make the run successful from the cradle to the grave," soared through their miserable night, powered by notes of youth, tones of raw faith in the inherent goodness of existence. Old-time gospel had a healing power bloodless intellectual faith could not lay claim to.

Sleep came before the song ended, not in the pleasant drift Anna was accustomed to, but with the suddenness of a trapdoor falling shut. Deep and dreamless, a little death, it held her paralyzed for a time, then loosed her into the conscious world as rudely as it had snatched her from it.

In an instant she was hideously awake, clawing at the air above in a vain attempt to rip away the suffocating tonnage of bedrock. Her heart pounded and her breath came in staccato gasps. A light, she needed a light in order to breathe. Elbowing her companions, she dug into her pockets for the little Maglite she had rescued from her pack.

A heavy hand closed on her shoulder, the weight of an arm was laid across her chest. "Anna, it's Curt," came a whisper in her ear. "Are you okay? Do you know where you are?"

Whether it was the human contact or the fact her fingers closed around the shaft of the Maglite, she wasn't sure, but the panic ebbed slightly.

"The twilight zone?" she whispered back.

He must have smiled; she felt his beard tickle her cheek. "Do you have to go to the bathroom? Do you want a drink of water?"

Reassured by the childhood litany, Anna breathed out slowly. "I'm old enough to be your mother," she said to cover the fact his simple stratagem was working.

"You're old enough to be my sister," he corrected her. "I always thought she was pretty hot stuff. If you let me watch you put on your makeup, I'll be your slave."

"Believe it or not, I've been known to wear it." Lipstick and perfume seemed far away, artifacts from a past life. Reflexively she raised her hand to touch her face, count the creases time had carved there. A furry brush stroked her cheek, and she realized she clutched a feathery rope-end in her fist, caught up, no doubt, in her scrabble from sleep. It took a second to figure out where she'd come by such an oddment. It was the end of one of Lisa's braids. Stealthily, though the darkness had masked her thievery, Anna put the pigtail back on its owner's chest.

Rolling onto her shoulder, she groaned as the bruised flesh reminded her of her transgressions.

"If I let you use me as a pillow will you stop squirming and go back to sleep?" Curt whispered.

"I'll try," Anna promised.

Schatz raised his arm so she could move onto her uninjured side and rest her head on his shoulder. Anna didn't know if he was a Boy Scout, an opportunist, or a friend when she needed one. She didn't much care. His warmth brought her courage, the sound of his heart beating soothed her like the ticking of a clock is said to soothe orphaned puppies.

Curt's breathing evened out, but sleep refused to return for Anna. Shielding the glow so it wouldn't disturb her bedmates, Anna flicked on the Mag. Brent was missing, and down the stoop-walk corridor to the rift she could see the water bottle in the "occupied" position. Even the time-honored remedy for insomnia of going to the bathroom and getting a snack was denied her.

Encased in perfect darkness the meager brilliance of her covered light showed everything clearly. Pressed between Lisa and Holden, Peter lay next to Zeddie. Like she and Curt, they'd found a degree of solace in each other's arms. Zeddie's head nestled in the crook of Peter's neck. His arm and one knee were thrown across her body. The embrace looked practiced; there was an ease of familiarity in the intimacy. Embarrassed, Anna turned off the light. She remembered Sondra's accusations. "Everybody's laughing themselves sick at my expense," Sondra had said, and, "Is there anything you wouldn't do to make yourself necessary to women?" That smacked of a fight over infidelity. Peter had said something about Frieda, then Sondra said, "Maybe I wasn't talking about Frieda." Zeddie. She'd been talking about Zeddie.

Homicide by avalanche struck Anna as a little over the top to get time alone with one's inamorata, but if avoiding an ugly divorce was thrown in as an added inducement it might tip the scales.

The absurdity hit Anna with its obvious counterpart. Peter wasn't the one with something to gain in the rockfall. Sondra said she was going ahead. As far as they knew, she was the last to head up for the Distributor Cap. An avalanche had started. She was out free. Her husband and his lover were trapped, possibly dead.

Holy smoke, Anna thought, consciously using one of the newly proffered cowboy curses. Following this epiphany was a wave of white-hot fury that shook her so hard she clenched her fists in Schatz's shirt and he swatted at her like a man conditioned to sleeping with pesky felines. An act of God or Mother Nature, Anna would accept. The deadly conniving of her fellow man, never. She could live with the fact that Frieda had lost her life, but not that she'd been robbed of it. Holden was not the only one anxious to know just what had caused the avalanche.

In a perverse way, Anna hoped it was Sondra. Unless she wanted to spend the rest of her days in jail, she would have to forgo the pleasure of wringing Sondra's neck but, given the mood she was in, it would feel good to knock her around a bit. Surely a jury would allow her that. After Lechuguilla, a plea of temporary insanity would sound not only believable but probably downright conservative.

Fantasies of revenge did what counting sheep could not. When next Anna stirred, the others were up and moving. Curt had slipped his bulk from under her and left a cold place at her side. Lying on the dirt floor of the cave, letting the pain of her shoulder bring her slowly into the new "day," she thought about how long it had been since she'd slept curled in a man's arms. More than a year. Two summers before, a long-distance affair with an FBI agent had dribbled unspectacularly to a close. On some level, Anna had known it was for the best—too many old wounds on both sides—but she'd never properly laid the affair to rest. Except for the final good-bye over the phone she'd not seen or heard from Frederick again. It was as if they'd never happened. Even her sister, Molly, wasn't keen to talk about it. That was where Anna might have found what the modern how-to books were calling closure. Without being able to talk a thing to death with her sister, it was hard to truly put it to bed.

The pure, unadulterated male warmth of Curt's expedient embrace had awakened dormant memories. Anna groaned and piled her aching self into a sitting position. As near as she could figure, it had been approximately ten thousand years since she'd last seen the sun. Her love life was the least of her worries.

Holden was already up. Flashlights were set butt-down on the cave floor, forming a makeshift campfire. The dark held few terrors for Tillman; he traded batteries for morale. Anna looked at her watch. They'd slept seven hours. Tillman looked as if he had never closed his eyes, and when he spoke it was a cross between a rasp and a whisper. Stress and the injury to his ankle were costing him. Running on empty, Anna noted, or close to it. The idea alarmed her. She'd worked with guys like Holden before. They'd literally work till they dropped in the traces.

We'll be out of here before then, she promised herself. Then she remembered she had a gift for Holden: Sondra McCarty. She would tell him of the suspicions Frieda had had, of her own. If she could prove his choice of anchors hadn't killed Frieda, she knew a weight the immensity of which she could only guess at would be lifted from him. Even if Sondra was innocent, Anna would gladly throw her to the wolves for Tillman's peace of mind.

Opportunity didn't knock for several hours. Tapping what had to be toxic doses of instant coffee crystals into his lower lip, Holden kept the team together and working. Camp was cleaned and the logistics of what had now become a body recovery were hammered out. The traverse was rerigged using the bridge as an anchor. Because of Holden's own decency and the sensibilities he granted those around him, Frieda's remains were handled as if they still housed her soul. Delicacy was the respect the living paid the dead and the respect Tillman showed the cavers who had known Frieda.

Anna considered herself to be of the "lights out" persuasion; life is there, then it's gone, as if a switch was flipped. No afterlife, no hauntings, nothing. Here today, gone tomorrow. Regardless of this cherished hardness of heart, she was touched by the care shown the corpse. It allowed her to hold Frieda close a few hours longer if only in tending a home her friend had long since abandoned.

Taking landmarks from earlier surveys and comparing those measurements with the measurements of the newly existing gout of debris, Holden was estimating the thickness of the slide. Ten hours had passed since the rock had fallen. From his calculations and the sounds from the far side, he predicted it would be less than an hour before the rescuers broke through. As soon as Frieda was retrieved from the bottom of the Pigtail, he would detail three people to dig toward them. More than three could become a danger to one another.

Suggesting he rest his broken ankle got Anna nowhere. To slow him down enough so she could tell her story, she had to appeal to his gallantry. She didn't need to feign fatigue, merely to capitalize on it. Sitting on the bridge, feet dangling over the abyss, she told him everything. Reproach pulled down his mouth and her heart, but she refused to justify herself for keeping silent about their suspicions. The decision had been Frieda's. Had the situation been reversed, she would have wanted her wishes respected.

"You think the doctor's wife might have started the slide?" he asked after she'd finished.

"It crossed my mind."

"How do you figure she did it?"

"Pried out a key rock," Anna suggested. "A rock other rocks hinged on."

Holden thought about that for a while, then shook his head. "Pried with what? We didn't come equipped with shovels or crowbars. A spoon handle is about the biggest lever she could have gotten her hands on."

Anna didn't say anything. She hadn't thought of that. "Maybe she started it from above the entrance to the Distributor Cap, at the apex of the slide area. Pushed something."

"I don't see how she could have started it, then gotten below it to safety in the Cap."

"Maybe she's buried underneath."

Holden nodded slowly. He was too generous to admit that murder, the disintegration of a marriage, were more appealing than the idea that he'd screwed up and lost a patient, but Anna could see the concept growing on him.

"Well, you know, I could have sworn that anchor was bombproof," he said finally.

She waited.

"Okay. You check it out. With this bum ankle I'm likely to stir up too much trouble. Be careful. Test every step before you trust it. I'll keep folks clear till you get back. Then we dig."

Anna left before he could change his mind.

The slide was comprised of loam as fine as ash, and rocks with unblunted edges. For each step up she slid half a step back. Dust boiled from under her boots and hands, and she could hear the steady rain of dirt and debris from below. The slide had wiped clean all trace of human passage. Orange tape, footprints, everything was buried. Anna crawled on, wondering just what it was she hoped to find. Instead of cluttering her mind with what-ifs, she opened her eyes to let any and all information register.

The slide narrowed near the top in an abbreviated cone of loose rubble about twenty feet across. If anything remained to indicate cause, it would be here. Anna stopped, turned, and planted her rump in the soft soil to slow her heart and still her mind before she began tainting the scene with her presence.

"Got something?" Holden called.

"Just catching my breath." From her vantage point she could see the length of the Pigtail. Dust had been carried away on Lechuguilla's air currents, and the helmet lights of the cavers working on the body recovery moved and winked like fireflies. In a different context Anna might have found it beautiful. At present it served only to remind her how much she'd give for one more glimpse of a summer's night.

The last few feet of the climb were the hardest. The way grew increasingly steep and the cushion of soil thinner at each step. Bracing toes and knees in the dirt, she shined her light along the uneven curtain of new-fallen silt. The dirt was uniformly smooth, packed down slightly at one place where it ran the thinnest. No scars indicated rock had been scratched or pried.

"Anything?"

"Looking," she hollered.

"Come on down. From the sound of things we're going to have company real soon." Holden's voice had gone utterly flat. The small spark that hope of a reprieve had ignited within him had gone out.

"In a minute." Anna was determined to find something.

"Make it short."

Anna moved her light across the wall again, but nothing new was revealed. The pitter-patter of earthen rain grew louder.

"Anna. Now."

Loath to give up, she pushed her luck for half a minute more but was none the wiser for it. Before Holden had to embarrass them both by yelling at her a third time, she turned to skitter down. Her light fell on the spot where she'd sat admiring Lucifer's fireflies. In the soft loam was a smooth-packed place, a perfect butt-print in the silt.

"Got it," Anna shouted. "Ten seconds more." Forgetting she could start another slide, she crawled quickly back up the slope. It was there; the slightly smooth, lightly packed place near the center. Knowing she was onto something she risked the slide potential of the last few feet and pushed herself up near the top of the fall. A butt-print remained where someone had sat, braced their back against the wall, and shoved with their feet. In the fragile drift of fine sand she could make out wrinkles in the fabric and the line of a seam on a rear pocket.

"Anna!" Below her the dirt was beginning to shift, she was being pulled down. She knew if she fought it she would start another slide that would take her and Lord knew how many pounds of dirt down onto the heads of their saviors.

Before her eyes the print was vanishing, eaten away as a footprint on the beach is drawn into the sea by the waves.

"Coming," she hollered, and turned to slide down on fanny and heels, oblivious to the sharp-edged fragments of limestone that tore at her trousers and arms.

Someone had been up there, probably had started the slide. Anna must cling to that. With the dark and the dust, the evidence drained into dirt, it could so easily seem a figment of her imagination.

She would keep it real for herself, for Holden, for Frieda. And she would find who'd made the mark if she had to examine every posterior in New Mexico.

10

THE NEXT SEVEN hours passed like a fever dream.
With Frieda dead, Anna felt no compunction about rotating
out. She climbed, crawled, and crept, a zombie clawing her
way from the grave. Under protest but accepting the inevitable, Holden went out with her. Brent, too, took the opportunity to escape. Oscar, Peter, Curt, and Zeddie chose to
remain with the new team and continue the body recovery.

The closer they got to the entrance of Lechuguilla the
more desperate Anna became to get out. Emotions, long
held in tight rein, began to break their bonds. Claustrophobia returned in force, and she chafed and sweated at each
delay. Only the ominous threat of appearing a fool or a
blackguard kept her from abandoning Holden and the others to bolt for the surface. By the time they reached the
culvert that would release them into the confines of Old
Misery Pit, waiting her turn to ascend she had to count in
Spanish and recite poems to hold on to the ragged edge of
patience. At last the iron trapdoor was closed behind her,
and she could smell the world, cold and dry with a faint

perfume of desert plants. Ascending the last sixty feet to the surface, she forgot the steady ache from her shoulder in unadulterated joy. Even the dirt smelled alive. Gone was the dank sepulchral odor of soil unblessed by life or light. When she saw her first stars, she croaked out her delight from tired lungs. Night, real honest-to-God night, with planets and dead suns, clouds and breezes. After so long a sojourn underground, even the moonless sky appeared bright and welcoming.

The glare and hubbub that awaited as she climbed into the narrow oak-filled gap protecting the cave's entrance was overwhelming. In anticipation of a heartwarming celebration of heroism and perseverance, a great crowd had gathered. News media from all over the country were there with harsh lights and makeup to herald the triumphant return. The news that Frieda died had surfaced only moments before Anna, and the party was in a confusion of changing gears, rewriting copy.

Nobody wanted to be left out of the limelight; all the NPS brass was in attendance: CACA's superintendent, the head of resource management, the chief ranger, a sprinkling of bigwigs from Guadalupe Mountains, an hour to the west. A tent had been set up for the rescuers, both those going and those returning. Beer and pizza had been hauled out onto the desert hillside.

Anna survived a grueling gauntlet of questions, condolences, and congratulations as she stumbled over the uneven ground toward the tent, where she hoped to hide. As a little fish, she gauged she should be able to slip through the net of cameras and well-wishers without too much difficulty. Not so Holden. Notoriety and a crippled ankle made him an easy target. The last Anna saw of him, he was pinned down by hot lights and microphones. Though sympathetic, she had to laugh. The man was worn out, his mind turned to putty, as was hers. Floodlights had brought down a host of moths, and as the news anchor asked deep and meaningful questions, Holden's eyes flitted here and there following the flying insects. He looked less like a hero than a complete lunatic. Anna hoped somebody with a VCR was taping the interview. When he'd recovered, she suspected he would enjoy the joke. Any laughter they could glean from this debacle was to be treasured.

The cavers' tent, probably borrowed from CACA's fire cache, was a twenty-by-twenty-foot canvas shelter with flaps that opened at either end. Free of media types and, no doubt because of that, free of brass, the welcome was low key. No amount of hype could seduce them from the single fact that they had gone in to save a fellow caver and they had failed. Anna was hugged by strangers, some smelling nearly as bad as she did; kind words were murmured and a cold beer was pressed into her hands. They seemed to understand that she could not talk and could not stay. No overbearing do-gooder tried to stop her when she slipped out of the rear of the tent.

The December air was cold on her arms and back. Clad only in tee-shirt and trousers—and those soaked with sweat—she emerged into a winter night, forty-five degrees at best, with a slight wind. Sweat turned to icy patches on her shirt, and the hair on her arms was raised by goose-bumps. Anna revelled in it. Intellectually, she knew the honeymoon would be short-lived, but at the moment she felt she would never again resent the cold of the wind or the heat of the sun. So long as she could feel it, it would remind her that she was alive and aboveground.

When she'd gone far enough she could still see yet was hidden by the night from prying eyes, she sat down with her back to a small boulder weathered into a thousand tiny crevices, potential homes for all manner of beasties that might be attracted by her warmth: snakes, scorpions, tarantulas, centipedes, lizards. In her exalted state, Anna welcomed them all. Like some deviant Disney heroine, she would spread her metaphorical skirts for all the stinging, biting, scaly creatures of the world. She smiled at the thought of waltzing with a horned lizard to the plaintive strains of "Someday My Prince Will Come," a bevy of mud wasps holding up the gossamer train of her soiled tee-shirt.

Numbness in her fingers reminded her she still clutched a beer. Years had passed since she'd given up the stuff. Not a drop had crossed her lips since the first summer she'd worked at Mesa Verde. Visions of blackouts and delirium tremens and inappropriate remarks had kept her sober.

Deliberately, she took a long drink. It wasn't as good as she remembered it, but then little was. She caught herself in that thought and was ashamed. Cynicism was okay, bitterness a pain in the neck. The hairline difference between the two was hope and humor. The cynic had both, the embittered, nothing. She took another drink and enjoyed the sensation of alcohol and rebellion. Eventually she would have to confess to Molly. The whole point of being a recovering alcoholic was making sure there was a healthy dose of guilt and the catharsis of confession as a chaser for each drink. But for tonight none of that could touch her. She felt as if she'd squirmed out of the ground into a world where she was only partially committed, as if she were a ghost or the invisible woman. Shock might have explained the sense of detachment, but, as it was not altogether unpleasant, she chose not to question it.

Despite Anna's rebirth on this higher plane, the cold was beginning to seep through the seat of her trousers, penetrate beneath the wet patches on her shirt. Soon she'd have to go back. Freezing to death ten yards from the tent would be humiliating to say the least.

Till I finish the beer, she told herself, and stayed where she was, watching the drama under the lights unfold. Mouthing lines she could not hear, people three inches tall, as measured between thumb and forefinger, marched about in a purposeful manner getting absolutely nowhere. George Laymon, CACA's resource management specialist, pushed his way into the camera's frame between Holden and Brent for his moment of fame, then was hustled offstage with the geologist. The superintendent, resplendent as was Laymon in a Class-A dress uniform, joined them momentarily. Brent was released, and the two National Park Service men gravitated back toward the limelight.

Brent bobbed this way and that, a man who had no place to go yet could not decide which direction would get him there the fastest. Suddenly his head jerked up, and the indecision left him. Anna watched as he walked, then ran, into the darkness beyond the floods. A minute later he reappeared, his fretful face transformed, almost handsome. In the crook of each arm he carried a little girl. The children were two or three years old. They were dressed identically in frilly pink dresses, white tights, tiny red cowboy boots, and little blue parkas with the pointiest hoods Anna'd seen this side of the Macy's Thanksgiving Day parade. Twins, she guessed, probably Roxbury's daughters by the way they clung and chattered and he laughed and nuzzled. A fourth member of the party dragged out of the shadows. Mrs. Roxbury, Anna presumed. She didn't seem to share the children's rejoicing in their father's safe return from the depths. Possibly she hung back only to give them their moment together.

The beer was gone; hypothermia was just around the corner. Time to go back. It was all Anna could do to rise from the ground, and that wasn't accomplished in one fluid motion but in a series of grunting stages from fanny to knees, knees to feet. With cold and inaction her muscles had shut down. She was so stiff it surprised her she didn't creak like a rusty gate at every move.

A bath. The concept gave her renewed strength. Now that she'd joined the ranks of the topsiders such luxuries were not unheard of. With this in mind she limped more or less cheerfully back toward the milling humanity.

Each and every wish of Anna's had come true. Zeddie's house had been given to her with Zeddie's permission granted over the newly functioning field phone. There was a bath, solitude, beer in the refrigerator. Even a cat, a sleek white female with a gray saddle and ears so pink they were translucent. Calcite, she'd been told, was the cat's name.

Anna had soaked till her skin shriveled, quaffed a second beer, and now sat on the sofa cocooned in Zeddie's sweatpants and hooded sweatshirt. The Austin Lounge Lizards poured forth musical nostalgia from an environmental movement that was over before Zeddie had graduated from high school. All was as it should be, yet Anna could not shake a restlessness so close to the bone her wiggling and twitching had alienated the cat. Despite overtired muscles, Anna wandered from room to room, stopping to stare out windows, gaze into the refrigerator, read the spines of books. More than once she braved the dropping temperature and padded onto the back patio in stockinged feet to look over the starlit expanse of the ancient reef and imagine, below it, the struggling forms of Oscar, Curt, and Zeddie, carrying Frieda's remains through dark and twisting channels.

Shortly before the ten o'clock news, she devolved from stalking to outright snooping. Access with permission and no supervision to the home of one of the five people who could have had a hand—or a butt—in Frieda's demise: this was opportunity knocking loud and clear. Anna would have been a fool to ignore it. Or so she told herself as she poked through her generous hostess's private things.

The photos weren't hidden away like a dirty secret but proudly displayed on bedside table and mantel: Zeddie and Peter McCarty grinning out from hot-colored Polartec pullovers on a ski slope. Zeddie in back of Peter hugging his neck, her chin on his shoulder, behind them autumn leaves vivid and plentiful—St. Paul, most likely.

Did this flaunting of an adulterous relationship indicate that Zeddie knew it would soon be on the road to legit? Did she hope Mrs. McCarty might drop by to borrow a cup of carabiners, see the pictures, and run screaming for a divorce lawyer? Was it indicative of a sixties-like scorn for traditional values in keeping with Ms. Dillard's nuevo-hippie armpit hair? Or was it as simple as a girl wanting to show off her boyfriend and trusting that a twelve-hundred-mile separation from his significant other would keep her from getting caught?

The skiing picture was several years old, judging by the length of Zeddie's hair, a good six to eight inches shorter than she wore it now. The autumn leaves shot was more recent, not last autumn but this one. Zeddie had been with McCarty before and during his marriage. It wasn't unlikely she had plans to be around after. Would those plans include pushing several dump trucks' worth of dirt down on his bride? Earlier suspicions to the contrary, Sondra McCarty was nowhere to be found, and Zeddie had spent the night in her husband's arms. If Sondra had counted on the rock slide to solve her marital woes, she'd been sorely disappointed. Zeddie, on the other hand, had come out smelling like a rose.

Experience told Anna the odds against two unrelated murder plots hatched in a small space and over a short period of time were astronomical. Going on the assumption Frieda had been correct, and someone had pushed a rock down on her, then statistics dictated Frieda was the one and only target both times.

Unless Zeddie thought Sondra was down in the hole when she shoved the rock. Unless Sondra thought it was Zeddie when *she* pushed the rock. In the perilous midnight of a cave, a case of mistaken identity wasn't too far-fetched. But the second time someone had actually died: Frieda. Coincidence? Luck of the draw? Frieda and Anna had been easily the most vulnerable. Could the pusher-of-stones have been so cold as to write off extraneous casualties as the cost of doing business?

The mechanism of the crimes carried with it no gender connotations. Opportunistic, unprofessional sabotage—possibly even spur of the moment—was as likely to be attempted by a woman as a man. Like poison, it wasn't hands-on violence. If one was agile, no blood need spatter on one's person.

Circular thinking; it tired Anna and she shelved the line of thought for the time being.

Other than the photos, she found little of interest. Zeddie had submerged herself more or less completely into the NPS lifestyle. Wall pictures were of wilderness views and sports, magazines focused on wildlife and land management issues. Anna did find one outdated *Allure* stuffed down behind the toilet like a shameful bit of pornography. Even the most stalwart feminist was entitled to the occasional slip into girlishness.

She was back out on the patio, basking in the light from the stars and ignoring the increasing cold when the telephone began ringing. Though she'd spent less than forty-eight hours buried in Lechuguilla, the things of the world had become alien to her. The phone bell jarred, a mildly upsetting intrusion that had little to do with her. Any moment now the caller would hang up or the machine would answer. She turned back to the desert, a breathtaking vista separated from her only by a low cinder-block wall. Zeddie's house was on a rise; her patio looked down over the Carlsbad complex, across miles of silvered desert to the shadowy beak of El Capitan, forty miles away in Texas.

The ringing continued. Anna cursed Zeddie's fundamentalism. Even Ed Abbey would have an answering machine, for Christ's sake. Stomping back into the house, she snatched the receiver from the cradle.

"Yeah?" Phone etiquette had deserted her.

"Anna?"

It had never crossed her mind that the call might be for her. Staying in another woman's house in another woman's park, she'd felt as isolated as if she'd borrowed a condo on Pluto.

"This is she," she said formally, phone etiquette returning with a vengeance. "May I ask who is calling?"

"It's Frederick."

Anna said nothing, both the English and the Spanish languages gone from her head.

"Frederick Stanton?" she blurted out after a painfully long silence.

"Come on, Anna, it hasn't been that long." His voice was rich with intimacy and humor.

Hers wasn't. "It has." Excitement, the sick variety, wallowed in her belly, mixing with anxiety, embarrassment, and cheap beer.

"I guess it has," he admitted, and she relaxed a degree or two. She knew she was spoiling for a fight: with him, with Mother Teresa, with anybody. This conversation was a tightrope she must walk, a high wire between the maudlin and the shrewish. Unarmed, in a stranger's sweats, she felt unequal to the task. She felt unequal to anything but a cup of cocoa and a Perry Mason rerun.

Groping for a neutral remark, she said, "How did you find me?"

"I'm the FBI guy, remember?"

"It's coming back to me." Self-preservation kept her from saying anything more.

"You were on the news," he said. "Coming out of that cave. They said Frieda didn't survive."

Anna had forgotten that Frederick had met Frieda the summer they worked a case together in Mesa Verde. A couple of emotions did brief battle with her. Guilt because he was a fellow mourner, and anger that he, who scarcely knew Frieda, had the unmitigated gall to presume on his brief acquaintance to reach out and touch Anna in her hiding place.

Guilt won. It was amazing that a Methodist childhood could be so completely eclipsed by four years at a Catholic high school.

"The anchor we'd tied into gave out. Frieda and I fell thirty feet. I landed on top of her, my knee on her windpipe. My weight crushed her larynx. Either she suffocated or I snapped her spine." Anna heard herself, angry and cruel, and knew she lashed out at both of them. Herself for the deed, and Frederick for not loving Frieda sufficiently in the brief time he'd known her.

"Do you want me to beat you up about it?" he asked calmly.

That was a shrink question, a Molly question. Guilt vanished to be replaced by tears. Anger was still very much extant.

Anna took a deep pull on the beer she'd carried in with her. The problem wasn't that she'd consumed alcohol after abstaining so long, but that she hadn't consumed enough. *Alcoholic thinking,* came the words of a mentor she'd lost contact with. *Eat my shorts,* she told the memory, borrowing an epithet from Holden's accepted vocabulary list.

"I've had a real bad day," she said, and laughed. Laughter turned to tears. She hid them with silence. Zach, her husband, lover, soulmate, so many years dead she'd almost managed to lose count, would have known why that was funny. 1988, Broadway, *Crimes of the Heart.* Mom hanged herself in the cellar, along with the family cat. Why? She'd had a real bad day.

Feeling doomed to a lifetime of loneliness, Anna sucked down another draught of beer. Mentally, she removed a cold chisel from an imaginary toolbox. With it she chipped the tears from her face and voice.

"Thanks for calling, Frederick," she said evenly, and was rewarded by a brief frisson of pride. "I didn't know I'd made the news. I'd better call Molly and let her know I'm okay."

A silence followed, one so awkward that even through the miasma of alcohol and weirdness Anna generated, unspoken messages pounded like invisible radio waves.

"I've already called her," Frederick said, his voice curiously devoid of expression.

At the time Anna had sensed there was something bizarre about the end of her and Frederick's relationship. Anna was snapped back two years, held in the time warp of flashback. At her request Frederick had traveled to New York City to help her sister with a series of threatening letters. That was when things had gotten strange.

With the impact of an Old Testament revelation, Anna knew: Frederick had had an affair with Molly.

The knowledge, accurate or not, broke on her consciousness with the force of lightning. A pit beside which Lechuguilla paled opened in Anna's befuddled mind. The least breath of air would topple her into it. A vision of her sister's face dropped like a lifeline, and Anna grabbed on to it. Molly could be—indeed had been—trusted with Anna's life. A cornea, a kidney, a loan, a place to sleep; if Anna needed it, Molly would provide it. Were there a single drop of water in the Sahara, a last bite of ankle bone among the Donner party, Molly would give it to Anna. She knew this the way she knew her heart pumped blood.

Had Frederick Stanton been the proverbial last man on earth and Molly the recipient of the last fabled Spanish fly, there wouldn't have been an affair.

The pit closed. Sanity resurfaced.

"And?" Anna said.

"She wasn't home," Frederick admitted.

Of course she was home. It was 11:40 P.M. New York time on a Tuesday night. Molly was drinking Scotch and watching Leno. She was a woman of regular habits. Nothing short of a patient crisis or a seventy-five-percent-off sale at Bergdorf Goodman could lure her out from one of her sacred "at home" nights. She'd refused to pick up. She'd probably refused to pick up for two years.

"She'll be home for me," Anna said unkindly, and, "Thanks for calling." As a courtesy, she let him say good-bye and hang up first.

Three times she tried to dial Molly. On the third attempt her fumbling fingers pushed all the right numbers. As expected, the machine answered.

"It's me, Anna."

A clatter of plastic followed as Anna's older sister grabbed up the phone.

"Anna. Thank God."

"I've been drinking," Anna said. It was the last piece of information she'd intended to communicate that night.

"It happens," Molly said.

"And thinking about Zach."

"Oh, my. Sounds like you've had a *real* bad day."

Not alone, Anna thought. Not alone at all.

11

HER PART IN the rescue at an end, Anna had no business remaining at Carlsbad Caverns and no intention of returning to Mesa Verde until she had unraveled what had happened to Frieda. At best guess the body recovery would take another twelve to twenty-four hours. Till then she had a place to stay. Pleading injury, exhaustion, and all manner of unprovable but debilitating ills, she'd asked for and received sick leave. Hills Dutton, her district ranger—indeed, all the staff at Mesa Verde—was reeling from Frieda's death. Winter was the slow season, and Anna was not really needed. She could easily beg a week or more and get it.

Beer and bruises had given her a fitful night's sleep. Thrashing around in Zeddie's down comforter, she stalked and was stalked by killers of all stripes. More than once she woke up in a panic, fighting a ceiling of stone that was no longer there. Around three in the morning she'd dragged her bedding out onto the back patio to feel the reassuring cold of starlight on her skin as she slept. When day finally dawned she was relieved, if not rested.

Between her first cup of coffee and her morning shower she formulated a modest plan. Or the first stumbling steps of a plan. Sondra needed to be tracked down, information on the other members of the team to be ferreted out. Bundled up in a sweater of Zeddie's and a battered leather jacket she'd inherited when Zachary died, she walked from the housing area to the cluster of neat stone buildings that housed Carlsbad's administrative offices.

Clouds hung heavy over the desert, adding a pervasive damp to winter's chill, dulling the light of the sun to a gray throb in the south. To Anna the day was made beautiful by its mere existence. Cold embraced and invigorated her. A sharp wind from the northwest reminded her how magnificently alive even this barren chunk of earth was. Down a steep slope from the cave resource building where she'd originally been assigned to man the telephones were the offices of George Laymon and the superintendent. Anna hoped for a low-profile schmooze with the secretaries. In a park as small and isolated as Carlsbad Caverns there would be few secrets. Whose car was parked too long in front of whose home, who drank and, perhaps more damningly, who didn't, would be common knowledge. It seemed as good a place as any to begin.

That assumption couldn't have been more wrong. Once in the door she was caught up in the machinery of government.

In the wake of the failed rescue attempt and the blaring media coverage, administration was buzzing with activity. Each decision would be reviewed, all plans reconsidered in a new light that would change as the political winds changed. Blame might be assigned, selected heads might roll but, most important, a dense layer of paper would be generated. Like a frightened squid obscuring the past with ink, the NPS would muffle the incident in memos, reports, and revised operating procedures.

As Anna walked in the door, Jewel, George Laymon's secretary, said, "Just the person I was looking for." Never a good sign. "George wants to talk to you. He's in with Brent, but they should be pretty close to done."

The implication that Anna would, of course, sit and wait docilely till summoned was strong. At an early age a serious streak of contrariness had been discovered in Anna. The only two stickers she'd ever considered slathering on her Rambler's bumper read "God Bless John Wayne" and "Question Authority." Today she chose not to rise to the occasion. Claiming a folding chair near Jewel's desk, she sat and composed her face along cooperative lines.

Jewel was a stocky woman in her early thirties with an abundance of black hair curling down her back to bra-fastener level. Not a glint of a shine escaped the careful tangle of curls, not a thread of gray or red or brown. The hair was black as construction paper, flat and rough. Bangs and sides were cut short and teased high on the crown. Hair was molded into flying wings above each ear with industrial-strength hair spray. From the front the coif looked big, a lion's mane. From the side the effect was lost. The volume was two-dimensional; the popular style always made Anna think of the false fronts on buildings along movie Main Streets of the Old West.

"What's up?" she asked in hopes of opening channels of communication.

The secretary was more interested in her computer screen than in gossiping with Anna. "Debriefing," she said without bothering to turn around.

"Critical incident stress debriefing?"

"Something like that."

After incidents in which rangers were exposed to unusually stressful situations—the death of children or fellow employees, long rescues in which the victim died, or messy accidents with burned or mutilated bodies—the National Park Service had instituted debriefing sessions, times when the rangers involved could theoretically come to terms with their own personal trauma. Undoubtedly the idea was a sound one, but Anna'd never been to a session that proved helpful. It's just me, she thought, not for the first time.

She eyed Laymon's office door suspiciously. Jewel had just said Brent, not a whole host of cavers. One-on-one was unusual unless it was with a bona fide psychologist. Laypeople trained to run the sessions always had all the participants in at the same time. Part of the therapy: sharing fears, inadequacies, strengths. Coming to know you weren't alone, that the bizarre things that passed through your mind weren't an indication of a character flaw. She turned her attention back to the secretary.

Jewel typed like a fury, stiffened tresses quivering with the impact of lacquered nails on the keyboard.

The office was cold and boring. Anna squirmed around, but comfort on a metal folding chair was elusive. "I thought it would be a group thing," she said, hoping Jewel would relent and amuse her.

"Nope." Jewel typed on.

There were no magazines to be seen. Anna's shoulder began to ache. She laid her injured limb along the edge of the secretary's desk.

"Do you happen to know where Sondra McCarty is? Peter McCarty's wife?" Anna asked.

"All nonessential personnel have been demobbed."

For all the expression Jewel put into the practiced words, she could have been one of those dolls with a ring in its back one pulled to make it talk.

"She's a civilian. Peter asked me to check on her," Anna lied.

"Packed and gone."

A punch, a poke, and paper was sucked into the printer next to Jewel's elbow. Still she typed; she didn't miss a beat. Anna didn't think anyone outside the confines of the big city could type that fast. It was a talent best kept under wraps in the Park Service, or ham-handed rangers would endlessly be pestering one to type up their reports. Probably not an issue; Jewel looked pesterproof.

"Are you sure Sondra's gone?" Anna asked, testing the theory.

Flying fingers stopped midword and began a slow drum. Not pesterproof. Jewel screwed her chair around till she was facing her desk—not all the way around to face Anna, that would have constituted too great a commitment.

"Absolutely positive." She whipped a pile from her "out" basket and, dabbing the pad of her index finger into a little pot of waxy stuff, flipped through it quickly, keeping her fingers stiff so the acrylic of her nails would not be compromised.

"Packed and gone," she repeated with satisfaction, and shoved a list in Anna's direction. "She was given a ride down to the airport yesterday with some other guys. Guess she couldn't wait for her husband to come out."

A note of humanity crept into Jewel's voice, suggesting she would have waited for a husband until hell froze over.

"Good job, Brent, I mean that. Hang tough." The words wafted from Laymon's office as he pushed the door open to usher the geologist out.

Brent mumbled something. He looked bad. Pale and unshaven, the haggard eyes of a man who'd been sleeping badly. Anna guessed she didn't look so hot herself.

"Is Holden here yet?" Laymon asked Jewel. Anna could tell he'd seen her. Draped as she was over the end of his secretary's desk, it would have been impossible not to. He chose to pretend he didn't. A man who liked to deal with one thing at a time.

"He can't come in," Jewel told her boss. She didn't look at him, but turned back to the computer screen. Her fingers rested on the keys, but she was neither reading nor typing. The screen had gone blank. She either had lost her text or had touched a magic computer hide-it button.

Laymon wasn't in the mood to take no for an answer. "Did he call? I told you to interrupt me if he called."

"His wife, she tol' me he gotta go to the doctor's about his foot."

Jewel's articulation, her posture, her vocabulary, all were disintegrating under Laymon's disapproval. Anna wondered if it was personal or if the secretary habitually cowered in the glare of the opposite sex.

"I got Anna Pigeon," she said with the air of a shop-keeper offering inferior but available merchandise.

"Keep trying the Tillmans'," Laymon said. "Talk to the man himself, not his wife."

Only after this exchange had been completed and a nod of acquiescence wrung from Jewel's bowed neck did George Laymon officially "see" Anna.

"Good of you to come by," he said, managing to gather power unto himself by conferring obedience upon her.

"I just sort of wandered in," Anna said. "I wasn't aware there was a critical—"

"I appreciate your coming down so early," he said, and waved her into his office. Closing the door he winked con-spiratorially and shook his head. "For a woman who types that fast, Jewel doesn't seem to get a whole lot done. How're you doing?"

Laymon's attention, a focused beacon, lighted and warmed. Despite a natural aversion to being wooed by politicians, Anna had to admit the effect was flattering. Laymon ushered her gallantly—but ever so correctly, without a hint of condescension or sexism—to the single chair in his office. Padded, the seat and back covered with nubbly brown fabric, the visitor's chair, though significantly less grand, matched his desk chair. The desk matched a com-puter credenza behind it, against the windowed wall. The carpet was new, the potted plant in the corner alive. George Laymon obviously rated. Anna had been in superintendents' offices that weren't so well appointed.

Laymon didn't retreat behind the pseudomahogany of his desk but perched on the side, one haunch on the wood, one booted foot swinging free. He actually must have paid attention in those management classes the NPS was always shipping the higher-ups off to. Putting me at my ease, Anna thought. She decided if he crouched down to her level the way one was taught to interact with children, she was going to leave.

Laymon was a spectacularly average individual. Height, weight, color of hair and eyes: everything fell in the neutral zone. Because true average is a mathematical concept and not a class, he didn't vanish into the woodwork. Graying hair, good build, and regular features made him a handsome man. Anna guessed he was fifty-five or sixty, and had little doubt he could still have been quite the ladies' man but for one thing: he wasn't interested.

She wasn't vain enough to think because a man wasn't flashing lights and sounding sirens the minute she walked into a room he was gay or asexual. Laymon's lack of interest was beyond the personal and had nothing to do with the expected photo of the lovely wife and two appropriately scrubbed kids framed on the desktop. Anna guessed it was something harder to come by than sex or affection that fueled his inner fires. Imposing order. Maybe knowledge. Attributes that could make him good at his job. Controlled zealots were just the people needed for the daunting task of saving what was left of the environment.

"Brent sure looks like shit," Anna said, making conversation.

"Brent's taking this hard," Laymon told Anna. "He's a sensitive man. One of the things that makes him the best in his business. Attention to detail and a straight answer no matter who it costs. But he takes a lot on himself. He feels somehow responsible for Miss Dierkz's death."

Anna understood. After all, she was the one who had killed Frieda. "We all do," she said.

"It's to be expected. How are you doing?"

Anna gave him the short answer to that and several more questions designed to show her he was a caring administrator. Then he got down to the meat of his inquiry. Laymon had no interest in critical stress debriefing—there were procedures for that and they did not fall within his job description. What he wanted from Anna was a detailed account of his resource, Lechuguilla Cavern.

"I'm from the 'Show Me' state," Laymon said. Exactly what had she seen? How far had she explored the Paddock? What had others told her of holes blowing, going leads? Who carried the survey and the sketches? How clear was Lake Rapunzel? How deep the slide? How unstable the Pigtail?

Anna told him she was not the best person to ask. As a neophyte, a claustrophobe, and a close friend of the deceased, her powers of observation had been at a low ebb. Claiming to understand her limitations, he was still keen to hear her views, so she answered the questions as best she could. He pressed her for detail on Tinker's, Rapunzel, and the Pigtail—parts of the cave to which he had never been. Anna struggled to remember as much as she could and, in a childish desire to please, came close to making up answers—a human trait that made eyewitnesses so unreliable. Time after time she drew blanks and he pushed harder.

Laymon was digging in a vein that had been mined out in the first few minutes of their interview. She could tell he wanted more, but there wasn't any more she could give. It made her feel stupid. Stupid was turning to annoyed before he finally gave up.

Anna had said nothing about Frieda's death being not an accident but murder. In the light of day, she was unsure, hyperaware there was no hard evidence. In honor of Frieda, she had to try.

Clearly, Laymon felt the interview to be at an end. He stood. Anna kept her seat. "Frieda thought the rock was pushed on her. Not fell. Pushed."

The words out, she waited. Laymon looked blank, then, as the import struck, shock twisted his even features. Lines cut between his eyes and around his mouth. He sat down, this time in his official chair and in his official capacity.

Anna told her story. Laymon took notes and didn't interrupt. When she finished he stared for a time out his window.

"You realize how serious this is?"

She did.

"You've given us nothing to go on—not your fault," he added quickly. "Just the nature of the beast. Frieda was sure?"

Anna admitted she was not.

"And this print in the dirt, you're a hundred percent sure of that?"

Anna stuck to her guns. The butt-print was real.

The chief of resource management blew out a lungful of air and turned to face her squarely across the desk. "Holden is coming in later. I'll meet with him, the superintendent, and Oscar when he gets out of Lechuguilla. We'll take it from there."

"Thanks," Anna said, relieved to have passed the buck.

Now the interview was indeed over. Laymon rose and walked around his desk, nudging her toward the door with repeated thanks.

She managed one question of her own before it was closed between them.

"What next?" The question was purposefully vague. She wanted to take the temperature of resource management, to find out if Holden, Oscar, Zeddie, or anyone else was going to be targeted as scapegoat. Her cynicism was uncalled for. Laymon was thinking only of the cave. A rescue, even one as carefully orchestrated as Frieda's, could go sour. Despite Holden's care, damage had been done. Possibly irreparable damage. Even without the rock slide, that many people, that much equipment couldn't be dragged through the fragile and pristine underground without leaving a mark. Since there was no way of guaranteeing that cavers would not injure themselves, and since the American public would never condone the idea of a "no rescue" wilderness where visitors went in at their own risk to come out or die as the gods and their own skills decreed, the only way to protect the cave, at least this newest and most virginal part, was to close it off. Until a truly compelling reason to allow people in arose, the cave could rest. Unlike the surface of the earth it would not be able to regenerate, to cure the wounds they'd left behind—or not on a timeline short-lived humanity could appreciate—but further impact would be stopped.

That was fine by Anna. Holden would be miffed, and she could sympathize. Had Lassen Volcanic, Big Bend, Isle Royale—any of a dozen parks she could name without thinking—been closed to her she would be bereft, resentful. Caves she could comfortably leave in the dark.

Cavers were another matter. Before she could get a clearer picture of the survey team that had been with Frieda, she needed to know more about the personalities involved. She had little idea how to go about gleaning background information. They were such a disparate bunch. Curt was a New York university professor, Brent a geologist for somebody, Peter a midwestern gynecologist. Who would she call, the AMA, the PTA? Sondra, at least, had a face, address, and phone number.

Anna was in the middle of wheedling the McCartys' home address out of Jewel when a series of interrupting phone calls brought Laymon back out of his office.

"Ah, good, you're still here," he said, and Anna knew she was about to be volunteered for something. "Could you do us a favor and pick Mrs. Dierkz up at the airport? She wanted to be here when the body was brought out."

The body.

Laymon was businesslike, nothing disrespectful in word or manner. Yet Anna bristled. As far as she knew, Laymon wasn't acquainted with either Frieda or her mother. It would have been bizarre had he beat his breast or rent his garments. Still, she would have preferred it to this cold dispatch.

What she said was, "Sure," and, "Vehicle?"

Laymon nodded at his secretary. "Jewel?" Without waiting for her to respond, he shut himself back into his office.

Not only was Anna's sick day to be co-opted but her solitude as well. Jewel informed her that what visitors' quarters existed were filled with cavers, specialists, and media. Frieda's mother would bunk with her at Zeddie's house until she left with the corpse of her daughter or more suitable arrangements could be made.

Jewel saw to it Anna was provided with a not-too-bad sedan. The battered 4 × 4s and pickup trucks struck them both as frivolous for the task at hand.

Clouds were as thick over the town of Carlsbad as they were over the caverns, but, as the town was considerably lower in elevation, small planes were able to sneak in below the overcast. It was in one of these puddle-jumpers that Dottie Dierkz arrived. Anna had no trouble finding her in the tiny waiting room. It wasn't that she was one of only three people. She looked like a woman who had recently sustained a killing blow and had not yet had the luxury of falling down.

Frieda's mother was tall, five-foot-ten or so, and impeccably groomed. Money and taste were evident in the perfectly brown, perfectly styled hair, the cashmere mock turtleneck in fuchsia, and the tailored navy jacket. Unlike her daughter, Mrs. Dierkz was thin and angular with high cheekbones and a clean fine jawline, bone structure that would keep her beautiful as long as she lived. From the look of her, Anna wondered how long that might be. Her settled beauty was brittle with the effort of holding grief in. She smiled brightly, showing perfect teeth behind exquisitely painted lips. The eyes remained as lifeless as mannequin's glass.

"Flying! Ooh!" Mrs. Dierkz mock shuddered as Anna carried her one bag out to the waiting sedan. "I can't count how many hours I've spent in the air. Dad—Gordon—and I have been to Europe I don't know how many times. I never got used to it. Goodness! It's good to be on the ground."

This and similar flight-related comments got them across the parking lot and out toward the highway. Anna had done little besides introduce herself. She and Mrs. Dierkz had never met, but they had become acquainted as those who share a loved one tend to. Once or twice, Anna had answered the phone at the office when it was Mrs. Dierkz calling for her daughter. Stories had been told on both sides. More to Anna. Daughters so love to gossip about their moms. Frieda had adored hers and, less common, had enjoyed her company and looked forward to visits home.

As Anna turned the car onto the National Parks Highway, out of town toward the park, the wind turned vicious. Buffeting the sedan, it skinned away the fragile warmth. Mrs. Dierkz sat in the passenger seat, her shoulders hunched and her hands pressed between her knees. Anna turned up the heat, though she doubted mere Btus had a prayer of warming the cold that held Mrs. Dierkz. The smile was still switched on. Not to impress—Anna'd been forgotten—but because she had simply neglected to turn it off. Emotions were no longer attached to facial expression. Had they been, the world might have seen a mask of tragedy best reserved for Greek plays.

"Frieda—" Anna began, needing to say something.

Mrs. Dierkz plucked one hand from between her knees and fluttered it; a woman batting away gnats. The hand was in keeping with the rest of her: nails shaped and painted, a heavy gold wedding band embracing a few carats' worth of engagement ring. Tasteful, affluent, but not off-putting. Anna knew a little of Frieda's childhood, enough to know her mother was not a stranger to hard work. She and her husband had started a used-car dealership in 1951. Four daughters and nearly half a century later, they were rich. More power to them.

"Call me Dottie," Frieda's mother offered unexpectedly.

"Dottie," Anna repeated. Without Frieda as a subject, she was at a loss for words.

Mrs. Dierkz—Dottie—tried to keep up a semblance of conversation. As much, Anna suspected, to keep thoughts of her daughter at bay as to fulfill any sort of social obligation. The vagaries of air travel exhausted, she hit upon landscape as a safe topic. The desert was less than helpful. Anna couldn't but feel that it had put on its bleakest aspect. Thin rain fell in fitful spates, providing no moisture, only adding to the gloom. Without sunlight or any lingering touch of summer, the sage showed black and spiny against soil gray as ash.

It wasn't long before Mrs. Dierkz gave up. Her last sentence, an admirable attempt to liken the black scrub to the graceful lines of Chinese brush paintings, skidded to a halt midsentence. A heartbeat's silence followed, then she admitted, "I've always liked a little more green. So restful on the eyes."

Anna nodded. She kept her attention on the road. Grief is such a naked emotion, and she wanted to respect Dottie Dierkz's natural modesty.

"Frieda?" Mrs. Dierkz said then, inviting Anna to take up where she'd been fluttered to silence some minutes before.

Anna was more than happy to do things on Dottie's terms. Never having had children, she could not fathom the sort of pain the woman must be suffering. She knew only the loss of a husband, a father, and several very good cats. If it was worse than that, she was impressed that Dottie remained upright and coherent.

"Frieda," she began again, as asked. Monitoring Dottie from the corner of her eye as she talked, trying to gauge what to tell, what to omit, whether to go on or turn the subject to other matters, Anna told her of the accident, the rescue, the second and fatal fall. She left out the part where her knee crushed the life from Frieda. Maybe she did it to protect Dottie, maybe to protect herself. There was nothing in it but gratuitous angst for all concerned. Mostly she focused on Frida's love for the underground, her courage, her humor, and how deeply admired she was by her fellows. Or all but one of her fellows, an addendum Anna kept to herself.

By the time they started the twisting ascent to the park quarters, Anna had pretty much talked herself out. Whether or not Dottie had taken all she could of Frieda's last days, Anna certainly had. Lumps formed like salt licks in her throat, and tears burned beneath her eyelids. The last thing Dottie needed was to see Anna break down.

Yet abandoning the topic altogether seemed not only callous but impossible. Now, and for a while, it was the only topic in the world. So Anna skewed the tales around till she was gossiping about the other members of the survey team. Curt Schatz's claim to mouse bones, Tillman's mainlining caffeine—anything to distract herself or Dottie for a moment. She described Brent Roxbury's caving ensemble and elicited a small smile, brief but genuine, a break from the bigger brighter ones. Mrs. Dierkz didn't recognize Roxbury's name and that surprised Anna somewhat. Brent had been so upset by Frieda's injury and then her death, Anna assumed they'd been close. Perhaps they had. Mothers weren't necessarily privy to all information. Time and distance made them strangers even in the best of relationships. And, too, Brent's distress could have been just the stress of the situation or the sensitivity of one caver for another.

Zeddie Dillard was an old family friend. Her older sister and Frieda had gone to college together. When her own sister died, Zeddie had attached herself to Frieda and her sister.

Dottie knew Curt, but "just to say hello to." They had met in Minnesota. Dr. McCarty she had known for years. He'd inherited her when her gynecologist retired. Dottie had recommended him to her daughter.

Dottie and her husband, Gordon, had been invited to his wedding. They'd been in Italy at the time and hadn't gone, but she'd heard it had been beautiful. "Quite lavish," she said, and managed to convey disapproval without so much as a lifted eyebrow or a lowered tone. "I don't know his wife well." She sounded like she didn't care to rectify that situation in the foreseeable future.

Piqued, Anna pushed a little. "I only just met her," she said. "But I got a feeling there was trouble in paradise."

For a minute it seemed Mrs. Dierkz was too dull with grief or too refined to go for the bait. A need to keep her mind off worse things won out. "I think it might have been one of those hurry-up deals," Dottie said without much interest. "Gilda, Frieda's . . . my youngest girl knew her from graduate school. Just to say hi to, you know. They didn't travel with the same crowd. I guess there was some trouble with one of the professors and this girl. Then we hear Dr. McCarty's marrying her."

"You think she was pregnant?" Anna asked bluntly.

Too bluntly for Dottie Dierkz. "Who can know?" she said. "We've all got to live our own lives, I guess. Me as much as anybody."

Anna left it alone. It would be easy enough to find out if there'd been a baby. What that might tell her, she was uncertain. Having babies out of wedlock was an epidemic among the poor and a fashion trend among the rich. Not the weapon for serious blackmail it had once been.

"I thought they might get together at one point," Dottie said wistfully.

"Sondra and Peter?" Anna asked.

"Peter and Frieda." Staring out the rain-streaked window at the broken hillsides they climbed through, her face was turned away, perhaps mourning not only her daughter but grandchildren she would never know.

"Dr. McCarty and Frieda," Anna repeated, more sharply than she'd intended.

"They went together for a year or two. Frieda seemed like she might be getting serious at one point. Both Dad and I would have liked that. Frieda was always an independent girl. A little too independent to be a doctor's wife, I think."

McCarty and Frieda.

McCarty and Sondra.

McCarty and Zeddie Dillard.

Anna was beginning to wonder if she was the only woman in the western hemisphere who'd not enjoyed the doctor's bedside manner.

A GOOD DEED actually paid off, and Anna was enjoying a mildly righteous glow of virtue's own reward. This good deed had begun as the lesser of two evils; to hang around Zeddie's and soak in the palpable pain of Frieda's mother or to make a cowardly retreat to town with the excuse of checking on Holden Tillman.

Her first choice, pursuing background information on the members of Frieda's survey team, had ended against several blank walls. Sondra wasn't answering her phone in St. Paul, and, since she was freelance, there was no place of business whose business it was to keep tabs on her whereabouts. Just for the hell of it Anna had called the *St. Paul Pioneer Press.* The fourth person she'd been forwarded to had actually heard of Sondra McCarty—the doctor's wife wasn't as regular a contributor as she liked people to believe—but had no inkling as to where she could be found. Anna left messages and Zeddie's phone number. As for the rest, she hadn't the foggiest idea where to begin. She doubted McCarty's medical colleagues would know much about his caving contacts. The same went for Curt's academic associates. That left Zeddie and Brent. Zeddie was a little too close to home. Staying in her house, on the heels of the disaster, with her still underground toiling to bring Frieda's body out to her mother, Anna wasn't comfortable questioning her friends. The park was too small, the mood too highly charged. As Anna's grandmother would have phrased it, she was liable to get a thick finger stirring in that pot. A little time needed to pass before she could cast her aspersions before peers.

Brent, Anna could and did get to. The man wanted to talk. She could hear the craving over the phone. Till then she'd not realized how strong the need was in her to talk it all over with someone who had been *there.* In a way, had the cave not been growing ever tighter and more malevolent, staying with the body recovery team would have been a comfort.

Unfortunately, when Anna reached him, Roxbury was on a cellular phone in a Jeep on BLM land adjacent to the park. His cure for the crazies had been to throw himself into his work. Their phone connection started out bad and rapidly went to worse. The last intelligible words were mutually desperate promises to get in touch.

Dead ends.

That was when, faced with an afternoon basking in Dottie Dierkz's grief, Anna had decided to hang on to the borrowed sedan a few more hours and call on the Tillmans. She didn't phone ahead for the obvious reason that she didn't want to be told not to come and thus have an honorable avenue of escape denied her.

Holden and his wife lived in a modest house on the outskirts of the town of Carlsbad. Outbuildings, a requisite in the West, cluttered the lot beside and behind the house: an old garage with a door that wouldn't close, two trucks, a horse trailer with one flat tire, a barn with a horse without sense enough to get in out of the rain standing miserably nearby, and a dog house, sans dog, with a peeling tar-paper roof. Other items scattered around completed a look that Anna, through long familiarity, had come to find homey. Rubber tires, a staple of western decor, were tumbled near the woodpile; an aluminum canoe, partly filled with brackish water, was grounded under a leafless tree.

She parked the sedan in front of a picket fence denuded of paint by wind-blown sand and let herself through the gate. The tiny porch was overflowing with cowboy detritus: deer antlers, rusting metal pieces of machinery that, like bleached skulls and pine cones, created their own artistic statement. To one side of the door a square picture window framed a book-covered table lit by a single lamp. On such a gray day, the golden glow was welcoming. Anna was glad she'd come.

The door was opened before her knuckles could fall a second time. A woman a good ten or fifteen years Holden's junior smiled at her with the hushed apologetic look that unmistakably says "nap time." Anna had forgotten the Tillmans' four-year-old. Waking the boy was a sin on two counts, once against the child and once against his mom. Anna found herself whispering.

Holden was napping as well. He and Andrew were curled up together on the boy's little bed. Anna was warmed by a glimpse of them as Rhonda Tillman closed the door off the kitchen.

Tillman's wife was classically beautiful, with thick lustrous hair that fell past her shoulders and wide-set green eyes under winged brows that had probably never known a pair of tweezers. She was model-thin, with long slender arms and tapered fingers. When she talked her hands sketched graceful pictures in the air to accompany her words. Holden's wife was young enough and pretty enough to dislike on sight, but she gave Anna two homemade oatmeal cookies and a glass of white Zinfandel so Anna decided to overlook her faults.

Rhonda pushed aside a paper plate full of multicolored Play-Doh and put her elbows on the painted wood of the kitchen table. "Holden's driving me nuts," she said, and she and Anna fell into the easy camaraderie women often do when left to themselves. "I thought I was going to have to wrap him in a towel and shove the painkillers down his throat the way I do with the cats."

Anna broke off a chunk of cookie and washed it down with the wine. Beer last night, wine now. Two years of abstinence poured away. She just didn't give a damn. The terrors of the bottle had faded, the attendant weirdness an unreal memory. Not to mention, the stuff didn't seem to work anymore. Three beers had left her with a full bladder and no buzz. Still, she drank Rhonda's Zinfandel, was eager to drink it. A memory of comfort? Of forgetfulness? Maybe it was the only way she knew of handling death. Nobody important had kicked the bucket in a long time. No wonder sobriety had been a piece of cake.

"How's Holden doing?" Anna asked, tired of asking the same thing of herself.

"Not good," Rhonda replied in her hushed nap-time voice. The softness made Anna lean across the table, her and Rhonda's heads together like conspirators. It was a nice feeling. Rhonda picked up a cookie with both hands, holding it between fingertips and thumbs as if it were a sandwich. Nibbling around the edge with little squirrel bites, she thought about her husband. "Very bad, in fact," she said at last. "He's convinced himself he killed Frieda Dierkz. Now he's working on convincing himself he can't trust his own decisions. This morning he had Andrew in fits dithering about whether to let the little guy ride in the front seat. Poor old Holden. I can read him like a book. No, like a newspaper. His emotions are headlines. He was scared he'd crash the car, hurt Andrew." She took a delicate sip of wine and resumed torturing her cookie to death.

"Tain't so," Anna said. "That's not how it happened." She decided now was not the time for secrecy. "Did he tell you what I found?"

Rhonda nodded, her hair shining in the overhead light. "Holden no longer believes in your butt-print," she said. "It's like he won't let himself believe. Some sort of punishment. He said he would have known if somebody had gone up there."

"No, he wouldn't have," Anna argued. "Sixty feet above him, in the blackety-black of that frigging cave, Godzilla and Puff the Magic Dragon could have been perched up there the whole time and none of us would have seen them."

"Not seen," Rhonda said. "*Known.* He's getting metaphysical in his delusions."

"Damn it." Anna was annoyed. "It was my butt-print. I saw it. I should know. It was there. I could see pocket seams. It was an ideal, perfect, unassailable butt-print."

"Talk to him?" Rhonda asked.

"Sure."

"It won't do any good."

"Probably not." They sat in companionable silence for a while. A fat white cat with Siamese markings from one ancestor cut into tiger rings from another jumped up on the table and stretched out full length, his paws pushing gently against the base of Anna's glass.

"You know you're not allowed on the table when we have company," Rhonda said. The cat twitched its tail in disdain.

"Are you a caver?" Anna asked.

"I used to be. Not so much anymore. When you're married to *the* Holden Tillman it gets old." There was a tinge of bitterness there, but Anna knew the feeling. Some battles weren't worth fighting. "I still do some," Rhonda said in self-defense. "I just backed out of the whole political side of it."

Anna had not considered caving as having a political side. Naïve of her; everything touched by humans was touched by politics. "How so?" she asked to keep the visit from ending.

"I used to go to all the grotto meetings. Get involved in all that. My last year I was president of the local grotto. No more."

Grottos. Local groups of cavers. That was the key. Anna had overlooked the inevitable: people couldn't resist joining up and forming clubs. Cavers were no different. She could let the AMA and the PTA alone. "Grotto meetings!" she said as one might say "Eureka!" "Is Brent Roxbury a member? Is Zeddie?"

"Are you going to help Holden?"

Anna laughed. "Unless he really did kill Frieda."

"Not a problem. Holden hasn't killed anybody in years. He puts spiders outside. Even big hairy ones." Rhonda got more cookies from a jar on the counter and refilled their wineglasses. "Fire away."

Anna outlined her theories. It didn't take long. If someone had attempted to kill, then finally had succeeded in killing Frieda, the list of suspects was mercifully short: the members of the core group with the exception of Oscar, Holden, and herself. If the fall in the Pigtail was unrelated to the rock that had broken Frieda's leg, then they were all suspects. Anna felt duty-bound to mention that but didn't give it much credence. The law of averages was meant to be broken, but it served as a fairly trustworthy guide.

"I don't know what I'm fishing for," she admitted in the end. "I need more information. More to go on. Other than Dr. McCarty's tendency to drop trou at the slightest provocation, I know almost nothing about anybody. With zip in the way of physical evidence, motive is the only thing I've got."

Despite Rhonda's desire to be of help, the pickings were pretty slim. Frieda had a reputation in some circles for "scooping booty," the highly unpopular practice of dashing headlong down new passages to be the first without addressing the needs of the cave, i.e., surveying each new portion as it was explored. Rhonda assured Anna that emotions ran high when it came to scooping booty, but neither of them could see it as a motive for murder. Tinker's Hell was a dead end or, as Holden would have said, an end in itself. All the leads surveyed petered out. No booty to scoop.

Sondra McCarty was a neophyte, a whiner, not well liked. No news there.

Brent was well thought of by cavers. He was active with children's groups, taking even very little kids into the caves to teach them about bats and crickets, instill in them awe instead of fear of things subterranean. Brent was a good father—high praise from the mother of a four-year-old. Rhonda said Andrew sometimes played with his daughters. They had a house in town a couple of miles from the Tillmans'.

Rumor had it Brent had exaggerated reports on occasion to protect the underground resource. The caving community loved him for it. The petroleum interests would have had a significantly different take on the issue, but Rhonda said it was just gossip. She doubted it had penetrated much outside the grotto.

Zeddie was new to caving. Enthusiastic, young, idealistic, she had all the makings of a life-long devotee. No rumors attached themselves to her, but Rhonda seemed reluctant to write her off as squeaky clean. They weren't too far apart in age. Zeddie a caver, Rhonda a mommy—Anna guessed it was just a natural jealousy.

Peter McCarty was known to be skilled and experienced. By some he was considered a lightweight—a bit of a dilettante—but Rhonda had never heard much against him besides the occasional snipe because his wife was too young, his equipment too new, his hair too well cut.

Schatz, Rhonda didn't know. She'd met him a couple times, but he was mostly an eastern caver, and she hadn't heard any stories about him either way.

This pleasant, if fruitless, exchange was brought to a close by the intrusion of the telephone bell.

"That tears it," Rhonda said in exasperation.

"Is that the phone?" Holden's voice emanated from Andrew's room.

"See? Too good to last," Rhonda muttered. "I got it."

Andrew slept on. Holden stumped out on crutches as Rhonda was hanging up.

"That was George Laymon," she said. "They're bringing out the body."

12

FIVE HOURS PASSED before Frieda was brought into the open air. This time the reception was subdued. There were no floodlights, only one media crew, and the brass had thinned out considerably. Not a single caver had left. Standing in rain rapidly turning to sleet, a dismal army dotted the stony hillside.

Anna had no task to occupy her; when Frieda no longer needed her, she'd become superfluous. Knowing she'd failed her friend, Anna felt a crushing self-consciousness. The eyes of the surviving cavers seemed to follow her like the vacant sockets of so many masks. With a visible shake of her head, she told herself it was grief and guilt deluding her. The cavers' eyes followed Holden, too. On crutches, lower leg in a cast, he'd hobbled the mile and a half over rain-slicked desert. Pain too deep to be accounted for by broken bones paralyzed his muscles as surely as if he'd suffered a stroke.

Darkness hid the faces of the watchers, but Anna had little doubt that they looked on with respect and sympathy.

Because she was with Holden, she was allowed down into the boulder-choked mouth of Lechuguilla. Desirous of staying out of the way, she found a niche in the rock behind the stunted oak that served as an anchor.

Flanked by George Laymon and the superintendent, Mrs. Dierkz was below her, partially sheltered from the rain by scrawny branches. An attempt had been made to convince Dottie to wait in a warm dry car down in the parking area, but she'd been firm. She'd walked all over Europe and China, she told the superintendent. She would walk this last little ways. Her leather shoes were soaked and muddied, her hair flattened beneath a yellow so'wester-style rain bonnet, but she stood straight and, as near as Anna could tell in the rain, didn't weep.

One by one the recovery team crawled up from darkness, their progress robbed of grace by a need to navigate boulders and spiny plants while roped in at waist, knee, and ankle. Oscar Iverson was first, wide-eyed with fatigue. McCarty was next, his features closed down, as stony as Holden Tillman's. Curt Schatz was third. His strength was wonderful to watch, the muscles fluid as they brought the Stokes to the surface. Frieda had been wrapped up in toto as befitted her new status as a corpse: a faceless, shapeless bundle lashed in the wire basket. Not a scrap of flesh or hair or clothing was left visible to remind them of the woman inside.

As it should be, Anna thought. The woman was gone, the husk itself become an empty casket, deserving of respect but not reverence.

Zeddie and Kelly Munk followed the Stokes. Zeddie had more life in her than the rest. Relief wasn't evident, or sorrow. Anger was fueling her. In one so young it was impossible to mistake. She'd not yet learned to hide her feelings from the world's freezing indifference.

The source of her aggravation wasn't hard to find. Kelly Munk, close on her heels, got a snarl in return for his offer to help her off with her gear. "Anna," she snapped, seeing her hunched vulturelike in the rocks. "Make yourself useful."

Anna jumped down to help her derig, happy to be of service and happy to share in the snubbing of Munk. The man was unchastened. His face worked overtime. "Chewing up the scenery." Anna dredged up a phrase from Zach's theatrical lexicon. Kelly Munk labored under the delusion that all dramatic incidents were centered around Kelly Munk. As he hauled himself up the rocks at Anna's shoulder, she could see him trying on expressions. He settled on a look of heroic exhaustion, affixing it firmly in place as he made a beeline for the media.

Zeddie shot an evil look after his retreating form. "When I'm queen, different people are going to die," she said.

Anna scavenged a raincoat for Zeddie and gave back the sweater she'd worn all day. After so much time underground, none of the recovery team was prepared for the winter weather. Zeddie paid her respects to Frieda's mother, then cleared out. Anna stayed till the litter, with fresh bearers and a frighteningly stoic Dottie Dierkz, started down the hill. A handful of cavers from among those keeping vigil amid the rocks came to take over the derigging. Anna fell in step beside Curt and went with him to the cavers' tent. No pizza this time but beer and coffee and a plate of sandwiches that Dottie had insisted on providing. Blessing the woman's graciousness, the team fell on them as if they'd not eaten in a week.

Brent, Holden, Oscar, and Anna stood at the edges of the tent, wall-flowers at the dance. Feeling bereft, Anna took a cup of coffee to be companionable. The sensation wasn't unfamiliar. Twice before in her career she'd pushed—once eighteen hours and once nearly twenty-four—bringing victims out of the backcountry only to have them die on her within sight of modern medical facilities. Too much time had passed; they hadn't been strangers anymore. Too much hope had been invested, and ego and energy. A strange and cosmic coitus interruptus; perfect communion denied. From the way the team wolfed down their food, backs to one another, little left to say, Anna knew she wasn't the only one feeling isolated.

Kelly Munk was the exception. Beer in one hand, untouched sandwich in the other, he was holding court. Most of the older cavers ignored him, but he'd gathered a newsman and a coterie of the less-experienced cavers. With becoming modesty, he outlined how he'd taken over the medical care of Frieda, explained how his rigging could have saved her life, and, at risk of losing his audience, moved on to a tale of paranormal prowess implying he heard Frieda's spirit crying in the darkness of the Pigtail. Zeddie looked as if she might be contemplating a queenly prerogative, and Brent Roxbury was so pale Anna was afraid he was going to faint. "I can't take this," she heard him murmuring. Even Schatz, who normally would allow Munk to make as much of a fool of himself as he wished, had taken on a look of if not malevolence then peevish irritation.

The story was in the worst possible taste. Not because of the grandstanding, trading on tragedy for a moment in the spotlight, but because there were those, Anna among them, who would have dearly loved a last word with Frieda. That Munk could suggest her spirit would have frittered it away on an ass like himself was too much to bear on freeze-dried food and too little sleep.

Hands were bunching into fists, faces screwing up for harsh words. Oscar stepped in. Anna thought Holden would do the honors, but he was too wrapped up in his own misery. With little fuss, Oscar herded Munk toward the tent's exit. Kelly didn't thank Iverson, but he should have. The men might have maintained a veneer of civility but Zeddie was ready to punch somebody's lights out. Tempered by two years on rope and rock, her fists would carry quite a wallop. Anna was sorry to see the fracas averted. Abusing Kelly Munk would have proved a catharsis. But Oscar, older, wiser, not nearly so much fun, spirited Kelly Munk away before the newsman got anything interesting to train his camera on.

Beer and sandwiches buoyed the team up sufficiently to make the hike back to the waiting vehicles, trudging along without speaking. With the exception of Oscar, Holden, and Brent, the core group gathered at Zeddie's home. None of them had anywhere else to go, and, with the instinct of a flock of birds or a battalion that's seen action, they needed to stay together.

Zeddie pulled an answering machine from a drawer, hooked it up, unplugged the phone, and turned the volume on the machine down so they could sleep in. McCarty didn't call home to let his wife know he was out of the cave. He behaved as if he and Zeddie were an accepted couple. In this age of technology Anna doubted a thousand miles of real estate could have given him such a feeling of privacy. Gossip traveled faster than light, faster than e-mail. Sins in New Mexico could be news in Minnesota before they'd had time to be properly committed. It could be that he just didn't care anymore. It could be that he knew for one reason or another that Sondra was beyond the grapevine, her threats no longer viable.

Anna and Curt bunked on the couch, heads at opposite ends, limbs vying for space in the middle. Mrs. Dierkz slept on the single bed in the spare room. In keeping with Peter's suddenly single status, he and Zeddie retired to the double bed in the master bedroom. Under the circumstances adultery seemed, if not natural, then inevitable, and no one commented. Frontline morality, Anna thought as she felt Calcite stomp up her belly to lie on her chest. Eat, drink, and be merry, for tomorrow you die. There was an attraction in that. The stuff of movies, the reason wars continued to delight in retrospect, if not in reality. To be so alive, so of the moment. No tedious consequences. No tawdry loose ends.

In this atmosphere of opportunistic hedonism, Anna noticed the warmth of Schatz's thigh pressed against hers. She could hear the hush of his breath and smell the soap he'd showered with. A lovely young man, she thought, and felt a pleasant tingle.

"Get thee behind me, Satan," she whispered.

"Anna?" Schatz said, and she felt her already weak resolve vanish utterly.

"What?" Her voice was husky, cliché; it embarrassed her.

"Are you going to hog the cat?"

She would have laughed but for the fact it might have disturbed Calcite. "She chose me. Get your own damn cat." Disappointment was canceled by relief. This wasn't war. Tomorrow they would all still be alive, and there would be pipers demanding to be paid. Best not to run up too much of a tab.

MORNING CAME LIKE a hangover. Everybody seemed lost. The survey Frieda's team had embarked on was scheduled to last four more days. No one had flights booked out till then. For a few days at least, Zeddie would have houseguests. Anna was glad. She could lose herself in the crowd.

Curt seemed content to stay where he was, though Anna couldn't tell whether it was due to her questionable charms, Calcite's allure, or the fact that he had nothing waiting for him at home. Peter McCarty opted to stay as well, but his motives were more transparent. Mrs. Dierkz had the corpse of her daughter waiting on ice in Carlsbad.

Peter reattached the phone line and made a duty call to his home in Minneapolis. The machine answered. He didn't strike Anna as worried, angry, relieved—he didn't strike her in any way at all. Did he know Sondra wouldn't be answering the phone? Sondra had flown out with the first group, but nobody had checked to see what her destination was. She could have gone any direction. Maybe McCarty had reasons he wasn't sharing for knowing she had bolted. Sondra could be running from the law or from her husband, or simply screening her calls.

During the night Zeddie's answering machine had taken one call. At 1:27 A.M., according to the impersonal voice of the recording, Brent Roxbury had called for Anna. He'd be at Big Manhole from noon till around three, checking reports of unauthorized digging. He needed to talk. From the late hour of the call, Anna inferred some urgency. While she had a car she would meet him and see if what he needed to tell had any relation to what she needed to hear.

According to Zeddie's map, Big Manhole was less than an hour's walk from park housing. There was no trail, but the way was not difficult, much the same as the terrain to Lechuguilla. A walk would do Anna good. Exercise underground was a different discipline, and she longed for the hard stretch of movement, feeling the world go by, seeing the earth pay out beneath her boots. A bitterly cold wind and the necessity of delivering Dottie Dierkz to town dissuaded her. Paved roads out of Carlsbad would take her most of the way, dirt tracks the rest.

Big Manhole was a cave on BLM land adjacent to the park, an unprepossessing hole more than fifty feet deep, the entrance a mere crack beside a low brow of stone. About ten feet down, the aperture widened abruptly into a bell-shaped cavern. On its own, Big Manhole had little to recommend it, but there were a number of people who believed it would prove to be a second entrance into Lechuguilla Cavern. Toward that end, various tunnels had been bored into the bottom of the cave. Some were dug with the knowledge and blessing of the Bureau of Land Management. Some were not. Holden had once remarked to Oscar that he always carried an extra padlock when he visited because, often as not, the last lock used to secure the gate closing the cave would have been pried off.

North of the park the country was beautiful only to an eye acclimatized to the desert's idiosyncratic allure. Broken hills, scabbed with rock and cactus, spread out to a horizon composed of faint blue mountain silhouettes. Dry washes, ancient stream- and riverbeds, slashed through, exposing the bones of the earth in stratifications of gray, white, and dun. Nothing eased the eye: no green trees, sparkle of water, or carpet of grasses. The sky failed to soften the blow. Cold and scoured by the icy winds, its blue was as unyielding as lapis luzuli.

North northwest of the park boundary Anna ran out of pavement. Turning off Highway 137, she edged the sedan over a gravel road. For a dirt track it was in good condition, recently resurfaced and leveled. Potholes, massive and unannounced, suggested heavy use. That and dust forced her to slow to an irritating creep. Dust was ubiquitous. Anna had spent a lot of years in a lot of deserts, and she couldn't remember seeing dust this bad. It was as if the land had been ground exceedingly fine, pulverized into white powder that settled over everything. Rocks, bushes, the few stalks of sparse grass were featureless under a suffocating blanket of grayish white. Clouds boiled from beneath the sedan's tires.

Suddenly a wind sucked the powdered earth up and wove it into veils, wings, plumes, fantastic blinding shapes. Anna stomped on the brake, and the car shuddered to a halt. The whirling devil wind that engulfed her in earthen fog pummeled the car, velvet fists pounding first one door, then another. The radio antenna whipped so hard she could hear its high faint singing over the wind. With a last, playful swat, a broken sage bush rolling tumbleweed fashion over the car's hood, the tiny tornado moved on.

Anna watched its progress, a jaunty white funnel skipping over the catsclaw. A dust devil in the steady winds that had raked the desert since morning was unusual but not the greatest of the natural phenomena spawned by the rugged landscape. The twister carried off only a drop in the ocean of dust that continued to pour across the roadway in a steady stream.

A rough track forked to the south. No signs marked the way. Anna guided herself by counting. Unless she'd missed a road during the bizarre storm, this was the third; the road that would carry her to Big Manhole.

Seconds after she left the gravel the dust was gone. Winds raged unabated. The road began to deteriorate. Zeddie had warned her she'd need a high-clearance, four-wheel-drive vehicle to navigate the backcountry. Anna would have preferred it. What she had was a 1993 Chevrolet and she would have to make do. Had it been her own car, she would have been more circumspect. Muttering a quick apology to the taxpayers, she forced the car over an imbedded spine of limestone that threatened to disembowel it.

Twenty minutes later she knew she'd have to abandon the car and walk the last couple of miles or risk having to walk the entire sixty back to Carlsbad. Despite her leather jacket and another of Zeddie's sweaters, wind found ways into her bones. Leaning into it, she shoved her hands in her pockets, lowered her head, and barged up the bleak hills. By the time she reached the last bump in a line of thick places along a low ridge, she felt a kinship with a baked Alaska. Exertion had raised her body temperature till, beneath her layers, she'd begun to sweat, but the bite of the wind had nearly frozen the flesh from her cheeks and ears.

Over the years she'd nearly forgotten the unceasing winds of a Trans-Pecos winter. Moaning, godless winds that ripped through, carrying away sanity. Jason's harpies could have taken lessons from the Texas wind. Relentless, it tore at human nerves, snatching hats, doors, packages, whipping people with their own hair, scouring with sand and cold, never letting up, never letting go, sawing at the eaves in the night and the mind in the day.

"The wind is my friend," Anna remembered a conservationist in Guadalupe telling her. "It blows the tourists away."

Sensible tourists, she thought as she pushed over the nub of the last hill. The sight of a four-wheel-drive Blazer rewarded her. If, after all the effort, Brent had stood her up, she might have been less than perfectly gracious when next they met.

Caves were well camouflaged in New Mexico. The entrances blended in with the scenery. One could easily pass within a foot of a major cavern and never notice it. Anna followed Zeddie's directions to the letter. She walked to the middle of the barren knoll where Brent had left the Blazer, pulled out her compass, and turned till she was facing south southeast. If she'd done it right, park headquarters should be several miles away, hidden by a swelling of the ground. Crossing to where the knoll rounded down into one of the shallow ravines that carried away water from the short but fierce monsoons, she looked for the cave.

Gray-brown hillsides rolled away in all directions, marked only by fragments of lichen-speckled stone and the unwelcoming beauty of desert plants. Anna turned her attention to the ground at her feet. At first nothing presented itself, but she was used to that. The desert was a mosaic; changes were subtle. After a moment a faint trail began to emerge as her eye picked out minute changes in color and texture. The experience was not unlike staring at a 3-D pattern. First there's nothing; then, once the picture forms, it's unmistakable. Enjoying the childlike delight this simple magic never failed to produce, she ran lightly down the trail, the wind at her back threatening to give her wings.

Fifty yards later the trail didn't so much stop as dwindle to nothing, and still Anna couldn't see anything suggesting a cave. What finally tipped her off that she was in the right place was a boot, an old hiking boot, protruding from the snarly fingers of a catsclaw bush. Beyond this unnatural formation she saw Big Manhole. Tucked up beside a low serrated bench of stone, the entrance was right out of *The Patchwork Girl of Oz*, a place designed for the incarceration of flesh-eating ogres. Flush with the ground, a hole roughly the size of a hope chest leaked black shadow through whitened limestone. Rusted iron bars cemented into the rock formed a grid over the opening. A trapdoor of the same rusted iron was welded in, a heavy hasp wanting a padlock to secure it. To see the hairy knuckles of a giant poking elephantine fingers through the grid didn't take too great a stretch of the imagination.

"Brent?" Anna hollered as she stepped around the grabbing thorns of catsclaw. The wind snatched the words from her lips and hurled them over the desert. As it happened, they would have fallen on deaf ears anyway. The battered boot was not an ancient artifact. It was firmly laced to the foot of Brent Roxbury.

There are postures that the human body does not adopt in life. Roxbury had the broken-doll look of someone struck down from a standing position and dead or unconscious before he hit the ground. His feet were splayed at uncomfortable angles, legs bent when the knees buckled. He'd landed on his hip, his left arm flung back from his torso and falling behind him. His right was trapped beneath; his face pressed against the grid over the cave.

"Brent?" Anna said again, but she was talking to herself. Crouching over his inert form she felt for a carotid pulse. Finding none, she took the liberty of rolling him onto his back. Spinal injuries were the least of his worries. Her hand came away from his navy windbreaker dripping with blood. Not marked or smeared but dripping as if she'd dipped it in a bucket. She could feel the salt sting of it in the myriad scrapes and cuts her Lechuguilla adventure had left on her knuckles.

"Yet who would have thought the old man to have had so much blood in him?" came a line from Shakespeare's Scottish play, one in which her husband had carried a spear. Brent's soul had been gored from his body by a bullet from a high-powered weapon. No neat black hole between the eyes had let his life leak away. A furrow chewed up from his clavical into his neck, severing the carotid artery on the left side of the pharynx, then continued up till it blew away the point of his jaw, much of his dental work, and his left cheekbone.

Due to the severe facial trauma there was no way Anna could have effected an airtight seal to begin rescue breathing. It was a moot point. Without blood to carry it, oxygen had no way of reaching the vital organs. The throat wound no longer spurted but merely seeped. No heart left to push the blood, no blood left to flow.

Feeling mildly insensitive, Anna wiped the gore from her hands on the dead man's trousers. Nothing else was available, and she sure as hell wasn't going to wipe it on her own.

Blood had become toxic waste. Paper trail: if she played out the paranoia, there'd be reports and doctors' offices visited to leave a record in case she tested positive for HIV after the incident. Every class, every lecture drummed precaution into the brain. The greater danger of being mowed down by a drunk driver did not worry the public. Maybe because it did not carry with it the horror of death by inches.

A crack of sound and the sting of needle-fine pieces of stone sown into her cheek jerked her back to more imminent danger. What with one thing and another, she'd overlooked the obvious. The shooter was not necessarily gone, nor was he necessarily finished. Not daring to look around for the rifleman, she flattened herself on top of Brent Roxbury. Blood, warm as bathwater, drenched her face and neck. He couldn't have been dead more than a minute or two. A second shot cracked, then sang high and angry off the rock inches beyond Anna's skull. She could feel—or imagined she could—the stirring of its wind in her hair.

She had two choices for cover: behind Roxbury's corpse or down through the rusted bars wiring the jaws of Big Manhole. As tempting as Brent's company was, a wall of flesh and bone would scarcely slow a bullet down. Unpleasant images of WWII executions clicked behind her eyes.

Quick as a wounded snake, she writhed over to the iron-barred trap and dropped through. The black enclosed well of the cave held no terrors for her. She figured the fall would kill her before claustrophobia could set in. Knuckles wrapped around the grid, she looked down expecting to see nothing but darkness. Today the gods were kind—or in a playful mood. The neck of the immense limestone bottle was not neat and sheer but a ragged crevice with plenty of ledges upon which a small and determined woman could find footholds.

Where Anna dangled, the aperture was no more than three feet across. Jamming both boots on a ledge eight inches wide, she planted her back against the opposite wall. Wedged in, she could wait a good long time. Confident she was secure, she peeled her hands from the metal of the bars. Her fingers weren't slippery with Roxbury's blood. The man was a good coagulator. His plasma glued her skin to the iron.

Two more shots rang out, lending the scream of lead and limestone to the shriek of the wind. Both times Anna winced, though she knew her cover was complete. In the security of the newfound shelter, her mind changed gears from instinct to intellect. Who would shoot Brent Roxbury? In the Southwest, particularly New Mexico, local militia groups had threatened to shoot BLM rangers on sight. Militia. Bubbas with IQs lower than the caliber of their handguns. Guys who felt cheated because "varmint hunts," the senseless competitive slaughter of coyotes that lived so far out on the desert they'd never so much as tasted chicken or lamb, had been interfered with. Men dispossessed because bicycle trails were infringing on traditional shooting ranges, and the government, afraid a few of the Spandex-and-ponytail set would catch a stray bullet, had closed more than one.

As near as Anna could remember, most of the ill will was centered in northern New Mexico, near Farmington. Southern New Mexico had been spared that particular ugliness. At least it had in the past.

That train of thought derailed. She loved the novels of Thomas Hardy and was a great believer in coincidence. But never when one needed it. Two members of the survey team meeting untimely ends from unrelated sources was highly unlikely.

Brent had been with them when Frieda died. He had been much distraught by her death. He'd wanted to speak with Anna and had foolishly left a message to that effect on the answering machine at Zeddie Dillard's. Everyone there—all the members of the core group, with the exception of Sondra—had heard it, right down to where and when he and Anna could meet. Zeddie had conveniently pointed out that it was an easy walk from park housing to Big Manhole. Before Brent had an opportunity to talk, he'd been killed. It didn't take a great thinker to trace the thread. Brent knew something about Frieda's "accident." Possibly he'd seen or suspected who had made Anna's cherished butt-print. That person had decided Brent was to carry his secret to the grave. A one-way ticket had been provided.

Lost in thought, Anna let a minute's silence tick by, then two. The shooter had given up. She would wait till he'd gone, then come out of hiding. Minute three passed and with it Anna's illusion of safety. She had no reason to believe the rifleman would slink away in defeat. Why should he? A glance disabused her of any hope she might have harbored regarding cover or alternative egress. The slot where she hid was eight feet long, two to four feet wide, and bottomless. Anna had incarcerated herself in the ideal trap. No place to hide, no place to go but down, and no way to get there but fall. Big Manhole, having no cause for regular visitation, didn't boast a standing line, and Brent had been gunned down before he'd rigged a descent.

Options skittered through her mind. They were few in number and low on appeal. She could remain in her chimney and wait to be shot. Slim possibilities occurred to her: the would-be attacker might make a mistake, create an opening she could parlay into an escape. A mistake of that magnitude would require a gunman both unbelievably stupid and a tad psychotic. Judging by the deadly efficiency with which Brent had been dispatched, this fellow was probably neither. There would be no long cinematic tortures or lengthy rationalizations. Chances were he'd not poke the rifle barrel through the bars to prod his caged quarry so she could wrest the weapon from him in a moment of glorious heroics. He'd point, shoot; she'd fall, die; a crumpled, dead, middle-aged lady on a heap of antique bat shit. No glamour there.

"Shit," Anna whispered, then, with a nod to the Hodags, "Shucks." She needed all the help she could get. The saw of the wind precluded any possibility of listening for approaching footsteps. Not that early warning would do her any good. Diving into a hole had been a serious error in judgment. Odds were, running, she'd have made it, if not unscathed, then at least alive. Moving targets were devilishly hard to hit with any kind of accuracy.

Now whoever it was would be closer, know precisely where she was, where she could and could not go.

Anna eyed the rectangular chunk of uncut blue in the iron grid. She was in fairly good physical shape, but climbing out was going to be considerably slower than dropping in. At best guess, there would be thirty to sixty seconds during which she'd be a tempting target.

Still, there was nothing but to do it, and she tensed up, gauging the distance with the concentration of an Olympic gymnast: eighteen inches, a jerk, a push, a scramble. Readying her muscles, she shifted her weight and flexed her fingers, mimicking the tiny nervous movements of a cat preparing to pounce. On three, she told herself.

Before she'd begun her countdown, a glittering ruby detached from the sky and fell to a narrow shelf of white limestone. The red was unreal, luminous. Blood, Brent's blood, dripping through the bars with mesmerizing slowness.

A second drop, perfect and beautiful in the harsh light of the winter sun, formed on the underside of the iron, quivered, sending thousands of microscopic reflections across its scarlet surface. Caught up in this minuscule drama, she watched as it grew too great to support its own weight, then fell three feet to explode in sudden and sparkling splendor. In this brief life and death of a droplet Anna's mind had time to paint a grisly future: her grabbing for the bars on either side of the trap, ramming her boots into the sides of her rock prison, and shoving her head and shoulders up through the grate. A bullet ripping through her spine, bits of bone, white and sharp as shrapnel splattering the rock beside her. Her bowels letting loose and her legs going numb as the nerves were severed. Fingers uncurling and the weight of her dead legs dragging her down. Light receding to a pinpoint as she fell to the bottom of Big Manhole.

The vision sucked the breath from her. She shook free of it and began to scream like a berserker warrior reminding himself of his own bravery. Intellect was over. Time for instinct.

She lunged upward toward the light.

13

TACKY WITH BRENT'S fast-drying blood, Anna's hands caught the metal and held as if mated with Velcro. No small blessing under the circumstances. Without a glance at Roxbury's corpse, she kicked up from the limestone, pulling with all her strength. Adrenaline made her virtually shoot upward; half her body cleared the grid in a heartbeat. In another she had one knee on the iron bars and was scrambling on all fours over the ledge of stone that backed the entrance to Big Manhole.

Moving too fast for balance, she was unable to straighten up, and loped along on hands and feet. Wind tried to push her back, but fear made her unstoppable. She was a stampede of one. Rock and lechuguilla raced past a mere foot or two from her eyes as if she swooped over the desert in a low-flying plane. "Serpentine! Serpentine!" A line from an old Peter Falk movie blossomed in her mind. Had she had breath, she would have laughed. Had she time, she would have complied and zigzagged to avoid the sniper's bullets.

A moment more and she found her balance, pulled

herself up, claiming her ancestry as a Homo sapiens, and began to sprint up the hill. This tiny evolution had transpired in seconds. That was as long as the honeymoon was to last. The time had been purchased by the element of surprise. Evidently her attacker didn't think she'd have the courage—or the cowardice, depending on how one looked at it—to make a run for it across the open country.

A shot cracked behind her. Energy in the form of liquid panic spurted into her gut, but her body was already performing at its peak. There was no more speed to be gotten from her legs. The next noise brought her down. Whether the crack was from bullet or bone, she couldn't tell. Both feet flew to one side, and she smashed down on hip and shoulder. With the breath knocked half out of her and her brain skidding in her skull, she considered for a moment lying where she fell. An instant's betrayal of life and those who loved her, and it would all be over.

Oblivion's temptation flickered out in a gust of anger. She clawed at the rock, determined to drag herself as far as she could. The gunman could damn well work for this kill. Though hurting—a fact she vaguely sensed through the insulating layers of nature's own anesthetic—everything seemed in decent working order. Again she scrambled animal fashion over the ground, wondering with an odd detachment where she'd been hit and waiting with the same carelessness for the bullet that would end her life. The spill she had taken had been of long enough duration the shooter could take careful aim for the follow-up shot.

None came. A clue. What kind of rifle carried only that many bullets? How many? Worthless. Anna couldn't remember if the gun had fired twice or a dozen times, and she didn't know for a fact that Brent had been killed with a single shot. Didn't matter. The shooter was reloading. She had time. Hope did what fear could not, and she squeezed more speed from her muscles.

The top of the knoll had been graded flat to provide parking space. A low berm of dirt around the crown of the hill resulted. Anna hurled herself over it and rolled. When her belly came under her once again, she pushed to elbows and knees and wriggled toward the Blazer. Another shot rang out, but she didn't hear or feel it hit. If her guess was right, and the rifleman had come to the cave's mouth to kill her, he'd put himself on the downhill slope. As long as she stayed low she'd be out of range till he climbed to the top of the hill.

By then she'd be gone.

Unless Brent had taken the keys with him.

Anal retentive, Anna thought as she dragged open the Chevy's door and crawled lizardlike onto the seat. "I'll bet the son of a bitch—" Keys dangled from the ignition. "All is forgiven," she said aloud. Swinging into position, she cranked the key over while muttering a mantra of "please-pleaseplease" left over from a childhood in which begging occasionally produced favorable results.

The engine fired up without complaint, and she promised herself she'd write General Motors a thank-you note if she made it back to a post office alive. Haste precluded finesse. Dropping the Blazer in reverse, she floored the gas pedal and jerked the Chevy in a tight arc, its tailpipe pointed about where her stalker would be coming over the hill if he'd continued on her trail. Before the truck came to a full stop, she jammed the gear lever into first and poured on the gas. Gravel flew from beneath all four tires as they scratched down through the dirt to find purchase. Then the Blazer leapt forward, its power fishtailing the body over the ruts of the road and down the far side of the hill.

The jolting knocked Anna from one side of the cab nearly to the other. Without seatbelt and shoulder strap it was a battle to keep her feet on the pedals and the car on the road. If there were any more gunshots the racket of the engine drowned them out. She didn't so much drive as ride the bucking, skidding beast of metal until she'd put a lump of hillock between her and the knoll she'd left behind.

Unable to control the raging jitters, she mashed on the

brakes rather than easing to a civilized stop. The Blazer skidded, shuddered, and died. Gasping for breath, Anna clung to the steering wheel and studied the rearview mirror for any sign of pursuit. Reaching up, she wrenched the little mirror this way and that, widening the scope of her search. Vanity stopped her from simply turning around and looking out the Blazer's rear window. Should she take a bullet, she'd just as soon it wasn't in the face. That was too personal. Brent wasn't merely dead; he had been ruined. Though it probably mattered not at all to the dead, it bothered the living, and, at least for the moment, that was the side she was on.

No lumpish hostile appeared. Anna would have been surprised if one had. She had escaped, but so had the shooter. He still had his anonymity. He'd be a fool to risk it just to shoot someone who might or might not be a threat to him.

Or her.

Anna tried that out. No sense being close-minded about things. Cowboy movies had trained her to think of rifles as boys' toys. Usually true, but women in law enforcement were out-shooting their male counterparts on the rifle and pistol range. They seemed to have a natural aptitude for it. Lining up a bead on a target was not unlike threading a needle, plucking a splinter from a toddler's finger, dotting the "i" in icing on a birthday cake: hand to eye, steady nerves. They were born to it.

With a last long look into the mirror to guarantee the coast was indeed clear, she finally shoved open the Blazer's door and stepped out. Her foot buckled under her, and pain, kept at bay by necessity, crippled her. Screaming at the suddenness of it, she fell to her knees beside the truck. When the shock cleared she dragged herself around till she was sitting, back against the front tire, to assess the damage. A bullet had struck her left foot. It was that which had downed her with such vicious abruptness on the hillside. Lead had torn away the heavy lug heel of her hiking boot and pulled the leather away from the sole. Near as she could tell without taking the boot off, it hadn't drawn blood, but the force had twisted her ankle sufficiently to break or sprain it.

"Dagnabbit," Anna said, then ground her teeth lightly. Cowboy cursing reminded her of low-fat ice cream: mildly ridiculous and totally unsatisfying.

Having unlaced the offending boot, she considered it for a moment. Her first instinct was to remove it, run her fingers over her foot to reassure herself it was all there. Intellectually she knew it was; there was no blood, and, though it hurt, she could wiggle everything that was supposed to wiggle. The ankle would undoubtedly swell. Once she got the boot off she might not be able to get it on again. With a lame foot she'd be useless, and there was something more she needed to do. Lacing the boot back up, she cinched it tight, splinting the ankle. Given good support, she could push herself a little further.

The ankle hurt, but she could put her weight on it. Not broken, she told herself, and limped away from the Blazer. She had taken the keys from the ignition and snapped them in the outside pocket of her jacket. Donating her vehicle to her attacker and spending the night under a juniper would not be a happy ending.

Anna was banking on the fact that her would-be murderer didn't think she'd stop once she got clear of his sights; that he'd turned and run the minute she'd disappeared over that second hill and would be hightailing it back to the park to cover his tracks. All Anna wanted was a glimpse of him. Or her.

That's all she got.

Having circled three-quarters of the way around the hill she saw, half a mile or more away, a tiny figure. Blurred and indistinct in khaki clothes or desert camouflage, it trotted over a ridge and down out of her line of sight. The shooter could have been six feet tall or six inches, black or white, male or female. All the hard-won sighting told her was that he was probably headed back toward Carlsbad's headquarters, and she'd already guessed that much.

Adrenaline, vengeance, hope all abandoned her at once, and suddenly she was so tired it was an effort to draw breath. Her ankle throbbed, drumming its dissatisfaction at the recent abuse. Cold poked icy fingers into her ears, irritating the eardrums. Brent's blood caked and itched on the skin of her face and neck. Eschewing cowboy delicacy, she called down vile imprecations on all things living and dead, on the wind and the cold, the uneven dirt and the knife-edged plants. By the time she'd reached the truck she'd used up the vocabularies of several generations of sailors and, had there been any truth to the conceit, would have left a blue streak as wide as the Danube in her wake.

Brent didn't carry a radio in his vehicle. As he wasn't BLM or NPS, it made sense. Anna cursed him anyway, because she was in that sort of mood. Every jolt and rut pained her. Her ankle complained so bitterly that pushing in the clutch pedal was torture. She cursed Roxbury for having a manual transmission. Cursing him was easier than remembering him, than feeling his blood on her flesh and knowing somebody was going to have to break the news to his wife.

When she reached the highway she goaded the Blazer along at sixty-five miles per hour in third gear rather than trash her ankle further. Finally she could stand the whine of the engine no longer and used her right foot to shove in the clutch. The Blazer careened into the oncoming lane. "Never a cop around when you need one," she growled as she righted the vehicle; then she smiled. Anything taken to absurd extremes ran the risk of becoming ludicrous. Even ambient crankiness.

The Bureau of Land Management offices were on the east side of town, off the main drag. On impulse, Anna drove into their lot. It was just before five and almost dark, but there were still cars parked in front of the building and lights in the windows. She was taking the chance that Holden had gone to work today. Holden would have all the numbers: the sheriff, the coroner, BLM law enforcement. She yearned to dump the whole thing in his lap, run back to

Zeddie's, crawl in the hot tub, and drink the forbidden juice of the grape.

Cunning and baffling, her mentor in AA had quoted the accepted wisdom on alcohol to an alcoholic. So be it, Anna thought unrepentantly. She'd been cunningly baffled by events for coming on a week now, and none of them were remotely as rewarding as a glass of good wine.

The BLM offices were as lackluster as could be expected of new government buildings. Efficient and featureless in neutral tones and cubicled spaces. The receptionist, a young Navajo man with shoulder-length black hair tied neatly in a ponytail, squeaked like a rabbit when Anna appeared in front of his desk. She'd spent all her time with the rearview mirror looking for the sniper. Had she bothered to take a look at herself, she might have cleaned up a bit before returning to civilization. The receptionist reached for the phone, and Anna laid a hand on his wrist. "Don't worry," she said. "It's not my blood."

He was not reassured. Hand halfway to the receiver he froze, staring at her blood-black fingernails on his arm. In vain, she tried to find the words that would ease his mind. Finally, she said, "Is Holden Tillman here? He'll know what to do with me."

Magic words, "Holden Tillman." Anna made a mental note to give him a bad time about their open-sesame effect someday when they both recovered their senses of humor.

The receptionist returned, Holden swinging on crutches at his heels.

"Sorry, Holden," Anna said stupidly. "Are you in the middle of anything?"

He took in her bloodstained person, the dusty clothes, her crippled stance. "A local's been complaining about traffic noise on the northwest boundary, but I expect it can wait." He smiled his slow smile, and Anna's heart lifted a little.

"I've just come from there," she said. "And the only traffic was me, but I did stir up a bit of dust."

Holden did everything right, wearing all hats at once: EMT, bureaucrat, husband, father, friend. Hot coffee was fetched. Anna's bloody jacket was peeled off. A kindly woman in the gray-brown BLM shirt with the American flag sewn on the shoulder took her to the ladies' room so she could wash the last traces of Roxbury from her face and hands. Calls were made to the right agencies. The sheriff was alerted. Her boot was cut off and her foot elevated. Ice was found for the ankle.

Holden underwent a marvelous metamorphosis. As he tended her, she watched him change from the uncertain palsied man who'd killed his patient through negligence to the confident man of understated command he'd been when she'd first met him. Roxbury's death was not good news to Holden; there was nothing of relief or relish in his new attitude. It was that he saw the shooting as Anna did, linked somehow with the death of Frieda Dierkz. This second murder proved the first. Holden was a born-again believer in the sacred butt-print. He hadn't killed Frieda. It made a new man of him.

Only after she'd been cared for and was firmly on the road to being human again, did Holden begin to dig for details. The sheriff had come. Holden had timed it so she'd only have to tell her story once.

Anna told her tale, notes were taken, questions asked. When she finished, Holden arranged everything as she would have herself: the NPS car would be picked up and delivered back to the park by a sheriff's deputy. Rhonda and Holden would give her a ride back to Zeddie's that night. Rhonda arrived in the midst of these plans and took on her new duties with good-natured grumbles. Since Holden's ankle was broken she'd been playing chauffeur. Now she had two gimps to squire around. Their son, Andrew, had come with her. It was the first time Anna had seen him conscious. He didn't look like either his mother or his father but was one of those children who appear to have been fashioned by the fairies. There was an irrepressible impishness about him that delighted Anna even as she was glad she wouldn't have to raise the boy.

That impish spark in the child's eyes was the only physical resemblance he had to his dad. Anna laughed to see the twin gleams when Holden pulled his son onto his lap. Rhonda looked both surprised and pleased. That twinkle had been gone from her husband for a while.

Rhonda drove, Anna rode shotgun, and Holden and Andrew were tucked in the cramped seats in the back of the truck's "king" cab. From the scraps of conversation and high-pitched squeals, Anna guessed they played at some game involving toy bats and tickling.

Anna found herself telling her adventure again, not because she had to but because she needed to. It was a story of such magnitude, at least to her, that she would need to tell it several more times to dissipate its power, to get some kind of hold on it. Rhonda asked all the right questions, questions the sheriff would never think of: Were you scared? Did it hurt? Did you think you were going to die? Under this gentle probing, emotions quashed by pride or necessity welled up with such force they threatened to choke Anna. No wonder men were often frightened of women. They had a way of getting to the heart of things, a dangerous place sometimes.

Lest she betray her weaknesses, Anna stopped talking. Giving her time to recover, Rhonda told how she had spent this cold and windy day. She'd not been chased, shot at, or dipped in blood, but she'd ferreted out a whole lot more information than Anna had.

"I spent the day on the phone," Rhonda said. "No mean feat with Andrew around. I'll send you my phone bill when we get it. All calls during prime time. Yikes. Most of the stuff was just gossip, but I did come up with a few interesting items."

They'd turned off the National Parks Highway and onto the park lands. In the headlights a jagged line of road flanked by low stone walls was sliced from the night. Play in the backseat became one-sided. Anna could tell Holden was listening. Rhonda sensed it too and went on talking with no change in tone, as if she was afraid of frightening away some shy wild thing. Anna could have told her her husband was back for good, but she figured Rhonda would know that soon enough.

"Whether these bits and pieces will help, you'll have to tell me," Rhonda continued. "Brent's last job was in West Virginia. He worked as a geologist for a coal company there for a couple of years. Holden and I met the president of their local grotto at a cavers' convention in Albuquerque. I called him because he'd seemed down on Brent the one time his name came up. I figured he'd be a good candidate for dirt. According to him, Brent had a dishonorable discharge from the army in 1972. That's what this guy had against him. He's a Vietnam vet and proud of it. His guess was Brent was discharged for desertion or maybe cowardice, so he's never liked him. Does that help?"

She sounded so hopeful that Anna didn't like to discourage her. "You never know what's going to help," she said.

"Hah!" Rhonda snorted. "Too bad. That was some of my best stuff. Want to hear the rest?"

Anna did.

"This is more sad than pertinent, but it's what I got."

"Shoot," Anna said.

"Careful what you wish for," Holden said from the backseat.

"Careful what you wish for," Andrew echoed in a sweet piping voice.

"Who's telling this story?" Rhonda asked with mock severity.

"You are, baby," said Holden.

"You are, Momma," said Andrew.

"More sad than pertinent," Anna said to get things rolling.

"Yes. Thank you. This is from the Minnesota connection. I called the secretary of the grotto up there. She's in love with Holden."

"Unrequited!" came from the backseat.

"A healthy choice," Rhonda told her husband. "The secretary, Sarah or Susie or somebody—"

"Sally," Holden interjected. A tactical error. "Or maybe it was Silly . . ."

"Nice save," Rhonda said, and laughed. "*Sally* told me Zeddie had an older sister who was killed in a climbing accident when Zeddie was in high school. Her sister was a lot older, close to thirty at the time."

"Sondra's age," Anna said idly.

"You think it means anything?" Rhonda asked.

"I wouldn't know what," Anna admitted. "It would have to have happened more than ten years ago. Did this Sally know any details? Who was there, what happened, that sort of thing?"

"No. I thought of that. Like maybe Frieda was there and screwed up, got Zeddie's sister killed or something?"

"Frieda would have been twenty-five or so. She was already working for the Park Service. I suppose she could have gone home. Her mom said she was friends with Zeddie's sister. And the accident didn't have to take place in Minnesota. I don't know if there's any place to climb in Minnesota that's high enough you could kill yourself falling off of it."

"I'll find out," Rhonda promised.

Holden made squirmy uncomfortable noises from the rear seat. "Daddy, you're squishing my bat," came a complaining note.

"Sorry, son. Rhonda, I don't know if that's such a good idea," Holden began. "What with guns going off and avalanches and what not. I don't want you and Andrew—"

"What?" Rhonda cut him off. "Talking long distance on the phone? This from Mr. Crawl-Down-Holes-and-Break-an-Ankle? Mr. Spit-in-the-Face-of-Danger?"

"Aww, that's not how it is," Holden said, but Rhonda had won her point.

"Is that all?" Anna asked. Her words sounded niggardly and ungrateful even in her own ears, but she was so tired.

Reaching into her reserves she dredged up a few more. "Not that it's not a lot," she managed.

"Gee, thanks a heap," Rhonda said, and, "Ringtail!" She put on the brakes, her high beams spotlighting a graceful little brandy-colored cat with a black-and-white tail as long as its body crouched atop the stone wall beside the road.

Enraptured, the four of them watched as the cat studied them, gauged the personal danger, opted for the better part of valor, and disappeared over the far side of the stones.

"Pretty neat, eh, Andrew?" Holden asked.

"Pretty neat," the little boy agreed. "Can I have one?"

"They're wild animals, sweetie," Rhonda told him. "They only like to be seen once in a while like this. They wouldn't be happy in a cage."

"I wouldn't keep him in a cage," Andrew said stubbornly. "I'd keep him in my room."

The adults laughed. Offended, Andrew returned to his stuffed bat, carrying on a whispered conversation they clearly were not meant to be privy to.

Rhonda started the truck moving again. "And, since you asked," she said picking up the thread of conversation, "no, that is not all. I saved the best for last. I mean the best if any of this is of any use. *Sally* was a veritable fount of information. Dr. McCarty may not be Marcus Welby material after all. Twelve years ago he was brought up on charges. She seemed to think pretty serious ones—lose-your-medical-license serious. But he settled out of court, and the charges were dropped. And no," she said before Anna could speak, "she didn't know what he'd been charged with."

THERE WAS A party going on at Zeddie's house. Anna almost whimpered at the blaze of lights and babble of voices that blasted her when she opened the door. Rhonda and Holden had slunk away under cover of darkness as soon as they'd seen the symptoms of revelry. Tonight Anna wished she could have gone home with them, hidden out in their cozy little house. The Tillmans were a family. Childhood with mother and father, dinners around the table, chores and games, was decades past. If Anna'd ever really known what family meant, she'd long since forgotten. In her world it was merely a mechanism of exclusion, shutting out those who weren't connected. Anna had her sister, whom she dearly loved. Once she'd had a husband. There was closeness, trust, companionship—all the stuff of Hallmark cards. But did two constitute a family? Somehow it didn't, not quite. For family, more than one generation needed to be represented.

You have your NPS family, a saccharine voice in her head chanted as she hung her scabrous leather coat on a peg by the door. Looking as sour as she felt, she limped into the front room. The festivities weren't as vile as her tired mind had painted them. Oscar was there, Peter and Zeddie, Curt, and a young couple Anna didn't recognize: a handsome lithe man in his mid twenties with a beard close-cropped in the fashion of Curt's, his olive-skinned wife and their toddler, a child so apple-cheeked and curly-topped she would have been a shoo-in for a Gerber's ad from the fifties.

Zeddie was on the sofa with a guitar. Calcite curled up in a ball at her hip, apparently a devotee of stringed instruments. The young woman's hair was loose and clean. Anna realized it was the first time she'd seen Zeddie without a bandana tied buccaneer-style around her head. This night she looked impossibly young and strong, a willow, wide and rooted deep, able to withstand any of life's storms. In her rich contralto she was belting out an intricate ballad, the refrain of which was "and I want a shot of whiskey!" From the laughter, Anna surmised Zeddie made up the lyrics as she went along, poking fun at the business of rangering and the politics of caving.

Peter McCarty leaned on the mantel of a fireplace that hadn't been used in so long it had been converted to a storage place for magazines. On his handsome face was a look of proprietorship and reflected glory that he had in no way earned. Not by matrimony, at any rate, or by any basic honesty that Anna had noted. Tonight she found the hypocrisy irritating.

Oscar was giving full attention either to the performance or the performer and spared Anna the barest of nods. The two strangers smiled politely, then glanced away. Curt Schatz held the apple-cheeked baby girl on his lap, looking almost as happy as if she'd been a cat. Perhaps all nonverbal animals share the same charm. Schatz dangled his keys in front of chubby grasping fingers in lieu of paws, percolating giggles taking the place of purring.

Anna caught his eye and he stood immediately, shifting the child to his hip in a practiced movement. A smile illuminated the shadows of his beard, and behind horn-rimmed spectacles, his eyes were welcoming.

Warmth brought Anna unpleasantly close to tears. If you want somebody who's glad to see you so damned bad, why don't you get a dog? she mocked herself. The self-inflicted cruelty stemmed the waterworks for only a moment. Then she remembered she had a dog. Frieda's dog, Taco, a trusting, slobbering, jowly, loving, jumping golden retriever.

"And I want a shot of whiskey!" Zeddie wailed, the depth of her voice filling the small room and pouring like hot wax into one's bones.

Anna's eyes filled.

"Uh-oh," Curt said. "Don't *do* that. I'll get you a beer if you'll stop," he coaxed.

"Wine," Anna said. "And it's a deal."

Schatz deposited the baby girl with her mother and vanished around the corner into Zeddie's kitchen-cum-dining area. The song came to an end in laughter and a spattering of applause. Faces turned toward Anna. She stood just barely inside the door. For a moment she believed Brent Roxbury's blood still stained her face and hands and that was the reason for the stares. Then she remembered it had been washed away in the ladies' bathroom at the BLM offices.

"What?" she said. "What?"

An embarrassing silence descended. Mouths moved like those of grounded goldfish, but no one spoke. It occurred to Anna that one of them must be her gunman. Who else could it be? Sondra McCarty, only pretending to be gone, stalking the desert with a high-powered rifle? Maybe.

"Your wish. My command. All that shit," Curt said, returning with a water glass full of red wine.

The spell was broken. People moved. They talked. They drank. And if any of them wanted Anna dead, she couldn't read it in their faces.

14

A LITTLE WINE, a little music, the cat transferred to her lap, Curt sitting at her feet playing with the baby, and Anna was willing to believe she had imagined the whole thing: the funky stares at the door, the shooting, Brent's blood, even Frieda's murder. Willing but not quite able. Normalcy, instead of making violence seem unreal, was itself made unreal by that violence. Despite the purring Calcite and the warm cabernet, Anna was on edge.

Zeddie strummed her guitar, humming snatches of tunes Anna didn't recognize. With a thump, Zeddie dropped the flat of her hand onto the strings, cutting off the music. "So what did you think of Big Manhole?" she asked.

Anna twitched as if she'd been struck.

Peter dropped his pose at the mantel and took two steps across the room. Hands on knees, he peered into her face. "Are you all right?" He laid the back of his hand across her forehead as a mother checking a child for fever might. Anna would have flinched again, but she managed to control it. McCarty's face ballooned in front of her, bobbing and weaving. Cold sweat pricked in her armpits. Noises sounded distorted.

"I'm fine," she said, and heard her words as from a distance. An anxiety attack; Anna'd never had one, but she'd sat with enough displaced tourists suffering the symptoms to recognize it for what it was: an all-encompassing physical fear reaction that came from nowhere. Pain was better, exhaustion, depression, toothache, the dry heaves, herpes, hives. Breathing slowly through her nose, she rode the horror like a breaking wave. It'll pass, she told herself and, for the first time, understood why those words of wisdom always failed to comfort.

McCarty was still in her face. It was all she could do not to shove him back. Deliberately she stroked Calcite, concentrated on the warmth of the cat's fur under her hand. When she could lift the glass and find her mouth, she drank wine. Every eye was on her. It made things immeasurably worse.

To keep from rushing screaming from the room, Anna began to talk. "Big Manhole was . . ." Her voice sounded hollow and distant. She tried again. "Brent was at Big Manhole." Better. "Somebody shot him. Killed him outright. Half his face was blown off." Her intention had not been to shock, yet she slapped the morbid images across the party faces of those with her. Even as she was disgusted with herself for tracking her misery into someone else's home, she watched for any reaction that might say, "It's me; I am your shooter."

Oscar looked as if he'd sustained a physical blow. The young mother nestled under her husband's arm. Curt appeared annoyed at this emotional breech of etiquette, but he closed his free hand over the arch of Anna's uninjured foot in a show of support. Zeddie and Peter pounced on her offering succor. Zeddie's strong arms hugged Anna. McCarty propped her feet up on the sofa. Curt was sent to make hot drinks—the outdoorsman's cure for whatever ails.

Anxiety was carried away in the hubbub, leaving Anna drained and nervous. Cat still intact, she was pampered and enthroned. From her place of honor she told the story a third time. Not once, not from anyone, did she feel a flicker of guilt, see a hint of foreknowledge or an iota of ill will. Either the sniper wasn't there, or he or she was desperately clever and a practiced deceiver.

Her tale of gore effectively killed the party. The young couple were the first to go. The woman scooped her child from Schatz's lap as if merely being in Anna's vicinity might give the baby bad dreams. Oscar lingered awhile longer. He'd known Roxbury, had worked with him. Though Brent hadn't been killed in the park, the superintendent would want to be told, as would George Laymon. The Bureau of Land Management would take the brunt of police and media attention, but it would be a courtesy to inform the people at Carlsbad who had been connected with Roxbury. "Courtesy" was Oscar's polite term. The underlying message was understood. Park employees learned it almost as soon as they learned where to pin their name tags and the appropriate way to wear the flat-brimmed Smokey Bear hat. Like brass anywhere, NPS bigwigs hated being blindsided. The underling who failed to inform them of approaching disaster was severely frowned upon. More than once Anna had avoided much-deserved punishment by the simple expedient of telling her district ranger she'd screwed up before an irate citizen could give him the same information in a less palatable manner.

Oscar ended with the NPS's standard warning. "I doubt newspeople will call you. This isn't a park-related incident. If they do, refer them to me, George, or the superintendent."

Don't talk to them. Everybody got that.

"I want to talk to George," Anna said.

Iverson was at the door, holding it ajar, letting the heat out in the tradition of winter guests. A pained expression met her words.

"I think Brent's killing is linked to Frieda's," Anna pushed.

Oscar looked weary. "I'll set it up in the morning, okay? First thing."

Anna nodded. Oscar left. For a long minute the four of them stayed where they were, scattered around Zeddie's living room, no one wanting to meet Anna's eye.

"You think Frieda was killed on purpose? You think one of the core group killed Frieda?" Zeddie asked. There was belligerence as well as incredulity in her voice. "One of us?"

Anna said nothing till their combined silence undid her. "Nobody else was there."

"Maybe it was Brent," Peter said, trying to make peace. "He was up near the head of the Pigtail. Maybe he got to feeling bad about it and shot himself."

Anna gave him a withering look. "Then shot at me?"

Peter glanced over her head at Zeddie and shrugged as if to say, "I tried."

"Well," Zeddie ended a silence grown too long. "I'm hitting the hay. Murdering people in cold blood really wears me out." She left without bidding anyone good night. Peter followed, leaving Anna and Curt to each other's company.

"You don't really think that, do you?" Curt asked.

"I don't know what to think," Anna told him.

Curt levered himself up from his position near the sofa. "I'll sleep on the floor," he said. "Don't want to accidentally kick your bad ankle."

Calcite jumped off Anna's lap, clawing her in the process. She hadn't made any friends tonight.

JUST AFTER SEVEN, the sun not yet up, they were awakened by the phone. Stumbling off the couch, Anna was reminded of her ankle. A night's sleep had done wonders. It was stiff and sore, but she could tell it would loosen up with use.

"Dillard residence," she said into the receiver. The call was for her: Oscar Iverson. George Laymon would see her in his office at eight o'clock. That was what she wanted, yet she hung up feeling dissatisfied.

Curt shambled by clad in boxer shorts and a hand-crocheted afghan in lime green and pink squares. "Who was it?" he croaked as he fumbled with Zeddie's coffee-maker.

"Oscar," Anna said, and it came to her why she'd been disappointed. Some corner of her brain had hoped it would be Sondra tracking down an errant husband and providing a few answers.

Padding after Curt in a tee-shirt, underpants, and ragg wool socks, she asked, "Did Peter ever get a hold of his wife?" Two days underground and the campout feel of group sleepovers had made them informal.

"Not that I know of. Why? Do you want to pin your pet theories on Sondra?" Curt loaded the pot expertly and poked the "on" button. Anna crawled onto a stool on one side of a counter that separated kitchen from dining space. Curt settled on the other. Both stared hopefully at the pot filling between them.

"That would be nice, wouldn't it?" Anna said.

"Pinning it on Sondra?"

"She's such a twit."

Curt laughed, and Anna felt forgiven. They sat without talking till there was enough liquid in the pot to fill two coffee cups. Curt poured and Anna fetched a pint of heavy cream from the refrigerator. Curt's eyebrows rose. "No soy milk?"

Anna didn't share Zeddie's taste for good health. "I smuggled it up while you guys were still in Lechuguilla. How well do you know Sondra?" she asked as she poured cream into her cup.

"You're going to make me do something, aren't you? Something sleuthy and embarrassing. Something that will probably get my face slapped. If I just confess to shooting you in the foot and murdering whoever you think was mur-dered, can I be excused?"

Anna refused to be diverted. "Are you good friends, medium friends, friendly acquaintances, what?"

Curt groaned.

Anna waited.

"Between medium and friendly acquaintances," he said warily.

"Could you call her?"

"*You* could call her."

"Do you know people she knows? Family, friends, whatever?"

Curt sipped his coffee. Anna sipped hers. He looked over the rim of his cup. "I smell a trap. I'm not answering any more questions until you tell me what it's going to cost me."

"Since you're in the Minnesota connection, I thought maybe you could make some calls," Anna said. "Find out where she is. I'm getting a bad feeling about her."

"Why don't you ask Peter to do it? He knows more about where his wife might be than I would."

"Peter's part of the bad feeling."

"Jeez. I guess I should be honored you don't suspect me."

"Not yet." Anna wondered if she was only kidding.

"Sure. I'll do it," Curt said at last. "After all, it's not like I have a life or anything."

GEORGE LAYMON WAS if not pleased then anxious to talk with Anna. Ushering her into his office the moment she arrived at park headquarters, he sat her down in the visitor's chair. From his familiar perch on the edge of his desk, he towered over her. His face was an interesting amalgam of aggravation and concern.

"Oscar called last night, and I talked with Holden Tillman at the BLM this morning," he said. "The sheriff's department is taking care of returning the government vehicle." Laymon didn't change the tone of his voice, yet much was conveyed in that simple sentence: the knowledge that Anna had used an NPS vehicle in an unauthorized manner, a threat of reprisals if the sedan was damaged, the hint that he now held the upper hand in this conversation.

"I think Brent's murder and Frieda's are connected," she said baldly.

Moving as if a weight had settled on his shoulders, Laymon put his desk between them. "You said Frieda changed her story, didn't remember anybody trying to kill her." Anna started to protest, but Laymon silenced her with a raised hand. "I know. You thought you might have seen something near the site of the rock slide. We went over that with Holden and Oscar," he said patiently. "Oscar felt, given the place, the conditions, and the stress levels you were all operating under, a fleeting impression in shifting loam wasn't significant. Holden agreed with him."

"He's changed his mind," Anna said. She was pushing her luck. Concern was growing rigid, cracking across Laymon's cheekbones.

He looked out the window for a minute, the cloudless sky bluing his eyes. His fingers drummed softly on the desk blotter. "I'm not surprised," he said. "Losing a patient is hard on anybody and harder on Holden than most." His focus returned to the room, the chair, Anna. Reasoning with her was at an end. Folding his hands in front of him, he told her how it was going to be.

"In using a government vehicle in an unauthorized manner, you have overstepped your bounds considerably. You have made remarks without substantiation that do not reflect well on the people here, people who worked so hard to save your friend. You have no authority in Carlsbad. You are a guest of this park. Until now we have been willing to cut you a good deal of slack because of what you have been through. You've used that slack, Anna. I can put you in touch with human resources either here or, better yet, in your home park, and we'll get some counseling for you. Other than that, there is nothing we can do. Oscar and I have talked it over with the superintendent. This latest incident is a BLM matter. Your statement has been taken, but, as you arrived after the fact, you aren't a material witness."

"Attempted murder, assault on a federal officer, illegal discharge of a firearm," Anna said. "Whoever it was shot at me more than once. Malice."

George Laymon's eyes strayed again out the window. "You had a bad scare," he said carefully.

"You think I'm making this up?" Anger boiled so hot the image of steam pouring from her ears didn't seem so much ludicrous as inevitable. What saved her from an unladylike outburst that would have gotten her tossed out of Laymon's office was the sheer profusion of hostile remarks that clogged her brain and tied her tongue.

"I didn't say that, Anna. Some of these good old boys around here get carried away. Look at any road sign. They are all riddled with bullet holes."

"My boot heel—"

"Could have been broken off on a rock. That's rough country out there. Or it could have been shot off like you say," he said placatingly.

Anna was not placated.

"I just think there are many explanations you haven't considered. You're too close to this. Too personally involved. To put it bluntly, you're out of line. It's time you went home."

A brief maelstrom of emotions ranging from acute humiliation to homicidal rage seethed. Because she was female, her body's natural response to the onslaught was tears, tears of anger that, had she allowed them to fall, surely would have burnt holes in the carpet like droplets of battery acid. Determinedly impassive, she waited for the storm to abate. She hadn't a leg to stand on. Everything George Laymon said was true. A Chinese aphorism came to mind: *If you keep going the way you're going, eventually you'll get where you're headed.* Where she was headed was out of town, if not tarred and feathered riding on a rail, then the modern-day equivalent.

Going home to Mesa Verde, her tower house, her cat,

tempted Anna to the very soul. It was, as the bard had said, peevish and self-willed harlotry that bade her stay. Self-willed harlotry won. The time had come to grovel fetchingly.

Anna sighed and rubbed now-dry eyes. "Thanks, George. A counselor would be good. I know I've been a pain in the neck. I guess I needed to blame Frieda's death on somebody human. God is so unsatisfying." She laughed, and it took no effort to sound shaky and uncertain. "I'll talk to a shrink, get some rest, and get this ankle stable. I'd like to be here for Brent's funeral, get some closure. Then I'll head home." Laymon couldn't very well refuse to let her stay for the funeral of a coworker whose body she had found. That and a shrink appointment would buy her a few more days in which to continue wearing out her welcome. "Thanks again for listening," she said. "This has been a rough week."

Laymon was relenting, though his eyes were still wary. Anna didn't want to overplay her hand. Pushing herself up from her chair and limping more than was called for by her rapidly healing ankle, she allowed herself to be shunted from his office.

Outside the building, she stood in the thin winter sunlight pretending she felt some heat from it. Sheltered from the wind, it was almost true. She turned her face to the light the way a sunflower will. The day was young. Laymon was a professional; he'd managed to rake her over the coals in less than a quarter of an hour. One thing was sure: she was officially on foot. CACA wouldn't be giving her a vehicle in the near future. Later she would consider bumming a ride into town and renting a car. Since 1994 when the NPS had bumped most of their law-enforcement rangers up to GS-9s, her poverty days were over. Anna made thirty thousand and change annually. For a single woman living forty-five miles from the nearest retail store, thirty grand stretched a long ways. A rental car wouldn't break the bank.

Maybe tomorrow, she thought. Today she was going on a hike.

ZEDDIE'S HOUSE WAS empty. She was working the Big Room down in Carlsbad Cavern till noon, then roving a section of trail in the twilight zone after lunch. Peter would be hanging about, within whispering distance. Where Schatz was was anybody's guess. Solitude was a relief. Having alienated her hostess with accusations of murder, Anna didn't relish getting caught raiding her refrigerator for a packed lunch. A bottle of Dos Equis beckoned with its long and graceful neck, but she declined, taking an Orange Crush instead. Demon alcohol would have to wait till she didn't have so much on her mind.

A quick forage through the bathroom cabinets produced an Ace bandage. Ankle taped, food and water in a purloined daypack, Anna left the housing area and started cross-country in the direction of Big Manhole. A mile's walk took her over a rise in the earth that effectively blocked the Carlsbad buildings from view. Out of sight of headquarters, she ceased to move in a straight line and began making slow wide arcs, her eyes fixed on the ground.

CACA's backcountry was rugged and not well traveled. The park was known for its cavern; visitors came to see the cave, not to hike. Little money was dedicated to the creation and upkeep of trails. Anna hoped this would simplify her task. In a hiking park the plethora of footprints would have rendered tracking nearly impossible.

The desert was not good country for finding sign. The earth was hard-baked and covered with stones, though recent rains had softened it somewhat. On that Anna pinned her hopes. That and the shooter's mind-set. He hadn't planned on leaving any witnesses. Maybe he'd not bothered to cover his trail. With her escape, he'd been thrown off balance. The glimpse she'd had of him, he'd been running. Runners left good prints.

Two hours' careful traverse of sand and rock turned up little besides weathered litter and game trails. Cold drove the life of the desert underground, and she hadn't seen so much as a jack rabbit or a horned lizard. Three times she'd come across recently made footprints, and three times the trails turned away from her objective: shooting distance to Big Manhole. Anna remained unconcerned. Tracking was slow business, two hours scarcely a beginning.

Wind, cutting in an endless blade across the exposed skin of her face, was an irritant, but she chose to use rather than fight it. This time of year it blew unwaveringly from the northwest. By keeping it first to one quarter, then, when she turned and began tracking in the opposite direction, to the other, she could stay on course without bothering to lift her eyes from the ground.

Two more hours passed without producing results. Anna found a fold in the earth to deflect the wind and lunched on a peanut butter and jelly sandwich, Doritos, and the orange soda. From her niche she could see what she believed was the hill that housed the entrance to Big Manhole. In an unending landscape of fawn-colored hills it was hard to be sure without digging out the binoculars she'd pilfered from Zeddie's mantel. Beyond the hill a valley had been carved by a now-dry watercourse. The riverbed writhed like a snake through scabby hills and up under cliffs of white limestone. In an ancient oxbow, dry for centuries, was a pipe sticking out of the ground, a "dry hole" marker, where a well had been. A quarter of a mile beyond was another well, this one up and running. A black speck, followed by a comet's tail of white, barreled down the road toward the wells. A truck fighting the same choking dust that had engulfed Anna.

She retrieved Zeddie's field glasses. A cement truck, no doubt laying a well pad somewhere in the hills. She followed the trail of dust back to where the rutted dirt to Big Manhole forked off from the gravel, then traced it up to the bald hillock where she'd found Brent's Blazer. A cream-colored pickup was parked there. Because of its protective coloring she hadn't noticed it with the naked eye.

Interest rejuvenated, she moved the glasses slowly down the hill till she rested them on the entrance to the cave.

Brent's blood, black now, stained the rock, but the body was gone. The sheriff would have taken care of that. Big Manhole was locked, or at least closed. The driver of the pickup was nowhere in sight.

A minute's watch, and he appeared. Walking up from the gully separating Anna from Big Manhole came the rangy weathered form of Oscar Iverson. He was in uniform and so on duty. This wasn't a recreational jaunt. Probably he was there for the same reason she was: to see what he could find about the shooter who'd killed Roxbury. He'd driven around to the cave to backtrack.

Anna deliberated on whether to show herself or not. Laymon had made it abundantly clear that she was persona non grata in these parts, and the previous night, Oscar had seemed none too pleased with her either. From her protected crevice she would be all but invisible unless she purposely called attention to herself.

In times past she'd learned a good deal more from watching people than from talking with them. Words were used to obfuscate as often as to communicate. She decided on the role of unseen spy and cupped both hands around the end of the binoculars lest they catch the sun and flash out her whereabouts.

Oscar wasn't a tracker. He moved quickly, his long legs eating up the terrain. She guessed he was following a fairly clear trail and cringed as his great booted feet slapped down, obliterating traces of the shooter. Halfway up the long slope, not more than fifty yards from where she hid, Iverson came to a stop and squatted down, his long green-clad legs poking out at the knees in a fair imitation of a praying mantis. For a while he stared at the ground, then he poked at something with a stick he found nearby. Whatever it was that he had unearthed, he picked up gingerly with two fingers and dropped into a plastic bag that he tucked away in the pocket of his coat. That done, he straightened up again and appeared to be searching the area.

"Stomp, stomp, stomp," Anna whispered. Iverson's boots were falling with the oblivious regularity of the non-tracker. Once the obvious had been snatched up, the scene was treated like dirt. There'd be precious little left to see by the time she got there. She wished she'd not stopped for lunch, not commenced her tracking on the far end. Railing against past decisions petered out the way it always had to: when she reached Eve wishing she'd not played with the snake, regret vanished. There are no alternate life paths.

Finally Iverson moved on, and Anna allowed herself to exhale. He didn't go much farther. On higher, drier ground he lost the trail. After a few stabs into the brush, he gave up and returned the way he had come, over the same trail.

"Stomp, stomp, stomp," Anna lamented.

Briefly he stopped at the mouth of Big Manhole. Bowing his head, he dragged off his hat, a green billed cap with earflaps that tied beneath the chin. Ridiculous-looking garment, but Anna wished she had one. The wind was causing her ears to ache.

Iverson stood combing his straw-colored hair with his fingers till it stood out in the wind. Anna wondered if he was paying his respects to Brent Roxbury's ghost or merely cooling his brains the better to think with. Whatever the phenomenon, it was short-lived. Pulling the hat back on, he made short work of the walk up to his truck and drove off. Anna waited till a plume of white told her he was headed out toward the main highway, then she packed up the leavings of her lunch and started down the hillside to see if anything was left of the shooter's trail.

In minutes she reached the place where Iverson had stopped, a small clearing ringed with low growth and boasting a line of sight to the cave, an ideal place to lie in wait with a rifle. Anna paused just outside the clearing and hunkered down on her heels to study the ground. It didn't look as if the sheriff's men or any BLM people had visited the scene. Darkness would have prevented any serious investigation when they'd come to fetch the body the previous night. Either they'd be out later in the day, or they'd already come and gone but had failed to track the sniper.

Iverson's prints were all over the clearing, the easily

identifiable marks of a corrugated lug sole, the kind found on every pair of firefighting boots made by White's, the choice of elite wild-land firefighters from every land-management agency in the country.

To one side of the clearing she could see where he'd crouched down and gouged the earth with his twig. In the dirt was a smooth indentation about an inch long with a slight T-shaped mark at one end. A rifle shell, overlooked by the gunman, had left its impression in the soil. That was what Oscar had bagged and pocketed. Several minutes' careful study was unproductive. If the shooter had left other tracks, Iverson's overlay them. With a snort of disgust, Anna turned her attention to the trail Iverson had followed up the slope for such a short distance. Again lug-soled foot-prints were all she found. Either they all belonged to the heavy-footed Iverson, or the shooter also had been wearing White's boots. Near the ridge she lost the trail. The crown of this hill and the next were stripped bare of earth. Pol-ished limestone remained, untracked and untrackable.

Plunking herself down on the rock, Anna looked back toward the cave's mouth. A number of possibilities occurred to her. The shooter might not have left any tracks, or the tracks had been destroyed by Iverson. The shooter could have been wearing fire boots. They were common enough. She owned a pair. Zeddie probably did. Holden would. Curt, Peter, and Sondra wouldn't. But then she was wearing Zeddie's clothes. Borrowing or stealing wasn't out of the question.

An extremely unpleasant thought intruded. Maybe the shooter had worn Iverson's boots. Oscar had come directly up to the sniper's lair. Was he tracking, or did he know precisely where to come? The stomping and shuffling: insensitive investigation or intentional destruction of evidence? It wouldn't have been difficult to discover where and when Anna was to meet with Brent. Everyone at Zeddie's had known. They might have told. It wasn't a secret. Brent's choice to leave the message could be telling. Was it that he trusted the members of the core group, knew they had nothing to do with the killing? Or was he careless, overwrought, or overconfident?

The first attempt on Frieda's life had failed. It was not beyond the realm of possibility that Oscar Iverson had gone down into Lechuguilla not to rescue Frieda but to finish the job. If Brent had started to kill Frieda, then lost his nerve and decided to spill the beans to Anna, it made sense. Would an experienced caver like Oscar start an avalanche? Maybe. There was no way of knowing the whole side of the Pigtail would come down. With Holden watching every moment of the rigging, it would have been easier than sabotaging the ropes.

Unless Holden did that himself.

The thought made Anna physically ill. With a surge of relief, she remembered his broken ankle. He'd been at the bottom of the rock slide, not the top. And the person she'd seen scurrying away after the shots were fired was not lame. Suddenly she felt tired and scared.

One person to trust, and a cripple at that.

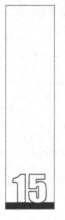

15

BY EARLY AFTERNOON Anna was back in Zeddie's house. To her delight, but for Calcite, it remained uninhabited. The hike had taken a toll on her weak ankle. Some of the swelling had returned, and she was glad to put her foot up and rest. Trust in one's fellows is like the net beneath the highwire. The act can be done without it, but the effort becomes considerably more taxing. Considering that, the ankle, and the cold, the morning's work had been tiring. Anna was feeling her age, measured not in years but in acquired cynicism and human frailty.

The message light on Zeddie's answering machine was blinking. Brazenly, Anna played back the messages. None was from Sondra. One was for her from Rhonda Tillman. Either a terse or a careful woman, Rhonda said only, "Call me."

Full of good intentions, Anna dragged the cordless phone, along with a cup of hot tea, to the sofa. Wrapped in the ghastly pink-and green afghan, she sipped her tea and contemplated the instrument. There were several people she would have liked to talk with. Of course, her sister, Molly. Jennifer, a friend of hers and a ranger at Mesa Verde. It was Jennifer who was looking after Anna's cat, Piedmont, and the newly orphaned Taco. Frederick the Fed, her ex-whatever, crossed her mind. After two years' silence he'd intruded back into her life. Knowing he'd fallen for her sister didn't lower him in her estimation. To her way of thinking, Molly was quite a catch. But it did render Frederick off-limits forever. Without knowing he was doing so, Frederick Stanton had banished himself from the affections of the Pigeon sisters. Molly would never touch a man Anna was interested in. Anna wouldn't dream of a man interested in her sister.

Besides, she had nothing to say to him.

She had nothing to say to anyone.

Words not related to the deaths of Frieda or Brent balled up and slid off her mind like liquid mercury. Sick as she was of the subject, it consumed her. Rhonda Tillman was the only person with whom she could trust herself to maintain a coherent conversation.

Soon she would call. Till then she would rest, drink her tea, and order her fragmented thoughts. The demographics of the suspect pool had broadened. Caving's isolated nature had blinded her to other possibilities. Even for an imagination as willing to invent monsters as Anna's, it stretched credibility to think of someone creeping deep into the earth over forbidding terrain to kill Frieda when she could be so easily run over in a parking lot or gunned down at the mall. That had left only the core group. Iverson's activities today opened a new line of thought. A member of the core group had to have pushed the rock that had landed Frieda in the Stokes. Given that, Anna had been pursuing her investigation from the angle that something that happened in the cave had fomented an opportunistic attempt on Frieda's life. But there had been a second and successful attempt. Oscar had been there, and Anna and Holden. They'd come down knowing Frieda was helpless. Completion of a failed murder attempt could have been decided upon before the expedition went underground.

For the life of her, Anna couldn't imagine why anyone would want to kill Frieda. Frieda Dierkz wasn't even the sort of woman a stalker would fancy. She was a solid, straightforward, midwestern farm girl who had intelligence without cunning, discretion without guile. Her favorite drugs were legal. She didn't gamble, steal, smuggle weapons, or traffic in illegally obtained artifacts. She was dispatcher and secretary to the chief ranger at Mesa Verde. Professionally she was indispensable, but she was not in a position to give or withhold anything worth killing for. If she had slept with married men, she had been as silent as the tomb. Anyway, Anna would have known. Everybody would have known. Parks made fishbowls look like the heart and soul of privacy.

Murder insisted on a motive. Because Anna couldn't find it, or couldn't understand it, didn't change the fact. For the moment she would set aside motive and paint mind pictures in hopes of seeing something new. Assuming Brent had pushed the stone onto Frieda in Tinker's Hell cleared up a number of things. Roxbury had been unnaturally perturbed by the injury and subsequent death of a woman he ostensibly didn't know. Guilt over his part in her death might account for that. Had that guilt preyed on him significantly, he might have lost his nerve after the first attempt and refused to try again. So Frieda lay helpless, yet unharmed, till assistance arrived in the persons of Anna, Oscar Iverson, and Holden Tillman.

Other cavers had cycled in and out during the rescue. How many, Anna didn't know. None of them had been in place when the avalanche started. It let them off the hook.

But Oscar had been there.

If Brent was bent on killing Frieda, he had plenty of opportunity. He didn't do it. Therefore someone else had to be factored in. Who did Brent have any opportunity to communicate with other than Holden, Oscar, and Anna? So:

Oscar comes down. Brent refuses to finish the job. Oscar finishes it for him. Brent can't live with the guilt and decides to tell Anna. He leaves a message on Zeddie's machine. One of the group mentions it to Oscar. He hikes out from the park, shoots Brent, and tries to shoot Anna for good measure. The next day he drives out to Big Manhole, covers up his trail, and retrieves the rifle shell he left behind.

On the surface the story held together, but, without knowing the why of it, Anna remained unsatisfied. There was no reason for Oscar to want Frieda dead that badly. Unless he was one hell of an actor, Anna was sure he didn't know Frieda except as a name on a research list.

The other aspect of this scenario that bothered her was personal. Oscar Iverson didn't strike her as the murdering kind. She was well aware that to spout that philosophy on the witness stand would get her crucified in any court in the country. Ted Bundy, criminologists were fond of pointing out, struck everybody as a heck of a swell fella. Anna wasn't so deluded as to think she'd know a murderer if she saw one. A few had crossed her path, and she'd not felt a cold wind on the back of her neck or sensed a darkness entering the room.

Under the right pressure anyone could become a killer. For someone to kill with this premeditation bespoke either great vanity, overriding fear, or both. Oscar Iverson exhibited neither. At least not to Anna. Still waters and all that, she told herself, and decided to leave Oscar in the running.

Picking up the cordless phone, she punched in the Tillmans' number. The machine answered. Anna was halfway through her message when Rhonda picked up.

"Sorry," she said. "I was hiding."

"Who from?"

"Oh. Everybody but you, Holden, and maybe my sister. No reason. I just get this way. If it makes people crazy, tough."

Anna laughed. "Get that way? I was born that way."

"Then you know what I mean."

Anna did and was duly honored to be on Rhonda's short-list with her husband and sister.

"You doggone well better appreciate this," Rhonda said. "I haven't gossiped this much since high school. There's got to be ears burning in three states. And, if gossip is a sin like Andrew's Foursquare Baptist grandmother says, I'll burn in hell for the next zillion years."

"I went to Catholic school," Anna told her. "I know nuns. They know people in high places. I'll get them to intercede for you if the gossip is good."

"It's good," Rhonda promised. "Unless you're Dr. Peter McCarty." A gulp of something was imbibed, and Rhonda went on, "Old girlfriends love to talk, and your darling Peter has his share. Miss *Sally* poked around for me—well, not for me. I had to promise I'd say 'hi' to Holden for her, which I won't, but she doesn't know that. I found out what the dropped charges were all about. Rape."

"You're kidding." Anna was taken aback. Rape was a power crime. Armed with charm, good looks, and money, McCarty had such built-in power over women, rape seemed redundant. Rape was also about hatred, and much of McCarty's appeal came from the fact that he genuinely seemed to like women.

"Not *rape* rape," Rhonda told her once she'd gleaned the drama from her announcement. "Statutory rape. Of Sondra. She was a patient of his, not quiet eighteen, and they had an affair. Her daddy went ballistic, as you might imagine. From what *Sally* said it took a sizable chunk of McCarty's money to smooth the ruffled feathers. Sondra kind of banged around after that—'bang' being the operative word. All her beaus were older and had money. It sounds like she was shopping for a sugar daddy. She was all set to marry a college professor about twenty years older than her, but something went wrong. He left her at the altar. This was more than two years ago. Peter was in an on-again off-again relationship with Zeddie at the time. Then bingo, bango, bongo, six months later he's walking down the aisle with

Sondra at a Barbie-doll dream wedding with yards of white lace and three or four hundred close friends. Weird, no?"

"Blackmail, you think?" Anna asked.

"Either that or an old statutory flame fanned into a sudden blaze."

Anna remembered the conversation she'd overheard as she lay squashed in the long passage out of Tinker's Hell. Sondra said she knew things about Peter that could get his medical license revoked. Had she been talking about a twelve-year-old rape case? Anna doubted it. Those charges were dropped. Given that Sondra had taken his money, then married the man, if she made a stink it would be she, not the doctor, who would end up looking the fool.

Sondra, at seventeen. Frieda at twenty-three or -four. Zeddie at the same age. Dr. McCarty had a history of seducing his young patients. If Sondra had discovered she wasn't the only one, that McCarty was continuing the pattern, and she had gotten her hands on proof, that might do it. Whether or not McCarty lost his medical license, the publicity would damage his practice or lose him his position if he wasn't in business for himself. As Rhonda had said, this was good. Anna assured her she'd receive absolution for the sin of gossiping.

An impatient wail cut over the phone line. "Oops. Gotta go," Rhonda said. "Andrew is awake." The line went dead. Anna wasn't done talking. She needed to bounce these new thoughts off another brain. Expose the obvious flaws. Air out her thinking lest it become circular and self-perpetuating.

The empty house, so recently a boon, began to chafe on her nerves. Where was Curt? Had he made the calls? Where was Iverson? What had he done with the rifle shell? Had there been an autopsy of Brent Roxbury? Anna was out of the loop, out of her park, out of her jurisdiction, and possibly out of her league.

For a quarter of an hour she stalked from room to room, gazed out over tracts of desert, of street, of employee housing. Able to stand her own company no longer, she put on a coat and limped down to headquarters to see if she couldn't mooch a ride into town.

Jewel was typing furiously as Anna let herself into the chief of resource management's office. Her face was screwed up as if she went for a speed record. Loath to break her concentration in case she was training for the secretarial Olympics, Anna closed the door softly and walked soundlessly across the room on moccasined feet. She was at Jewel's desk before the secretary noticed her.

With a start and a squawk, Jewel banged the screen button and blacked out her computer. She wasn't fast enough, and Anna smiled. "Aren't you the sneaky snake," Jewel said, and tried to regain her composure by preening hair-sprayed wings with porcelain nails.

"Sorry," Anna said.

"You here to be chewed out too?" Jewel asked with evident satisfaction.

"Too?"

"George told me Oscar was in hot water, messing over at Big Manhole. Seems you're a girl who can't resist hot water."

"Not this time," Anna said, and told her why she'd come. A few phone calls, and Jewel found a maintenance man who was driving into town to get machine parts. He picked up Anna on his way out of the compound. Being a pariah had its upside; Anna doubted Jewel would have been so forthcoming had virtue's reward not been the removal of Anna Pigeon.

Sixty-five minutes later she was outfitted with a Dodge Neon the color and stature of the average aphid, along with a full tank of gasoline. Credit cards were wonderful things. Anna drove to the BLM building on the eastern edge of town and again presented herself to the receptionist. Sans blood and dust, he didn't recognize her until she asked for Holden. Without bothering to phone ahead, the young man walked her back to Tillman's desk. On the way he asked questions about the shooting: How loud? How much blood? Color? Texture? Just as Anna was writing him off as a ghoul, he explained he was an amateur filmmaker—documentaries, mostly—but he wanted to make movies à la the Coen brothers in Minnesota. He was studying visual images. Anna laughed, not because she found his ambition amusing but because with that information she'd instantly forgiven him his prying. He was an artist not a busybody—as if that mattered one whit in the giant scheme of things.

Behind the fabric-covered partition that marked out his work space in a room of like spaces, Tillman was packing to leave. "Hey, Anna," he said. He was pleased to see her. It took her by surprise. She'd begun to think she'd alienated every living soul in New Mexico.

"Bad timing," he went on. "You caught me on my way out the door. What with one thing and another I got swamped. I'm in the field this afternoon."

"Can I ride along?" she asked on impulse.

Holden acted glad of the company. Foot encased in a walking cast, he took a BLM truck with an automatic transmission and drove out of town on the highway Anna had taken to Big Manhole. She found it hard to believe she'd made the journey only the day before. Corpse, bullets, wind—it felt as if it had happened years ago, or perhaps in a dream.

Holden told her everything he knew about the Roxbury Incident, as he now called it, a name to depersonalize uncomfortable memories. Along with the sheriff and the county coroner, Holden had gone out to Big Manhole. They'd arrived around eight o'clock, full dark, so there hadn't been much to see. The coroner pronounced Brent dead of a gunshot wound. A deputy recovered the rifle slug that killed him. The shot had ripped through Roxbury at a shallow angle and emerged where jawbone met ear. Much of its power spent, the slug lodged in the limestone lip above the cave entrance. As evidence it was of little value. Rock and bone had worked on it until it was simply a misshapen hunk of lead sporting fragments of Roxbury's flesh. Any rifling that might have been used to match it to the murder weapon was destroyed.

Anna told Holden of watching Iverson take the rifle shell, and he nodded as at old news. "George Laymon called and told us. The shell will be fingerprinted as soon as the park gets it to town. The sheriff wanted his own guys to do the work."

Turning in the shell didn't mean much. If it produced the killer's prints, it might be telling. If it had none there would be no way of knowing whether the shooter had wiped it before he loaded his weapon or if Iverson had wiped it clean of fingerprints before turning it over to the police.

"That's BLM land," Anna said as a thought occurred to her. "What was Oscar doing over there anyway?"

"It's only a few hundred yards from the park boundary. The superintendent wanted to know if any damage had been done, that sort of thing."

"Makes sense." Anna wondered why she used that phrase whenever she was particularly confused. "Oscar really trampled the scene," she said after a while.

Tillman laughed. "Captain Lightfoot. We kid him that he'll never get lost. That boy could leave tracks in concrete. Old Laymon won't let him anywhere near the more delicate crystal formations. Scared his feet'll hit high enough on the Richter scale it'd shatter anything within a fifteen-foot radius. He wouldn't have found much anyway. That whole ridge is nothing but one big rock."

"So I discovered." Holden didn't ask her what she had been doing there, and in her heart, she thanked him. Justifying herself was becoming a habit she'd just as soon break.

Because she needed to talk to someone and Holden was the only person whom she didn't suspect and who was still speaking to her, Anna shared her ideas about Oscar and Brent working together or in tandem to effect the death of Frieda Dierkz. Oscar and Holden were friends. Metaphorically speaking, Anna trod on eggs. She kept her statements theoretical, hypothetical, intellectual, trying her damnedest to convey suspicion without offending. After she finished her story Holden was silent for so long she began to get nervous.

"I'll have to think on this," he said in his slow, deliberate way. "I don't believe Oscar's got it in him to kick a cat out of the middle of the dinner table. But there might be something in what you say. I've got to think on it."

Anna had to be satisfied with that. She dropped the subject. "Are we going up to Big Manhole?" she asked as he turned the truck off the highway onto a gravel road that looked familiar.

"Not unless you want to. I was headed out to the Blacktail to go over some reports."

Anna had no desire to go to Big Manhole.

THE BLACKTAIL WAS like many other gas wells dotting the landscape of the Southwest. The Bureau of Land Management was not dedicated to conservation. Like the United States Forest Service, they were a multiple-use organization. Public lands were not only used for recreation and wildlife preserves but were leased to ranchers for grazing livestock, miners seeking precious metals, lumber interests, hunters, and companies drilling for oil and gas. By some estimates, 30 percent of the gas reserves in the lower forty-eight states were located under New Mexico. It was a boom and bust economy. The doomsayers predicted the petroleum would be pumped out by the year 2040. Advocates of preservation used these predictions to push for the development of alternate energy sources. Oil interests used them to try to force Congress into opening wilderness areas in Alaska to drilling. So far the oil interests were winning. Anna had been on the fringes of the ongoing battle for so long she was more than casually interested to see the inner workings of a producing well.

Several wells outside the town of Carlsbad were close enough to the highway that she had already seen them. They were past the drilling stage; casings were in place, and the business of draining the petroleum pockets was in progress. Little remained but pipes and tanks built low to the ground and painted a neutral grayish-yellow. As far as Anna could tell, they were unmanned. The Blacktail was still in the process of drilling. A metal tower, much like those Texas was famous for, had been erected in the middle of a pad a hundred feet on a side. Piles of pipe in various sizes were stacked around the outbuildings. One of these was a corrugated aluminum shack that might have been for storage, and the other was a trailer house. A short piece of pipe chocked with rocks served as a front step. A flatbed was parked beside the road to the well, pipe waiting to be unloaded. Two concrete mixing trucks were behind the trailer.

"How close to the park boundary?" Anna asked as Holden drew to a stop beside the trailer. A fog of dust, churned up in their wake, overtook the truck, and they sat a moment waiting for it to clear.

"Pretty close," he said. "But strictly legit. They got a lease. They can sink a line straight down beside the fence if they want to. The Blacktail's not that bad. See that beaky-looking rock sticking out?" He pointed to a wedge of limestone protruding from a slope an eighth of a mile distant. "That's where the boundary line runs. And don't think it's not checked regularly. Carlsbad is a stickler. So are we."

For Holden it was a long speech. Anna'd struck a nerve. Land management agencies with differing goals sharing a border tended to be exceedingly careful of each other. The politicians might wrangle over use issues at a higher level. Those on the ground knew they had to work together.

Moving to more neutral territory, she asked, "What are you checking the Blacktail for?"

"We check all the wells every now and then. By law, they've got to file regular reports on the drilling. How deep. How long. Pipes. Casings. That sort of thing. The Blacktail's last report mentioned a loss of returns. When they are drilling, the drill fluids bring up mud and rock cuttings. A loss of return means they're drilling all right, but nothing is coming back. Could mean a lot of things. Could mean they've hit open space. A cavern. The Blacktail is along the same lineament as Big Manhole. There's logic to cave formations." Holden winked at Anna. "Maybe another entrance to Lechuguilla. I like telling George and Oscar that when we find it, we'll sink an elevator and set up a tour concession."

Anna laughed. Holden would oppose the commercialization of Lechuguilla as strongly as any park ranger. Had that not been true, those might have been fighting words, if not to Anna on principle, then to cavers from love of the resource.

A barrel-chested man introducing himself as "just plain Gus" emerged from the trailer to greet them. Gus was covered in filthy dungarees and a coat that looked as if it had survived the Exxon Valdez oil spill. He ushered them into the trailer. To Anna's surprise it was crammed with instruments. Lighting a cigarette, he offered coffee all around; then he and Holden began to talk in a language Anna wasn't conversant in: WOC, whipstock, dry-drilling, thribble, lost circulation, stabbing board. Boredom and cigarette smoke drove her back out of doors.

For once she appreciated the wind. Facing north, she shook her head, letting the cold strip away the nicotine residue. Four men, bundled in layers and hard-hatted, had appeared from somewhere and were occupied unloading pipe from the flatbed. Mouths moved, orders were shouted, but the roar of the forklift engine and the whine of the wind drowned out the words.

Anna walked to the edge of the pad, put the storage shed between herself and the wind, and looked across the wash toward Big Manhole. From here she could see the lineament Holden had mentioned as clear as a line drawn on a map. A shift in subterranean layers created a marked change in vegetation density on the surface. She traced it as far as the bald knob of hill above the cave. Always in a murder there was a reason, however twisted, why the victim had to die. Sometimes there was a reason the victim died where he did. Was Brent killed because he was at Big Manhole, or was it merely an opportune place for a spot of homicide?

"A guy was killed up there, you know."

The voice at her shoulder so closely echoed her thoughts, Anna wasn't startled at the unexpected company. A driller, shapeless in overalls and a down vest, a sweatshirt with the hood up under a bright yellow hard hat, leaned against the shed and cupped his hands to light a cigarette. Two days' stubble covered his jaws, each coarse whisker coated with gray dust.

"Some broad found him," the man went on, words coming out with smoke. "Guy had got his head blowed off."

"No kidding?" Anna said.

A chance to stand out of the wind and impress the girls must have been the highlight of this driller's day. He looked pleased with himself and his situation. Taking another drag, he embellished. "I knew the guy. We all did. Brent somebody or other. He used to come around. A geologist or some damn thing. Worked for Lattimore and Douglas out of Midland, Texas. They own the Blacktail."

Now that her memory had been jogged, Anna remembered Brent had done freelance work for local oil companies. "What did he do?" she asked.

"The dead guy?"

She nodded.

"Oh, he was a rock hound. Looked at the core samples. Stuff like that."

"Ah." Anna would ask Holden.

"Scuttlebutt was they were going to unload him. He got himself in bad odor with somebody." The man laughed, and fine particles of dust sifted down from his beard to settle like powdered sugar on his coat front. "Maybe they 'terminated' him the old-fashioned way."

A bellow bored through the wind to their ears. "Break's over." The man crushed his cigarette under a steel-toed boot. "Good talking with you." He touched the brim of his hard hat.

"Likewise," Anna assured him as he disappeared around the corner of the shed.

Returning to the shelter of the truck, she waited for Holden and turned the murder of Brent Roxbury over in her mind. By the time Holden emerged from the trailer and joined her, she'd kneaded and stretched a few disparate facts into a theory.

Holden Tillman listened with his customary politeness as she outlined it. Half a minute more elapsed while he digested her words and chose his own. "I don't think that's going to fly," he said at last. By the strained edge to his patience, Anna knew he'd not quite forgiven her the attack on Oscar. She understood. She was out of patience with herself. Changing theories every ten minutes smacked of grasping at straws.

"So now you're saying Brent might have been shot because he was working for Lattimore and Douglas? He was shot near here. I'll give you that." His tone was noncommittal.

"I was just thinking aloud." Anna defended herself. "Couldn't Brent have found something out that they didn't want found out and been killed?"

"The Blacktail is legal," Holden told her. "They've got a ten-year lease. They're in a place it's legal to drill. They're drilling for what they say they are. The well could produce upwards of three to five million cubic feet of gas a day. You can like the drilling or not, but they've got every legal right to drill as long as they file the reports and abide by the lease stipulations. What happened to your idea that Brent and Frieda's deaths were connected?"

Anna didn't have an answer for that. Frieda's demise in a rock slide deep in a cave on park lands and Brent's shooting aboveground on BLM land were hard to tie together. Different locales. Different causes of death. Brent was connected to the Blacktail, and the driller's gossip pointed a finger, but Anna had no way of putting Frieda into the picture. Frieda was NPS, from Colorado. As far as Anna knew, she'd neither seen nor heard of the Blacktail or any other gas well. No more had they seen, heard, or cared about a secretary from Mesa Verde on holiday in Carlsbad.

"Did you get your problems settled?" she asked just to end the silence.

"Yup. They lost circulation, then weren't getting any returns. They pumped down a little cement and pea gravel ten days ago. The drilling is about over. They hit paydirt. They'll be moving in a completion rig soon. From the sound of it this is going to be a hot well. Good thing too. Probably saved Gus's job. That boy ordered *way* too much of everything. Once pipe and gravel's been delivered, it's yours. Folks get real persnickety if you try and return it. Maybe that's where Brent ran afoul of them. He'd have recommended how much, how far, how deep. Could be he was off."

"Would they have shot him for it?"

"Nope. Happens all the time. Drilling is a gambler's game. If it happened too often they just wouldn't use Roxbury anymore. They'd get themselves a new boy. We're barking up the wrong tree."

Anna appreciated the "we."

Dust overwhelmed them then, and Holden needed all of his concentration just to stay on the road.

NIGHT HAD COME to further obscure the mysteries of the desert by the time they returned to Holden's office. There were three messages on his desk: a courtesy call from the sheriff's office telling him the only print lifted from the shell casing was Oscar's. Iverson had picked it up by the ends, planting his thumb on the base of the shell. A call from Laymon's secretary informed Holden the Roxbury funeral would be in Carlsbad the following day, with a short graveside ceremony at the Santa Catarina Cemetery. The last message was from Rhonda. By the way Holden smiled and folded the scrap of pink paper into his shirt pocket, Anna deduced he treasured up every communiqué from his wife.

Holden limped to his truck and Anna to her Neon aphid. Letting the engine warm up, she fiddled with the radio tuner trying to decide between half a dozen country-western stations playing more or less the same song. The day had been long, tiring, and confusing, but not a waste of time. Though she was no closer to knowing the identity of Frieda's killer, or Brent's, she was compiling a stock of information. Most of it would prove useless, but she was accustomed to that. Somewhere in this miasma of gossip, observation, and speculation, there would be answers.

Roxbury's ledger was filling fast: a dishonorable discharge from the army, bad information to a drilling company, a reputation for falsifying data, a presence at the first attempt, the opportunity to talk with Oscar Iverson during the rescue, on site at Frieda's death, and the victim of the second murder.

Oscar had the opportunity to conspire with Brent after the attempt and before Frieda's death. He was in the neighborhood, could have known Brent was meeting Anna at Big Manhole, and he'd screwed up the evidence either intentionally or accidentally.

Zeddie was present for the attempt and at Frieda's death. She knew where Brent was to meet Anna and how to get there. The love of her young life, Peter McCarty, had been blackmailed from her side by another woman. If Sondra had been the victim instead of Frieda, Zeddie would have been at the top of Anna's list.

The picture was skewed. Either the pieces of more than one puzzle had been mixed, or a piece was missing.

Anna backed the Neon into the deserted parking lot and fumbled with an unfamiliar dashboard in hopes of locating the headlights. Each time she laid out her thoughts, going over old information or incorporating new, she always ended back at the same blank wall: Sondra McCarty. A fugitive on the lam? A runaway wife? A frightened witness? Another victim?

After Brent's funeral Anna would dedicate her time to tracking down the doctor's wife.

16

FUNERALS GAVE ANNA a displaced feeling, a sense of purposeless rattling through life. Since the death of a boy her junior year in high school, during the aftermath of which most of the class sat in the back of the funeral parlor undecided between giggles and tears, she'd managed to avoid them. Despite her connection with the corpse, she would have weaseled out of this one had she not wanted to study the other attendees.

For a rotten afternoon, cold and cloudy with a flaying north wind, a goodly number of people turned out. They looked as miserable as she felt. To focus on the casket with its decaying reminder of mortality was morbid. To think of anything else was irreverent. Mourners turned up their collars against the wind, settled their faces into neutral solemnity, and stared at the ground. Not where it erupted in new earth to receive Roxbury's remains but the little safe patches of brown grass in front of their toes.

The caving community was represented by a motley assortment of poorly dressed individuals. Those who had come to Carlsbad to work or study underground had not arrived with a wardrobe suitable for weddings or funerals. Anna had ridden down with Zeddie, Peter, and Curt. On behalf of the park, George Laymon and Oscar Iverson were there. Holden had come and with him Rhonda. A dozen others were in attendance. People Anna didn't recognize, friends and business associates of the deceased.

Roxbury didn't leave this earth awash in tears. Every eye in the place was as dry as the north wind. Brent's wife looked on with the drawn face of shock but without any indication of great sorrow. A wide-bodied man in a good suit seemed bent on protecting her not only from the wind but from the storms of life. Imposing in a calf-length black wool coat, he stood at her side, his shoulder touching hers. Mrs. Roxbury's head was inclined toward him as if it was there she sought comfort. The saddest note in this bleak formality was Brent's little girls. At three, they were too young to understand what was happening. Identically clad in tiny navy blue coats, double-breasted and buttoned up, they hung one on each of their mother's hands. Well-behaved little creatures, they didn't whine or pull away, but time and strangeness weighed upon them. They wiggled, peevish and playful by turns.

Arsonists liked to hang around to watch the firetrucks arrive. Serial killers often enjoyed reading about their exploits in the newspaper. Had Brent's killer come to his funeral? The possibility was there. Not so much to return in some way to the scene of the crime or to gloat over the finality of the act, but because most murderers know their victim. Often they are close friends or family. In that situation, not to appear at the funeral could be cause for comment.

Anna studied the faces. Uniformly grim, pinched with cold, and red-nosed from the wind, the mourners listened to the preacher's words. With the exception of Brent's wife, the mourners were uninteresting. She clung too close to her male companion to win any awards in the grieving widows category.

"What's with the fat man in the expensive coat?" Anna whispered to Zeddie as Mrs. Roxbury stepped forward to drop a handful of dirt on the dearly departed.

"That's the boyfriend," Zeddie told her. "He's a local dentist."

"Did Brent know?"

"Yeah. The marriage was over. They were just dickering over the details."

"What details?"

"Kids, dogs, house. Shh."

Anna hushed and, jamming her hands deep in pockets devoid of warmth, watched her suspect pool flood over its banks.

An estranged wife, a new boyfriend, a custody battle; as potentially illuminating as these bits of information were, Anna did not welcome them. Like an obsessed scientist, she wanted only data that proved her theory. This new twist could indicate Brent Roxbury's death had no connection whatsoever to Frieda's. Anna had used the Roxbury incident to prove that Dierkz was murdered. If it was freak coincidence, she was back to Frieda's testimony—recanted—and the butt-print—buried. Holden, her one ally in this quest, would desert her for the seductive realm of the guilt-ridden.

A sickening possibility stirred her thoughts with an icy finger. Could it be she was dead wrong and making a world-class ass of herself? A shudder vibrated her bones. Curt's strong arm threaded between her elbow and her ribs. He snugged her up against his side and kept her there till the last clods were thrown and the mourners were allowed to escape the grave.

"What's the matter, don't you like dead people?" he asked as they followed Peter and Zeddie back to Zeddie's rusting Volvo. "They seem inordinately fond of you, judging by the numbers dropping at your feet."

"I like them fine," Anna replied distractedly. "It just occurred to me that I might be totally mistaken about nearly everything."

"I wouldn't have any idea what that was like," Curt said with apparent sincerity.

"Bloody awful."

"I love it when you talk dirty in foreign languages."

In the car, Anna pressed Zeddie for details regarding the Roxburys' marriage.

"I thought I shot Brent," she said. "Don't tell me you're going to bump me in favor of his wife? I've already opened negotiations with Meryl Streep to play me in the movie."

Anna squirmed uncomfortably in the backseat. Curt, who'd retained her arm, gave it a squeeze. "C'mon, Zeddie," he said. "One teensy-weensy little murder accusation and you get all bent out of shape. Where's your sense of humor?"

To Anna's relief, both Zeddie and Dr. McCarty laughed. The cold shoulder was still there but, Anna dared hope, a shade less glacial. Caught up in the mood of generosity, Anna admitted she could have been wrong.

"Gee, yuh *think*?" Zeddie returned. A second laugh at Anna's expense warmed the car's interior. "Brent's marriage has been on the rocks for a while. The divorce papers are in the works. I don't think his heart was too badly broken over the whole deal. He just wanted his kids," Zeddie said.

"Would he have gotten them?"

"Ah ha! You have replaced me. What do you think, little Mrs. Roxbury toddled over the desert in her high heels with the dentist's deer rifle?"

"Maybe the dentist did it for her," Peter suggested.

"Right. 'Local Dentist Goes Berserk in Love Triangle.' He's got three kids of his own. I doubt he'd risk everything to bring the total up to five. She was the one who ended the marriage," Zeddie admitted. "My bet is the dentist has been fixing more than her teeth. She might have lost a custody battle."

Not wanting to waste a perfectly good trip to town, Zeddie pulled in at the supermarket before they started back up for the park. As soon as she and Peter wandered off down aisle six, Anna asked Curt if he'd made the calls, located Sondra.

"You never give up, do you?" he said with a hint of exasperation.

"I may have to," Anna said. "But not quite yet. Did you?"

Curt sighed, took the basket from her arm, and began sniffing apples. "I called a bunch of people. Pete's mom, Sondra's dad. The *Pioneer Press* and the YMCA. Pete and I work out there. Well, Pete does. I sit in the sauna. Sondra's an aerobics fanatic. It's great. They wear those thong things and you're not even considered a pervert if you watch. Just admiring glute definition." Two apples passed muster and made it to the basket. "Nobody's seen or heard from her."

THE BAD NEWS was waiting for Anna when they got back to the park. George Laymon had taken the liberty of making an appointment for her with a psychologist in Carlsbad. Whatever plans she'd made for the afternoon had to be postponed. To keep her credit good and her lies all in a row, she was duty-bound to go.

Anna swallowed a little lunch, climbed into the Neon, and started back down the long and twisting road out of the park. Desert views, usually captivating, failed to interest her. Lost in thought, she drove like an automaton. A list formed in her mind: things to do in town. As it grew, her resentment toward Laymon for wasting half her day began to wane. She would stop at the airport and see if she could unearth any record of when Sondra had flown out and what her destination was. On one pretext or another she would worm her way into the Roxburys' house and have a chat with the widow. Coincidences were part of life. They happened with a regularity that flew in the face of statistics and common sense. Bad things quite often did come in threes.

It wasn't beyond the realm of possibility that Brent's shooting was in no way connected with Frieda's death. Should that be the case, Anna swore she would bow out, leave the investigation to the sheriff's department or the BLM—whoever had jurisdiction over that particular part of the desert.

And Sondra's disappearance?

Anna pondered that while the pseudo-frontier village of White's City, a tourist town clinging to the shirttails of the park, flashed by the Neon's windows. Was that yet another coincidence? The third in a string of evils? A hoax designed to bring a straying husband to heel?

The clock set into the Neon's dash read 1:27. Anna's appointment with Dr. Coontz was at 1:45. She had no idea what she would say to the guy. Yes, her knee had crushed the esophagus of her friend. No, she didn't feel guilty about it. Yes, she thought the fall had been orchestrated. No, she had no proof. No, she didn't know who did it. No, nobody else agreed with her. Yes, she had been under a psychiatrist's care before. Yes, she was an alcoholic. Yes, she was drinking again.

The litany clicked through her mind with the familiar resonance of rosary beads, and Anna laughed out loud. An hour wouldn't even scratch the surface of her psyche. Visions of weekly visits for the next thirty years would dance sugarplumlike through the psychologist's head. Coontz would think he'd stumbled onto a veritable gold mine.

No sense getting his hopes up.

Deciding to be late, Anna turned off the highway into the Carlsbad municipal air terminal. The airstrip wasn't much different from a dozen other small-town airstrips she had flown into for one reason or another. Meager landscape vegetation, planted with the best intentions then abandoned, clung to life around the front of the terminal. Small aircraft, belonging to those with the money or the passion to support a private plane, were tied down beside the taxiway.

Anna parked in the same spot she'd used when she came to fetch Frieda's mother and went inside. A young woman stood behind the counter, her chin propped in her hands, talking to a boy dressed in the uniform of the West: cowboy boots, Levi's, western shirt, and tractor cap.

As Anna blew in on a gust of cold wind, the conversation stopped. Wide intelligent eyes lit up a face already half smiling and ready to be of assistance; someone who enjoyed her work and was good at it. Given that Anna wanted rules broken, this was not an auspicious sign.

With patience and unfailing good manners Becky—or so the name tag on her chest proclaimed—repeated the regulations about divulging the contents of passenger lists on commercial flights. Anna pushed until the woman began running out of new ways to say the same thing, then accepted that this cat would have to be skinned another way.

Having no appreciable weight to throw around in New Mexico, she couldn't lean on Becky. But she could lean on Jewel. Before Laymon's secretary had managed to blank her computer screen, Anna had gotten a glimpse and an inkling as to why she was such a mumbling idiot around her boss. When she got back up the hill, she would approach this issue from another angle.

DR. COONTZ WAS a woman. The hour went quickly, and Anna enjoyed herself. She walked a thin line trying to maintain her integrity, to show just enough neurosis to be of interest but not so much she'd have to live it down later. Another visit wouldn't be a bad thing if it bought her more time in Carlsbad. They parted with mutual assurances of goodwill.

Roxbury wasn't a common name, and Carlsbad was a small town. So small, in fact, the public phones actually had phone books attached to them. Only one Roxbury was listed. Having neither pen nor pencil, Anna started to rip the page from the directory, an act prompted by seeing it done repeatedly in the movies. Before the tear was half an inch long, she had to stop. Lying, stealing, mayhem, adultery—

all those were crimes she had committed or might commit if the wind was blowing from the right quarter and she was so inclined. But petty vandalism was right up there with littering. An unpardonable breach of personal etiquette and public decorum. Making up a nonsense rhyme to cement 10672 Luna Vista in her mind, Anna left the phone book only slightly worse for having known her.

It didn't take long to put herself and the Neon outside the cyclone fence around the widow's house on the north-western edge of town. Low to the ground and built of brick, the Roxburys' home was indistinguishable from the others in the same tract built in the sixties. A bricksided carport, the bricks mortared in an open lattice to the windward side, housed a dusty burgundy 1985 Honda Accord, the kind Anna would have chosen was she organizing a vehicular tail. Make, model, and color were so common as to render it invisible.

This aggressive tedium didn't cause her to question the accuracy of the address she'd memorized. Two tricycles with identical pink ribbons feathering down from the handlebars were parked to one side of the front door. Two kiddie swings with offensive but safety-minded plastic bucket chairs hung from a branch of a leafless tree in the front yard. Two child-restraint seats peeked through the rear window of the Honda.

Mary Chapin Carpenter's "I Feel Lucky" was on the Neon's radio. Anna waited till the end of the song, procrastinating because she didn't. Visiting widows was a chore she'd been given more than once. Logic being since she was a woman and a widow, she could help. No one could help, nothing. Even women who'd lost husbands they didn't love or didn't like—drunkards, philanderers, bums, and bores—staggered under the blow of their death. Most from that category recovered to flourish—or found another man to hate—in fairly short order. For the first few days though, widows of all stripes shared similar fear of the future and brutal severance from the past.

Mrs. Roxbury would be no different. Because of the

boyfriend she'd have a giant chip on her shoulder that was bound to be dislodged by Anna's first question. Bracing herself for an unpleasant interview, Anna tripped the child-proof latch on the gate and walked to the front door. A benevolent cover would be best, she decided. Questions pertaining to marital problems and infidelity would usually be answered more truthfully by the gossips than by those directly involved.

Mrs. Roxbury answered the bell almost the instant Anna rang. She was attended by two identical yapping shih tzus, a house of twins. Brent's wife was a small woman, well proportioned and carefully made-up. Her hair was cut short and layered, an easy cut to maintain for the mother of toddlers. Her features were ordinary but pleasant, like the house and the car.

"I'm Anna Pigeon," she introduced herself as the woman quieted the dogs. "I was caving with Brent."

"I recognize you from the funeral," Mrs. Roxbury said politely, her voice a soft Southern drawl. "Won't you come in?" The children, lying on their identical bellies in front of a television set alive with the abrasive colors of a cartoon show, didn't even turn to see who was calling. Anna was led across neutral tan carpeting into a tidy kitchen that smelled of coffee and roasting meat.

"Brent did so much work with the Park Service we wanted to write an obituary for him for *Ranger Magazine*," Anna lied easily. "People who knew him would like a chance to say good-bye." To her own ears she sounded treacly, but Mrs. Roxbury seemed not to mind. She refilled her own coffee cup, poured one for Anna, and shoved two bowls of white powder in her direction. Guessing which one was the cream substitute, Anna spooned a gob into her cup.

"That's very nice," Mrs. Roxbury said, and sat down, leaning slightly forward, eyes wide, the personification of being "all ears."

"How long had your husband been interested in caving?" Anna asked to prime the pump.

"Oh, forever," the Mrs. said. She looked expectantly at Anna, then asked, "Don't you want to take notes? I always forget things if I don't take notes."

"I forgot pen and paper," Anna admitted sheepishly. Roxbury's wife smiled suddenly, and Anna knew why the dentist loved her. She had perfect teeth, square and white and even, not in the least feral. Totally beguiling.

"I'll get some." She hopped happily to her feet and bustled out of the kitchen.

Ineptness, a wonderful tool. Guaranteed to take people off their guard. And in this instance Anna didn't even have to feign it. Settled again with a Woody Woodpecker pencil and a Leonardo Da Doodle pad between them, Anna resumed the "interview."

Brent was a graduate in geology from a college "somewhere in Virginia." He was an only child, his mother was dead and his father "long gone." Anna took that to mean he'd left the family in some fashion other than feet first. Brent and Amy—as the woman invited Anna to call her—had been married for four years. They'd met in Springfield, Missouri, where Amy worked as a dental hygienist. Both had wanted children. From the way Amy looked first in the direction of her daughters then down at her coffee, Anna suspected this had been a strong motivator on her part. Maybe on Brent's as well. Amy would have been somewhere between thirty-three and thirty-six, the ticking of the biological clock growing ever louder.

"Previous marriages?" Anna asked, trying to sound professional.

"No," Amy answered readily. "A first for the both of us."

Anna kept quiet, in the hope silence would goad her into telling more than she intended.

"Brent was a late bloomer. His mother suffered a long illness. He stayed with her. I never knew Mother Roxbury. She died before we met."

"Do you still work?" Anna asked, her pencil poised as if the answer was relevant to the obituary.

"I'm a hygienist for a dentist here in town," she said, and she blushed. "But I'm hoping to quit soon so I can spend more time at home with the girls. Brent and I just never had the money."

Anna didn't need to ask where the money was to come from. Roxbury might have had life insurance, but that would be icing on the cake. The blush pretty much told it all. Though death, violence, and infidelity intruded, Anna couldn't but envy Amy. She loved her fat dentist with transparent girlish adoration.

"I don't like it here," Amy said with sudden candor. Coffee, chat, and an interested ear fooled her into thinking she'd found a friend. Stifling a stab of conscience, Anna mimicked the "all ears" posture and made listening noises, the indistinct murmurs of reassurance her sister had taught her.

"It's too . . . too everything. Except green. Everything just dries up and blows away. Even the people are dry. Tough and strong. Stringy." She laughed. "I guess you can tell I'm a southern girl. I don't want to climb and ride horses and fight rattlesnakes. And nobody goes to church. Not that I'm a real churchy person, but it's good for children to be raised in the church, a community, something to give them a sense of morals, of their place in God's world. Potluck is a dirty word here, and only Indians play bingo. Jeff . . . my boss . . . well, I've got a chance to move to Memphis. Now that—" Realizing too late she'd chattered beyond the limits set by a formal interview, Amy buried her nose in her coffee cup. When Amy came up for air, Anna could tell she was embarrassed. She rose partway out of her chair, suddenly desperate to get rid of her company.

Anna glanced over her shoulder at the clock on the kitchen wall, pretending to notice how time had flown. "Oh dear, I've taken up way too much of your time," she said to calm Amy's nerves. "One more quick question, then I guess I'd really better go." The end in sight, her faux pas apparently unnoticed, Amy lowered her round behind to the chair seat again.

"Did Brent have a military record? Lots of our readers are vets," Anna explained. "They set a lot of store by that sort of thing."

"I think he had a high draft number or maybe one of those college deferments," Amy told her, and Anna could detect nothing to suggest she lied. "Anyway, he never had to go. They were drafting people back then."

Amy wasn't aware of her husband's dishonorable discharge.

Anna thanked her and promised to send her a copy of the bogus obituary. Remembering to take the worthless notes, she left the widow to her coffee, her dogs, and her children.

Several things of interest had been disclosed. Amy wanted out of Carlsbad, and Jeff, her boss, the boyfriend, was a ticket back to the lush Christian greenery of the South. Moving out of state would have upped the stakes in the custody battle. A separation of a thousand miles rendered joint custody impossible on any practical level. Somebody was going to lose their children, the children they had come together for the purpose of creating.

As the adulteress, Amy might have lost that battle. Might have. A weak motive for murder. The scene just wouldn't play out in Anna's head. Amy would possibly kill to protect her children, but Anna couldn't see her doing it with a high-powered rifle. A self-professed southern girl with a hatred of the desert wouldn't be likely to have the knowledge or the canniness to traverse several miles of damp soil without leaving a single track for Anna to find. Though Anna hadn't peeked into the woman's closet, she doubted she'd find a pair of fire boots among the Reeboks and Liz Claibornes. McCarty had suggested the dentist boyfriend for the role of the shooter, but the man at the funeral had been too fat. The figure in camo retreating from Big Manhole had not been fat.

On the surface, the things Anna had learned were not illuminating, but she cranked over the Neon's engine with a light heart and rising optimism. Nothing Amy said went against her original theory. Brent's death was not a freak coincidence. A jealous boyfriend hadn't shot him. A crazed wife hadn't hired it done. Brent had been killed because Frieda was killed.

Yearning for Guy Clark and settling for Clint Black, Anna switched on the country-western station. Compared to the past few days, she was feeling positively gay.

17

DARKNESS HAD FOLDED quietly around the buildings by the time Anna arrived back in the park. A thread of gold leaked from the blind on the window to the right of the doorway. Within, there was wine and food, a cat, and the companionship of three murder suspects. It felt like home to Anna. Parking the Neon beside Zeddie's Volvo, she sat for a minute enjoying the night. Much of her adult life had been lived alone. For society, she had her work and the telephone. Half-read books remained undisturbed till she returned for them. Food in the refrigerator waited till she, or mold, ate it. No one snatched her covers, hogged her bed, used her toothbrush, or maladjusted the driver's seat in her car.

Loneliness became a way of life after Zachary was killed. At some point the stings and barbs had worn away until all that remained was a soothing aloneness. Periodically Anna invited men possessing charm or wit or lovely physiques to share her space. Visitors only, passersby; she'd never allowed anyone to grow too comfortable in her quarters.

Sitting in the night's stillness, she prodded into dusty corners of her mind to see if this was healthy. Nostalgia for the past was there, mental pictures of Zachary blurred by the river of years that had poured over them since they were new-made. Nostalgia not only for the husband she had loved but for the youth they had lived. She'd been a young woman when she was widowed, not yet thirty-four. From the vantage point of her forties, that seemed young. At the time she'd felt too old to go on living.

Beyond this mist of memory there existed fragile hopes of finding a man with whom she could combine the littles of her life. Pictures of the animals going joyously two-by-two were created as much by the media as by personal need. Songs, billboards, movies, sit-coms, liquor ads repeated the mantra. Rock and roll summed it up concisely: even a bad love is better than no love at all.

A sharp rap on the window jerked Anna from her brown study, and she cracked her knee against the steering wheel.

"I thought I heard you pull up," Curt said as he opened the car door. "Can't you get out? If you push that little red button it'll undo your seatbelt." He took in the cramped interior of the Neon and added, "Sort of like unbuckling your roller skates."

Anna was glad to see him, so much so it alarmed her. Declaring it an official night off, she put aside the dirty particulars of double homicide and went with him into the house.

Supper was spaghetti and red wine. *A Fish Called Wanda* was the evening's entertainment. At ten thirty Peter and Zeddie vanished down the hall. Wrapped in pajamas, sweatshirts, and candlelight, Curt and Anna retired to their sofa. Her head rested on the arm near the door, his at the opposite end. The cat cemented their thighs together where they crossed midway. Until past two in the morning they talked of nothing: nieces and nephews, cats and dogs, clothes, cars, college, alcohol, tobacco, and firearms. Curt told elephant jokes. Anna remembered knock-knock jokes. They invented How-many-university-professors-would-it-take?

jokes. Anna fell asleep first and dreamed no dreams. When she got up just after dawn to go to the bathroom, she noticed Curt had blown out the candles. So soundly had she slept, she'd not felt him get off the couch.

In the morning she was left alone in the house. Zeddie was giving an off-trail tour in Carlsbad Caverns; a trek of three or four hours crawling through rock-gutted wormholes to an immense cavern boasting an enormous ghostly formation and called the Hall of the White Giant. Curt and Peter responded as was appropriate to such an unexpected treat. Anna declined in her most polite and inoffensive manner, yet the three cavers looked upon her with the condescending pity a beer drinker might expect at a wine-tasting convention.

If the snub bruised her delicate sensibilities, they were soon salved. Nobody bothered to shower. In a few short minutes they would be burrowing through the dirt like so many grubs. All the hot water was Anna's, and she used every drop. The drum of water for backup, she belted out half a dozen verses of "We'll Sing in the Sunshine" and laughed because, despite the clichéd behavior, she had not gotten laid the night before. They had talked. And they had slept. A combination any woman worth her salt had to admit was better than sex three times out of five and a good deal harder to come by.

In the sanctity of the shower stall, she entertained pleasantly impure thoughts. Curt was, for lack of a better word, such a *dear,* his smile so deliciously canine. Opportunities had been presented on silver platters, but he'd never made a pass. For an instant Anna wondered if she was losing her touch. She dismissed it. Her mother always told her and Molly that a woman needed only two physical attributes to be pretty: good face, nice legs. Great breasts, fine hair. Terrific hands, lush hips. Anna could still lay claim to two out of three.

Contradicting her macha nature-girl image, Zeddie's bath was stocked with enticing shampoos, scented soaps, creams, unguents, conditioners, and perfumes. Without suffering so much as a qualm of guilt, Anna partook of the sensual goodies. Lingering over her toilette, she dabbed on enough blush, brow pencil, and mascara that she could pass for unadorned while banishing ghastly.

Painted and perfumed, she let herself into the administration building at half past nine. Not one to be caught out twice, Jewel blacked out her computer screen before Anna was halfway across the room.

"You still here?" she said by way of greeting.

"Still here," Anna replied cheerfully, and plopped herself down in the chair at the end of the secretary's desk.

Jewel fidgeted, glanced pointedly at her computer, then drummed lacquered nails on the blotter. "I got things I gotta do," she said when Anna refused to take a hint.

"I was hoping you could help me," Anna said.

Jewel's face twisted from the mouth out as if smart-ass retorts were trying to escape the carmine lips. "Whaddya want?"

"I haven't had any luck getting in touch with Sondra McCarty," Anna told her.

"I don't have her phone number or nothing."

"I've got all that. She's not answering. You said she flew out of here the day after she came out of Lechuguilla."

"Yeah?" Jewel was getting antsy. She sensed the net closing around her but hadn't a clue as to what kind or why.

"Did you see her?"

"Whaddya think, I run a taxi service to the airport?"

"You didn't see her after the accident, didn't talk to her on the phone, didn't hand her a ticket, anything?"

Anna took Jewel's mute stare for a negative.

"Why are you so sure she left?"

Another glance at the blind screen, another at her nemesis, and Jewel apparently decided the only way to get rid of Anna was to answer. "Her name was on a list." The satisfaction in her voice suggested that what was written was fact, a result of living in a world of secondhand information.

"But you didn't see her?"

"Would ya quit?" Jewel snapped in exasperation.

"Who put her name on the list?"

"I did."

"All by yourself?" The words were out before Anna realized how patronizing they would sound. She was punished by a baleful glare from eyes so black the pupils were indistinguishable from the irises.

"I typed it," Jewel said tersely.

"Who wrote it?"

"Oscar gave it to me. Why don't you go badger him?"

Anna would probably get around to that, but for the moment she was perfectly happy badgering Jewel. "Did you—the park—make the plane reservations?"

"We don't make 'em for cavers."

Anna digested that. Becky—or whoever filled Becky's loafers at Carlsbad's airport this morning—would be no more likely to hand over passenger manifests to Jewel than to Anna. "So you only know who was scheduled to go down to the airport, not who went?"

"Like I been telling you. Can I get back to work now?"

"Can I see the list?"

Petty triumph glowed in Jewel's midnight stare. "Sorry. That's personnel stuff. Nobody gets to mess with it."

Anna doubted that. Maybe this was one of those situations her grandmother had warned her about where more flies were caught with honey. Too late; the vinegar had already been served.

"How is class going?" Anna asked.

Jewel's demeanor transformed. Sullenness was replaced with excitement. Tension went out of the taloned fingers on the desktop. "Good. I've got—" Suspicion clouded the briefly sunny disposition. "What class?"

"Yesterday I noticed you were working on—what? Your master's thesis? Too many footnotes for anything else. Looks like you've put in a lot of hours on it."

Jewel's right hand skittered furtively toward the keyboard. A spider in crimson shoes, it seemed to move without her permission. "There's nothing says I can't educate myself." Jewel was on the defensive. That was where Anna wanted her. Saying nothing, she let the silence weigh down. Jewel was using government time to do personal work. Maybe not a firing offense, but most certainly one that would get her a stern lecture and, worse, put her under Laymon's careful eye. Her activities would be curtailed.

"Maybe I still got that list somewhere," Jewel said coldly.

Anna was careful not to smile or show any sort of gloating. Her edge was tenuous. Jewel wasn't the sort of woman to be jerked around too often. A sheet of paper was smacked down at Anna's elbow. "This is a terrific help," she said as if Jewel had handed it over in the spirit of cooperation. "Can I copy it?"

Jewel pointed toward the copier.

Anna ran off a copy, folded it, and tucked it in her hip pocket. The original she brought back to Jewel's desk. "Thanks a million."

"You're welcome." Jewel snatched the paper and crammed it in the out part of her in-out basket.

"There's one other little thing."

"Oh, Jeez . . ."

"Brent Roxbury's SF-171."

"We don't use 'em no more."

"Brent would have. He's worked here off and on for four years. He'd have had to fill one out to get his first position." The SF-171 was an agonizingly detailed application form the Park Service had required for most of Anna's career. Pages of constipated little boxes for the answering of complex questions.

"You can't look at that," Jewel said. "It really is a personnel thing."

"What are you getting your master's in?" Anna asked interestedly.

"Oh, give it a rest," Jewel growled. Then, because she couldn't hide her pride, she said, "Abnormal psychology."

"Cool," Anna said, and meant it.

"I've got two kids. I got no time at home," Jewel said. Then, "George doesn't know."

"I won't tell him," Anna promised. "I wouldn't have anyway. I just need a break on this Frieda thing. It's making me crazy."

"So I noticed. We studied people like you second semester."

Anna laughed. "Will you look up Roxbury for me?"

Jewel thought about it. Anna had called her own bluff and waited without much hope. "What the heck," Jewel said after Anna had suffered a sufficient length of time. "It's not like the guy's not dead."

ARMED WITH BRENT'S SF-171, the list of cavers with whom Sondra had presumably flown out, and her AT&T credit card number, Anna settled down at Zeddie's dining table for an afternoon of telephonic sleuthing. Midmorning on a weekday it took her thirty minutes before a real live human being answered in place of a machine. Stan Daggert, the long-bearded caver from Kentucky, worked the graveyard shift at a plant producing electrical cable. Anna dragged him out of a sound sleep and had to talk a minute till the fog cleared. Once he was oriented to time, place, and task, he was very clear. Sondra had not been with the group on Jewel's list. She'd not ridden down the hill with them; she'd not flown with them. He remembered her, "a leggy looker." He had not seen her when leaving Lechuguilla or at any point thereafter.

Lisa, the lady with the looping braids, was Anna's next success. She was at home in Palo Alto, grading papers. With the exception of describing Sondra as "a looker," she echoed Daggert's words. Sondra had not been with them. Lisa, like Daggert, insisted she would have remembered Sondra but for entirely different reasons: "Sondra was a royal pain in the patootie."

Of the five others on the list, Anna tracked down the phone numbers of four and left messages asking them to call her at Zeddie's. Their ratification of events would be nice, but she didn't need it. Sondra had not flown home or anywhere else.

Brent's SF-171 was next. From it she verified everything Amy Roxbury had told her and filled in some of the blanks. Brent was born in Black Gap, Pennsylvania, and raised in Charlottesville, Virginia. He'd been drafted in 1971. As a private in the army he was stationed at Fort Leonard Wood, a base in Missouri. He'd served seventeen months. The dishonorable discharge box on his application was checked. Beneath, in the meager space allotted for explanations, he had written "conscientious objector." A good choice. It explained nothing yet came off sounding morally righteous.

Tracking down a fact a quarter of a century old, even one that was a matter of public record, proved harder than anticipated. During the military downsizing of the early nineties, the army base in Missouri was decimated. Personnel, already nomadic by profession, had been scattered all over the world.

Anna was forwarded, patched through, brushed off, put on hold, and disconnected until she finally landed in an office of records in Washington, D.C. A mealy-voiced man went to some length to let her know that, though he worked for the army, he wasn't an army man. Why she was supposed to care was beyond her, but she made a few appreciative noises so as not to alienate the fellow. His civilian status established, he was willing to look up the information she requested. Seconds ticked by like dimes clinking into a pay phone while he muttered and fiddled with his computer. "Got it," he said at last. Anna was not yet allowed to relax. Hemming and hawing, he fussed, pretending the matter might be sensitive or classified. He was bored. He was unimportant. He wanted to be cajoled. Pepper-spraying him being out of the question, Anna grasped the ragged edge of patience and cajoled.

Brent Roxbury had been discharged for conduct unbecoming an enlisted man. He'd been caught exposing himself. Local law enforcement suspected he'd been at it for some time. Reports of a man fitting his description flashing women in parks and on bike paths near the base had been coming in for a year and a half—roughly the amount of time Roxbury had served. When he inadvertently flashed Lieutenant Marsha Coleman of the military police while she was jogging with her cocker spaniel, she arrested him. Securing him with the dog's leash, she delivered him to the town's constabulary. Dog tags were found, military connections noted, and he was turned back over to the army for discipline.

Anna thanked her informant, withstood a couple minutes more of his voice, then got him off the line. Her right ear was sore from being pressed so long against the receiver, and she had the beginnings of a headache that strenuous games of phone tag always engendered.

A brief raid on Zeddie's medicine cabinet produced two Advil. Anna washed them down with cold coffee and returned to the SF-171. Evidently Brent had liked the area. After his discharge his home addresses all had been in Missouri. The last was in Springfield, where he'd met and married Amy.

Since coming to New Mexico he'd eked out a living by working with the various agencies and the oil and gas companies. His SF-171 had the required three names to call for references. They were all people from the petroleum industry. The last was the man responsible for managing the Blacktail. Anna circled it. Seldom was a shooting brought on by something in the distant past. Long planned and finally executed revenges or a sudden irresistible opportunity to redress an old wrong did happen, but usually the reason was closer to home, closer to the now. People had long memories, but they had short fuses. Rarely did anyone exhibit the patience and discipline of the Count of Monte Cristo.

Like a kaleidoscope, each time the information spun, the pieces created new patterns. Chances were good Brent had outgrown his antisocial form of self-expression—or gotten terrifically good at it. A few calls to the police departments of the previous Missouri addresses assured Anna there'd been no further arrests on that score. Unless one was psycho, flashing was hardly a killing offense. Certainly not for Amy. Brent's early career as a pervert for Uncle Sam further exonerated her and her dentist. Few courts would quibble over giving Mom custody when Dad was a convicted sex offender, even of the most benign variety.

Brent's indiscretions got his ex off the hook and in no way linked him to Frieda, or to Oscar as his shooter. Yet, try as she might, Anna couldn't let go of the subject. Something niggled in the back of her brain wanting to link Roxbury's military history with events in New Mexico. Maybe it was just that she was so sick of questions she was beginning to hallucinate answers.

There would be another skeleton, she promised herself. She just hadn't looked in the right closet.

In the case of Sondra McCarty, Anna had no doubt she was in the appropriate closet. The form the skeleton would take remained to be seen. At the start of the investigation she had considered the possibility that Sondra didn't survive the rock fall. After Jewel assured her the woman was alive and well and winging her way homeward, she'd dropped the idea. Now evidence was mounting that Sondra had never left Lechuguilla, had never gotten any farther than Katie's Pigtail.

Zeddie and Peter wrapped together in the darkness; such a sudden coupling after the separation of husband and wife spoke of great need or great assurance. Anna had assumed it was the wall of dirt between Peter and his spouse that gave them the confidence to turn to each other so publicly. A wall of dirt on top of that same spouse would be just as reassuring and a whole lot more final.

Trying to tie them to Frieda was what had kept them on the back burner of Anna's mind. Both had had ample opportunity to kill her.

Peter was her physician for the first forty-eight hours after the rock had struck her. Their culpability in her eventual death was too great a stretch. Factoring out the original attempt on Frieda's life—an opinion held by nearly everyone but Anna—and putting Sondra in the place of the corpse du jour, it was no stretch at all. Brent's shooting could be explained as well. Peter and or Zeddie arranged for Sondra's death in the ill-begotten rock fall. Brent saw something. Brent was silenced. Zeddie made a much better suspect for desert stalking and sharpshooting than either Amy or the boyfriend.

"Damn." Anna had only just been forgiven for accusing Zeddie and Peter of murder. To do it again was liable to get her thrown off her couch. Or killed. Shoving herself up from the table, she stared at the winter-bleak patio. Wandering through the kitchen, she blindly looked into the refrigerator. Hopeful, Calcite swished around her ankles. Anna picked her up and set her abstractedly on the kitchen counter. The cat twitched her tail, and Anna caught it. Loose ends. The Zeddie-McCarty-Sondra triangle tied up a lot of loose ends.

Calcite jumped to the floor when a sigh gusted from Anna's lungs. The solution didn't sit well. The sequence of events rendered Frieda's death so unnecessary, so peripheral. Was that what was bothering her? The idea that her friend's death had been meaningless, a by-product? Anna shook off the thought. No one else had seen Frieda's face, heard the tremor of certainty and horror as she described looking up, seeing her headlamp flash over a gloved hand rolling down a stone, the fear and the sadness born of knowing someone wished to take her life from her.

Anna cleared her mind. Like it or not, she would have to tackle Zeddie.

18

SONDRA WAS, AS advertised, a royal pain in the patootie. Possibly not above blackmailing a man into marrying her. An ambitious woman who wanted to do it the old-fashioned way, climbing the ladder one man at a time. From what Rhonda had uncovered, she had used her evil wiles to snatch another woman's beau. Plenty of reasons to hate her. More than enough never to have her over for dinner. But murder? Intelligent people—at least sane intelligent people—realized that murder was doing it the hard way. Zeddie and Peter were worldly enough to know things could be lived through, faced down, or bought off with less backlash than murder. Breaking that strongest of taboos was usually a step taken in desperation. Adultery, fornication—the stuff of love triangles—just weren't that big a deal anymore. Photos on Zeddie's mantel indicated she and Peter had been together since his marriage. Clearly it was not necessary to do so over his wife's dead body. Either they were not as sane as Anna presumed, or there was something she was missing.

Why had McCarty allowed himself to be blackmailed into matrimony? Why had he gone on vacation with his wife, girlfriend, and ex-girlfriend? Did he like the fireworks? Was it a game, one that had taken an unexpectedly ugly turn?

Tawdry questions, half answered with half-truths, jammed Anna's brain like sand poured into a piston engine. Before she blew a gasket, she decided to stop thinking. Her stomach reminded her it was past lunch. Her watch told her it was one thirty. Zeddie, Peter, and Curt should have crawled out of the arteries of New Mexico by now. Curt and Peter would be home shortly, eager for hot showers and clean clothes. They would probably spend the afternoon watching a ball game. December: Anna couldn't remember if it was baseball, football, or basketball season, but undoubtedly Madison Avenue had arranged for one sport or another to peddle beer and cars on a Sunday afternoon. Mere fire and brimstone, a murder investigation couldn't compete. She would have to postpone Peter and start with Zeddie. She had a feeling the "something more" she sought lurked in that quarter.

Due to a small flu epidemic thinning the ranks of interpretive rangers, Zeddie said she had "one bitch of a day." Closing her eyes, Anna focused on the morning's breakfast banter. Like children on holiday, Zeddie and Peter had milkshakes for breakfast. Shoulder to shoulder, they sipped through candy-cane-striped plastic straws. Each time Zeddie looked away, Peter snaked his straw over at an angle and snorkeled up her ice cream. The picture triggered something, but not the information she wanted. What was it Zeddie had been saying while Peter pilfered her milkshake? "Off-trail in the morning and the Urinal in the afternoon."

From the scuttlebutt, Anna had deduced that the Urinal was a stretch of trail above the Big Room in Carlsbad Caverns. It was so named by the interpreters because it was about ninety minutes into the cave, the length of time the male bladder could comfortably transport a couple cups of coffee. A dark and twisty portion of trail afforded an irresistible temptation.

YEARS HAD PASSED since Anna had been in Carlsbad Caverns. Walking out of the twilight zone, she smelled the musty breath of the underground home of a dwindling but still impressive population of Mexican freetail bats. After the initial unpleasantness of leaving behind real air and the light of day, she was overwhelmed by the intricacy and immensity of the cavern. Wide and well kept, with discreet lighting, the path curved down through glossy formations and vaulted ceilings dripping with icicles of stone. Long buried, a statistic floated into her mind. Someone had once told her that more than two thousand formations a year were destroyed or stolen by visitors. On some level, she'd been expecting the cavern to appear tired, more shopworn than she remembered. The opposite was true. The park had rejuvenated the cave and the trails. Along the way she saw teams of volunteers unobtrusively tending to the resource. Four women in soft-soled shoes painstakingly tweezed lint from the rugged rock faces. Tons of lint and hair from tourists circulated on air currents. Without constant intervention the innards of the cave would take on the aspect of an overused clothes dryer. Another group, armed with sponges, brushes, and pails, erased muddy footprints of those insensitive enough to walk off the paved trail.

The expected pinch of claustrophobia failed to materialize, and Anna enjoyed the trip. After the suffocating confines of parts of Lechuguilla, the light, airy cavern felt like what it was: a walk in the park. Spiraling ever downward, each turn producing a view more splendid than the last, Anna considered the words she would use to share it with Molly. Inadequate metaphors were all she could muster: a cathedral, a ballroom, a whale's belly, a set for *The Phantom of the Opera*. In its uniqueness and magnificence, Carlsbad paupered the imagination. Unremitting opulence jaded the eye until it became possible to wander this unsung wonderland without seeing any but formations so stupendous they forced one away from the conversation of one's fellows or the contemplation of the dinner to be had when one returned to the world above.

Periodically Anna drifted by a troglodyte in the green and gray of the NPS uniform: rangers roving the trail, providing information, assistance, and a watchful eye for a resource so domesticated it could no longer protect itself. Cloaked in darkness and civilian clothes, she passed with a nod or a wave, happy to be another faceless tourist.

On a zigzagging segment where the path descended steeply toward the Big Room, a chamber the size of fourteen football fields according to the brochure, Anna found Zeddie Dillard. One foot on the low stone wall with which the Park Service bordered the asphalt—an attempt to keep people from stomping the entire cave floor into a likeness of a Safeway parking lot—she addressed a group of girls. Blue Birds or Brownies, something organized by age. Mellifluous in speech as in song, her voice hummed warmly in the dim cavern.

They were stopped at a natural viewpoint. A thoughtful government had provided a tasteful stone bench by the trail. Anna sat, half listening to the lecture and marveling at the panorama. The trail was considerably above the Big Room. Several more twists, turns, and tunnels would have to be negotiated before reaching the promised land. The zig where Anna sat provided a sneak preview, a peek from the stone-shrouded mountainside into the valley. Faint lights marked a sinuous path through a vast plain dotted with unimaginable monsters frozen for all eternity. Seen from above, it reminded Anna of flying into a strange city by night: pinpricks of light, canyons of darkness, mystery, unvoiced hopes and veiled threats.

The gaggle of girls trickled downhill. Zeddie turned, the professional smile of the tour guide barely discernible even to eyes accustomed to the dark.

"Hey, Anna," she said with what sounded like relief.

Dropping heavily onto the bench at her side, she said, "Boy, am I beat. I've got half a mind to come down with the flu myself. I could use the time in bed."

Both of them thought of Peter McCarty. Anna didn't so much as snicker, but Zeddie felt the vibrations. "Rest. Sleep. Hell . . ." Her words petered out. Then Anna did laugh.

Sniffing audibly, Zeddie said, "Do I smell Plumeria?"

"I've been playing with your toys," Anna admitted.

"Good for the soul. Even Xena the Warrior Princess wears a little eye shadow. I'm bored with men who think strong and sexy is an oxymoron."

"Heavy on the moron?" Anna suggested. Zeddie leaned over, bumping her with a shoulder that was no longer cold. Anna was touched. She liked Zeddie, liked to think well of her and be thought well of in return.

Two tourists, twined together like unpruned ivy, walked past. They smiled and nodded at Zeddie. The flat hat, the uniform, brought that out in people. Rangers, like firemen and comic-strip bears, were considered benevolent creatures. That as much as anything made Anna wince when she had to bust somebody. It was bad for the image.

"I oughtn't to be sitting," Zeddie said idly. "It looks bad." She made no move to get up. The morning's tour would have taken a toll even on such a robust specimen as Zeddie Dillard. She was tired, vulnerable. Anna might not get a better opportunity.

"Have you ever sung in the Big Room?" Anna asked, putting off the inevitable dissolution of their budding friendship.

" 'Ghost Riders in the Sky.' "

Leaning her head back, Anna stared into a heaven eternally dark. Thunderheads, canyons, spires, defied gravity. Utah's Canyon Lands in a Salvador Dalí nightmare. "Good choice," she said.

Carlsbad, the destination of as many as three-quarters of a million tourists each year, had none of the baffling silence of Lechuguilla. She and Zeddie were no more isolated than two women on a bench at the Guggenheim on a Sunday afternoon. In exposing the visual grandeur of the cavern, the soul of the cave had been compromised, as outer space was compromised by the bits of metal flung into it. Once man intruded, perfect solitude was banished. In this instance, Anna felt it was an improvement. Safety in numbers.

The comfortable quiet on the bench grew strained. Zeddie broke it first. "Dare I hope this is purely a social call?"

"I wish it were," Anna replied wearily.

"Are you going to accuse me of murder again?"

"More or less."

Zeddie snorted, but there was humor in the rude noise, and Anna took heart.

"Well, let's have it," Zeddie said. "Jealousy? A fortune in jewels? An inheritance: Frieda was my secret twin separated at birth?"

Anna searched for the words that would convey meanings only slowly becoming clear. "It's kind of a two-parter," she said. "There's Frieda. Then there's Sondra McCarty."

"Sondra's gone," Zeddie said with a frankness that caught Anna off guard. "And good riddance. That woman was a boil on the butt of humanity."

"Gone?" Anna tensed for a confession laced with hardcore rationalizations.

"Peter got rid of her," Zeddie said, pride of ownership in her voice. " 'Bout damn time."

She was too open, cheery. Anna was getting confused and a little nervous. What she had here was either a misunderstanding or an undiagnosed psychopath. She sought clarification with a gentle probe. "I hate to pry—"

"Hah!"

"Okay. I like to pry. How about this: Why in God's name did Peter think it was such a terrific idea to go on an expedition with his wife and his girlfriend and his ex-girlfriend?"

"The ex is no big deal," Zeddie said. "That was years ago. Frieda and Peter were friends. Shoot, Frieda and I were friends. With the notable exception of the Boil, I've always liked Pete's taste in women."

A clutter of tourists, jangling cameras and Anna's nerves, clattered down the trail. Duty calling, Zeddie left the bench and answered questions for a few minutes. Anna's favorite came from a scrawny youth in trousers so large the crotch hobbled him at the knees. "What does the cave weigh?"

The group was swallowed by the shadows, and Zeddie returned to the bench. "What do you want to bet that boy'll piss in the Urinal?"

Bowing to Zeddie's greater experience in things scatological, Anna declined the wager.

"Where were we?" Zeddie said, then, "Oh, right, you were interrogating me about the most intimate personal aspects of my life that are none of your business."

"That's it in a nutshell," Anna conceded. "You, Peter, and the Mrs. along on the same trip. That's where we left off."

"It does sound kinky when you put it like that. I was going through a bad time. Peter wanted to be with me. The sentiment was mutual. This survey came up. I wangled two places on it through Frieda. At the last minute Sondra dug in her heels. It was bring her or call the whole thing off. He brought her. Peter and I have known each other a long time, been through a lot together. We don't have to sleep in the same bed—though I've got to admit it's nice. Just being together, having a chance to talk, was enough."

"I take it Sondra didn't know about you two?"

"We were broken up when they got married."

"Why did he marry her, blackmail?"

"Rebound. I broke up with him. He's older than I am, established. I'm not ready to become Mrs. Doctor anybody. There are things I want to do. To make it stick, I made it brutal. Just fooling myself. I'm as addicted to Peter as he is to me. But I'm damned if I'll marry him. He was beginning to feel like an aging Warren Beatty with no Annette Bening in sight. Sondra showed up and waltzed him down the aisle. Therapy waiting to happen."

"Does he want a divorce?"

"Yeah. It embarrasses the hell out of him. They haven't been married all that long. He did make a fool of himself.

We all do now and again. But he wants out. She was just too much of a bitch."

Anna let the information soak in. Zeddie genuinely seemed not to care that Peter was wed, not to want to marry him herself. It fit with the other things Anna had observed: the free spiritedness, the fierce independence, the hint of tie-dye and incense. According to her—and the story had the mundane ring of truth—Sondra had not blackmailed Peter into matrimony. She'd caught him on the bounce and parlayed it into a white veil and a wedding band. Blackmail must have come later, been used not to acquire the husband but to control him.

Zeddie was kidding herself if she believed Sondra was not aware of her relationship with the doctor. In the beginning Sondra may not have known, but after the forced intimacy of several days underground she would have figured it out. Secret lovers seldom fool anyone but themselves. The discipline of an Olivier is required to lie with body language over a protracted period. There's too much to control: looks, gestures, position, voice. Women are especially adept at reading the signs. When a husband and a younger woman are involved, the senses become preternaturally acute. Sondra knew. A few questions to Frieda or Curt would have told her Zeddie, like herself and Frieda, had once been a patient of Dr. McCarty's. Two would be added to two, and Sondra would have enough leverage to keep Peter married to her or walk away with a hefty divorce settlement.

Anna had heard her threaten Peter with those choices. During that part of the rescue the team had been strung out along the route, each with a job to perform in the problematic evacuation. Peter would not have had a chance to talk with Zeddie, not before Katie's Pigtail. Zeddie wouldn't have known Sondra was going to play hardball.

". . . was too much of a bitch . . . was a boil . . ." Zeddie had used the past tense when speaking of the doctor's wife.

"*Was* a boil. You said 'was.' "

"Too crude for you?" Zeddie asked offhandedly. "Too bad. It's about the nicest thing I can think of to say about her."

"Was. Not is. Why the past tense?"

"Okay. Is."

Not a flicker of self-consciousness. Anna got no inkling that Zeddie had been caught in a trap, given herself away.

"As long as she's not a boil on my personal butt, I couldn't care less. What're you, her press agent?"

"I only asked because Sondra never came out of Lechuguilla."

Zeddie snorted her truncated laugh. "Yes she did."

"Nope. Never came out, never rode down to town, never flew out of the Carlsbad Airport."

"You're kidding." Zeddie sounded hopeful.

"Not kidding."

"Jesus." Zeddie took off her flat hat so she could lean back against the stone. Stretching her heavy legs, she drummed her heels softly against the asphalt; an obstruction just waiting for a tourist to trip over it. Anna sat without speaking, watching gray ghostly visitors glide along pathways below.

"Sondra never came out?"

"Never did."

"Jesus," Zeddie repeated. "Is this the part where you accuse me of murder?"

"No," Anna said. "Not quite yet." She was thinking of that something else that had been troubling her. "You said Peter came down because you were going through a bad time."

Zeddie didn't reply, and for the first time since they'd sat down together Anna sensed wariness. "What was that about?" she pressed.

"Just some personal demons. I intend to keep them that way."

Warning was clear in her voice. Anna chose to ignore it. "You had an older sister?"

"Darla," Zeddie said dully.

"She was killed in a climbing accident, wasn't she?"

Zeddie didn't say anything. Had they not been so close, Anna wouldn't have seen her nod. Her chin dipped toward her chest in acquiescence or defeat.

"Ten years or thereabouts?" Anna asked.

"Ten years this month."

The tenth anniversary of her sister's death; Anna could understand how that would cause a bad patch, emotionally speaking. "Was Frieda there when it happened?"

Again the nod. Before Anna could go on, Zeddie looked up like a woman coming out of anesthesia. Anna didn't need light to see the anger burning in her face. "What are you saying?" Zeddie demanded. The hard edge to her voice should have tipped Anna off, but it didn't.

"That maybe what happened to your sister happened to Frieda."

Anna never saw the blow coming. Suddenly she was facedown on the path with a buzzing in her right ear and a feeling the world had fallen in on her. Imposing as a limestone formation, Zeddie towered above her. In the velvet semidark Anna could not see her face. She could see strong hands bunched into fists next to muscular thighs and the broad expanse of shoulder looming between her and the vastness of the cavern's ceiling. The shadowed bulk moved back. Anna curled into a tight ball, readying for a kick in the ribs.

"Oh my gosh! What happened?" A voice piped through the gloom. Half a dozen tourists, smelling of catsup and cologne, pattered down. The herd closed around Anna.

Zeddie reached down. Anna clasped her wrist and was hauled to her feet. "I tripped," she said to the concerned crowd.

"Watch your footing," Zeddie said to the visitors. "These paths can be treacherous. Are you all right?" she asked Anna because the audience expected it of her in her role as the ranger.

"Right as rain," Anna said. The clout behind her ear had

been delivered by the meaty part of Zeddie's forearm. No harm was done, but she was stunned and disconcerted.

When the group passed out of earshot, Zeddie turned. Not willing to take another hit, Anna stepped back. Evidently Zeddie thought better of fisticuffs, but her rage was undiminished.

"Get out," she said. "Out of my cave, out of my house, out of my park. Stay the fuck away from me."

There was no give in her face, no chinks in her armor. Anna didn't precisely turn tail and run, but a hasty departure was the only option she'd left herself. Having backed out of range, lest Zeddie change her mind about using physical violence, she walked through the Urinal, cut across a corner of the Big Room, and caught an elevator back up the seven hundred fifty feet to the real world.

No question about it, Anna had hit a nerve. For that matter, so had Zeddie. A pervasive ache was spreading from behind Anna's ear up to her temple and down her neck into her shoulder.

AS PREDICTED, PETER and Curt were crumpled in front of the television, Calcite stretched along the back of the sofa, one paw kneading the bristle of hair on Curt's cheek. Greetings were grunted. Surreptitiously, Anna gathered up her things. It took all of three minutes. Standing at the door, she said, "I've got to say good-bye."

Like drunks emerging from stupor, the men tore their eyes from the TV and refocused on Anna. "Going?" Curt said stupidly.

"It's time. I can catch a flight out to somewhere—Las Vegas or Phoenix or Dallas—and be in Durango late tonight or tomorrow."

"This is sudden," Curt said. A roar erupted from the crowd on the television, and his eyes strayed back to the set.

"Not really. Walk me to the car, Curt," Anna said firmly.

It wasn't until the door closed between them and the game that the spell was broken, and Anna noted signs of intelligence returning to Curt's brown eyes.

BOOKED INTO A charming but cold cabin in White's City, Anna telephoned Dottie Dierkz. She remembered when Darla had been killed. Yes, Frieda had been there. The death of Darla Dillard was only half the tragedy. Anna thanked her and replaced the receiver in its cradle.

Zeddie and Peter at breakfast, Peter sneaking sips of her milkshake: the meaningless particles that had been floating in Anna's mind like dust motes settled into a pattern.

"Holy smoke," she said. She had been way the hell off base.

19

I HOPE YOU realize you're putting me in an awkward position."

By the light of the flashlight Anna held, Curt was tying an anchor line around the stunted oak at Lechuguilla's mouth. "I realize," she said. "Arrest, fines. You're a pal."

"Not that. Going to jail would lend me a certain cachet with my students. And you are going to pay any and all fines incurred, including the speeding tickets we get while running from the law à la *Thelma and Louise.* No, this goes deeper than that. It's dangerously close to midnight. We are about to descend into utter isolation. Isolation, I might add, from which your screams will not be heard. I am the only one whom you trust completely. Are you with me so far?"

"Hurry up." December was breathing ice down Anna's collar. Mixed with a bad case of nerves, it was all she could do to keep teeth from chattering and knees from knocking.

"I'm duty-bound to try to kill you," Curt said. He stopped

twisting the nut on the locking carabiner and looked up. His eyes were masked in shadow, but the glow from the flashlight illuminated small white teeth bared in a wolfish smile. A chill deeper than that of the north wind worked its way toward Anna's bone marrow.

"What?" she said stupidly.

"That's the way it is," Curt said. He went back to his anchor. "Hold the light still."

Anna's hand was shaking. She grabbed her wrist to steady it.

"In the next to the last chapter the only guy the hero—or heroine, in this case—trusts undergoes a sudden and total personality transplant. Sort of the literary equivalent of growing fangs and hair on his palms. And it turns out he was the killer all along. Voilà!" This was in mild celebration of the completed anchor. "You first or me?"

Anna was unable to speak. Like a child by the campfire, she had been scared by the ghost story. When she was twelve, her parents had left her home alone. A city council meeting, the results of which could affect their business, required their joint attendance. Anna had the flu but, wanting to be grown-up, she hadn't told them. To pass the evening, she'd curled up in her dad's big chair by the fire and read Bram Stoker's *Dracula*. Somewhere around ten P.M., fever and Stoker's genius combined to raise the undead. Vampires whined on the wind under the eaves, skritched at the windows with bony twig fingers, hid in shadows behind the piano and at the end of the hall. To put even a foot from her father's chair was to court disaster. There was but one way to exorcize her febrile demons. Knowing she committed the unthinkable, Anna had thrown the hardbound book into the fire and watched until even the cardboard curled in, completing the black rose-petal ruin of pages.

That same feverish terror gripped her on the limestone ledge above the gateway to Lechuguilla. This time there was no book, no symbolic crucifix to frighten away the bogeyman.

"Anna! You or me?" Curt's voice cut through the sludge of remembered horrors.

"That wasn't funny," Anna said.

Curt registered mild confusion, then laughed. "Sorry." He didn't sound it. "My sisters used to take me out for walks at night when we were little, then stop and say, 'Did you hear that? What was that!' then run shrieking away, me shrieking right behind them. I fell for it every time. Till now I didn't know I'd inherited the knack."

"Not funny. I'll go first." Anna handed him the light. They traded places, and she straddled the rope where it snaked over boulders hinting at white in the truculent light from the stars. Having clipped her safety to the line, she began threading rope through the ladderlike rack for the descent.

"You're sure this is a good idea?" This was not the first time Curt had asked that question since Anna had stolen the key to Lechuguilla from the pegboard behind Oscar Iverson's desk.

"Nope." She gave the usual answer. "But Holden knows all the details. He'll know where to come looking."

"Tell me you didn't leave him a letter marked 'To Be Opened in the Event of My Death.' "

"Something like that. On-rope." The circle of gold from her headlamp dancing giddily across her boots, Anna walked backward down the face of a boulder the size of a small Airstream and providing only slightly more traction than polished aluminum. Among Holden, Rhonda, endless phone calls, and a short stint as a burglar, the day had been tiring. Closeted in her cold cabin in White's City she had tried for a few hours' sleep. Though her body ached for rest, her mind refused to cooperate.

Much as she liked Curt and—morbid fantasies aside—trusted the man, she wished Holden Tillman were with them. The broken foot rendered it out of the question. Superstitiously she couldn't but believe the cave wouldn't hurt Holden. Her it might devour. Like a dog or a horse, it would smell her fear and turn on her.

"Cut that out," she said aloud.

"I didn't say a word," Curt complained.

Anna didn't have sufficient concentration to explain that it wasn't he but her own subconscious she ordered to silence.

The night below sucked her inexorably from the night above, darkness swallowing darkness till even the hope of day was lost. Fleetingly, she wished she were a religious woman. Perhaps it would be a comfort to have a blessed congregation lobbying a beneficent deity on her behalf.

Descending into a forbidden pit at midnight was ridiculously melodramatic. The sheer theatricality of it helped keep reality at bay. For half the afternoon Anna and Holden had gone around and around trying to find another way. She'd laid out her thoughts, and they'd spent an hour going over reports from the Blacktail well, Brent's recommendations for concrete and pipe, and the desert road, pulverized to a choking dust. Holden agreed that the key to Frieda's death would most likely be found in Lechuguilla. Between them they pieced together a picture of what must have occurred, though not one so clear they could identify all the players. Adding the Blacktail to the mix implicated half the brass in Carlsbad Caverns National Park. There was no one they could safely tell until they had proof.

And there was still the question of Sondra McCarty. How she fit in was unclear. The woman had literally vanished off the face of the earth, never to be seen again. If she, like Brent, had been involved and then disposed of, the field was somewhat narrowed. If not, then the number of people who would want Anna kept out of the cave and permanently silenced increased by at least one.

As Anna dropped down the last forty feet, the now-familiar musk of the underground filled her nostrils. A dank cellar smell, it put her on alert like a jittery cat. For Holden, Zeddie—true cavers—it was perfume, the scent of adventure, of untapped potential in the earth and within their own souls. To Anna it smelled of trouble, the olfactory hallucination that warned of a coming seizure. Once inside the cave it would be gone. Lechuguilla didn't have bat colonies to provide guano, no ready exchange with the surface to promote mold or insect life.

The floor of Old Misery Pit was below. Spinning like a spider on its web, Anna suffered a moment of vertigo. Her helmet light moved across one wall, was lost in a hole that fell sharply to one side, then flickered to life again on the ridge between the drop-off and the subtler exit that led into Lechuguilla. Giving in to momentary dizziness, she landed not lightly on her feet but firmly and solidly on her butt. She'd been right to descend first. This was not an entrance she would care to have witnessed by a pretty young man. Feeling all thumbs, she freed herself from the rope. In her limited but intense caving experience, she'd noticed a phenomenon she could always count on. Regardless of how often she changed batteries or switched lamps, the light from her helmet always appeared dirty brown, possessing only half the wattage of that of the other cavers.

"Off-rope," she hollered into the void. On hands and knees, she crawled to the side of the pit, trailing the end of the rope so she could steady it when Curt neared the bottom.

"On-rope," filtered down from above.

Less than ten minutes later she and Curt had negotiated the ten-foot nuisance drop from the floor of the pit. They crouched in the cramped chamber, where a trapdoor sealed the throat of Carlsbad's other world-class cave. The stolen key fitted the lock, and Anna pulled on the iron trapdoor. It gave easily, the heavy octagon springing upward. A blast of wind screamed out of the bowels of the earth as if the cave howled in rage. Blinded by dust, she staggered back, tripped over Curt's feet, and fell heavily.

"Holy smoke," she muttered, trying to rub the grit from her eyes. Wind continued to pour from the pipe at forty to fifty knots, filling the tiny earthen room with its own noxious brand of weather. "What the hell—"

"Pressure equalization," Curt said, unperturbed. "Must

be a low-pressure zone passing over New Mexico. Still want to do this?"

"No. You first or me?"

Curt went first, giving Anna time to weep the dirt from her eyes. After he called clear of the ladder, she followed. Standing on the second of the rungs welded inside the culvert, she had to use all her strength to force the trapdoor down against the gale. A muffled clang and sudden absolute peace let her know she'd succeeded.

Careful not to think more than was necessary, she hurried down the pipe and crawled out the dirt tunnel into the cave. Curt waited in the wide corridor that had once before ushered her into Lechuguilla. Corkscrewing away in the shadowed and toothy way of limestone passages, it was surprisingly comforting. For the first time she felt a glimmer of the passion that had cavers crawling into holes since the beginning of time. A fortress sense of safety surrounded her. The knowledge that bombs could fall, stock markets crash, and hemlines go up again, and none of it could touch her. Not in this world. Holding her breath, she waited for the familiar bite of claustrophobia to gnaw away this tenuous truce. It never came, and she breathed out her relief. Maybe she was cured. Chalk up a victory for aversion therapy. She made a mental note to tell Molly when next they talked.

Swept along by Holden Tillman's grace and expertise, Anna had made the trip from Old Misery Pit to Tinker's Hell in just over six hours. Curt was not so lithe, and neither she nor he so sublimely confident. A steady and careful trudge brought them to the rift in four hours. The traverse that had raised Anna's blood pressure the first time brought her close to a heart attack the second. When Curt finally dragged her into the constricting coils of the Wormhole, she was almost relieved. To the list of classic choices—rock and a hard place, devil and the deep blue sea—she added abyss and wormhole.

Minutes after dawn in a world that grew increasingly unimaginable with each slithered mile, they were at the egress from the Distributor Cap by the exit that would take them down the newly fallen rock and into Katie's Pigtail. There was just room in the opening for the two of them to sit side by side, their feet dangling over the lip, like children sitting on a tailgate.

After six hours' hard travel without a night's sleep to bolster her, Anna was tired. Muscles quivered on bones that felt brittle and old. In dire need of refueling, she spooned cold beans into her mouth from a foam cup. Curt drank noisily, his elbow jostling her each time he hoisted his water bottle. Close quarters foment love or war. Anna was unsure which way she was going to fall. "Nudge me one more time and you're meat for cave crickets," she said before it came to a decision.

"You're little. You don't need any space," Curt returned. "Airplanes, ironing boards, shower stalls—all made for Munchkins. I've got to be somewhere."

Several suggestions came to mind, but Anna left them unvoiced.

True to the tradition of light leaches, Curt had turned his headlamp off to preserve batteries. Anna's burned a lonely hole in the darkness of the Pigtail. Below them, a fifty-foot slope of powdery silt and rock spread in an apron filling the Pigtail to the bridge from which Holden had called his orders. Tracks from their exodus and the subsequent extrication of Frieda's body were perfect, ageless in the soft soil. This internal hillside remained unstable. Another rock slide poised to tumble down at the least provocation. Untried by the vicissitudes of the surface, much of the underground teetered on this edge for eons, awaiting that first tip of the scales: an earthquake, the flicked wing of a lost bat, the footfall of an unwary caver.

"Would you think less of me if I pretty much said, 'you're on your own,' and went home?" Curt asked. Another drink, another bump of the elbow against Anna's sweaty shoulder.

"Oh, yeah," she said. "Absolutely. Left alone and helpless I would naturally have to accompany you out and blacken your name on ladies' room walls forever after. Are you going to back out?" she asked hopefully.

"Not now."

"Damn."

The light from her helmet had dimmed to a myopic eye, a dull yellow-brown iris around a darker center. With the movement of her head the watery orb wandered across the rockfall. " 'S'pose she's under there?"

"Could be."

"Want to dig?"

"We'd be digging for days."

"Days," Anna agreed. The bottom of the slide, where one might reasonably expect Sondra's body to have been carried by multitudinous tons of loosed soil, was bulldozer and backhoe country. Two people with small folding shovels could dig till retirement and not find a thing.

"Not Zeddie?" Curt said.

"I don't think so. Maybe Peter. Zeddie didn't know Sondra was going for the jugular over the divorce issue. Peter did. Besides, Zeddie didn't have much of a motive. Neither money nor marriage rings her chimes."

"She's young," Curt said. "Give her a few years. They will."

"Too true." Anna remembered her aunt Peg telling her when she was in college, "Of course you're not conservative. You have *nothing to conserve*." Zeddie was still at an age at which "security" and "tedium" were synonyms.

"If you tell me about Zeddie and Frieda, I'll go down first," Curt offered.

Anna followed his gaze over the delicately balanced hill of loam. "I have to go first," she said. "I'm lighter."

"And I can dig faster."

"Good point." Anna didn't relish the image, but it was good to know he'd be standing by with a shovel. "Five more minutes." Screwing her courage to the sticking place, she switched off her headlamp to save the batteries. Total darkness closed around them. She touched Curt's knee, then the cool stone in the passage beside her to reassure herself that space had not vanished with light. Curt scooted closer, brushing her shoulder with his, letting her know she wasn't alone. Anna appreciated it. Fear of the dark had never been a problem for her. Since beginning her reluctant caving career, she understood why. She'd never been in the dark. Night was a kindly living entity. Darkness was not. Darkness was an invitation to the bottom dwellers of the id to come out and play.

"Frieda and Zeddie," she said, her voice sounding odd in her ears, as if the going of the light had altered the acoustics of Katie's Pigtail. Or those of her own skull. Resisting an impulse to feel her cranial bones to see if they had shifted, she went on. "Frieda's mom told me the story. It's Zeddie's secret to share or to keep, not mine."

Curt didn't say anything. Without light, not only space was rendered a bizarre and changeable entity, so was time. A blunt-edged clod of it tumbled by to a ticking in Anna's head.

"Strictly *entre nous?*" she said when a brief struggle between ethics and temptation had concluded.

"*Oui, oui,*" Curt replied. "Sub rosa and all that good stuff."

Anna laughed. The noise rebounded from unseen walls, frightening her. Returning to a murmur, she told Curt the story Dottie Dierkz had related over the phone.

"Short and sad," she said, and in her blindness felt as if she spoke only to herself. "Zeddie was a sophomore in high school. Her sister was home from college on spring break. She and Frieda took Zeddie climbing with a group of other college kids up to some rocks on the Yellow River, north of Minneapolis. There was ice. There was beer. There was a lot of general horsing around. Zeddie was belaying her sister. The anchor didn't hold. Zeddie wasn't strong enough. Her sister fell sixty-five feet and broke her back and neck. Eight days later they pulled the plug on the life-support machines, and she died."

A moment passed, then Curt said, "Like I'd dine out on that story."

Drowning in cave ink, Anna nodded.

"No wonder she went ballistic when you so rudely brought the subject up."

"I said maybe Frieda had died like her sister. I meant killed for revenge. Zeddie must have thought I was suggesting she'd screwed up."

"She was always anal retentive about rigging."

"Nobody was going to die on her watch again."

"Maybe that's why Zeddie got so strong," Curt suggested. "The woman is an ox."

A tremor took Anna as she saw herself, too weak to hold on, dropping Molly half a hundred feet to shatter on icy river rocks.

Time for the monsters to scuttle back under their stones. She flicked the button and turned on her lamp. A pool of light no bigger than a Frisbee and the color of mud feebly illuminated their boots.

"Why do people bury their dead?" Anna growled. "It's redundant." She pulled her helmet off and turned the switch, extinguishing the pathetic beam. Fresh batteries were in her sidepack and a Maglite was Velcroed in a canvas pocket on her belt. Before she could free it, a thin ululating wail stopped her hand. Caught in the Never-Never Land of Lechuguilla's night, the sound was directionless, without substance, a frail lament of the cave. Anna hadn't heard its like before: the keening of a child lost to hope, a meager, broken, madhouse moan. Prickling spread up her scalp as the vestiges of primordial muscles tried to raise the hackles on her neck.

"Did you hear that?" she whispered.

"No. God, no. And I never want to hear it again," Curt breathed, a voiceless warmth in her ear. Fear shook through his words. Anna's own ratcheted up a notch. She clung to his arm, Becky to his Tom Sawyer, listening for Indian Joe.

"Wind?" she managed.

"No."

"Kelly's ghost?" She was thinking of the obnoxious grandstanding of the man swearing he heard Frieda calling from beyond the grave.

"Get a grip," Curt hissed. Veiled by a testosterone version of the heebie-jeebies, his irritation failed to bolster her courage.

"Light!" Anna fumbled out her flashlight, felt it tip from her fingers to fall away soundlessly. "Fuck. Light!" she demanded.

Curt sat too still. She wanted to pound him. Fractured visions from movies her mother had told her not to watch flickered through her brain. "It" had gotten him. She sat next to a headless corpse. Possessed by an evil spirit, even now he lifted his hands to close around her throat.

Anna punched him.

"Doggone it, Anna, I'm trying to find that little switch thing."

Relief tugged a giggle from her throat. A thin heartless wail trailed on after her laughter stopped. Adrenaline worked its way to her bowels. The phrase "having the shit scared out of you" took on a sudden and graphic interpretation.

Curt's headlamp came on, pushing the cave back where it belonged. With the return of the sense of sight, the chilling cry seemed an unreal memory. Panic subsided, and thought resurfaced; still, every cell in Anna's body quivered.

At their feet the Pigtail yawned. The long rift looked bottomless in the imperfect light. Curtains of stone, rounded and draping from ages of gentle erosion, filled the chamber with theatrical shadows, a stage where the most impossible fantasies were rendered credible.

"You did hear it?" Anna begged. There was something about the bend and waver of the sinuous limestone walls that brought back memories of acid nights and flashback days. She needed reality ratified.

"I heard. Let's get out of here."

A good idea. A great idea. Probably the best idea Anna had heard in weeks.

"We can't," she said finally.

"Why not?"

"We're grown-ups."

"Now you tell me."

20

ANNA AND CURT sat without speaking. Breathing deep and slow to return her heart rate to normal, Anna listened until her ears ached with the silence.

"Maybe we should turn the light out again," Curt suggested.

"No," she said too quickly, then relented. "Try it." Entombed in darkness they waited. The eerie cry was not repeated.

"An aural hallucination?" Curt took a stab at explanation.

"We both heard it."

"Jesus. It's been nearly four days."

Anna said nothing. She doubted she herself would have lasted four days.

"Doggone that Kelly," Curt exploded. It was as close to swearing as Anna'd heard him come. "I hate people who can't grasp the obvious. If you think you hear a woman wailing in the dark, there's *probably a woman wailing in the dark.*"

"Sondra!" Anna shouted.

The name ricocheted from tiers of limestone. A tiny avalanche broke loose to their left, skittering furtively as far as gravity would take it.

Curt turned his lamp back on. By its light Anna replaced the batteries in hers and added its inadequate glow.

"Let's keep the hollering down until we're clear of the Pigtail," Curt whispered. "Ulterior motives aside, resource management was right to close this section. It's wanting to come down; I can feel it."

Anna could too, or thought she could, a pregnant heaviness in the atmosphere that was only partially accounted for by an overactive imagination. Once, snowshoeing in the Rockies under an unstable drift of spring snow, she had had the same sensation, as if the air between her and ten thousand tons of snow was being compressed.

Talking only when they had to, and then with an eye to the boulders preying on them from above, she and Curt rigged a rudimentary belay using his body as anchor. The descent was not so steep that Anna needed to be roped up, but, should the dirt begin to shift, Curt might be able to pull her free. Failing that, he could dig along the line, confident that at least a part of her would be waiting at the end of it.

The claustrophobia from which Anna had recently declared herself cured thundered back and took up residence behind her breastbone. Lechuguilla no longer seemed a benevolent fortress. With each trickle of stone set in motion by her boots, Anna heard the chuckle of a mountain waiting to bury her alive.

Then the Pigtail was at her feet. Crabbing sideways she set foot on solid rock. Leaving the line secured to her web gear, she picked a trail along the side of the chasm following the goat track that would never see a goat. To her left the rift dropped away, sheer on one side and vicious with broken rock on the other. Her light didn't reach the bottom, but the Pigtail's terrors were all in memory. Falling no longer frightened her. At this point in the journey it was the lesser of half a dozen evils.

When she was far enough away that a second slide would not reach her, she tied the line to a stalactite, moist and growing in its imperceptible way, and called gently, "Off-rope." With his greater weight, should he trigger a slide, Curt could drag Anna down with him. The stalactite would hold. Intellectually she knew this was appropriate. Viscerally she would have preferred to station herself directly below Curt. Standing at ground zero when the bomb dropped would be a quicker and easier end than being left alive to deal with the fallout.

Schatz's light winked as he turned his back, following the route she had taken. Though streaked with mud and darkened with sweat, his tee-shirt shone a rich emerald green. Color. Anna longed for the sight of color. Above-ground the bleakest desert landscape was alight against the blue of the sky at midday, dyed in hues of red and ocher with the setting of the sun. The darkest nights sparked silver from the sand. As a child she'd learned color was only a trick of the light, a wavelength reflected back to the human eye. Till entering a lightless realm, the truth of that hadn't come home to her.

Curt reached bottom. Years of caving made his big feet fall with such delicacy he dislodged scarcely half a cup of soil. Winding line as he came, he made his way down the rift to where she waited.

Pride, a favorite sin of Anna's, wasn't operative this deep in the earth. Content to let the younger, stronger, more experienced Schatz take the lead, she concentrated on where she put feet and hands. As they worked along the sketchy traverse, she kept an ear open for a recommencement of the haunting cry. If it came, she didn't hear it over the rasp of labored breathing.

From the repetitive clutching required in cave travel, the muscles in the palms and fingers of her hands ached as if she'd opened dozens of recalcitrant peanut-butter jars at a single sitting. By the time the Pigtail was behind them, Anna was wringing her hands in an unconscious parody of Lady Macbeth. Twenty feet into the dirty and uninteresting passage connecting the Pigtail to Lake Rapunzel, Curt stopped abruptly.

"It's gone."

Anna came up beside him, cramped under his arm by a pinch of stone.

"The tape is gone. Somebody took it."

The monomania of sustained movement cleared from her mind. The orange plastic surveyor's tape marking both sides of the trade routes through Lechuguilla was missing. Without it as a guide, the cave became a treacherous maze, each junction in the sinuous underground indistinguishable from the last. The way was not linear. Jagged rips in the limestone, some big enough to drive a truck through, others providing only wiggle room, were above, below, all around. Only one led out. A hundred such junctions, each with its myriad possibilities, rendered the odds of consistently making the right decision virtually nil.

"Why would Sondra take up the tape?" Curt asked.

Anna remembered when, during the carry-out, they'd finally reached the field phone: Frieda talking to her folks, Oscar Iverson and Brent Roxbury on the phone, Sondra sitting too close, taking notes.

"She didn't," Anna said with certainty. "She was eavesdropping. Something Oscar or Brent said must have struck her as that big news story she was so hungry for. She went back to find it. Somebody must have followed, pulled the tape, and left her."

"Gad, but that's cold."

"Or desperate."

Curt dug through his pack for a roll of tape. Anna carried some as well, part of the rudimentary kit for cavers in new environments. Following footprints and scuff marks, they moved on but much more slowly, leaving orange ribbon to mark the way back.

On a natural balcony overlooking Lake Rapunzel, they cried Sondra's name but could not scare up the ghost of the cave a third time. Urgency was growing in Anna, a need to find the woman, to reach Tinker's Hell, to get out of the realm of the dead before she started seeing three-headed dogs and smelling sulphur. Had Curt not insisted on a rest, she would have pushed on.

They sat; they drank. They did not speculate. It took too much energy, and even Curt was beginning to flag. Anna shined her light down glistening red-gold flowstone and ignited the perfect topaz of Rapunzel. That serene and liquid jewel, cradled in its basket of burnished limestone, made her doubly glad for the invention of the buddy system. Without Curt to curb her baser instincts, she knew, with what would have been shame had she not been too tired to care, she might have plunged in, clothes and all, introducing a cloud of grime into the pristine waters. Tracing her light up the far side of the sunken lake to Razor Blade Run, she remembered the glassine forest of aragonite crystals yet to be threaded through. She hoped she'd never be so brain-dead she would bull her way through that china shop. She liked to think that even without witnesses there was a limit to her fatigue-induced evil.

They moved without incident through the descents and ascents of Rapunzel and the dry pit of encrusted pillars called the Cocktail Lounge. The two rooms and their connecting passages were simple by Lechuguilla's standards. Few openings existed that hinted at further trails. At the mouth of each they called and listened lest Sondra had wandered in and become disoriented.

In the long and crushing passage that linked the Cocktail Lounge with Tinker's Hell, their shouting at last elicited a response. Standing upright in the chamber where Sondra and Peter had argued, they froze, willing the sound to come again. Just beyond was the belly-crawl where Anna had lain newtlike and eavesdropped. Anna's muscles twitched and her psyche trembled. Holding the reincarnated claustrophobia at bay took energy, akin to carrying a pit viper in a cotton pillowcase, ever vigilant, ever careful not to let it get too close.

"Sondra!" Curt shouted.

Moaning from hearts of stone dripped into their ears.

The chamber where they stood was not so much a room as an irregular void left behind by the shifting of immense blocks imperfectly mortared with lime. Walls were not smooth, not unbroken. The floor was not flat. The ceiling was dizzy-making with fractured planes. Cracks gaped from every angle. More were hidden by shadows. The one, true, going lead, the exit that would take a traveler to the Lounge and on, was one of these. Anna had recently crawled through it. She stood with her back to the bib of stone camouflaging it, yet she couldn't say with absolute certainty she'd find it again without the orange flagging.

No wonder Sondra hadn't made it out. Without tape she was lost. Without light she was doomed. Her batteries wouldn't have lasted four days. The miracle was that they had heard her through the rooms and passages between this forsaken rent in the earth and Katie's Pigtail. Either there was a crack somewhere high in the rock that carried sound, or Frieda had indeed been whispering, trying to summon help.

Whimpering oozed from all directions. Curt pointed with his light to a triangular opening five feet up and slanting away to the right. "I'm guessing that one. What do you think?"

"We've got to start somewhere."

Ten minutes in, the lead dead-ended. No room to turn, the two of them backed out. Curt gathered up the tape as they retreated. Sweat ran from Anna's hairline in blinding streams. Her shirt hinted at a life of wet tee-shirt contests and mud wrestling. Humidity and exertion were as deadly as the dehydrating sun of the Trans-Pecos. Every time she thought of it, she drank. Every time Curt told her to, she drank. Fortunately, with Lake Rapunzel and several other designated watering holes, getting enough liquid wasn't a problem.

Despite renewed shouting, the whimpering came no more.

Curt marked the failed lead, and methodically the two of them began following the others, moving counterclockwise around the room. To save time, they split up, each leaving a trail of tape. On Anna's third solo crawl she found Sondra McCarty.

Before she'd squirmed twenty feet, the smell met her, a vile odor of excrement and human despair, the odor of prisons, hospitals, and madhouses. A smell that can be masked but never completely expunged. Fighting nausea, Anna pulled the neck of her shirt over her nose and mouth, Joe Bazooka style, and crawled on. Sweat soaked through the rip-stop covers on her elbow and knee pads. Mud formed, creating minuscule dams that broke and reformed as she moved.

Trailing a lifeline of surveyor's tape, she heaved herself over a fall of flowstone. Stench hit her in full force. Her light shone into a room more spacious than any they'd found since leaving the Lounge. Twelve to fifteen feet high and twice that long, it stretched into the darkness. Blocks of limestone broke it into a maze. Piles of human waste dotted the flat areas. Paper and foam cartons were scattered around. A sidepack and helmet, cast off as in anger, hung precariously on an abutment halfway down the room.

At the far end, a wall glistened with water. Seepage formed a pool at its base. The body of a woman was beside it, curled into a fetal position so tight her head was hidden. All Anna could see were arms, legs, and butt. Having lowered her feet into the room, she slid down till she stood on the floor.

"Sondra?"

The fetus began to unwind with painful slowness, limbs like sticks, stiff as a puppet's, unfolding. Matted hair was pushed back by skeletal fingers to reveal eyes as devoid of humanity as any Anna had ever seen. They closed against the unbearable brightness of her lamp. No spark of recognition had registered, no gleam of incipient sanity.

Hunkered down on her heels so she would present a less alarming figure, Anna said, "Sondra, it's me, Anna. One of the cavers who came down to help carry Frieda out. Do you remember?" She kept her light just off Sondra's face. No intelligence was burgeoning. The vague, soulless stare continued. "You've been lost down here for four days." She spoke softly, easing Sondra back into the world of the living. "I see you found a water source. I'm impressed. You've kept yourself alive. That took courage. We're here now. We're going to take you home. Can you get up? Can you do that for me? Are you hurt?"

With a suddenness that caught Anna off guard, Sondra uncoiled, rose to feet and hands, and charged. Guttural cries rumbled behind bared teeth. Anna tried to stand, to jump clear, but legs too long without rest had cramped in the crouching position. She fell, rolling helplessly onto her back.

In an instant, Sondra was upon her, hands clawing, the growl becoming a staccato bleat.

Though moderately painful, the assault turned out to be friendly in nature. The tall, once haughty young woman held on, trying to burrow into Anna's arms, crawl into her pockets, hide in the warm safety of her.

Anna held her and muttered a slightly profane version of "there, there" till Sondra's hysterical flailing ceased. Bit by bit the grunts began to form into words, an ongoing litany of "Oh, God. You're real. So long. God. Don't let go."

Just as Anna began to think she would soon be able to form complete sentences, Sondra dissolved in racking sobs, her body jerking as if an electric current surged through it. Any attempt on Anna's part to pull away triggered such a fit of violent grasping that in the end she just hung on to the quivering mess that was Sondra McCarty and waited for the storm to blow itself out.

"Mind if I join you? Or is three a crowd?"

Anna looked up from where Sondra had her pinned in the dirt to see Schatz's most-welcome face.

"My lead dead-ended. I followed the bellowing." He slid down beside them and looked around, his lamp raking over the filth. "Not exactly the Hilton."

"She found water and stayed with it. Good girl," Anna

said in that peculiar voice usually reserved for dogs and horses.

"Hi, Sondra. Everybody's been missing you," Curt lied without a hitch.

Pulling her face away from Anna's chest at the sound of her name, Sondra stared at Curt. Face streaked with tears, hair in dreadlocks from sleeping and living in the mud, she looked every inch the tragic refugee. Momentarily her hands loosened their grip.

Opportunity was knocking. Aiming Mrs. McCarty at Curt's broad chest, Anna gave her a shove. Neat as a flying squirrel, Sondra let go of Anna and smacked into Curt, fingers, toes, every prehensile inch of her reattaching to the new savior.

"Thanks a heap," Curt said dryly, eyeing Anna over Sondra's head where it wedged between his jaw and neck.

"Don't mention it." Rubbery legs took Anna's weight. Rubbing clutch marks from her arms, she tried to shake free of the insanity if not the stink of it.

Affixed to Curt, Sondra made gurgling noises and hid her face. A line from an old Travis McGee novel came to mind: "You girl, do you dither? Do you bleat and snuffle and carry on?" Anna looked away. The woman had earned the right to a breakdown. Batteries would have gone dead on the first day. Food run out on the second. Without water Sondra would have died on the third. Carlsbad's volunteers were going to have fun cleaning up after this adventure.

Turning her back on what had become a prison for Sondra, Anna knelt. The younger woman's shoulders grasped between her hands, she gently pulled her several inches away from her human rock.

"Time to go. You've been here plenty long, don't you think?"

Childish in extremity, Sondra nodded and pawed away tears with one hand. The other had a fistful of Curt's tee-shirt and looked in no way ready to let go.

"You must be real hungry," Anna said coaxingly. "I've

got a whole bunch of food in my pack. If you can come just a little ways, back out to the real trail, we'll eat something. Then go home." To Curt she said, "Take her hand. The one on your shirtfront if you can get it. Hold it till you can't anymore. I'll be right behind you with her gear."

Schatz did as he was asked. In the confined crawl space leading back to the Trade Route, there was a scuffle and some wailing when he tried to detach himself so he could move ahead. Anna took a bandana from her pocket, tied one corner to the end of Curt's bootlace, and gave the other to Sondra. Tenuous as the tether was, it gave her confidence to go on.

Back in the crumpled space whence this side trip had begun, Anna got a container of ravioli from her pack and let Sondra eat half of it. The rest she set aside to see if her patient could keep the food down.

Anna had brought Sondra's helmet and pack out. Curt put fresh batteries in her headlamp. With her own light strapped to her head, she calmed down significantly. Given light, food, and the promise of salvation, she showed signs of regaining the rudiments of human intercourse.

The ravioli stayed down. Anna let Sondra have what was left, her cautions to eat slowly totally disregarded.

"Can you tell us what happened?" she asked.

The brown eyes filled with tears fat as summer raindrops. They dripped from the narrow jaw, splashing onto her trousered thighs with audible plops. Tears were an improvement. Tears were human; they helped to melt the unnatural rictus of her face. Still, Anna didn't want to risk a setback.

"You don't have to talk about it," she said quickly. "You just eat and get your strength back."

Curiosity might have rendered her less kindly, but she had a pretty good idea what must have transpired. Sondra had heard someone—Brent or Oscar, or Brent and Oscar—talking about the original injury to Frieda. She'd put together that Frieda had been attacked to keep her from finding something they didn't want found. Sondra sneaked away in search of an exclusive story. Her disappearance was noted by someone wishing her ill. During the night the rescuers had been trapped in the Pigtail, this person had slipped away while the others slept. By the simple expedient of removing the tape, he had seen to it that Sondra would not come out.

Anna had awakened that night. Brent had been gone from his sleeping place. Another reason guilt might have driven him to what became his own death. Killing would be hard to live with. Burial alive, impossible.

"Did you get all the way to Tinker's Hell?" Anna asked.

Sondra shook her head, her mouth full of ravioli. In a shuddering gulp she swallowed it. Her eyes refilled, and she whimpered, "There was somebody following me." Memory, mixed with trauma, was drawing a veil over her mind.

"Don't," Anna said sharply. "Stay right here. Right now. With us. Eat. Talk to her, Curt."

Curt, still tied to their acquisition by Anna's handkerchief, began telling stories of the incredible abuses perpetrated on the English language by his students. The talk was pointless, mildly amusing, and just what the doctor might have ordered. That is, if the doctor wanted his wife back.

Harmless male chatter was a balm to frayed nerves. Sondra's eating slowed, and her eyes dried. Stretching her legs, Anna mingled the muddy soles of her boots with those of her companions. Closing her eyes she invited a catnap to recharge her batteries. Tinker's Hell was close—no more than a twenty-minute trek from where they sat. She needed to get there; otherwise the whole trip was for nothing. Mentally, she apologized to Sondra. Saving a life, even one as irksome as Sondra McCarty's, was probably worth something. Mind drifted. It would be not only cruel but, more significantly, unwise to ask Sondra to go deeper into the cave. At best she'd be an anchor. At worst she'd flip out and become a serious liability. In her fragile state she couldn't be left alone. The briefest sentence back in solitary confinement could do irreparable harm. The mind-breaking solitude of the underground was stressful for the healthy and well balanced.

Anna enjoyed a peculiar sensation of simultaneously floating and weighing five hundred pounds. Ten hours' sleep would have been a boon, but if anything she'd read about long incarcerations in the dark was true, Sondra had been sleeping fifteen to twenty hours out of every twenty-four. Leaving her alone even through the act of becoming unconscious didn't sit well. Anna would have to make it out of Lechuguilla on catnaps. Once outside, she promised herself, she'd spread a sleeping bag on the open desert and sleep till Christmas.

"Christmas."

She'd been talking in her sleep. Curt's "Ho, ho, ho" woke her up.

"How long was I asleep?" she demanded.

"Maybe ten minutes," Curt told her.

"Ten years would be a drop in the bucket," she confessed. "How are you doing, Sondra? Do you feel up to heading out?"

"Is anybody there?" She sounded like a frightened child.

"Peter, you mean? He's there." Anna tried to reassure her.

Sondra pushed her face into her hands, hid behind a clotted mat of hair. "No. No. Not Peter." Her voice was creeping up the scale, on a collision course with hysteria.

At a loss, Anna got ready to slap her. Curt was quicker to understand.

"Not Peter," he said. "It wasn't Peter. Listen to me." Catching her by the wrists, he pried her hands away from her face. "Anna meant Peter is waiting for you outside. Nobody's waiting in the cave. Nobody's here but us. The guy who followed you is dead. Shot dead."

Anna thought the violence of the image might further derange Sondra, but she absorbed the words, then donned

an expression that looked a lot like smugness. Mrs. Mc-
Carty's personality was beginning to reassert itself.

"I've got to go into Tinker's Hell," Anna announced, putting it into words so she couldn't chicken out. Sondra
screwed up her face. Before she could weep or wail or
whatever it was she had in mind, Anna stopped her. "I'll go
alone. You guys go ahead and wait for me at the overlook
at the Cocktail Lounge. It's not more than a half hour back.
I shouldn't be more than two hours going and coming. Then
the three of us go home. What do you say?"

"No."

It took Anna ten minutes to argue Curt around, but she
finally did it. He took Sondra and began the tortuous wind
toward the Cocktail Lounge.

Tying one end of her surveyor's tape to his and anchor-
ing the knot with a rock, Anna pointed her lamp into the
dizzying tunnels.

Never had winning an argument left her in such a foul
mood.

21

FROM WHERE THE three of them split up it was a fairly straight shot to Tinker's Hell. Anna took it slow, leaving line in her wake. Fifteen minutes' scramble brought her to where the original tape had been severed. It hadn't taken Sondra long to become disoriented, then lost. Paranoia made Anna leave small pieces of her own tape in addition to what remained, strategically located at the junctions lest what befell Sondra should happen to her.

Tinker's Hell was bigger than she remembered, and more chaotic. Taking huge gulps of air in an attempt to assimilate the spaciousness into the recesses of her bones, she rested and drank. Twenty minutes more and she arrived at the base camp where Frieda had awaited rescue.

After several fruitless stabs under boulders all looking alike in shifting and limited light, she found the lead Frieda had been returning from when the rock struck her. Around the three-by-three-foot crack in the floor, the earth had been scuffed by those laboring to bring out the unconscious woman.

Having secured one end of the orange tape to a sizable rock, Anna chimneyed down an enclosed staircase designed by a mad Cubist. Five minutes in, it leveled off, a sloping belly-crawl. She tied her pack to her ankle and shimmied along, mentally marking off each foot claimed to keep her mind off greater evils. At what would turn out to be the halfway point, she lost her bearings. The space was big enough for her to sit upright. Two channels led through the rock. One slanted up and back toward Tinker's Hell, the other down and away. The faint breath of a living cave drifted through each; the stirring that cavers learn to wait for, moving air hinting at a going lead. With a nod to Alice's white rabbit, Anna chose the crawl down and away.

Perseverance was rewarded. After what seemed more time than her wristwatch assured her had elapsed, she was reborn in a chamber so vast that half a dozen rooms the size of Tinker's Hell could have been stored within it. Hardened as her heart was against all wonders remotely stygian, she was swept up by the unearthly beauty. After so long in a black and mud-brown world the illusion of light took her breath away. Chandeliers of snow-white selenite covered the ceiling. Like great inverted winter trees glittering with hoarfrost, branches grew down fifteen and twenty feet. This fairy forest was thick and extended. Grandeur, Anna suspected, unequaled anywhere on earth. At least anywhere human eyes had been. The cavern walls were draped in curtains of liquid stone, frozen in place one molecule at a time over the history of the world. Sheets of gold, burnt umber, ocher, ivory, and white spilled down hundreds of feet, folding in on themselves, then crumpling on the floor as gracefully as the satin skirts of a fine lady. Throughout the enormous room were columns, some joined to form arches, stalagmites grown up and stalactites down to meet in fantastic pillars hundreds of feet high. Some, still growing, had windows yet to be filled with dripping limestone. Within the windows were tiny worlds, variations on the grand scheme. Openings not more than two feet high and half that in width were encrusted with ferns of iridescent crystal and delicate popcorn formations in shades of copper and bronze. Through the midst of this enchanted land meandered a shallow stream, a collection of seeps and drips from a square mile of desert. Water so clear it seemed to be only the eye's distortion, flowed over rock looking no less liquid and mobile.

A caricature of a wonder-struck child, Anna sat on the lip of the tunnel, eyes wide, mouth agape. Millions of reflective surfaces caught her little light and magnified it. Drinking in the color she'd so yearned for, she muttered an unconscious prayer: "Holy shit."

Cavers the world over dreamed of, lived for, risked their lives in search of a room such as this. And she, a dirt-detesting claustrophobe, had found it. The fates have a wicked sense of humor.

Not the first, she reminded herself. This had to be what Frieda had discovered, what she was hurrying back to tell the others about. Anna had found the answer, and it made no sense. A room such as this was an incomparable good to all involved: a treasure for the park, a feather in the cap of every team member including Brent Roxbury. This miracle of miracles, located in the heart of protected public land, had no downside.

If the answer made no sense, Anna had yet to probe deeply enough.

Falling gracefully away, polished flowstone beckoned her to further exploration. At the first step onto the glassy walk, she heard Holden Tillman's cowboy cursing in her head. Lug-soled boots, caked with mud, had no place in this ballroom of the damned. Rubbery socks, the kind made for playing on rough beaches and rocky lake shores, were part of the kit of every caver allowed into Lechuguilla. They wore them on the delicate flowstone around Lake Rapunzel and anywhere else boots would destroy nature's artwork. The first cavers faced with this dilemma had doffed boots and traversed the fragile landscapes barefooted. Then it was noted that the oils from human skin disfigured pristine surfaces.

Rubber shoes in place, Anna sat a little longer, studying the ground. Tracking, reading the record of men or beasts, was something she did almost without thinking above-ground. In this alien environment she'd overlooked this fundamental skill. With limited light, the task was hard, but in a world without wind, automobiles, or creatures bigger than a microbe, there was little confusion. In front of her, nearly between her feet, was a partial print: mud on stone, the corrugated pattern of a hiking boot, small in size. There was but the single print. Either Frieda had turned back or, like Anna, had changed footgear.

Assuming Frieda would have taken the path of least re-sistance, Anna followed suit and flowed down with the stone into the great room. For fifty or sixty feet she saw no other evidence that Frieda had been there. Time was slip-ping by. She had already used more than half the time she'd promised Curt she'd be gone. She'd seen nothing of the cavern but that first stunning survey and the rock immedi-ately in front of her toes. Tracking was not conducive to sightseeing. Soon she must turn back. To date, all her sweat and fears had bought was a slightly used doctor's wife and an even greater mystery.

Squatting, she tried for a new perspective. In ribbons that ran through the yellow spectrum, rock spread out in three directions. One ended against a stalagmite older and more impressive than a giant redwood. To her right the flow slid under the water of the stream. On the left it ended in a mist of soil ground fine as flour. A minuscule imperfection cut through this internal desert. Closer inspection revealed a bootprint. Frieda had not changed boots for socks. But then where were the inevitable prints from the entrance tunnel? So untouched was the flowstone, the merest smear of mud would have been as obvious as a billboard on a stretch of virgin meadow.

Anna removed her helmet and held it high, increasing the spread of light. Half a dozen prints materialized, prints larger than the one left by Frieda Dierkz. Moving slowly, eyes to the ground, she followed. Two sets, one coming, one going, led across the silted patch and between curves of silky stone growing out from the wall like the roots of an immense tree. Scrapes and streaks of mud showed where the booted individual slid down, then climbed back up. Twenty feet above the cavern floor, maybe fourteen yards from where she emerged, was an oval of black overhung with liquid limestone.

Anna retraced her steps. Near the polished run of flowstone, at the base of a convenient chair-high rock, the silt was churned up. A logical place to slip off the offending boots to proceed on the more fragile surface in booties or stockinged feet.

The "how" of the first attack on Frieda became clear.

Brent Roxbury had been following a lead on the back wall of Tinker's Hell. Curt was waiting for him, working on sketches for the survey. Brent was gone a considerable time but returned to say the lead had petered out. It hadn't. The end wall of Tinker's was honeycombed with back doors, at least two of which exited into this undiscovered room. Brent had come out in the cavern and seen Frieda.

Anna would check on the return trip, but it was a good bet that the fork between here and Tinker's, where she'd felt the drift of air, opened into a passage connected with the route Brent had taken. As he crawled back toward Tinker's, he heard Frieda in the parallel passage and went through to meet her. He must have arrived before her in time and above her in elevation. He shoved the rock, then went back the way he had come to report nothing but a dead end.

That was how. "Why" was still at large. Anna looked at her watch again. She was going to be late. Hopefully Curt wouldn't panic, and Sondra wouldn't become any crazier than she already was.

Leaving the dead man's tracks, she walked back to the flowstone, an honest-to-God yellow brick road through a subterranean Oz.

Fatigue, awe, and fear combined to make the unreal surreal. Walking was upright, unhampered. It put to death the cavers' theory that there was no unbroken ground in this great cave. Vision was limited to the stingy reach of her lamp, but such was the glitter, she felt as if she walked in a moonlit garden. Stone flowed beneath the creek, and she waded across. Ice-cold water soothed feet too long confined in heavy leather. Beyond, she climbed a low rise and circled a formation of white spheres, piled one on another until the entirety of it resembled an elephant sitting on its haunches, forelegs raised the way she had seen them do in circus acts.

Past the Impressionist pachyderm lay what she had been seeking. Expectation did little to soften the blow. As she leaned against the elephant's cool flank, her eyes prickled with tears. The cavern extended another four or five hundred feet. Aragonite chandeliers had hung in defiant profusion from a ceiling of gold. The meandering stream had curved through formations looking more like cloud than solid earth. The end of the room had been cloaked in draperies of such delicacy it would have taken little imagination to see them moving in a nonexistent breeze. At their base, filled by a waterfall from the creek, was what had been the room's crowning jewel, a clear blue lake, garnished with lily pads of ruby-colored stone.

That was what had been. Before poison rained down from above, then was pumped back up in the form of double homicide. "Marble clouds, lily pads ruined," Frieda said that first night in Tinker's. She'd seen it. What remained was tragic, Philistines in the temple. Aragonite trees lay smashed on the cavern floor, their branches defiled with dirt and rock from a gout in the ceiling. The lake was full of mud, the lily pads broken. Half the lake and part of the waterfall were buried under cement and pea gravel. A pipe casing a foot in diameter cut through the ruined ceiling to plunge into the hideous pile and disappear.

The Blacktail, as Holden said, was drilling legally on a legal lease. But concrete trucks had run night and day, pulverizing the desert and causing the one neighbor in forty miles to complain of noise. Roxbury had ordered too much pipe. Inspired by the image of Peter angling his drinking straw into Zeddie's milkshake, Anna and Holden had pieced it together. The Blacktail drilled not straight down as required by the lease, but at an angle, pushing their pipe deep into the protected land of the park in search of gas.

When they'd hit open space, the cavern where Anna stood, and ceased to get any return—no mud or rock cuttings circulating back up—they didn't report it. When there was such an indication of underground spaces, regulations demanded a cease in drilling so the possibility of a cavern could be explored. The Blacktail couldn't afford to report it. They couldn't bear the scrutiny. In order to fill the hole so they could go on drilling, they pumped concrete and gravel into the earth day after day, night after night till they'd laid a new bed for their pipe. And destroyed a natural cavern that beggared man's proudest cathedrals.

Unanswered questions abounded. Why had Brent been part of it when he didn't have the courage—or the lack of morality—to go through with it? He'd ordered the extra pipe, the additional concrete and gravel, and had made a feeble attempt to falsify the data. So feeble, he must have wanted to get caught. Brent had pushed the stone to kill Frieda and might have been the one who started the slide that finished the job. Had he done it for money? From the way he lived, he hadn't gotten enough to make it worth killing over.

Anna took a thirty-five-millimeter camera from her pack. The camera was designed to capture Kodak moments: babies and birthdays. The flash would be lost in a room this size, but for her purposes it would suffice. She sought proof, not art. Armed with photos and an eyewitness, Holden could close down the Blacktail. With luck and hard work he could bring the owners or operators to task. They would not be sufficiently punished; drawing, quartering, and disemboweling were outlawed in New Mexico. They would be fined, the modern equivalent of the pound of flesh. Anna couldn't remember what Exxon paid for the Valdez incident, but she would keep her fingers crossed that this settlement would make the other look like pin money.

The soullessness of the business of business saddened her. One roll of film finished, she loaded a second. Crimes of passion committed by passionless men for money.

The Park Service would deal more harshly with participants within its own ranks. Jobs would be lost, reputations destroyed. Charges of conspiracy and racketeering might buy prison time for the perpetrator. For Oscar Iverson. He'd spoken with Brent in the Pigtail. He'd known Brent was meeting Anna at Big Manhole. As cliché dictated, he'd returned to the scene of the crime and taken away the one shred of evidence, the rifle shell. The shell had been carefully wiped clean of prints by the time the sheriff's department got their hands on it.

"Anna Pigeon."

So wrapped was she in her thoughts and belief in her solitude, she screeched like an owl and stumbled back. As she fell, her lamp was knocked askew. Light from an alien helmet struck her night-adjusted eyes with the force of an oncoming locomotive. Less than two yards away a man stood blanketed in darkness.

"You are in a great deal of trouble, Anna. A very great deal of trouble."

22

SHIELDING HER EYES, Anna took a guess. "George Laymon?" The intrusion had goosed her adrenal glands. Fatigue was gone. She was on her feet before the words were out.

"The same."

"Get the light out of my eyes."

He acted as if he didn't hear. Adjusting her headlamp to illuminate him, she joined the pissing contest.

"What are you doing here?" she demanded.

"The best defense is a good offense. I'm here to find you. Curt said you'd gone on alone, adding stupidity to your considerable list of transgressions. Lord! What a travesty."

His light had slipped beyond her and touched on the desecration of pipe and cement. "What an unholy mess." Trained on his face, Anna's lamp revealed shock and sadness in the slump of muscles. "Drilling," he said. "One leak in that gas pipe and not only is this room gone but all of Lechuguilla. The atmosphere poisoned."

Anna was losing her adrenaline high. Enough of an edge

remained to sharpen her voice if not her wits. "What made you come?"

Laymon turned his back on the mountain of cement and pea gravel. "My secretary went to Oscar's office. The key was missing from the board. You were gone. Mr. Schatz was gone. A quick check and we found the padlock cut on the gate to Lechuguilla's access road. So we put together what we hoped wasn't going to turn out to be a rescue team."

"We?"

"Oscar and the others stayed back with Curt and the woman. Finding Mrs. McCarty won't get you off the hook. The superintendent is not pleased. If there's a regulation in NPS-9 you failed to break, I've yet to find it."

After the words "Oscar's with Curt and the woman," Anna quit listening. Altruism—the safety of Curt and Sondra—sparked, then was lost in a blinding flash of self-interest. Oscar was between Anna and the culvert leading out of the cave.

"Oscar's involved," she said. "We've got to get back."

Laymon looked at her, then at the ruin behind her. "Surely not Oscar," he said, but she could see the idea was not completely foreign to him.

"I think Brent made a halfhearted attempt to silence Frieda, then backed off," Anna told him. "By the time we got to Katie's Pigtail, something had changed. Oscar talked to Brent. Pressured him somehow to try again."

Laymon looked weary, and every day of his sixty years showed. "All you have is a theory, Anna. I admit it sounds plausible, but without proof I wouldn't dare dignify it with any kind of formal accusation."

"Oscar's the cave resource manager. Oscar closed this wing of Lechuguilla."

"For the safety of the cave and the cavers. I concurred with the closure."

"Oscar stomped the scene of Brent's shooting and carried away the shell."

Laymon said nothing. He sat on a finger of dead gray

concrete that spilled out from the mass trashing the lake. Shoulders stooped, he flicked at the mud on his boot tops with one glove. "I sent a law-enforcement ranger. Oscar stopped him and went himself. I wrote it off as overzealousness. Everybody wants to play cop." He raised his head. "Present company not excluded. By your Wonder Woman act you endangered yourself, Curt Schatz, the resource, and those of us who've had to come after you. Since you didn't see fit to report any of your suspicions to the superintendent and myself, who did you work with? Or are you foolish enough to be working solo?"

"I told you I thought Frieda had been murdered," Anna said lamely.

"Laymon waved that away with an annoyed flick of his hand. "That's ancient history. Most of what you've told me is new. Did you work this out by yourself?"

The implied insult stung. The momentary sting of the lash covered up something else, a mild but gnawing sense of unease. Anna chose to ignore the question. "We've got to get back," she said bluntly.

"We do," he agreed, but he didn't move. He smiled. "Give an old man a chance to catch his breath. I'm an army brat, used to moving around, but I've done way too much of it these past few hours. I'm pooped."

Uneasiness grew. Half-formed ideas fluttered batwings in Anna's skull. Army brat. A fragment of casual conversation clicked in memory. During one of their meetings, Laymon said he was from the "Show Me" state. Missouri. George Laymon was from a military background in Missouri. He could easily have known of Brent's army career. Blackmail. That would account for why Roxbury, a known conservationist, might have covered up illicit drilling. One word about Brent's arrest for indecent exposure and he'd lose his little girls.

On the heels of these ugly thoughts came others: Laymon knew Oscar was heavy-footed; Holden had joked about it. Oscar might not have gone to Big Manhole on his own, but at Laymon's order. The "chewing out" Jewel reported wasn't something she'd witnessed but something she'd been told—by George Laymon. The rifle shell had been turned over to Laymon for delivery to the sheriff's office. Even the order closing the cave had come down from Laymon. Prior to the rock slide in Katie's Pigtail, Brent had spoken to someone outside the core group. Brent had placed a call on the landline. To Laymon? And Laymon had told him to finish what he started or lose his girls to Amy and her dentist?

The rapid-fire thought ended. Tired unto stupidity, Anna knew her revelations had trotted across her face for anyone to read. One look at Laymon ratified her fears. His face had changed. Charm was gone. Muscles bunched to lift him from the sitting position. There would be no playing the innocent and stringing him along until an opening for escape presented itself.

"What was in it for you?" Anna asked to distract him.

"Money. A whole lot of money."

"Oscar isn't with Curt and Sondra, is he? Nobody is."

"Smart girl," Laymon said. "Too much smarts isn't healthy in a woman."

Anna was in no position to argue the point. The cavalry had gone the way of John Wayne. The god from the machine was relegated to a line in Greek history. Screaming would be an exercise in futility. In the wake of two corpses and an elaborate coverup, the odds of talking him into repenting the error of his ways were nil. Sixty sounded old. But Laymon was in superb physical condition. He was rested. And he was a big man.

Throwing dignity to the wind, Anna ran. Behind her she could hear the smash of his boots on the flowstone. He'd not bothered changing footwear. That in itself should have tipped her off. No point in rearranging deck chairs when you know the ship's going down. Scrambling up the slide that had gentled her into this false paradise, she passed her boots, leather sentinels at the backdoor of Tinker's Hell. No time to retrieve them.

An explosion, intensified by the closed space, knifed through her eardrums. A piece of flowstone the size of a fist vanished from the rock by her left knee. The air shivered with a faint tinkling as of distant wind chimes: crystal trees trembling in the echo of the blast, and the high-pitched singing of rock and ricochet. Laymon had a gun. That possibility hadn't crossed her mind. On the surface it would have been one of her first considerations. Firearms didn't seem part of this world. "Whither thou goest, I shall go." Anna couldn't remember who'd said that to whom, but it would have made sense had the god of war whispered the words into the ear of man.

Like Br'er Rabbit, Anna dove into the confines of the exit tunnel, her personal briar patch. She'd railed against the claustrophobic embrace of Lechuguilla's tight places. Now she welcomed them. She was small; she could move quickly. Rocks cut through the rubber slippers. Razor-backed walls scraped her elbows as she pushed with feet, clawed with gloved hands. More than once she cracked her helmet hard enough that noise pinged in her vertebrae. There was no pain. That would come later. If she was lucky.

With each movement she made came the sound of pursuit, always right at her heels. So close, she looked for Laymon's light, expected his breath on the nape of her neck. The sidepack caught and dragged. In the long belly-crawl before the halfway point, the strap snagged and held her fast. Unhooking it, she squeezed on, sans water, food, surveyor's tape, and batteries.

Gone too was the insistent shuffle of her pursuer. The sounds that had driven her to the point at which heart and lungs threatened to burst were made by the contents of her pack shifting close to her ears.

Reaching the room with two leads, where Brent had cut off Frieda's return, Anna stopped, held her breath, and listened. Though not yet on her heels, Laymon was coming. At a guess, she was sixty seconds ahead. Beyond the tunnel was Tinker's Hell. Open areas with lots of places to hide. That was the obvious gambit. She would leave him to figure it out. Taking precious seconds for stealth, she crept not out toward Tinker's but up the passage that Brent had used to get from his elevated lead down to the passage Frieda traversed.

Having squeezed fifteen feet into the rocky maze, Anna wedged herself tightly into a crack and turned off her headlamp. Covering mouth and nose, she tried to smother the rasp of her breathing. As it ebbed, she was overwhelmed by a different, greater noise. Thrumming, distant and roaring, as if a dam had broken and water poured down into the rooms and passages of the cave. Water or gas. Could Laymon's bullets have damaged the pipe, killing him, her, and the cave? The sound grew more intense, an explosion forced through arteries and veins of stone.

Caught in a terror she could neither run from nor outsmart, she waited, mind curiously blank, muscles knotted as her body readied for an impossible battle.

The bellowing rush sustained, not growing closer, not receding. Through it, she heard gasping: Laymon prying himself out of the bellycrawl. With a start, she realized the roaring that had sounded like part of the earth itself was the beating of her own heart. She'd been told of the phenomenon, but didn't grasp how alien and frightening it would be. Hands clamped over her mouth, she fervently hoped the machinations of Laymon's own heart would mask the jungle-drumbeat of hers.

Furtive sounds penetrated the steady hum of blood in her ears. Whether he climbed toward her, moved on, or adjusted his pack, she couldn't tell. Inquisitive as a live thing, light streaked up the rock beyond her feet and across where the lead made a hard left creating the shelf on which she hid. The round of gold probed closer, Tinkerbell's evil twin. Cringing, she resisted an impulse to swat it away.

If the light sensed her presence, it had the good taste not to inform its master. Flickering, the gold slithered back down the rocky chute and was gone.

"Anna!"

Her name, shouted so close, startled her. Too tired for

perfect discipline, muscles twitched. Gravel skittered down the rock.

Maybe Laymon heard it. Maybe he didn't.

Maybe he knew she'd caused it. Maybe he blamed the resonance of his own voice.

She waited for the noises that would set her again to running till she was gunned down, could no longer lift one foot after another, or a better idea came to her. Reprising Brent's act with the stone was her first choice, but every rock in her cubbyhole was firmly attached.

The evil Tinkerbell light never came back. Laymon's skritching and scraping grew fainter. Anna took her hands from her mouth and breathed cautiously. Her legs were cramping, her feet beginning to tingle, but she was afraid to move. Playing possum wasn't exactly an innovative tactic. If she could think of it, so could he. He might be waiting not twenty feet away, light out, breath hushed, invisible.

Paralyzed by the idea, she stayed where she was. Utter darkness and exhaustion conspired against her. Morpheus wanted her. Minutes crept by, and she became less able to tell the difference between unconsciousness and sensory deprivation. Bodily aches and pains were apparently shared by both the waking and the sleeping states. She could not afford to fall asleep. The mental picture of waking alone padlocked in Lechuguilla spurred her to movement.

Switching on her light she waited a moment to see if it brought any response. It didn't. Two choices: go up, attempt to retrace Brent's trail, and emerge high on the wall above Tinker's Hell, or go back and take the more familiar trail Frieda had blazed. The first carried the risk of becoming lost, the second of stumbling into an ambush.

Anna opted for ambush. If one had to go down, it was cleaner to go down fighting than whimpering in the dark.

No Laymon.

No tape.

Anna blessed her paranoia. She'd not only left line but, in honor of Sondra and Hansel and Gretel, she'd continued to shove an inconspicuous scrap of flagging into a crack at each junction. Expecting every moment to have a rock crash on her or a hand shoot from a crevice to clutch at ankle or throat, she climbed, crawled, and wriggled through.

Sticking her head up into Tinker's required courage. Feeling slightly foolish, she reverted to the old cowboy trick of a hat on a stick. Lechuguilla having nothing in the way of vegetation, her arm took the place of the stick. She pushed her hard hat, lamp on, above floor level and rotated it as one would turn one's head. No shots were fired or stones thrown. She repeated the exercise with her head in the helmet. Near as the brownish orb could tell her, Laymon did not lie in wait, at least not in the immediate vicinity.

Several yards away, over more or less flat terrain, was a big friendly rock. Anna switched off her lamp, levered her body out of the hole, and crawled across the floor. Three yards—less than twice the length of her body—was an eternity. Mere seconds passed before disorientation set in. She banged body parts with painful results. Light on, she was a sitting duck. Light off, she was as good as dead. Her vision of night, of darkness, was shaped by a world aboveground. There, even indoors, there was light. It had occurred to her to sneak through Tinker's in darkness, the way she might slip through a midnight field or an unlit gymnasium. That was not a viable option. No light. None. No faint outlines. No lighter places. No rational angles and planes to follow. No architects or interior decorators to second guess. You traveled with your own light source, or you died.

She could wait Laymon out. If the falling pebble had tipped him off to the fact she was behind him, and he'd stopped short of the far wall, he could no more negotiate the remaining distance without giving himself away than she could. But if he'd made the exit, and, though Anna couldn't be sure, she guessed enough time had elapsed that it was possible, he could turn his back on Tinker's and walk away undetected, leaving her to wait till hell froze over. Anywhere along the way, at his leisure, he could stop again, rest, eat, drink some water, and wait. Anna would never know where until his bullet dropped her.

Already she was missing her pack. Thirst was nagging. Each time she moved, the lacerations on her feet made themselves felt. Suffocating darkness seeped into the crevices in her brain. If this was a waiting game, Laymon won; Anna had to go on.

The hat trick was the only one left in her depleted bag. She put it to use one more time. Having unbuckled her helmet, she turned on the lamp and held it away from her. Aimed at the light, Laymon's first shot should go wide. On some level she craved gunfire. It would let her know she wasn't alone.

The shot didn't come. She crossed Tinker's, drawing on reserves of strength she didn't know she had, climbing over an endless parade of table-sized boulders. Sweat no longer poured from her. Thirst was constant, and she chose not to think about it. From the way her feet hurt, she suspected she left bloody footprints. She didn't dwell too long on that either.

Reaching the far side, she rested, her lamp extinguished. There was no sound other than that of the life coursing through her body. Twice she turned on the lamp and waved her hard hat, fishing for Laymon. Nothing. Once she hollered his name but got only echoes in reply.

The conviction grew that he had heard the pebble, had known she was behind him; that he never intended to waste time lying in wait. He didn't need to. He only needed to leave her behind. The cave would do the rest. Numbing fear washed over her. She forced herself up on trembling legs. Caution was gone. Pushing as hard as her worn muscles would allow, she entered the twisting nest of passages that led from Tinker's to the relatively simple and open spaces beyond.

Her guess had been right. Laymon had already passed this way. The surveyor's taped she'd laid to mark the route was taken up. Not so the paranoid flags hidden at the junctions. As batteries dimmed and eyes fogged with weariness the flags became harder to find, but knowing they existed kept her from giving up. The last of these scraps was laid at the entrance to the area where she and Curt had stopped to seek the source of the crying.

Laymon couldn't have known it, but this was the one room in Lechuguilla with which Anna was intimate. On her first try she located the shadow-camouflaged exit. From there on, the route was less confusing. Within ten minutes she heard the unbelievably beautiful sound of human voices. Curt and Sondra were still alive. George and his two incognizant captives were waiting to descend into the spiky gullet of the Cocktail Lounge. Without gear, Anna doubted she could make a descent of nearly a hundred feet. She knew for a fact she could not freeclimb ninety feet up the far side. Along with bullets, burial, and bruised feet, that bit of information had been relegated to the dump reserved for things she wasn't thinking about.

Shrouding herself again in perfect darkness, she took off her hard hat and carefully set it down. Nothing else was left that might clank or jingle. A spill of light from ahead indicated direction. On hands and knees, she followed. The passage opened sufficiently that she could have walked on her hind legs, bent over simian-fashion. Afraid an over-used body would fail her and she'd stumble, she settled for the less evolved form of locomotion.

Above the Lounge was a recess where ancient waters pooled, releasing acids that ate away rock till the water could trickle down to form the pit. This subterranean aerie was oval, perhaps seven feet high and twenty across at the widest point. Pillars of limestone divided the room. On Anna's right a deep trough had been carved, a natural drainage. A low, ridged formation spiked by embryonic stalagmites separated it from the main body of the room.

Curt, Sondra, and George Laymon sat in the chamber's center, where flat space afforded them a modicum of comfort. Curt's lamp was off, Sondra's gleaming. The woman would probably sleep with a night-light for the rest of her natural life. Laymon's lamp had been extinguished, and

Anna saw him only when Sondra turned in his direction. Packs were off: Laymon's close by his side, Curt's near Sondra. Hers was back ten or fifteen feet as if she'd shed it precipitately on entering the rest stop. George and Curt were arguing. The heat of the words but not their meaning reached Anna.

Surreptitiously, she slunk into the trough. A painful inching process that seemed to wear on for hours and produce racket equivalent to that of gravel trucks speeding over railroad trestles brought her midway into the room. Raising herself up on her elbows, she hazarded a peek over the serrated bulwark of stone. Directly in front of her, less than ten feet away, was Laymon's broad back. Curt sat cross-legged to his left, his face visible in profile. Sondra was masked by her own light, merely a beacon teetering on a vaguely human form.

Laymon was talking, low, logical, intense. It was by Curt that the heat had been generated.

"She broke it all right, and maybe her collarbone as well. I left her with plenty of water and batteries. Anna will be better served by a quick rescue than by you getting yourself hurt and adding to the rescue effort."

George Laymon was one hell of an actor. Many people the Screen Actor's Guild would never hear of were brilliant practitioners of the art. Without lights and cameras, it was called lying. Laymon's lie was superb. He captured all the elements: drama, pathos, credibility, and tied it up neatly with an appeal to the listeners' better selves.

Anna had pushed on alone. An irresponsible act. Anna had injured herself and so, by her stupidity, would prove costly and dangerous to those who must bail her out.

Somebody to blame. Most people love to believe the worst of others. The rest worry, deep down, that it might be true.

Laymon had found her, made her comfortable, traveled out at a grueling pace to procure her safety. A hero. But only enough heroics to enhance credibility: he'd not added any spectacular flourishes to spark jealousy in other men or distrust in women.

And the final implication that whosoever disagreed with him was no better than, and would suffer the same fate as, the foolish and willful Anna.

"I don't like the idea of leaving her," Curt said. Anna was touched by his obstinacy. Given a performance the caliber of Laymon's, she'd have been the first in the audience on her feet yelling "Bravo!"

"I don't like it much either," Laymon said with just the right touch of sadness. "But it won't be for long. Oscar and the others went on down the North Rift in case that was the direction you two had taken. We're meeting this side of Glacier Bay in a couple of hours. We'll get Mrs. McCarty out of here. Oscar can go out with her and set the carry-out team in motion. You and I will come back to where Anna's resting. She shouldn't be alone for more than five hours. Six at the outside. She's prepared for it. I told her to meditate on her sins. This whole escapade is out of line. If I have any say about it, she will be billed for her rescue. The taxpayer shouldn't have to carry the burden for criminal negligence."

That last bit, reluctant sympathy tinged with righteous indignation, was stellar. Anna wondered if he intended to use his ill-gotten gains to finance a career in state politics. New Mexico wouldn't have a chance. In other circumstances, she would have voted for him herself and bragged to her friends of having met him once.

"Who all is with Oscar?" Curt asked. A barely discernible insecurity tinged the words. Anna heard it and had no doubt that Laymon did. It was the first step in capitulation. Anna was relieved. A falling-out now would end with two bullets and two more dead bodies. Without any warning, Curt's musculature and youthful reflexes would not save him.

"A can of worms," Laymon said regretfully. The big head nodded in a halo of light. "Anna told me her suspicions regarding Oscar. Frankly, I'm not sold. But we'll look into Oscar's activities. Send a team into Tinker's to find this mysterious secret. That's all I can do. And that's for later. Right now we need to concentrate on getting Mrs. McCarty home safe and getting a crew in to bring Anna out. God, what a day. I hope I don't have another like it anytime real soon."

Throughout this performance Sondra was unresponsive. Occasionally her light moved from face to face as the players entered the game, but always a beat or two late. Over the years Anna had been exposed to a number of mental aberrations fomented by stress and exposure. Burial alive was beyond her experience. Sondra's body was tight, muscles squeezing on bone, yet her movements were languid, as if she were in viscous liquid. She spoke now, and her voice projected the same lackluster retardation. It took Anna a second to realize what was missing: vibrato. Her voice was absolutely flat, like that of the most skilled medieval chanters. "I have to go to the bathroom." The words were as dead as a computer-generated warning. She looked only at Curt. For her, Laymon hardly existed, a mere ripple on the surface of her consciousness.

"You can go," Curt said. "It's all right." Patience blotted out the confusion he must have been feeling, and Anna was proud. He was what her mother would have called a natural husbandman. He took care of things: cars, cats, people, and did it in such a way it went unnoticed and unsung.

Sondra stared through him, a pained expression lending a spark of animation to her dirty face. All of them were so streaked with mud they resembled commandos in a B movie. Half a minute ticked by. By the spill of light from the lamp, Anna studied Laymon. The audience otherwise occupied, he'd dropped out of character. Behind eyes dark with shadow, she could sense an exceedingly busy mind. Curt and Sondra had to be disposed of.

His hand stole toward his pack. Anna pulled her feet under her to spring. Walled in stone, the only exit a one-hundred-foot drop, people would die regardless of the action taken. Shouting would only precipitate a massacre. Crouched on legs weak with fatigue, she hoped she had one good pounce left.

Curt broke the silence. "Do you want me to go with you?" he asked Sondra.

"I'm embarrassed." Same lifeless tone. Considering the content of the words, it was chilling. An emotional declaration made without emotion.

"Tell you what," Curt said. "I'll go with you. Then you go behind a rock or whatever, and I'll hold on to one end of Anna's hanky, and you hold the other. I'll be there but I won't be there, if you see what I mean."

Sondra thought it over, then nodded.

"Bottle or bag?" Curt asked in the offhand manner of a kindergarten teacher asking, "Number one or number two?"

"Bag," Sondra mumbled.

Good. They'd be a while. It would give Anna a few precious moments to figure out what in the hell she was going to do.

Murmuring banal encouragements, Curt followed Sondra, stoop-walking out the passage Anna'd crawled in. When they'd gone, their words an indistinguishable mutter, Laymon turned on his lamp and pulled his pack between his knees. As he reached in, Anna decided not to leap. Whether the decision was spawned by cowardice or good judgment, she would never know. She knew only that her little weight and exhausted efforts against his considerable bulk would end badly. Before she had time to consider whether the sacrifice could have saved Curt, Laymon drew his hand from the pack. He held not the anticipated handgun but a long, narrow package wrapped in brown waxy paper, and a coil of coarse gray wire.

Dynamite.

Anna found herself remembering the pistol with something akin to affection.

23

METICULOUSLY, LAYMON CHECKED the sticks of explosives and the fuse wire, stowed them back in the pack, and began removing climbing gear. There was no need to shoot anyone. Laymon was the de facto head of the group. Curt and Sondra would do as they were told. Curt, Anna guessed, was not entirely comfortable with the way things were shaping up. Discomfort and suspicions would not be enough to start a mutiny. Not where there was a crazy woman to be looked after.

Laymon would descend first, then the weak link, Sondra, then Curt, taking up the guard position. They would cross the Lounge. Laymon would climb the ninety feet to the narrow aperture that led to Razor Blade Run and on to Lake Rapunzel. In less time than it would take to tell it, he could cut the line, leaving Curt and Sondra marooned in a pit deeper and darker than Edgar Allan Poe ever imagined.

Safe from pursuit and unseemly interference, Laymon would continue on to Katie's Pigtail. In the slide area he would lay the dynamite and a good, long fuse. He'd be well clear when it closed off this wing of Lechuguilla permanently. Evidence and witnesses buried. The rockfall written off to natural causes. Laymon hailed as an insightful manager for closing an unstable part of the cavern before anyone else got hurt.

Sondra McCarty? She'd disappeared some time ago, something to do with a bad marriage. Anna and Curt? Laymon wouldn't need to explain. What had they to do with him? Given sufficient warning, the Blacktail would close up shop before Holden had a chance to investigate. Holden would tell of their entering Lechuguilla and why. A dig through the slide in the Pigtail would be considered, then rejected as too dangerous and costly. If anybody had to take a fall, Oscar Iverson would be chosen. Laymon, with Anna's invaluable assistance, had set him up.

As if he felt the menace behind him, Laymon stood suddenly and crossed to the far side of the room. Anna watched as he put the pack with the gun between his feet and sat on a ledge. The time for pouncing had been frittered away in indecision. Anna had deliberated too long. A minute ticked by to the unsuspecting murmur of Curt's voice down the passageway. Muttering harmless nothings to assure Sondra he was still there.

The mother of invention brought an idea. Though it promised little in the way of success, Anna embraced the opportunity to take action. Laymon guarded his pack with care. Curt's was closer but, gone missing, would cause alarm. Anna was counting on the fact that distraught women are never believed, even by the most well-meaning men. Unless they'd seen Sondra drop it themselves, they would assume she'd left her pack behind, lost it in one of the hiding places Lechuguilla offered in such abundance. Squelching a desire to rush, Anna weaseled quietly back the way she had come. Sondra's pack lay out in the room, only partially shielded from view by a formation. Laymon had his light on, but unless he trained it in that direction, she could maneuver the pack into her trough unnoticed.

As she dragged it, the pack made a faint grinding sound.

Light streaked toward the back of the room. A snatch, and the pack was clutched under Anna's chest. The light poked, preyed, faltered, then returned to Laymon's feet.

Scuttling backward with her prize, like an alligator with a Pekinese, Anna vanished into the trough. The water, she drank. The webbed belt, she wriggled into, graceless as a supine woman donning a wet girdle. Safety and rack were tethered to the webbed climbing belt. She was sliding the pack over her shoulder when she heard Curt and Sondra coming back from the ladies' room. Burrito bundle in hand, Sondra emerged first. Trusting the noise of their return to mask that of her crawl, Anna moved through the trough on elbows and knees. The pilfered water sloshed in her stomach, then was manifested as salt sweat in her eyes.

"Time to move out, kiddos," Laymon said. "The sooner we get to Glacier Bay, the sooner we can get back to your Miss Anna."

Belly flat against the rock, Miss Anna dropped onto an eighteen-inch ledge used as a jumping-off point for the descent. Two yards ahead she could see the rope, red and inviting, where it crossed the step and vanished into the pit.

"Suit up," Laymon said jovially. To others it might have seemed he strove to maintain morale. To Anna's ear the good cheer was that of a man who very soon would have the solution to all of his problems.

Gear grated, nylon rustled, carabiners clinked; then came a thin wail. "I can't find my stuff!" Sondra'd discovered the theft.

"Oh for Chrissake," Anna heard Laymon groan just above her. He rose to his feet and stalked back into the chamber. Anna dared one quick peek. He'd taken his pack with him.

Blessing the timely diversion, she scrabbled along the step and grabbed the rope. Ignoring her safety, she laced the rope through the rack. No mean feat without light.

"You two keep looking," Laymon said. He was returning to his former position. "I'll head down. If you don't come up with it, I'll send my gear back up and we'll sort of piggy-back from here on."

Anna's rigging was probably imperfect, possibly deadly, but it would have to do. With an unvoiced prayer to an unknown god that looked remarkably like her older sister, she swung over the edge. The rope was snug through the rack. Nothing snapped loose or flew open. Almost falling for the first few seconds, she descended rapidly. Without light she had no way of knowing where the bottom was.

When she found it, she wished she'd had the good sense to go more slowly. Her tailbone smacked into rock, sending a paralyzing jolt up her spine and down both legs. What a bad joke, to be lying crippled when Laymon dropped on her. Luck held. Everything worked. It hurt, but it worked. Daring one flick of her lamp, she sighted the ascension rope on the far side of the pit. Between the looming crusted tables, a red snakey tongue licked dead-white stone.

Hidden by darkness, she crawled in the direction she'd aimed herself. The crack of her helmet against the wall let her know she'd arrived.

"Did you hear something?" Curt, sounding hollow as he looked down into the dry well that was the Cocktail Lounge. Lamps appeared, weak and watery searchlights, scouring the pit. Anna lined herself up behind one of the flat-topped formations that gave the place its name. If they saw her the game was up. Shooting fish in a barrel.

Every cloud, and all that: Anna found a silver lining. In the light from the search and under cover of sound from conversation, she opened Sondra's pack and fished out her ascenders. Ascenders were complicated, made to go over boots, not rubber socks. Until they were properly attached to the rope, the angular devices of metal dragged on the ground, clattering at every step. Gloves in her teeth, Anna worked so fast her fingers fumbled one into the other, but she was rigged by the time she heard Laymon say, "Must've been Hodags," and the lights were snatched back from the deep.

Holding an ascender in each hand to muffle their noise, she knee-walked awkwardly along the wall till the elbow she skinned over the stone brushed against the rope. Working by feel, she wrestled the metal chest harness over her head and cinched it tight above her breasts. The fit wasn't bad. For so tall a woman, Sondra was small-boned. Taking the pin from the ascender on her right foot, she threaded rope through it, replaced the pin, and tugged on it to assure herself it was rigged solidly. The left foot went into a stirrup, the ascender at the knee. Anna threaded it, then double-looped the stirrup around her foot so it would stay in place without the rigidity of a boot for support.

Ready as she would ever be, she stretched the elastic line from her shoulder into the hook on the ascender and pulled herself upright on the rope.

The ascender wouldn't catch. Rope flailed impotently between her legs. Panic stopped her breath, and she heard the freight-train roar of blood behind her eardrums.

Easy does it. One step at a time. Walk before you run. Her mind chanted aphorisms to keep her body in touch with her brain. An ascender grabbed. She rope-walked up twelve inches. The other caught, the left, and the noose she'd tied around her foot tightened over the fine bones. Pain was bad; damage could be considerable. There was no time to re-think the plan.

Another few inches gained. By taking as much weight as she could with her arms, she eased the coils around her instep. Ten more inches. Maybe eight.

Step and step and do not scream. Behind her, scarcely ten yards across and thirty up, she could hear the others as clearly as over a good AT&T connection. Any minute, surely, one of them would turn their light on her and the shooting would begin.

A step, a lift, a grinding of bones. A step and another. With every lift of her feet, rope dragged across her ankles. Where once there had been leather there was only thin cotton. Her trousers were no match for the heft of rope and body. Skin was abraded away one thin slice at a time. Twenty-seven steps. Seventy-three left to go. Would seventy-three layers of flesh take the rope down to bone? Anna pondered that conundrum for eight more pulls in hopes the grisly picture would serve to block out the cutting.

Ascenders were designed to allow climbers to use thighs and butts rather than relying on the weaker muscles of the upper body. Trying to bull her way up with her biceps to keep the weight off her strangled foot, Anna burned out arms and shoulders. Each pull became feebler. Aching was replaced by sharp stabs of pain.

Fifty steps. Maybe. Anna lost count. Tears streamed down her face. She would have been tempted to stop had hanging not been nearly as painful as climbing, and the thought of Laymon winning more painful than both.

"On-rope." Laymon. Whirring followed as he dropped easily into the pit.

Eyes squeezed against salt sting, teeth clamped, Anna stepped and stepped again. Rock grated over her knuckles. She jammed her feet into the rope noose and shoved.

"Off-rope." Laymon was down and free of the line. Had she been able to hear over the pounding of her heart, she knew there'd be the crunch of boots as he crossed the Lounge.

A reprieve was granted. "Rack and seat sling on-line. Pull it up." Laymon was carrying through the charade. Curt and Sondra were to be allowed to descend. It made sense. Had Laymon gone on, Curt would have known something was wrong. He could descend in a fraction of the time it would take Laymon to climb the other side. With an angry man messing with one's rope, a climb would be seriously compromised. Younger and stronger, Curt might even be able to catch him before he reached the top.

Dimly, Anna was aware of Sondra descending, of talk back and forth. These things meant little to her. She'd entered her own world of hard pain and harder work. Her life was fighting this rope, easing the breaking hold on her foot, accepting the searing across her ankles. Other lives, other people, diminished to a memory, a dream of another life.

"On-rope." Curt Schatz. His voice penetrated Anna's red fog. He was close, over her shoulder, on the opposite side of the Lounge. She must be nearly to the top. With a last burst of strength she pushed herself up. The line curved. Air was mashed from her lungs. Her belly scraped over the lip. Locked at the knees, her legs poked over the pit. Gear tied her belly-down on the ledge near the anchor. Pulling gloves off, she jerked the quick-release pin from her chest wheel and felt some give. The buckle beneath her arm was yanked open. The metal-and-web harness let go, freeing her upper body. Crumpled facedown on the ground, she welcomed the cooling water on her face. A drip puddle edged the drop, and she had crawled into it. So drenched was she in sweat she could not feel wetness, only coolness.

The need to lie still, to lick her wounds, was as powerful as a drug. Bankrupt of fuel, her body was shutting down. Forcing herself to a sitting position, she pulled the pin from the ascender on her knee and shook the rope out.

"On-rope." Laymon.

The rope jerked, dragging Anna toward the edge of the cliff. Water, so recently her friend, reduced friction, and she slid easily over the slick rock.

"What's the problem?" Curt's voice floated up.

"The rope is snagged on something," Laymon said.

"Let me give you a hand."

Anna lurched for her right foot where the rope held it out over the pit. Grasping the ascender's release, she yanked, desperate as a man pulling the pin of a hand grenade.

"Now."

Her leg yanked painfully down. Throwing herself back from the edge, she clung to the anchor. Another jerk and the rope tore free of her foot. She reeled the leg in. Systems weren't working, limbs rebelled. She'd gotten ahead of Laymon, between him and the flawed exit from Katie's

Pigtail, but she was spent. In a wrestling match with a butterfly, she would have come out the loser.

The rope twitched: Laymon climbed. Shielding her light lest she lose the one playable card she held—surprise—Anna searched for a weapon. In a wonderland of rock there wasn't a stone to throw. Nothing bigger than a marble. His moment of greatest vulnerability would be when he floundered over the lip. She could kick him. Feet were bare and broken. Laymon's cranium was protected by a hard hat, his body secured to the rock face with rope and carabiner. All he'd have to do was catch hold of some part of her. A little leverage and she'd go over the edge like laundry down a chute.

Cupping her headlamp between her hands, she crawled away from the cliff. Tucked around a curtain of flowstone, behind the formation used as an anchor, she hid. Light off, she couldn't even tell if her eyes were tracking. She must catch her breath. Then she must think. The last of Sondra's water was sucked down, making her feel more alive. That was not necessarily a good thing.

Grating. Grunts. Laymon was up. Time had come to do something. Unable to think what, Anna stayed in her hole.

Metallic sounds followed. Laymon taking himself off-rope. He wouldn't bother to derig for the short journey through Razor Blade Run. The ascenders would be needed again to climb out of Lake Rapunzel. It no longer mattered that they could destroy a few million-year-old crystal formations in the Run. No one would ever know.

He was loose from the rope, but he said nothing to those below. Light flickered across the wall opposite Anna's niche. He was headed her direction. With more effort than it would have taken to lift a tractor, she eased to her feet. Leftover pride from watching Westerns as a child: die standing up. She wished she had her boots on.

Light winked out. Laymon had turned his back. On torn and bleeding feet, she stepped out. He was five or six feet away. Mesmerized, she watched as he took a Swiss Army knife from a nylon sheath on his belt. From below, Curt was calling his name. Wordlessly, Laymon began cutting the line.

The son of a bitch wasn't even going to say good-bye.

Anna lurched toward him. Her left foot buckled beneath her. A scream was stifled in her throat.

Laymon was turning.

Anna was stumbling, counting on momentum to do what strength could not.

Her shoulder caught him on the left hip. Light from his helmet fled erratically into the pit. A fist grazed Anna's jaw. Then he was gone. For a moment she lay in the cool of the water where he'd so recently stood, feeling it seeping into her eyes, mixing with tears and sweat. Muscles and mind in rebellion, she began shaking apart. Still there was something left to be done. For a long moment she tried to remember what. Finally it came to her.

Hanging her head over the drop, she called, "Off-rope."

24

ANNA WALKED A mile in the dead man's shoes. Burdened with a greater sensibility, Curt was squeamish about robbing the corpse, but Anna's feet were killing her. Packed with extra socks, Laymon's boots served as both protection and splint. Still, much of the exodus was accomplished on hands and knees.

They were welcomed back in the park with something less than open arms, an age-old need to kill the messengers and a bureaucratic loathing of independent action. In the subsequent furor over the defection of George Laymon and the destruction of that glorious chamber, Anna escaped punitive action. She was, however, invited to leave Carlsbad Caverns on the next available flight, and it was hinted that the personnel department there would not be a good choice should she need letters of recommendation in the future.

At the insistence of Carlsbad's superintendent and Holden Tillman, drilling at the Blacktail was stopped, pending investigation. A warrant was obtained to search George Laymon's office and home, but no papers were found to indicate with whom on the Blacktail staff he'd been conspiring. If the law never figured it out, the gas drilling company probably had a good idea. After paying the American public for damages, they would be inspired to take the difference out of the perpetrator's hide, if only metaphorically.

Sondra recovered quickly. The adventure had not mellowed her. Twenty-four hours after she was brought out of Lechuguilla, she and Peter returned to St. Paul. Peter wore a beaten, hangdog look, and Zeddie one of long-suffering patience. The divorce, if there was to be a divorce, would be every bit as ugly as Sondra could make it.

The day following the departure of the doctor and his wife, Curt drove Anna to the Carlsbad airport. Her left foot was in a cast, the lateral metatarsal bone broken during the ascent from the Lounge.

Since Curt had prodded, threatened, and cajoled her up the last climb out of Old Misery Pit, Anna had done little but eat, sleep, and watch TV. Depression as black as any room in Lechuguilla had settled over her mind. She didn't know if she grieved for the dead, despaired the endless plundering of the wild places, or just needed a vacation.

She wasn't sure she wanted to be a park ranger anymore. What other line of work she was suited for was unclear. At the moment, bagging groceries at the A&P or working the cosmetics counter at Wal-Mart looked tempting. A job where one was seldom called upon to kill anybody.

"Are you okay?" Curt asked.

Anna, ticket in hand, and he sat in the uniquely soulless environment of airport waiting areas.

"A week in a hot tub and I will be. You?" She asked to be polite but found that she cared about the answer. Of late, Curt Schatz was one of the few people on earth who didn't grate on her nerves.

"Anxious to get back to the university. There's only a week before Christmas break. Since we won't be allowing them to come to class for a month, I know my students will be eager to squeeze in every bit of learning they possibly can these last few days."

Outside, buffeted by December winds, a prop plane taxied onto the ramp's loading zone.

"We'll keep in touch?" Anna asked.

"You saved my life," Curt replied. "Now you're responsible for me."

The
"STUNNING"
(The Seattle Times)

"EXCEPTIONAL"
(The Denver Post)

"SUPERB"
(The New York Times Book Review)

ANNA PIGEON SERIES
by Nevada Barr

Blind Descent
Winter Study
Hard Truth
High Country
Flashback
Hunting Season
Blood Lure
Deep South
Blind Descent
Endangered Species
Firestorm
Ill Wind
A Superior Death
Track of the Cat

penguin.com

P.O. 0005273045 202

M473T0709